Suddenly it was too real. The fear of the meeting at arms was utterly gone from Jim; and with it the temptation to compete with his skill against a rider no more skillful then he. What was left was a surge of adrenaline all through him, and the realization that this land was solid as any earth he had walked or ridden on—and lance sweep or not, the aim of the Bright Knight was to kill him, either after he had been knocked out of the saddle or once he had been conquered and made prisoner.

He and his opponent drew together at what seemed a much faster pace than before. When he saw the white lance shaft of the other swinging out sideways, he crouched behind his shield, holding it as Brian had told him; and blindly, swung his own lance. It struck something so solidly that his hand quivered and stung as if he had tried to catch and hold the moving part of an engine.

He almost dropped the lance, but not quite. As he pulled Gorp to a skidding stop and turned the horse about, he saw the Bright Knight lying motionless on the grass. His horse, evidently as untrained as the knight himself, was running off toward the castle.

He took Gorp back to the fallen man and dismounted, tossing his reins ahead to the ground. Gorp instantly stood still. The Bright Knight still lay unmoving, his eyes shut, his face pale. Jim felt a sudden emptiness inside him; had he killed the other . . .

Tor Books by Gordon R. Dickson

NOVELS
Alien Art
The Alien Way
Arcturus Landing
The Far Call
Gremlins, Go Home! (with Ben Bova)
Hoka! (with Poul Anderson)
Home from the Shore
The Last Master
Masters of Everon
Mission to Universe
Naked to the Stars
On the Run
Other
Outposter
Planet Run (with Keith Laumer)
The Pritcher Mass
Pro
Secrets of the Deep
Sleepwalker's World
The Space Swimmers
The Space Winners
Spacepaw
Spacial Delivery
Way of the Pilgrim
Wolf and Iron

THE DORSAI SERIES
Necromancer
Tactics of Mistake
Lost Dorsai: The New Dorsai Companion
Soldier, Ask Not
The Spirit of Dorsai
Dorsai!
Young Bleys
The Final Encyclopedia, vol. 1 (rev. ed.)
The Final Encyclopedia, vol. 2 (rev. ed.)
The Chantry Guild

THE DRAGON SERIES
The Dragon Knight
The Dragon and the Gnarly King
The Dragon in Lyonesse

COLLECTIONS
Beyond the Dar al-Harb
Guided Tour
Love Not Human
The Man from Earth
The Man the Worlds Rejected
Steel Brother
Stranger

The Dragon in Lyonesse

Gordon R. Dickson

A TOM DOHERTY ASSOCIATES BOOK
NEW YORK

THE DRAGON IN LYONESSE

A Tor Book
Published by Tom Doherty Associates, LLC
175 Fifth Avenue
New York, NY 10010

www.tor.com

Tor® is a registered trademark of Tom Doherty Associates, LLC

ISBN: 0-812-56271-2
Library of Congress Card Catalog Number: 98-23490

First edition: October 1998
First mass market edition: August 1999

Printed in the United States of America

0 9 8 7 6 5 4 3 2 1

The Dragon in Lyonesse
is dedicated to Joe and Gay Haldeman

Chapter 1

"My *der frens,*" Sir John Chandos had written to the Lord and Lady of Castle Malencontri; in a small, crabbed hand, but at least also in plain English and without the flourishes of the scribes that usually made such letters hard to puzzle out for Malencontri's Lord, Baron Sir James Eckert. *"I writ thys secretly yn mine own hand to tell ye that the crown warrants for arests for treson of ye and others ye knaw be now at last witout noise in law witdrwn. So ye might knaw thys and so be mor at eese. May Goddes blesing be wit ye. Jon Chandos, knight."*

"It's a little confused near the end, there," said Sir James. He had passed the message to his Lady, Angela Eckert, and was rereading it over her shoulder as she went through it. "But it seems plain enough. Even though the Earl of Cumberland got the warrants signed by the King somehow, originally, now they've been erased from whatever record might be kept—or something like that. Don't you think? Well, say something, Angie!"

Angie—the Lady Angela—moved a little closer to the window of the Solar, their private apartment at the top of Malencontri's Tower, so that the light of the bright autumn morning could fall full on the unfolded piece of thick, grayish paper.

"It's very well written for someone of this fourteenth century, doing his own correspondence," she said. "Jim, do you recognize Chandos's handwriting?"

"Well, no," said Jim. "But then I've never had anything from him before that wasn't scribe-written. But if you stop and think what he does—being sort of unofficial head of whatever Intelligence Service the King has—he'd naturally have had some practice writing his own private letters. Besides, who else in the fourteenth century would send a letter just to stop us from worrying—or even stop to think we might be worrying? I don't think it'd even occur to Brian, good friend as he is. We'd better burn this letter, though, to protect Chandos."

"Not yet," said Angie, carefully folding the parchment; and tucking it into one of the thin wooden boxes attached to her accounts table, that was the closest the Castle's carpenter had been able to come up with, by way of a desk. "I'll keep it safe; and as far as Sir Brian Neville-Smythe goes, he's got worries enough of his own lately, over that father of Geronde."

Jim could hardly disagree. Brian—Lord of Smythe Castle, such as that run-down small holding was—knight and champion jouster, had been betrothed to the Lady Geronde Isabel de Chaney of the well-off hold of Malvern, since they had both been children. But Brian and Geronde had been unable to marry without the official consent of her father. So Jim and Brian, earlier this same year, had finally located him in the eastern lands, where he had gone adventuring some years before; and brought him home.

Their return should have been the beginning of a happy period. It had not been. As far back as when Geronde had been only eleven, it developed, she had never seen eye to eye with her father—or he with her.

"Oh, well," said Jim, "it's nice to get good news this

early, that's the important thing. Makes the day; and I think this is going to be a good one. Why don't we forget everything here, for once, and go for a stroll in the woods? After all, they're our woods."

"You're always suggesting that, and then we never do it," said Angie. "Besides, this isn't a world where you want to tempt fate by announcing what the future is going to be."

"Now, don't you, of all people, start overrating the magic they have here—" said Jim.

"I'm just using common sense, that's all."

"Common sense or not. We could end up as superstitious as everybody else is here; and you and I know that's just ignorance. There's got to be a logical reason for everything, even magic. Besides, I only said—"

There was a scratching at the door to the spacious single room that was their Solar. That room had originally taken in all the top floor, just under the battlemented roof of the Tower of Malencontri Castle; until they had partitioned off part of it to make a separate room for the baby, Robert Falon, who was now their ward.

They looked at each other.

"Come in!" called Jim. John Steward, erect, somewhat overstuffed, and just this side of being pompous as usual—but oddly wide-eyed—entered.

"M'Lord, m'Lady," he said stiffly, "the Master Archer Dafydd ap Hywel is in the Great Hall, and wishes to speak with you."

"Hall? Which hall?" echoed Jim—but there was really only one, unless you counted the large room, hidden on the ground floor among the quarters where the servants and men-at-arms lived, where they ate their meals, spent their leisure hours, and generally socialized. "How long has he been there? When did he get here?"

John Steward's heavy, pale, but meticulously shaven face took on an expression fleetingly divided between fear and embarrassment.

"Nobody knows, m'Lord. He was just there at the High Table, working on a bowstave, when Mary Light-the-Fire went in to start the wood in the Hall fireplaces."

"Why didn't somebody ask him?"

"No one thought of it, m'Lord."

This was a lie, of course. Either Dafydd had been asked and the questioner wanted nothing to do with the answer; or for some reason they had been afraid to ask. There was no point in pinning John down—probably superstition again, thought Jim.

"Well, how long had be been there? Did they find that out?"

"No, m'Lord."

"Well, how did he get into the Castle, then?"

But John was looking helpless.

There was nothing to be done with a Steward who looked helpless. With a less important servant, you could turn to his or her superior and say, "See if you can get an answer that makes sense," and walk off. Jim never did that, however, except in an emergency—the questioning of the less important one that followed tended to be a rough process.

"Magic," said Angie. "I'll bet you."

"Certainly not!" said Jim. "Dafydd's not a magician; and anyway, why would he need magic to get in when all he's ever needed to do was hail whoever was on night guard at the main gate? They all know him here."

"In this world magic probably had something to do with it," said Angie darkly. "If you hadn't gotten yourself mixed up in it—"

"The only reason I did it was because I had to rescue you from the Loathly Tower—remember?"

"True," said Angie. "I'm sorry, Jim. Forgive me—I'm vicious before I've had breakfast. Let's go down and get some; and find out for ourselves about Dafydd."

She linked her arm in his, and they headed toward the door. John Steward nipped through it ahead of them and stood aside.

"Anyway, I thought he was at an archery meet right now, in the North Country somewhere," Jim said as they started down the hall—John decorously following, five paces behind them.

At the High Table, raised on its dais at the inward end of the Hall, the cloth had been laid and foods set out. No longer working on a bowstave, Dafydd himself was eating; but he stopped politely and got to his feet as a mere archer should when Jim and Angie came toward him.

"Dafydd!" said Jim. "How did things go at that meet in the north?" Angie kissed the archer in the customary polite greeting of the age, in defiance of the fact that, officially, she was a lady and here he was only an archer, in spite of his great skills. Gentlemen, in obedience to the custom, could kiss women innkeepers and female servants—in fact, they often did—but ladies were not ordinarily obliged to lower themselves in that fashion.

For his part, Jim held back. Dafydd was an old friend, almost as much so as Sir Brian, who was the closest thing to a blood brother that Jim had in this fourteenth-century world, after their battle at the Loathly Tower. Dafydd, of course, had been there, too. Moreover, he was a guest, and, in principle, was owed a kiss of welcome. But Brian had never seemed to think that Dafydd would expect the courtesy from him—any more than any other archer might—and Jim was uncomfortable with the practice, anyway. He cleared his throat and seated himself at the table.

Angie and Dafydd also sat down.

"There were many good archers there, James," said Dafydd. "I saw much to admire."

Which meant, of course, that Dafydd had won everything in sight, as usual. He always avoided saying anything against a fellow archer; and in the rare case where he had been outdone (never more than once) by one of them, the information would be choking him until he could get it told. For all his casual, almost lazy habit of speaking, he could not bear the thought anyone might think he was afraid of admitting his failures.

"My servants—" began Jim, to change the subject; but was interrupted by the one of these nearest him starting to pour wine from a pitcher into his wine cup, temporarily blocking Dafydd from his sight. "—were surprised to find you here, already in the Hall."

"Indeed, they were so," said Dafydd. "But I had come in quietly of purpose, it being my aim to find out how well a watch was kept for you."

"But the main gate's doors in the curtain wall were closed and barred."

"It was so," said Dafydd. "Till dawn. But with the sunrise they were opened by sleepy guards who all drew open first one, then the other. So it was no labor for a man of woods and mountains like myself to slip past them unseen. Once in, there was only a short walk into the Hall, past others half-asleep still, to this table. It would not be hard for another like myself to do the same. I am not a man who tells another how he should live; but when you are away from here, yourself, it might be wisest to make sure a stricter watch is kept."

"Now you mention it, it probably would be," said Jim. "But what made you concerned after this much time with the guarding of our main gate?"

"You have not heard, then?" said Dafydd. "It is talked about all over England that Cumberland raises his own hired army, taking every hedge-knight, outlaw, and common wastrel that will go with him for hope of gain. Already it is said he has two or three hundred of such. With such force to his hand, it would not be surprising if he decided to pay off old scores. He is no friend of yours."

"You can say that, all right," Jim said. "He hates our—that is, you're right. He has little love for me, or Angie; and Agatha Falon, his leman, has even less—little love for any of us, including you and Brian and any belonging to either of you. But his coming against Malencontri with an army that large—"

"It does not require so much, look you. One man slipping inside the walls as I did can arrange to knife a sentry and let in a dozen more up a rope or through a small postern gate. That dozen can hold the gate, open it, and admit no more than thirty more to a sleeping castle, then kill most of those who could oppose them before they are half-awake. Then they who came are all gone again, like smoke; and no man knows who was responsible for the death or capture of you or Lady Angela."

"Hah!" said Jim, thoughtlessly out loud, and woke to the fact that both Dafydd and Angie were staring at his unusual use of the handy, all-purpose medieval exclamation. He looked directly at Angie.

"I thought it was a little too good to be true—someone like Chandos going to all the trouble of writing us a private letter just to tell us we were free of the warrants issued on us."

Angie nodded slowly.

"You're right," she said. "He had to know we'd hear what Dafydd just told us and put it together with the news in his letter."

Dafydd was looking at them both now with the appearance of only a mild interest in what they were saying—but both knew his look disguised a burning curiosity.

"You see, Dafydd," Jim said, "this morning we got this letter—"

"Let me tell it," said Angie. "I'm faster."

She was.

"You see, Dafydd," Jim said—after Angie, true to her promise, had filled their guest in with half the words Jim himself would have used—"how clever Chandos is? There's nothing in that letter, nothing at all that could compromise him; but he'd have known that we'd hear this news, too, sooner or later, and then all he had to tell us would be clear."

"Forgive my weakness of wit, James," said Dafydd, "but what is this 'all' you talk about?"

"Why, it has to be obvious to anyone that the only man in England who could raise a force of fighting men that size, and get away with it, would be the half brother of the King; which Cumberland is. Also, the King would not only have to know about it, but be in agreement with Cumberland's doing it; and there could be only one reason he'd agree. That'd be if he was actually planning an invasion of France; and what

Cumberland would be doing would be just the first quiet step toward drawing together an army for it."

"Your King Edward is well past the age of taking the field in war," said Dafydd.

"Exactly! And that's why Cumberland's being the front man. But there's more than invasion news in that message in Chandos's letter for us. It's a warning for us—me, you, Brian—to promise ourselves to fight with the part of the army Chandos will command."

"Me, he cannot have," said Dafydd. "I have a duty that goes before any other at this time. A duty of responsibility to those I love and danger to their land—the Drowned Land of my ancestors; and that is what brings me to you at this time, for it concerns magick."

"Magic?" said Jim. He looked suddenly and suspiciously at Angie. She raised her eyebrows questioningly.

"Magic?" she inquired.

"I say to you it is magick that threatens them," said Dafydd, "and of magick, as you know, I have none."

They looked at him.

"Magick?" Jim echoed once more, in as close to the way everybody pronounced it here as he could manage. "Whose magick?"

"That of what held the Loathly Tower and owned the creatures we encountered there."

"The Dark Powers?"

"It does no harm to say the name aloud? Very well, then, I speak of the Dark Powers. I venture you will tell me to consult Carolinus on this; but as we all know, he has been frail since his imprisonment by the former Gnarly King. It was in my mind that I speak to you first, my Lord."

"None of this 'my Lord' business, Dafydd," said Jim. "We're privy and friends together, friends who know you would be a prince if you moved down to those same ancestral lands under the ocean."

"You know that, Dafydd," said Angie.

The archer smiled a little sadly at both of them.

"I have not forgotten so," he said. "But archer though I

have chosen to be and am, you must remember I was raised to a certain touch of manners, James and Angela.''

''Good enough,'' said Jim. ''But why the excitement about the Dark Powers mixing in human affairs again? Carolinus says they do it all the time, trying to upset either Chance or History; so as to plunge us all either into Chaos or Stasis.''

''Whatever it is those names import,'' said Dafydd. ''But never like this since that matter at the Loathly Tower; and nothing so great as they now attempt, as long as the memory of man runneth, time out of mind. As I say, perhaps this should have been a matter for Carolinus.''

''You won't find Carolinus,'' said Jim. ''KinetetE's keeping him with her; and that's probably all for the best. He needs the attention of a magician as strong as himself to recover after what he went through—and all he put himself through.''

''Then long may he stay until he is full well again,'' replied Dafydd, ''and if strength is needed Mage KinetetE has it, as well as magickal wisdom.''

''Very true,'' said Angie.

''But help I still need.''

''I know,'' Jim said. ''I can't very well just take you to her without asking her first. But I can go to her and talk to her about it. It might be a little hard for you to get in touch with her. But what did you mean exactly about the Dark Powers' not trying anything and sayings like . . . *'time out of mind,'* and *'as the memory of man runneth backward'*?''

Jim was a little sensitive where those two phrases were concerned. They had been quoted at him a little too often by his tenants and Castle people, whenever those people opposed something he had ordered. Either phrase was universally accepted as the single, final, crushing argument to prove what he wanted done had never been done. It therefore could not be done, could never be done, and so there was no point even in talking any more about it.

''On second thought,'' he added hastily, since his own words had sounded more than a little harsh in his own ears, ''never mind that. I was just wondering why it concerns us.''

"Indeed, it does not concern you," said Dafydd, with a slight emphasis on the last word. "It concerns me and my people only, James. I am come as a petitioner to beg the grace of your aid and help."

"Well, you don't even need to ask for that! Anything I can do . . ." Angie was sending up signals, but Jim ignored them. "Look, why don't you just tell us all about it before I make any more bad guesses?"

"I am easier doing that," said Dafydd. "Well, then, two weeks past, it fell that I heard from the Drowned Land. Word came to me from my King there, whom you once met, with an urgency to see me now. I went below the waves, accordingly; and we two spoke privily. You must know that among us, those of the Old Blood feel things others do not; and he had not been alone there in feeling a presence—not quite yet upon his Drowned Land itself, but casting a growing shadow toward it; as the shadow of a thundercloud goes before it to darken the landscape."

"And did you feel that, too, when you were down there?" Angie said.

Dafydd looked quickly at her.

"I did that," he said, "from the moment I set foot on that ancient earth. The shadow of it has not left me since. I feel it even here, now, in your Hall."

He stopped speaking, looking at them.

Jim's and Angie's eyes went to each other unthinkingly. Jim could have sworn there had been nothing different about the Hall until Dafydd's last word. But now there was; and, gazing at each other, he and Angie each knew the other was also feeling whatever had come into it.

It was nothing visible or audible. The morning sun still streamed with September brilliance through the narrow windows from the bright sky outside. The freshly laid and kindled fires in the three big fireplaces still threw up their flames, doing their best to warm the overnight chill of the large, empty stone Hall in which they burned; but both Jim and Angie now felt darkness like a weightless finger laid upon them.

Jim's rebellious inner core, normally sleeping in him, woke suddenly and unexpectedly. He had argued with Angie and scorned his servants for their quickness to believe in things supernatural. But this was different.

This was an uninvited intrusion into the place that was his and Angie's—ALONE!

A fury as primeval and instinctive as that of Aargh, the English wolf, bared its teeth within him.

"Out!" he shouted to the empty air above him, careless of consequences. "Out of my Hall, my home! You've no power under this roof! GO!"

As he shouted, not even thinking of what the cost might be, in magical energy or life itself, he *thrust* with all the power of magic he had developed in him against what hung above them—and all at once, beneath the dark rooftrees, there was nothing where it had been. Nothing at all.

Chapter 2

For a long moment more, like a wolf filling the entrance of his den, teeth bared and snarling at an enemy, Jim went on staring up at what was no longer there under the shadow of the sharply slanted roof.

Then he became aware of a taste of blood in his mouth, felt with his tongue against his teeth and found he had bitten it. In spite of himself, he smiled; and, smiling, relaxed. The sudden, all-encompassing fire of rage that had come upon him began to sink, gutter, and die, like the flame of a fireplace log as the last of its burnable substance was consumed. He brought his eyes back to the High Table.

Angie and Dafydd were looking at him.

"Go on," he said to Dafydd, a little thickly. His tongue had already begun to swell, but not much. Angie relaxed in her seat.

Dafydd watched him for a second longer, the archer's face as calm as ever. Then he went on, as if nothing had happened.

"Of further facts I have none. But my King, like all my people now living apart on deep ocean floor, has spent all his life there and not only feels but reads more—and more correctly—into such feelings as we of the Old Blood have been gifted to sense. He reads the shadow as darkening to the west of our Drowned Land, beyond our borders, where is the fabled, ancient Land of Old Magic—Lyonesse; and it covers that country as far as the cliff-face you and I know, James, that is the beginning of the great underseas mountain which holds the Kingdom of the Gnarly people. There, where just a short time past Carolinus was held prisoner, and from which we carried him and your young ward back to this castle."

"The cliff-face has an entrance. Maybe the shadow's gone in there, too, where your people can't see or feel it?"

"No, James. It ends at the cliff with the entrance to that land. It is Lyonesse alone that is cloaked—an action such as the Dark Powers have never shown before, and for reasons known only to them. No doubt those reasons will show themselves in time—after they have truly won Lyonesse—for my King believes that winning still awaits a final test of their strength. Remember, Lyonesse is a land of old and strange magick—it may be older and stranger than even the Dark Powers understand. But reasons do not matter to my cousins beneath the waves, only that this darkness will be next neighbor to them if it succeeds."

Jim could think of nothing to say. Apparently, neither could Angie.

"I come to you, James," Dafydd went on, "because this is a foe my arrows cannot touch; and my King there is old, older than he looks; and not likely to go on being old forever even though he takes care not to be captured and misused as was Carolinus by the Gnarly King. It is the Drowned Land, not himself, for which he cares, you understand."

"Of course we understand!" said Angie. "He's worried about what will happen to the Kingdom once he's gone and there's no one capable in charge."

"Yes," said Dafydd; "and you likewise understand, I can see, James. I know this is none of your care or responsibility.

It is only I who bear an obligation and a duty to the Drowned Land."

"Never mind that. Go on," Jim said.

The entrance door to the Hall banged open; and, entering sideways because of a large gutted and cleaned stag on his shoulders, there came Brian, wearing his sword and an old mail shirt, but otherwise dressed in somewhat stained and well-worn everyday clothes. He turned to face the dais; and, still carrying the deer, marched down the aisle toward them. A quiver of arrows hung from one hip and the top end of a bowstave poked up between his left shoulder and the carcass.

"Heigh-ho!" he said cheerfully. "I was just out today, playing with my bow—shooting at rovers, you know—and damme if I didn't get this deer. Dropped him with one shot, as it happens. Well, I had an extra horse with me; but it struck me suddenly it was foolish to carry the meat back to my castle with Malencontri so close. So I thought I might gift it to you, as some small acknowledgment for the excellent dinners and other meals you have fed me here."

As he said these last words, he heaved the carcass from his shoulders onto the table they were sitting at, splashing wine out of the wine cups and nearly sending some of them, as well as other table settings, off onto the floor. No small feat, thought Jim, since the buck, even eviscerated, could weigh almost as much as Brian did himself.

It was instantly obvious to those at the table, who knew him, that Brian had been out since dawn or before—hunting on foot, most likely, his hounds all being too old and few for hunting from horseback in a more knightly manner; and that the deer had been taken with deliberate attempt to show he paid at least some of his debts, social or otherwise. It was also intended to show that there was no lack of food at Castle Smythe, which they all knew was not always the case.

"But now you're here, you'll sit and have a glass of wine, and maybe a bite of something with us, certainly?" said Angie, the quickest to recover.

"Now, I could never say nay to that!" Brian came around to the side of the dais behind the table, stepped up, and took his bowstave with its loose but ready string off his shoulder to put it aside before sitting down.

''Sir Brian, of your kindness may I see your bow, and perhaps your arrows as well?''

''Why—of course,'' said Brian, handing both over to the seated archer and obviously embarrassed. ''Just rough things, of course. Made them myself, with the help of Old Ned at my castle. Nothing to look at really—no real skill or time put into either—''

''My thanks for your graciousness,'' said Dafydd, taking them. ''It is that I am always learning from the way other men make these to their own purpose. Often I counsel young bowmen to do likewise; but many will not realize that, despite what skill they may have, they can always learn from any man who ever set knife to wood—were it only yesterday for the first time.''

''Hah! Yes, of course!'' said Brian, burying his face in the full wine cup Angie had just passed him. By this time servants were already there, taking away the deer and cleverly rolling up the old cloth with its stains of blood and other fluids, replacing it as it went with a new, clean cloth and extra food. Brian lost no time getting to work on the latter.

A stroke of luck, thought Jim, watching him. Brian would want to be invited to join any expedition such as Dafydd was proposing; and he had not needed to be messaged to join them here—which reminded Jim it would not hurt to ask Aargh, the English wolf, to keep an eye on the safety of Angie and Malencontri while Jim and the others were gone.

''By the way,'' he said to Brian, ''you didn't see Aargh while you were out, did you?''

Brian swallowed.

''Oh, yes. I always run across him in the woods—or he, me. I had wished to ask him the next time I saw him, if there was a smell to magick. So I did, less than an hour since, and he said there was, in fact an army of different scents; but being a two-legs, even if I could smell any of them, I wouldn't like them. Then he hung his jaw open—you will know, the way he does when he is laughing, but without a sound."

He paused to wash down another mouthful of food with a generous swallow of wine.

"The curious matter is," he went on, "that I have grown so used to the beast that what I would consider as a fighting insult from any other creature, thing or man, passes by me like a summer breeze, hardly noticed. But why should he be so sour and grim always? Do you know, James? Dafydd?"

"I think it comes from the life he has to live," answered Jim. "It's kill or be killed for him."

"Why, but so it is for us—" Brian broke off abruptly. "Forgive me, James. Such contention is not seemly. I must tell you how pleased I am to see you and Angela. And Dafydd, whom I had not expected to find here."

"The fact is," said Jim, "there's a problem that Dafydd has suddenly found; and I believe he meant to speak not only to me about it, but you as well."

"Ah?" said Brian, setting down his wine cup and looking all at once at Dafydd with concern and curiosity. "What is that, Dafydd?"

Not only Dafydd, but all of them told him.

"Another chance at the Dark Powers!" said Brian when they were all finished. "What merry news!"

However, he did not sound as if it was merry news. His voice was flat. Jim, Angie, and Dafydd looked at him.

"You need not be concerned about it, Brian," said Dafydd gently, omitting the *Sir* before Brian's name—something he did much less often with that knight than he did with Jim, and only in the most informal of moments. "I do not ask your help."

"But I would be happy to give it!" cried Brian. "If only it wasn't for this damn wedding—I mean, if it wasn't for Geronde's damn father—I mean, if it wasn't for the unfortunate situation of my father-in-law, right now, poor gentleman."

Jim tried to unravel this tangle of words, and ended by choosing the least damnable of them all.

"Would I be impertinent"—he was finally beginning to pick up some of the fourteenth-century verbal courtesies—"if I inquired what that unfortunate situation might be?"

"Oh, now it seems he owes money. An old debt, money he had long forgotten about. But his creditor, having learned Sir Geoffrey is back in England, threatens fire, brimstone, hanging, drawing and quartering if he is not paid back immediately. Geronde and I knew nothing of it until he suddenly confessed all, showing us a letter from the man."

"But he had this enormous palace and everything when you found him in the Holy Land," said Angie. "Didn't he manage to bring anything home with him?"

"None of it was his, you may remember," said Brian. "No, he came back to Malvern with Geronde and the rest of us, as penniless as a canting friar."

"And now that he has Malvern this creditor expects him to pay up?"

"Worse than that," said Brian. "He took it directly to a Justice of Assize, seeking an immediate payment from Malvern's movable wealth and valuables, which would ruin everything that Geronde has done to work it up in the years since her father went off to that so-called Crusade—to say nothing of leaving it all but empty of servants, empty indeed of cattle, horse, and tools of all sorts as well as stripping Geronde herself of all possessions except two dresses and a few other womanly necessities."

Jim and Dafydd were studiously silent. Angie was asking questions far more personal than either of them would have asked, even in a private one-on-one conversation; but they were eager to hear the answers. The rule amongst gentlemen worthy of the name was to perhaps hint at the knowledge wanted, but otherwise wait until it came voluntarily. But Brian seemed relieved to talk; and they were more than willing to listen.

"We can't let that happen—" Angie was looking at Jim. But it was Brian who interrupted her.

"No, no," he said. "It's all right. Quite all right. I took care of it. I put up a bond to the court for the debt."

Jim was ready to interrupt on his own, and slow Angie down on this personal questioning. He was all but certain she was about to go far beyond what was considered permissible between even the closest of old male friends in this society. If Brian really wanted to tell them, he should say so before she went any further. But she was too fast for Jim.

"Not your bride-price you earned from the Earl of Cumberland—"

"No, no," said Brian. "Geronde has that and would not give it if they dug up Malvern and carried its very stones away to settle the debt. No, I put as surety to the court some—some of my own property."

"Angie," said Jim, "I don't think we should ask Brian for any more details—"

"Quite all right, James," said Brian. "As a matter of fact, I went after a deer by intent this morning, to give me an excuse to come and tell you that other debts of honor I have to you might be beyond my power to pay, for now at least. What I put as surety was Smythe Castle and income from its lands, some of which is good crop or pastureland and could be rented out for some value. They're entailed, of course, to my oldest son, when I have one, and his oldest in due time and so on . . . but I could be excluded from there in my lifetime, or until the rents and other income on the property paid off the debt."

He paused and coughed, looking away from them all.

"As it happened," he said, "the Judge of Assize had never viewed Smythe Castle when he took my bond. Neither had the creditor."

There was a moment of silence while they all thought about this, Brian with obvious satisfaction.

"I understand now, Brian," said Dafydd, "why you cannot go to Lyonesse with James and myself."

"Jim—" began Angie, and checked herself abruptly. The three men looked inquiringly at her, but she only looked straight back at them as if one of their number had owned the voice they had just heard.

"Indeed," went on Dafydd, "there was no intention of

imposing on you at any time. It was simply that I thought—and I am sure James did as well—that you would wish at least to be invited."

"And I could use the exercise, I can tell you!" said Brian. "You have no idea how being involved, day after day, in house-bound problems—" .

He checked himself in turn, looking at his two friends, both of whom were married and each of whom had at least one child under his roof.

"Well, perhaps you can," he said, taking a long drink from his wine cup by way of putting a period to his words.

"Does Geronde know about all this?" asked Angie, in spite of Jim's frown.

"Oh, of course," said Brian, putting down his cup and looking at her with surprise. "That is to say, all but what we have spoken of just now—Dafydd's duty to his family in the Drowned Land, and that I have told him why, regretfully, I must be unhelpful at this moment."

"Well, I think she should know that, too. We should get her here, or all go to Malvern—whichever works best—so we can talk about this together. She's involved, too."

"Good idea!" said Jim, suddenly struck with an inspiration. "Why don't you send a pigeon to her right away, Angie; and meanwhile I'll go see if there isn't someone who could help us decide what to do about Lyonesse."

"Well," said Angie, "I suppose. But why don't you—"

"Be back very shortly," said Jim, and, visualizing the destination he had in mind, moved himself magically to it.

Chapter 3

Once again, he was in KinetetE's sitting room. It was exactly as he remembered it. As if he had left it only a second before. It was the same cozy-feeling place, all the comfortable overstuffed chairs placed at the same angle with the central carpet, the same warmly shaded lamps, the cheerful red-and-white wallpaper with tiny flowers—and above all the sampler on the wall, worked in green and red thread, that spelled out WHEN THY SHOE IS ON THY FOOT, TREAD UPON THORNS.

The only difference was a large, floppy-leaved green plant about four feet tall, standing in the middle of the room. Among its leaves was a trumpet-shaped growth that might have resembled a flower if it had not been more obviously a large, furled leaf. The plant could have been taken for a four-foot-high ornamental growth, if only it had been in some kind of pot or planter.

"Forgive me for thrusting myself upon your attention," it said to him unexpectedly, in a squeaky voice. "I am a *Dieffenbachia seguine cantans,* a singing plant. Not to be confused with the ordinary *Dieffenbachia seguine,* or dumbcane, as it is known in many kingdoms like the one you undoubtedly came from. I used to sing Merlin himself to sleep with a sweet lullaby—and now listen to me."

It began to squeak and shrill in a completely unbearable fashion; so that it was only by heroic effort that Jim kept from putting his hands over his ears to at least give his sense of hearing some protection.

It stopped, after what seemed a long time.

"Yes," said Jim, in the wonderful silence that followed, "that's bad. I take it you're here to get help from the Mage?"

"Ah, you know the Mage!" The dieffenbachia lowered its squeaky voice suddenly, and its large green leaves dipped shyly. "Would you possibly be a magickian yourself, honored sir?"

"A very low-class magician only."

"Ah, but still, you might know what has happened to my lovely voice. Sirens took lessons from me at one time. Nightingales dropped by regularly to brush up on the pitch of their notes. By any chance—"

"I'm afraid not."

"No," said the *Dieffenbachia cantans*, its single furled leaf drooping even farther. "Forgive me, Mage—"

"I'm not entitled to be addressed as Mage," said Jim.

"Oh. Forgive me, as I say, but I had to ask. Still, perhaps KinetetE—"

"Can do nothing for you," said KinetetE, suddenly appearing in the room. The tall, thin Mage's expression was stern, even severe; but then, Jim reflected, she always looked that way. "Only a Great Deed can give you back the voice you once had. Be patient, and perhaps in time there will be one."

"But the Land of Lyonesse is in parlous state!" squeaked the *Dieffenbachia cantans*. "I must help it and those of noble mind who will defend it. They must have the encouragement of my singing, else Lyonesse may be lost—"

"I doubt your loss of voice is quite that important," the Mage said. She gestured with one arm, the wide sleeve of her long, comfortable-looking dark-green gown flaring momentarily. The motion caused the tips of brown, slipperlike shoes to appear from beneath the hem of the garment. "In any case, attempts are being made by me and those like me to prevent the loss of Lyonesse," she went on. "In fact, that's what brings the Dragon Knight of Malencontri here to speak with me—and that is what he and I must be about now. It's time for you to go."

"Are you a dragon, sir?" asked the *Dieffenbachia cantans* curiously, turning to Jim.

"Begone!" said KinetetE—and it was.

"Weren't you"—Jim hesitated—"sort of hard on him—her—it . . . whatever the word would be?"

"Things have to be dealt with in their order of importance," said KinetetE; "but because he sang to Merlin and some others does not put him first in my attention when his personal trouble is only a part of the large problem you've come to speak to me about."

"That plant is a 'he,' then?"

"As it happens," said KinetetE. "The female *Dieffenbachia cantansae* are far less arrogant. To answer your first question, however—as you suspected, Carolinus must not be troubled at this time. Under such conditions it was quite proper for you to call on me."

"I hadn't asked any question yet."

"It wasn't necessary. You, Brian, and Dafydd are going to Lyonesse to stop the Dark Powers from conquering and owning it. You've simply come to me instead of Carolinus for aid in direction and the necessary increase in your own magick abilities for that task."

"Wait a minute," said Jim, as she paused. It was next to impossible to interrupt KinetetE when she was speaking. Each of her sentences was a statement that nailed any interlocutor to a wall of silence until she was done speaking. "You're jumping way ahead of what we've planned. In the first place, Brian can't go—"

"Nonsense!" said KinetetE, interrupting Jim without the least difficulty. "You should know better than that. In fact, you do. You landed in our world to find you could speak to and understand everybody you encountered; and ever since you've carried around the notion that therefore they felt and thought the same way you and Angie were used to. Well, we don't; and you'd better start keeping that in mind. Now, try to imagine you're Brian. If you were him, would you stay home while Dafydd and you go?"

"Not of his own free will, of course," said Jim. "But with this business of putting up Smythe Castle as surety, he hasn't any choice."

"Choice!" KinetetE did not sneer. She did not need to. The tone of her voice took care of everything. "Put yourself in Brian's place, as I say. You are Sir Brian Neville-Smythe. You are a great lance at spear-runnings and tournaments. You are known as one of the heroes who conquered the Dark Powers at the Loathly Tower. But here comes another chance to cross swords, metaphorically speaking, with the same Powers. The other two heroes are there, but not you. What will other knights—what will all England say?"

Jim almost blushed. He felt as if he was in third grade, having just been led into an unfair verbal trap by his teacher.

"That he was dodging this new battle," he answered. Now that the words were out, he was absolutely certain of what people of this time, particularly Brian's competitors, would say about his friend. "That he'd lost his nerve."

"You see? You can understand, but you've got to stop and look twice. Do so from now on."

"But how can he be absent now that he's promised to be available on this surety bond, or whatever it is, without notice?"

"You know the answer to that, too; and if you'd thought you'd have realized Brian would have asked you himself right out to use magick to warn you and send him back the moment he's required at Smythe. Return him in a twinkling. He hasn't asked you that yet because it might be an imposition on you. And, of course, that's another reason you're here now, pretending only to ask for advice from me—you want me to give you not only advice and more magick, but a way to use your magick in Lyonesse, against the laws of that and all other nonhuman Kingdoms."

Jim had now shrunk to kindergarten size in his own estimation.

"All right," he said, "I did want advice from you on some way of possibly carrying what magic I've got into Lyonesse—but that's if I go, myself. Angie will probably be against my going. For that matter, with their banns about to be published and their wedding as soon after that as possible, Geronde may not want Brian to go."

"Do you think she'll say anything to stop him?" said KinetetE. "Angie may say something to you if you talk about going; but she comes from a world where you have choices in such matters. Here, Geronde has her life and Brian has his, each with separate duties. Brian's chief duty is fighting and winning. Geronde's is to hold what is theirs. In each case, their duties come first. It would do her no good to tell him she doesn't want him to go. He would go anyway because there's no alternative. He'd be unhappy, but only because she's unhappy. I think you'll find Geronde will say nothing and spare him that."

Jim gave up.

"All right," he said. "Assuming we all go to the Drowned Land with Dafydd and end up in Lyonesse. How can I—or

Dafydd and I, and even if Brian was with us—hope to do anything about what the Dark Powers are at in Lyonesse?''

"I haven't the slightest idea,'' said KinetetE. "Neither would any other good magickian belonging to this world. Dark Powers, forsooth!'' For a moment she looked even more cadaverous than usual, her face seeming at odds with the homey comfort of her room and her gown.

"Chaos threatens,'' she went on, "in a new and more dangerous way; and History calls on you, Brian, and Dafydd to set right the balance. So says Carolinus, who sees more deeply into this endless struggle between those two forces than any of the rest of us. None of the rest of the Magickal Collegiate can imagine any hope of turning back this move toward Chaos. But Carolinus thinks you can do it, somehow, with your mad, otherworld ways.''

"What if we won't go?''

"Then we all suffer,'' said KinetetE coldly. "Every time one of the two Forces wins, the balance between them is broken. The winner becomes stronger and more likely to finally destroy the other completely. That affects all of us. But 'all' includes you and everyone you know. If Chaos rules, there'll be no more rules. You and Angie will most certainly be torn apart. So will Geronde and Brian, Dafydd, Danielle, and their children. Now, do you want me to give or help you now with what you'll want—and I'll give you anything I can in good magickal conscience—or would you rather call on me as you need me?''

Jim thought quickly. He was still determined not to go: but that argument could be settled later. Meanwhile, a door left continually open was much better than one open at just this moment. "I'll call on you.''

"I see. Along with everyone else. Carolinus never stops befriending everyone and everything he meets; and they all want a piece of him. Well, there's no changing him this late in the day. Farewell, then. All right—*you*! The dryad third oak from Carolinus's cottage. You're next—''

But Jim was already back at Malencontri. Everything looked the same—but different, somehow. It was still morning, but the Great Hall was lit differently. It was as if the sunlight was coming in from the high windows at a less bright and flatter angle than it had been when he left. Brian, Dafydd, and Angie were just as he had left them at the High Table. But so, inexplicably, was Geronde, who had been off in Malvern, nearly a day's ride away, when Jim had gone to call on KinetetE.

"Geronde!" said Jim. "How did you get here so quickly?"

He remembered just in time to give her the ritual kiss of greeting before sitting down. It was only when he released her that she had a chance to answer.

"I've been here since last night, James!"

"Oh?" he said. "Last night?"

"A pigeon came with a message from Angie and I got here by horse, riding fast, just before darkness fell," she answered, looking at him oddly.

"But—" began Jim, but checked himself. "Of course! I forgot to ask KinetetE to send me back here to the moment just after I'd left! I'll bet she had me in suspended animation until she spoke to half a dozen others who were waiting, like that dryad."

Geronde, Brian, and Dafydd looked at him with the polite, agreeable expressions adopted by people who are too mannerly to admit that they have no idea what "suspended animation" might mean—just in case it should have been something embarrassing or uncomfortable.

"Jim," said Angie, gently, "do you want to tell us what you're talking about? It was KinetetE you went to see?"

"Yes, she's seeing everyone who wants to see Carolinus—he's not up to visitors yet, evidently," said Jim.

They all waited for him to go on.

"Well, you see," he said, "I thought I'd get either Carolinus's or her opinion about this situation with the Dark Powers trying to take over Lyonesse. The magical community would be likely to know more about it than we would."

"And did you?" asked Angie.

"Yes—and no," said Jim. "They were way ahead of me; or at least KinetetE and Carolinus were, or are . . ."

His voice trailed off as his mind began replaying the conversation he had just held with KinetetE. He woke to the waiting faces around him.

"Apparently Carolinus thinks, and KinetetE believes"—he blurted out—"Dafydd—you, Brian, and I may be the only people who can stop the Dark Powers taking over Lyonesse; and things can become very bad then for your Drowned Land, to say nothing of the whole world if we don't."

They, all of them—even the usually self-contained Dafydd—began to speak at once.

"Hold it," said Jim. "That is, let me say something first."

They stopped speaking and waited.

"Look," he went on, "that's all KinetetE told me. She won't let anyone see Carolinus; and neither of them have any idea how I—how we might do it. That's all she said, all I know. Let's not try to hash it over just yet. Let's think about it and the situation each of us is in, maybe talk about it with whoever's closest to us; then meet here for supper and all of us discuss it."

"What about dinner?" said Brian.

Jim cursed himself. Even after these several years he kept getting the two meal terms mixed up. Here, of course, dinner was the noonday meal. Supper came at twilight, winter or summer; and everybody both went to bed and rose with the sun—more or less.

"I'll have the Serving Room set up this table as a table dormant," he told Brian. "There'll be food on it for whoever wants it, all the time."

"James," said Brian, "you are the best of hosts. I always think the better if my stomach is not empty."

He stood up. They all stood up. Angie linked her arm in Jim's.

"Come on," she said, "let's you and I take that walk you mentioned earlier—the one we never got around to. This is probably our best chance at the best of our autumn weather this year."

Chapter 4

Their feet made soft shushing sounds in the dry leaves as they walked under the great elms; and more leaves fell, twirling about them, as they went.

"You know . . ." Angie said. She had his arm linked in hers and held tightly to her. ". . . when we first decided to stay here, in those early days, I just wanted you to survive in this fourteenth-century world. Every time you went, I was afraid I might never see you again. I felt guilty about wanting to stay here myself—"

"You shouldn't have," said Jim. "I wanted to stay—badly. It was like a kid stepping into Toyland—the real Toyland—the people and everything about it."

"But if I'd said I didn't want to stay, you'd have at least stopped to think it over first. Anyway . . . the point is, after a while, I saw how well you were able to take care of yourself here; in spite of not being raised to weapons from the cradle the way Brian's been. I began to stop being afraid so much. But as that fear went, another one came. You haven't started to like it too much here, have you? These adventures, I mean; you haven't come to like the fighting and the killing?"

Jim stopped abruptly. They turned to face each other.

"No!" he said. "How could I, coming from where and when we were? And how could I change now, after all those years? I suppose I could; but I don't want to. No, what I *have* come to do is accept it . . . like the rain and the winter cold—and the people. The good ones, I mean."

Angie squeezed his arm.

"I love you so much," she said. "I didn't think you'd changed. I wouldn't want you to."

"And I love you!" he said. "We're lucky, that's all. Every so often two people win the lottery together. We did."

"Yes," said Angie. They walked on, side by side.

"No," said Jim, after a little silence, "what I liked from

the start—what made me want to stay so much I'd risk doing without dentists and modern medicines and all that—is the unbelievable will to live of these people. They try to make a good life out of it, under conditions where the chance of being killed is something you have to face without warning at any time—and often nothing you can do about it. It's just the way things are."

"I know what you mean," said Angie, watching her feet kick a thicker-than-usual pile of leaves out of their way.

"Now that I've recognized it," said Jim, "I realize that the same thing was there—plenty of it—in our native world and time; but born and brought up where we were, we could be blind to it in other places. If we'd gone back—but we didn't; and I'm still glad we didn't. A chance like this . . . well, it doesn't come to people. Anyway, we're here now with no way back, even if the situation here includes magic and things like the Dark Powers."

"Yes," said Angie. She reached out to catch a falling leaf that was twirling down at an angle toward her from one of the forest giants. She studied it for a few seconds, then passed it to Jim with a sudden smile.

"From me to you," she said, "good magic. Keep it safe, use it well."

Jim took it carefully, suddenly deeply moved.

"Angie!" he said. The leaf was completely yellow, but just beginning to turn dry and fragile. He held it cautiously in his hand.

"Thank you," he told her. From the moment she had smiled and handed it to him, he had been watching her closely. "You're worried about me now, and this thing with Dafydd."

Her smile went.

"Yes," she said. "I'm sorry—I just am."

"It won't be anything serious or dangerous, Angie. It can't be. I'll be completely protected by KinetetE's magic; and anyway, Dafydd just wants me because he thinks I'll understand the magic in the situation. I'm sort of like a lucky rabbit's foot to him. You heard him say he'd have spoken to Carolinus instead, if he could. Did you ever know Carolinus to run any risks?''

''Carolinus grew up in this world. He knows what the risks are—I'm sorry, Jim. Let's not talk about it. I know now you can take care of yourself. I've known that for a long time; and you were magnificent in the Hall yesterday, when the Dark Powers came.''

Magnificent was the last word Jim would have chosen to describe himself.

''I was mad, Angie, that's all. Mad clear through! If They'd just been something I could get my hands on—''

''Look at your hands now.''

He looked. They had curled into fists, and his forearms had raised to waist level parallel to the ground.

''If you could see yourself now,'' said Angie. She put her own hand on one of his tense forearms. ''Jim, don't look like that.''

He made his arms, his body, and his jaw muscles go through the motions of relaxing. By some miracle the leaf in his grasp had not been crushed. He reached down, pulled apart the opening of his purse—the small bag holding his coins and keys—and put the leaf reverently into it, then pulled the drawstrings tight again.

''There,'' he said. ''I'll keep it with me; and your leaf'll keep me sensible. It was just They came into our home, our castle—and I'd never thought it could be violated like that! I'd felt we were safe there.''

''So did I,'' Angie said. ''I never will again.''

''I'll fix it so you are!'' said Jim. ''Angie, it's me They were after. Once I'm off with Dafydd, They won't be back here. And I can handle them.''

''You're so sure?''

''Yes! I know I'm beginning to get a grip, in my own way, about the magic—or magick, whatever you want to call it—here. It's simple, basic. If certain things are possible, then there're other things that can't be. The Dark Powers are powerful in the sense of owning a lot of magical energy—but

They're limited in what They can do with it. We humans aren't limited."

"Are you sure you aren't talking yourself into something?"

"No. All Their powers—like the Naturals, there has to be a limit on Them. They can't move a single piece of straw by Themselves. The best They can do is work on some solid living thing to move it for them. Human magicians like me can use power to move things—admittedly the same thing applies to us. We're limited, too. Our magic won't cure sickness, though wounds, particularly battle wounds, we can heal. But on the other hand, we can use medicines, if we can find ones that'll work, to cure sickness. And any one of us can also pick up and move whole stacks of straw with everyday muscle. . . . We work in both areas."

"Why do all the Dark Powers and Demons and such seem more powerful than we do, then?"

"Because magic seems to be made out of a raw energy—that energy I mentioned. It isn't how much raw material you've got, it's how you can use it." He paused for a moment.

"Put it like this," he went on, "I'm going to be completely protected against attack, thanks to KinetetE, and I can attack Them because I can outthink Them. I don't think They've got anything more in the way of brains than some very primitive form of animal life."

He stopped speaking. It had been a pretty good statement on his part, he was thinking—and then, with the sensitivity of a well-trained husband (though he and Angie had only been married since they had come to this medieval world), suddenly he was sure it had been nothing of the sort, as far as convincing Angie had gone.

"Look," he added hastily, before she could say anything, "we humans actually have only a small scrap of the energy from which magic can be made here. The Kingdoms, like that of the King and Queen of the Dead, and Lyonesse itself, are full of it. Big devils like the Demon Ahriman have huge chunks by themselves." Angie frowned.

"I think," Jim continued hastily, "humans here started out with none at all, but have simply earned a small corner of it. I got my first chunk just by coming here to find you, out of our own world. Then I got a much larger chunk—but the Dark Powers would hardly notice it compared to Theirs—by winning the fight at the Loathly Tower. I've won against Them each time I've been up against Them, in a sense getting richer and gaining experience at the same time. But it's just lately I'm beginning to figure out how the whole thing works. My advantage is, you and I come from a time where we grew up feeling there had to be a reason, a pattern for everything that happened. Most people in this time don't think that way—so it gives me an edge."

He stopped talking again. He was not improving matters between Angie and himself. He gave up and prepared to listen.

"Tell me all the truth, then," said Angie; but she spoke gently. "What are you really up against? The dangers, everything. Magic for one thing, of course."

Jim looked at her affectionately.

"Nothing you'll have to worry about."

"I'm a lot happier knowing what I ought to be worrying about than I am sitting here at home and guessing at everything."

The beginning cheerfulness that had been lurking behind Jim's words went away.

"In all truth, then, Angie," he said, "there's the so-called Old Magic of Lyonesse. I don't know much about it, but it seems to be somehow different from the magic we've seen used. I think it works to help the Knights there, but I don't know if it'd be any help to me.

"But other than that I'm really not afraid to match magic with anyone—no, scrub that. What I mean is, I'm not afraid to match what magic I have, along with all I know from being born six hundred years later, against any other magic on this world. Every time I've been faced with that sort of thing so far I've always won. I haven't got it all sorted into words yet; but I've got an edge, something no one else has."

"An *edge*," said Angie.

"All right—an edge only, not a guarantee. But it's like anything else. Since I've been using it, I've gotten better at using what I have and the magic together. Trust me, Angie."

"Don't I always?"

"But you're determined to worry, anyway."

"Whether I worry or not's my own business. It wasn't your future knowledge and edge that you used to win at the Loathly Tower."

"No," said Jim soberly. "I won only because I was in Gorbash's dragon body. But I didn't know about magic, then."

"You did when we faced Ahriman; and it was only the magic in your staff that helped you win against that Demon."

"Not quite. It was that and the rest of you making a human chain with me to herd him back into the Kingdom of Devils and Demons. But that—"

"Was different, too. I know," she said. "All right, let's talk about this business of how you might get caught in Lyonesse and I'd never see you again?"

"Oh, that—" said Jim. "You mean what Dafydd told us the people of Drowned Land warned him about?"

"Yes, that."

"We're supposed to have warning before anything happens in any case, you know. I told you all about that. As long as the whole land and everything in it looks black and white, or silver, in color, there's no danger at all. It's only if you stay long enough to start seeing things in their ordinary colors that you're trapped and can never leave."

"And by that time it's too late. You can't leave."

"We're supposed to see it changing in time. Anything less than black-and-white . . . I'll have to keep my eyes open, that's all."

"You ought to be able to do better than that," Angie said. She reached out to catch another autumn leaf that was swirling down toward the ground; and studied it for a few seconds before dropping it. "Where's that future knowledge of yours? You need a warning device . . . let's see—I've got it! Glasses!

Glasses to warn you when the change starts so you can leave immediately!''

''Glasses?'' said Jim, staring at her. ''Pretty strange I'd look in Arthurian times, or even here, going around with glasses on my nose. What good would glasses do me, anyway?''

''Magic glasses, of course! And you don't care how you look!''

''Hah!''

''Besides, magickians are supposed to look strange.''

''Well, yes, I suppose so. But—''

''Anyway, I mean glasses that will make you notice your first tendency to see things differently. Just like shortsighted people see more clearly when they put on their glasses or lenses—the moment a hint of a color change becomes visible down there, your glasses would suddenly see everything in blaring, bright colors, everywhere, all around you! Or would something like that call for magic you haven't learned yet?''

''I don't think so,'' said Jim. ''In fact, I know I'm way ahead of most C+-class Apprentices—with all I've been mixed up in. None of them usually get the chance at things like Carolinus has let me run into on my own. I'd have asked him about rating me B-class before this, if he hadn't been so worn out and frail from what he went through in the Gnarly Kingdom.''

''Then make the glasses.''

''I can't just do it like that—right now,'' he said. ''I have to work up a concept of what I want before I can make the actual thing. I have to think of ways of going about it.''

''But you'll make them?''

Jim looked at her. She was very serious.

''Barring some reason that makes it impossible, that I can't even imagine now, I promise you—yes, I'll make them.''

''And wear them.''

''And wear them,'' he said resignedly.

''And you're really not worried at all about the Dark Powers you'll be meeting?''

''No. As I said, They can't do anything to me physically.

They can only work through other people or things. I can outthink the people and avoid the things."

"And there's nothing—nothing at all else . . . ?"

"No."

"What troubles you?" said an unexpected, but familiar, harsh voice behind them.

They turned, and it was the only individual that particular voice could possibly go with: Aargh, the English wolf, who had also been one of Jim's Companions and allies at the battle of the Loathly Tower—though Aargh would never admit being anything like a Companion to anyone. As usual he had come up behind them without a sound and had possibly been following them and listening to their conversation for more than a few minutes.

"What makes you think we're troubled?"

Aargh lifted his muzzle toward Jim.

"You were standing fight-ready," he said. "You have an enemy?"

Jim opened his mouth to point out that he had a number of enemies—Agatha Falon, the Earl of Cumberland . . . and so forth. Then he realized what Aargh must be talking about. He had been watching them as he usually did, for a small while, before making himself known; and this time he had been there to see Jim tense up and get angry all over again when Angie mentioned the Dark Powers's intruding on the Hall at Malencontri.

Most wolf language was body language; unless, like Aargh, the wolf could speak like a human—maybe it was not uncommon for them. Jim had met at least one other wolf who talked human-style. But the body language was still theirs. Aargh would have read Jim's body-remembered, absolute fury toward the invader of his home.

"The Dark Powers," Jim said.

"It will do no good to get your hackles up now," said Aargh. "Wait for the time when you can bite back."

"They came right into Malencontri!"

"No need to tell me," said Aargh. "I knew it. The deer know it, the birds know it—the forest knows it; and so I know it. Well, you can deal with it yourself this time. It's nothing to do with me."

"I didn't ask you for help," said Jim.

"You might have, as soon as you found me."

There was enough past evidence to warrant this assumption on Aargh's part. But the great wolf always had to pretend he cared for no one, rescued nobody. Jim was silent for a second, trying to think of a crushing answer. None came to mind.

"They're threatening the Drowned Land—but you probably don't know—"

"I know," said Aargh. "I know all places I can go. I know it also threatens Lyonesse."

"Put it this way, then," said Jim. "You wouldn't care, of course, if the whole world, including your territory here in Somerset, dissolved into Chaos?"

"It isn't going to. What you two-legs consider your world might do that; but for the rest of us, we'll hardly know it happened. For us, the earth is important, the sky, the wind, the trees—as we have always had them. Your Dark Powers can't touch those. If They could, we would all fight Them. Not otherwise."

"What makes you so sure?" said Jim.

"Why doesn't what you call your magick work on me, or others you call animals—it only works on two-legs and Naturals?"

Jim felt like a chess player who had just had the bishop he was counting on to gain him checkmate with the next move captured and swept away by a completely overlooked knight.

"It just doesn't. There's no particular 'why' to it—"

"Of course there is. What you lose means nothing to us. There's no History for us; and as long as we are alive, there can be no Chaos."

"Why not?" asked Angie.

Jim would have found that a challenge to answer. Aargh did not.

"Chaos is not an emptiness. It is everything moved out of place and connection with what was before. None of what humans call magick could move us and our world; and the kind of enemies who would bring on Chaos have only magick to work with, to move us—they cannot touch us."

"Hm," said Jim.

"However, if I am needed at Malencontri while you are gone," said Aargh, "Angie can set out the signal for me in the woods, the usual way."

He turned, fawned upon her for a brief moment, moved around her, and was gone.

Jim gazed into the trees in the direction where the wolf had vanished. Aargh must have been shadowing them silently and listening for longer than they had thought.

"I wonder if I made a mess of that," he said to himself, but aloud.

"You were fine," said Angie, slipping her arm through his. "Come on, let's look at the cattails down at the lake. There's still part of a beautiful day left, and the cold weather'll be here before you're home again. Let's roam a bit more and enjoy our lands in this best of fall weather, before we have to go back inside."

Chapter 5

The shadows of the tall elms at the edge of the forest were reaching out across the cleared space to touch the gray face of the western curtain wall of the castle, when they returned once more over the hollow-sounding drawbridge into a courtyard already deep in shadow.

Within the Great Hall the fireplaces were blazing; the cressets along the interior walls also brightly burning, shedding light and a welcome small amount of warmth from one end of the long room to the other. Candles set out in honor of the guests made even more light upon the High Table, at which Dafydd, Brian, and Geronde were already sitting.

They had been talking as Angie and Jim came through the door from the courtyard; but this broke off. There was silence as Jim and Angie sat down, and one servant poured wine for them, while another offered the trays of small foods that would start the supper. They helped themselves, drank, and then looked expectantly at the others.

"I must—but I cannot!" Brian burst out as if the conversation had already been going on for some time. "I am between two millstones, James."

The keen eyes of Geronde were upon him; and the candlelight had the effect of making almost invisible the scar where Hugh de Bois had slashed her cheek when she refused to marry him at sword's point. Jim was reminded suddenly he had meant to ask Carolinus, as soon as the Mage was well again, whether something could not be done, magically, to remove it. Even with the scar, though, Geronde's face was beautiful.

"—I swore an oath," Brian was going on, "to be at Castle Smythe whenever my creditors might come there to see me, the castle and the lands that I gave in surety for the debt!"

"Do you remember," asked Jim quietly, "the exact words you swore to?"

"Of course I do! I solemnly swore before God that should any officer of the court or the creditor come to Castle Smythe, they would see me there within the twenty-four hours after their arrival."

"Then I don't think there's anything to concern yourself about. Carolinus is still with KinetetE, as you know, recovering from what the old Gnarly King did to him. I could try to talk to him, or to KinetetE—in fact, I ought to try KinetetE anyway. Hold on—"

He tilted his head back and spoke to the dark rafters of the Hall, overhead.

"KinetetE—"

"Try looking for me then at the usual level, Jim," said the voice of KinetetE. "We're right here, under your nose."

He looked down; and, sure enough, just being seated at the table with them—no surprise at all—was KinetetE and—very much a surprise—Carolinus, with wine cups and appetizers now set out before each one of them.

"You wanted to speak to me?" KinetetE asked. "Carolinus insisted on coming. Don't tire him."

"Bah!" said Carolinus.

"Of course not," said Jim. "Yes, I—well, Brian, will you tell KinetetE your situation and what you have to do?"

"An honor," said Brian, "to speak to you again, Mage KinetetE; and Mage Carolinus, how it gladdens my heart to see you once more. Er—my problem is this . . ."

He told them, as he had told Jim just a short time before.

"That's quite in order, Brian," said Carolinus in a rusty version of his usual voice. "I'll—"

"No, you won't," said KinetetE. "I will! Brian, if it becomes necessary for you to return swiftly, have someone call out my name—"

"I'll take care of that," said Geronde.

"Very well. I'll then talk to you, Geronde. You'll inform me of the situation. I'll then speak to you, Brian, wherever you may be; and tell you your immediate return is prepared. You may not be able to leave the exact moment I call you; but it won't matter. All you need to do is click your heels together three times—"

Jim and Angie, who unfortunately were drinking a private toast together, both choked on their wine at the same moment.

"—clicking your heels together and saying to yourself three times—'Smythe, Smythe, Smythe.' May I ask what's got into you two, Jim and Angie?" KinetetE wound up in a steely voice.

"The servants poured the wrong wine for both of us," said Angie, who was quicker-tongued than Jim. "It was not the wine for our toast, and we didn't want to drink it."

"Ah!" said KinetetE, clearly annoyed and disbelieving, but also unable to find a polite formula to put these things into words. "—At any rate, Brian, you will find yourself back at your Castle immediately."

"I am forever in your debt, Mage."

"As for the two of us," KinetetE went on, "we just dropped by to show off Carolinus's recovery. Say something to them, Carolinus!"

"What the devil can I say?" replied Carolinus in the same rusty voice, but sounding more like his old, snappish self and warming the hearts of the rest at the table. "I'm perfectly all right, now. Be back in my cottage tomorrow!"

"By the end of the week hopefully, let us say," put in KinetetE. "Now we must go. Ah, Jim, Brian, Dafydd—may good chance go with you, down in the Drowned Land and Lyonesse, all of you."

She and Carolinus disappeared.

There was a long moment of silence in which all those still at the table looked happily at each other.

"So!" said Brian, breaking the silence and lifting his mazer so strongly the wine within almost sloshed out onto the tabletop, "I shall be going to the Drowned Land and mayhap to Lyonesse with you, Jim and Dafydd! This is a day to celebrate!"

"Within reason," said Geronde.

"Of course. Who would go forth on a task such as we three face with a head like a pumpkin and little sleep?"

"But what about your wedding, Brian?" Angie asked.

"Oh, this can hardly delay matters. After all, our battle at the Loathly Tower was accomplished in a day—"

"Hob!" said Jim.

"Yes, my Lord?" said a timid voice from the nearest fireplace; and the face of the castle hobgoblin appeared, upside down, peeking out from inside the top edge of the fireplace.

"Either," said Jim irritably, "come all the way in or go away. But stop popping into sight for a second and then out again. We all know you've been listening to everything said here, from the first moment Dafydd arrived."

"My Lord—"

"And, no, you can't go with me, this time. Your duty is here at the Castle." Any argument that would keep the hobgoblin at home was a good argument; it had reached the point that the little creature took it for granted he could go along any time Jim left home.

"Besides," added Jim, "you probably aren't allowed there. Remember, Rrrnlf had to leave us at the border of the

Drowned Land. Probably Naturals aren't allowed into the Drowned Land or Lyonesse."

"I know, my Lord," said Hob. "But the Sea Devil and other Naturals are different. They've got no proper place in the real world—and that's the only place they're allowed to go. But we Hobs are allowed to be with people. Then, there's some like that Demon Aroman—"

"Arhiman," said Angie helpfully.

"Thank you, my Lady—Arhiman, my Lord. He had to be summoned, even to come into the real world. Most Naturals who don't have their proper place there can go into the real world, but not into one of the Kingdoms of other Naturals. The only ones who can are those whose proper place is with people—like me—and, well . . ."

Hob gulped.

"Trolls, for instance. Their proper place is where they can eat humans—and other people—in the real world, and can go anywhere humans are. Besides, m'Lord forgets I was there with him before."

Jim *had* forgotten, remembering only while he and Hob had been talking, just now. He had ignored the memory, however, hoping Hob's memory had been equally faulty.

It was time to use his authority. Argument was getting nowhere.

"Hob," he said, "I order you to stay here."

Hob gulped again.

"Yes, m'Lord. Very well, m'Lord. May I ask, though, who will tell m'Lord what the QB is saying when he barks?"

Jim opened his mouth and then closed it again. The QB, of course, was the Questing Beast of Arthurian legend, a friendly creature that had literally saved their lives when they had been passing through Lyonesse before. He had come up to Jim after his rescue and barked—not with his famous sound like twenty couple of hounds questing, but with the single bark of a single dog; and Jim could not understand what he was trying to say until Hob translated.

Hob had a point. They might well be bumping into some

person or creature along the way with whom Hob could be useful in the same way again.

"QB? QB?" said Brian, conveniently filling the conversational gap. "Oh, you mean that mixture of several beasts, head of a snake, body of a leopard, and tail of a lion? Never expected to see such. It was the one hunted by King Pellinore, was it not, James?"

"It was," said Jim. "Remember how the youngest Sir Dinedan told us they liked to hunt together? But neither one was a good hunter; and they were always losing each other, so they spent most of their time hunting for each other rather than game—"

Jim caught himself up sharply. He had been about to plunge into a warm bath of reminiscences with an equally willing Brian; and for the first time he realized that the women at the table were being ominously silent.

"Essentially, you're correct, though, Brian," he wound up hastily; and put his mind back to what Hob had been asking. "Well, Hob"—he made his best effort at a smile and a conciliatory voice—"I'm glad you reminded me of that. Maybe you will have to come, after all."

"Oh, good!" caroled Hob, shooting up the chimney and out of sight like a rocket.

"I only said may—" Jim gave up. Reminding Hob of the escape clause in Jim's promise would only plunge the little Natural back into uncertainty and gloom. Might as well let him feel good while he could. Besides, Hob was most probably out of hearing range by now, anyway.

"James!" said Geronde sharply, "if the Mage can bring Brian back here to meet a court officer or a creditor, can you not also bring him back for the wedding and its celebration? It would only take three days."

"When's the wedding, then?" asked Jim; for the date had been moved forward, then back, then forward again, several times in the tug-of-war between Geronde's father—to have it done as quickly as possible so that he could leave on his latest adventure—and Geronde—in her determination that it should be done properly and only when everything was ready—including her wedding dress.

"Three weeks, two days, hence," she said.

"In that case, Jim," said Angie, "maybe it'd be a good idea to get started as soon as you can."

"I was just thinking that myself," said Jim. "I'd better get back to KinetetE right away. I'll try to come back here to almost this same moment—I mean, I'll hope to be back with answers almost before I've gone."

"You again?" said KinetetE, as Jim once more appeared in her waiting room. She was sitting there alone in one of the overstuffed chairs, sewing on what looked like another sampler.

Chapter 6

Jim gazed at her, fascinated.

"What are you staring at?" said KinetetE. "Didn't you ever see anyone sew before?"

"What? Oh, yes," said Jim. "I just didn't think of you as doing it."

"Anyone can do what they want—though most people fail at the dare," said KinetetE, laying cloth, needle, and thread aside on a tiny, fragile-looking end table. "I sew. Let who would stop me try it at will. Sit down."

Jim sat.

"I thought you'd be expecting me back without too much delay," he said. "No lineup of people or others to see you?"

"You were put to the head of the line," said KinetetE. "Also, I needed to do some thinking of my own. To answer your question, yes; knowing you, I was indeed expecting you back at any moment."

"Good. Then I'll just tell you what magic I'll need—"

"I know what magick you'll need as well as or better than you do. But to take things in their proper order, understand this will be magick from my own credit with the Accounting Department, not some of Carolinus's."

"Very well," said Jim.

"Furthermore," went on KinetetE, "never forget that it's being *lent* to you. Not given. The magick Carolinus gave you in the past was from his credit and it was lent, too—"

"He didn't tell me that."

"No doubt that was because, as your Master-in-Magick, he has control of your account and can pay himself back out of what you've earned from actions like the battle at the Loathly Tower, or your going to World's End to awaken the Phoenix. But, I'll expect you to remember—if you survive—that what you will have gotten from me was borrowed. You'll have to speak to the Accounting Office to pay me back. Can I count on that?"

"Of course you can," said Jim. But the matter-of-fact tone of the words "*. . . if you survive . . .*" had sent a chill down his back.

He had been in a number of dangerous situations since he had first come to this world. So far, he had always come out of them safely. But Carolinus had never treated him with the solemnity that KinetetE was showing. Now he remembered that time when, inhabiting the body of the dragon Gorbash, he had hung between life and death, with the lance of Sir Hugh de Bois all the way through his chest; and also the knife in his back from Edgar de Wiggin.

Perhaps he had come to think too much of himself as someone invulnerable. But there had been that cold note just now in KinetetE's voice as she mentioned his chance of survival. . . . He put it aside for the moment.

"Good. Then about this magic I'll need—" But KinetetE was already talking to thin air.

"Accounting Office?" she was now saying to the otherwise empty room. "Have you made a note of the agreement on this magick I have just lent the Apprentice, Jim Eckert?"

"I have," said the bass voice of the Accounting Office, as usual out of thin air, some five feet above the floor. And as usual, in spite of the fact he was expecting to hear it, Jim jumped.

"Duplicate to Carolinus's credit record."

"Yes, Mage."

KinetetE glared at the thin air.

"And copy to the Archives. If I remember correctly, once in King Tut's time—"

"That was an unfortunate error, Mage. A one-in-a-million—"

"Just so this matter doesn't become the second in that million. You can go now."

"Yes, Mage."

"Tell me," asked Jim, as the bass voice fell silent and before he thought, "why do you and Carolinus always give the Accounting Office such a hard time?"

"Is he gone?" KinetetE took another look at the thin air that the voice had been coming from. "Yes. Good. Keeps him in line. Tracking our magickal credit gives him no authority over us—rather vice-versa. But, now that the terms between us are settled, I've a lot to tell you about Lyonesse."

"Couldn't," Jim began, "I simply tell you what magic I need—"

"I'll tell you. After I've told you about Lyonesse. Now, sit still and listen."

"By the way, I'll need to get back to where I just came from, only a minute or so after I left there to come here. And when you send me back there, could you—"

"I could and will. Sit down."

Jim took a chair opposite her.

"Incidentally," he said, "I've been warned about the dangers of staying in Lyonesse too long—long enough that everything there stops being black and white, like a place in bright moonlight, and I can never leave. So I know about that."

"Do you? I hope so. Doubtless whoever told you that also told you it was a Land of Old Magic?"

"Yes, come to think of it," said Jim, remembering Carolinus's words, in the projection he had left for Jim to find on his last trip into Lyonesse. "I was told."

"Then suppose we start with that as the basics and enlarge on the matter from there. Old Magic—have you any idea what that means?"

About to say "Of course. It means magic that's old," Jim checked himself just in time.

"No," he said. "Tell me."

"Old Magic," said KinetetE, "is magick that is very old indeed. Old before all remembrance. Old before Lyonesse was upheaven from the abyss by fire, to sink into the abyss again—"

"Why," said Jim, "those're exactly the words Tennyson used to describe it."

"Who?"

"Alfred Lord Tennyson. A poet of the nineteenth—a poet whose poems we know back where I come from."

"He must have been there. At any rate, the point is that Old Magic is very, very old. So old, none of us in the Collegiate of Magickians has ever understood all of it." She paused briefly.

"When King Arthur and his army came to Lyonesse for the last battle with his son Modred, that delayed the land's sinking back into the abyss, which it otherwise would have done before now. But it's something that has to happen eventually—hopefully, not while you and your friends are there."

"Why should it happen then?"

"Because," said KinetetE, "the Dark Powers are single-minded, unthinking Natural Forces. But compared to the Old Magic They're no more than jumped-up latecomers who don't know the risk They're taking. They're playing with fire in trying to take over Lyonesse, though They don't suspect it. They could win Lyonesse, but by doing that destroy not only it but Themselves."

"How can you be so sure They don't suspect it?" asked Jim.

"Because They don't have our capabilities, Apprentice. Their power is only in the present, so that's where They live.

From Their viewpoint there never was a past and the word *future* means nothing," said KinetetE. "Obvious enough, I should think?"

"Yes," said Jim; and made up his mind to say no more for the moment.

"As far as They know, They only have to own Lyonesse to have a physical base in the real world, something They've never been able to have. A place. Hah! Little do They know what They may have to go through to win it. And little do we know what we'll have to go through if They do win it—"

"It could make that much difference?" said Jim, in spite of his determination to be quiet.

"How could it not? But to finish what I was trying to say—to win, the Powers at least realize They'll have to take it from those of the Round Table who are loyal to Arthur. But as far as the Powers understand it, if They just do that, They've got it. They can't conceive of the Old Magic refusing to let them hold it—possibly, They don't even realize the Old Magic exists. But, while They might win it, They won't be able to hold it except by agreement of the humans or Naturals occupying it. Bodiless forces can't possess earth."

"Makes sense," said Jim, forgetting again about his recent vow of silence.

"I'm glad to hear it. But—if the Dark Powers do manage to hold it, then with humans loyal to Them, They'll have a powerful base in Reality to launch future attacks on History and Chaos. In a word, They would come closer to being sentient beings, rather than just Forces—which would allow Them to think more like us who oppose Them by making History—a great advantage."

She stopped and stared hard at Jim.

"Ah, I see," said Jim, since clearly, now, at last, he was expected to speak.

"So you can understand," said KinetetE, "why the use of any outside magick by anyone, in Lyonesse, causes double danger. Not only is it subject to erasure or retaliation, but any transfer of the ownership of that Land from Arthur and his Knights—his original Knights of the Legends—to the Dark

Powers may disturb the precarious magickal balance that keeps the land itself from sinking in fire once more into the abyss.''

''Oh,'' said Jim.

''Not only that, but any improper use of magick from elsewhere may also upset the balance, with the same result.''

KinetetE paused and again looked hard at Jim.

''Any *irresponsible* use of magick by someone like yourself.''

''Yes, I understand,'' said Jim.

''All of which, of course,'' KinetetE continued in a more academic tone, ''rather limits the amount and kind of magick I can lend you. I expect you're planning to carry those two friends of yours—and I suppose that foolish little Hob—with you, plus horses and weapons and such; and I suppose we must expect at least a couple of emergency situations, in which you'll have to make at least two other uses of magick.'' Her voice took on an edge.

''I should warn you,'' she said, ''that if you are stripped of that magick while you're there, you must leave Lyonesse immediately, to resupply yourself. Do not take the risk of trying to recover what you have lost while you're there. But if I lend you the amount of magick needed for what I just mentioned, you should be amply supplied.''

''Except for one thing,'' said Jim.

''What one thing?''

''Well, perhaps I should say two. I know you have already agreed to call Brian back to Castle Smythe when Geronde asks; but for me, too, there may be a need to send one or both of my Companions back to the real world here and then recover them again, a little later, as well. Or myself, for that matter.''

''What for?''

A wild memory from his own twentieth-century world flashed into Jim's mind, of having watched, on television, as people being forced to testify invoked the Fifth Amendment. Impossible here, of course. But . . .

''I respectfully decline to answer,'' he said.

KinetetE stared at him.

"What?" she said.

"I realize," Jim went on stiffly, trying to take the attitude of someone standing firmly on his rights, "that this may result in your refusing to lend me the necessary magic. I further realize it may mean that it will make any attempt by me to go to the aid of Lyonesse at this important time impossible. Refusal to give me the magic necessary is, of course, your privilege.

"I will only say that the sort of magic I have used on several occasions, successfully up until now, requires that I have as much as is needed, and a free hand in using it. I estimate I could need at least double the amount you had in mind—or more. I'll also mention that at one time I had an unlimited drawing account; and when Carolinus arranged for me to have it, he made no stipulations about its use."

He folded his arms and sat looking as immovable as he could.

"I have never . . ." began KinetetE, and ran out of words.

They sat looking at each other for a long moment.

"Do you know what being an Apprentice means?" KinetetE asked at last.

"I think I do," said Jim. "I also think I am the best judge of what I might run into." He was beginning to feel ridiculous, sitting like this with his arms folded; but he could not think of an excuse to unfold them that would not give KinetetE the impression he was backing down.

"And you haven't forgotten who I am?"

"No."

"And you're continuing to demand—demand, I say—as much magickal credit again as I intend to lend you; but with no accountability?"

"That," said Jim, "is right."

There was a long, uncomfortable silence.

"If there was the slightest chance you could explain," said KinetetE. "I don't promise anything, you understand—I might—I just possibly might be willing to listen—"

"I'm afraid an explanation is not possible," said Jim.

"If you could simply give me *some* grounds for asking and acting like this. . . ."

"No," said Jim. "That's not possible, either." But he could feel his determination weakening.

"Then I have no choice but to refuse to help you in any way at this time."

"Very well," said Jim. He unfolded his arms and stood up.

"Sit down!" said KinetetE sharply. He sat down. She looked away from him into a corner of the room. "It's not the credit, it's the principle of the thing . . ." she said in a low voice, as if speaking to herself.

Jim continued to sit without saying anything. After a pause, she looked back at him.

"Tell me one thing," she said. "Did Carolinus actually never, at any time, require accountability from you?"

"He never did."

She sighed.

"Well," she said. "As the twig is bent, so grows the tree. That's Carolinus for you, through and through. Very well. I'm still only lending you this magick credit, remember; but you may have the amount you want, and do with it as you think necessary. *And the boy's only an Apprentice, in the name of all that's magick!*"

The last words were addressed only to the room in general. Jim scrambled mentally for the safest thing to say, under the circumstances.

"Thank you," he said.

"Very well," said KinetetE, "I'll do what you asked when I sent you back to the Royal Cave of the Gnarlies: send you to Lyonesse with a ward that includes some of the *Here* around you."

"That would be just what I was hoping," said Jim.

"—And I'll protect you as well as I can. But you must remember it's only while the ward holds that you'll have magick to strike out with; and once anyone or anything in Lyonesse senses you're warded, he, she, or it may wipe the ward out as easily as you breathe on a snowflake to melt it.

Also, remember what I said: no one, including me, knows all the Old Magic. Merlin might have, but there's no one like him today. So your powers can disappear without warning."

"Ah . . . yes," said Jim. "I'll remember everything you've had to tell me. But isn't it time now you gave me the magic and sent me off?"

"Very well," she said. "But recall this as well. I have a long memory, myself; and woe to you at my hands if you're careless or wasteful with the magick you borrow from me!"

"I'll have it in mind," said Jim stiffly.

"Very well," she said. "Then you're warded and equipped as of this second. Oh, by the way, the ward I gave you and the power to bring or send back and forth your friends; but you understand your own ward protects you only against magick. Good luck."

She had gotten back at him after all. Jim had simply assumed his ward would protect him against accident and unexpected wounds. That was an automatic coverage of the ordinary personal ward, in addition to whatever else it was set up to protect from. He had been a little surprised to get away with facing her down over Brian's transportation home in a hurry. He had been right to be surprised. He hadn't.

"Thank you," said Jim.

Graceful acknowledgment of being bested. Only thing to do.

And he was immediately back in the Great Hall of Malencontri, with Dafydd, Geronde, and Brian all looking at him.

"Something wrong?" he asked, sitting down.

"You were hardly gone a minute, Jim!" said Angie.

"Indeed," said Dafydd, "the time was very short. Did something go amiss?"

"Oh, no!" Jim said. "Everything went well. Piece of cake. I'm now prepared to send you home on a moment's notice, Brian. Or send all of us home on a moment's notice if it comes to that. The swiftness of it was just one of those things that happens when magic goes smoothly."

He laughed cheerfully. But the chill persisted as well. He kept up his outward smile. There were a number of uncomfortable possibilities, according to what she had said, waiting for them in Lyonesse.

He laughed, admiring KinetetE for the exactness with which she had returned him to the time he had asked for. She had not been exaggerating when she said she never forgot anything—but that thought was a sobering one. Her final words came back to him. If she was that good at keeping promises, there was that uncomfortable little bit about woe to him at her hands if he was careless or wasteful with the borrowed magic. Ah, well . . .

He kept his smile, firmly setting to one side memory of KinetetE's comments about his survival. Cross those bridges when he came to them.

That evening at bedtime, just before they settled down for the night, he showed Angie the magic glasses he had made. They were just about as good-looking as glasses for him could get, he thought—with thin gold rims and earpieces—"temples," he remembered the oculist calling them. They were about as unnoticeable as spectacles could be; but were protected against breakage by a ward.

"Jim, they look stunning!" said Angie, trying them on herself. "Oh, but Jim—you don't need bifocals yet, do you? There's some kind of a line between the upper and lower parts of the lenses!"

"An idea of my own, in fact," said Jim, feeling a touch of complacency. "You see, I had to make them so they'd react to any color around me, whether I was deliberately noticing or not; and I might not be noticing if—well, for example, if there was something like a glare in my eyes. So the lower halves are the part that shows color—more brightly than I'd see it with the naked eye, actually." He pointed a finger at a lens while she still wore the glasses.

"In contrast," he went on, "the upper half will still show the black-and-silver, but will shield me from glare, a bit. They're something like sunglasses, in principle—the kind that get darker the brighter the light is."

"That was clever of you," said Angie. She took the spectacles off and held them at arm's length toward the flame of their single candle on the candlestick stand of her side of the bed. "Yes, it does! Well, that was a good idea. Now all I have to worry about is your getting mixed up in something dangerous."

And KinetetE's promise about what would happen to him if he did not use his borrowed magic right, thought Jim. But there was no reason for Angie to have that worrying her.

He leaned over her, and blew the candle out.

Chapter 7

"I wish I could go in with you, too," said the Sea Devil, wistfully, looking at the green land under a bright yellow sun that lay beyond what seemed no more than the cliff-high edge of an atmosphere of ordinary air.

"We can take him, can't we, m'Lord?" asked Hob, who at the moment was riding on Jim's back—a feather's weight there, only.

"I'm afraid not," Jim said. "He's not allowed."

"That's right, very wee Hob," said Rrrnlf. "We Sea Devils can go anywhere—except where we're not allowed. Places like this Drowned Land are unallowed."

They were finally descending the last hundred of many hundred feet of deep salt ocean. The four horses—Gorp, Blanchard, Dafydd's light but courageous roan stallion, and Jim's sumpter horse—were enclosed in a calming enchantment and held in one enormous Sea Devil hand. Rrrnlf's other hand carried Jim, Brian, and Dafydd in another ward, but without the calming enchantment—which had a side effect of dulling the senses. Both sets of passengers were completely protected from the crushing pressure at this great depth—and the horses, at least, were completely indifferent to their surroundings. Brian and Dafydd appeared indifferent, too; but Jim knew that in any unusual place and situation, that was the way they would strive to appear.

—As for Jim, he was occupied.

He knew that a properly set-up ward was unbreakable, of course, so he could have been as indifferent as the horses; but at the moment he had gotten himself particularly interested in the manner in which they would enter the air-wall between sea and the Drowned Land. He had not thought to pay any attention to it the one time they had entered it before, on their way to the Gnarly Kingdom.

His attention was all on the approaching fields of the Drowned Land, and the feet of Rrrnlf's thirty-plus-foot body, as they crossed the seabed rapidly. If he just kept watching carefully . . . Jim told himself.

Rrrnlf stooped and pressed the two wards—invisible, of course, but undoubtedly very solid feeling in his two hands—and pushed them hard against the surface where water met air. They stopped moving suddenly.

"That's as far as I can take you, wee people," he said.

He turned his wrists around—widdershins, Jim noted—and the front surfaces of the wards went through the wall. Rrrnlf let them go and stepped back.

"That is all and more than needed, good Rrrnlf," Jim answered. The Sea Devil raised a hand, then simply vanished.

Jim was pleased with himself. Watching closely, with eyes now trained in magic, he had caught the briefest possible glint of a circular swirl in the air—like the swirl in the water made by a fish, just under the surface of a lake, when it turned suddenly in quick fright from a baited hook it had been investigating.

Then Dafydd's hand was through the air-wall into the land beyond, his body followed it, and Jim and Brian followed him. To their right the horses were following Dafydd's roan steed out in the same way.

"Hah!" said Jim, delighted and out loud, without thinking. "Of course. The simplest thing in the world! The Witch's Gate!"

"Witches?" said Brian, suddenly and sharply staring around him. "Where, James?"

"No. I mean, none, Brian. It was just a manner of speaking.

I was pondering on a point of magic, that was all, and spoke up without thinking."

"Shall we mount and go, sirs?" said Dafydd, almost sharply.

Mounting his roan as Jim and Brian also mounted, Dafydd led them inland from the shore onto the greensward.

"—Is this land all pastureland like this?" Brian asked Dafydd.

"No," said the archer. He had straightened somewhat since they had left their wards behind; and seemed taller than Jim was used to seeing him. "There are clumps of trees, but no real forests. But farther in, the land becomes rugged and rises to small mountains. As you start down the farther side of that you enter the Borderland—Drowned Land country, but a wild place where rough forest starts; and that forest becomes the forest of Lyonesse in no large distance."

Dafydd, as suited a prince in his own country—as he was here—now rode first, followed by Jim and Brian—Brian on a Blanchard who, for a wonder, this one time did not seem disposed to push himself ahead of Dafydd's roan. It was as if even the destrier was recognizing the present difference in rank. Now it was Brian who had tied to his saddle the lead rope of the sumpter horse that carried their baggage.

It was the same sumpter horse that had carried their baggage on their earlier trip through here to Gnarlyland. There had been a general feeling on the part of the stable hands at Malencontri that it would be bad luck to take a different horse if this mare was still able; so she went.

The horses, in fact, were all on their best manners. Jim had been half afraid the sudden change of scene might at least have spooked Brian's Blanchard—who could take offense at almost anything unexpected. But on this occasion, he had accepted the magical shift in scene with indifference.

The roan himself, beautiful but lighter than the two destriers of Brian and Jim, was typical of the horses they had seen on their previous trip through the Drowned Land. He plainly loved the man he carried; as, for that matter, did Blanchard love his own rider, Brian—once, Jim had seen the big destrier, for all his usual tantrums and demands for first place, refuse to take shelter one cold, rainy night, to stand in the open over his unconscious master. When Gorp had long since taken shelter under one of the heavy-leafed surrounding trees.

Dafydd, Jim and Brian had discovered, could ride, and ride well, when the need was there, although he preferred under ordinary conditions to travel afoot. In fact, Jim had never seen him on the roan until this last year; and it was only a few months back that he spoke about it to Dafydd, when it occurred to him to ask the name of the roan. The answer had been enlightening.

"Owen?" Jim had echoed the name—for Dafydd's life was spent among the English nowadays; and Owen had been the name of a Welsh leader who had been a real thorn in the side of those English trying to conquer and subdue Wales. "You named him Owen?"

"I did. He is named after Owen Glendower," Dafydd had replied.

"I guessed as much. But why that particular name?" asked Jim.

"I did that so when, as has happened, some Englishman might ask me his name, I could answer it was Owen. Then if the man should further ask how I should give a horse such a strange-sounding name, I could reply he was named after Owen Glendower; and if that same man should then wonder who Owen Glendower might be—then, if need be, I could take him aside and explain it to his full understanding."

Obviously, such an "explanation" might become a physically active one. Dafydd continually spoke of himself as "not a man of great dispute," but it was remarkable the way dispute came and found him. He was, in truth, always soft-voiced and polite to everyone. But even as an archer, he carried himself like a prince; and this was more than enough to make him a walking challenge to some other males.

Plainly, the name had been Dafydd's way of educating some of the English about a Welsh hero, the leader of the uprising there earlier in this century. It had been Wales's last strong bid to free itself from English rule, from what Jim remembered from his history—which, admittedly, was not always a perfect match for the history of *this* world.

Clearly, the horse Owen seemed to share much of the same attitude as his rider. At no time when they had been together had he challenged the larger Gorp or Blanchard, as stallions were sometimes prone to do—Blanchard very much so. But once when Blanchard had moved to domineer over him, Owen had responded like a screaming fury, attacking the heavier warhorse so swiftly he had appeared to be the one who had started the fight. Luckily, on that one occasion, the stable hands at Malencontri had got the two into separate stalls before any real damage was done on either side.

At any rate, so far, things had gone well. Hopefully, the King of the Drowned Land would be able to tell them more about the Dark Powers trying to take over Lyonesse—and his Kingdom, as well—

Jim's thoughts broke off suddenly; for a rider was coming toward them at a speed that raised a spreading cloud of dust from the unpaved road behind him. Dafydd raised a hand and reined Owen to a stop. Jim and Brian both rode forward a few steps to come up close to—but not quite level with—him, and also reined in to await the coming of the approaching rider.

He was with them in moments, and hauled his sweating, pawing horse to a stop. But the first words he spoke to Dafydd were in the language of the Drowned Land, which neither Jim nor Brian understood. Jim could have used his magic to interpret, but he felt vaguely that this might be a little like listening at keyholes. He and Brian waited.

The conversation was brief. Dafydd listened to what the horseman had to say and spoke to him briefly. Then he turned to Jim and Brian.

"Madog, here, will stay with you and guide you safely to the border of Lyonesse. He will take you to a different place on that border than the one we crossed at before to get to the entrance of the Gnarly Kingdom. I must leave you here."

"But you said nothing of this earlier!" said Brian. "I thought we would all pause while you saw your King—

perhaps a day or two—and then you would go on with us."

"Matters have arisen," said Dafydd. "In brief, the King is ill. Deathly ill; and his one living son, who has been hidden for his own safety, for reasons that are privy to those very close to the King—is now revealed. He is wise beyond his years, but still too young in my King's mind to take on the responsibility of the Kingdom, with this threat heavy above us. I must go to the King now, while he lives. Madog will see you well to the border and I will join you there in Lyonesse as soon as I can. Farewell for now."

He lifted the reins, and Owen broke almost immediately into a gallop, building to a swiftness that might well have given Blanchard a run for Brian's money. Jim had little doubt of which horse would win over a distance, however. Blanchard was so remarkable as to be almost a freak. In spite of his weight and size, endless power seemed stored in his great-chested body. It was almost visible, radiating from him, to any who saw him—the element that had made Chandos and others speak of him so highly.

Jim sat Gorp now, feeling strangely deserted and exposed by Dafydd's sudden leaving. He and Brian looked at Madog, sitting his wet horse and waiting for their attention.

The man was dressed exactly as had been others of the King's personal guards they had seen on their previous visit to the Drowned Land. In fact, he could have been one of those they had seen then, an escort mounted on beautiful, but small, bay horses—like the one he rode now. He carried a light spear held upright in a boot by his right toe, and was clad in armor of boiled leather reinforced by plates of metal. He also wore a helmet of antique style, with a nasal bar that left his facial area open. Hanging from his waist was a dark leather scabbard that held a slim, flat sword with a small silver hilt.

Behind the nasal bar, his face was tanned and sharp-boned, with keen brown eyes. There was something restless, eager, and potentially explosive—as Owen had been—about him.

"Do you speak English?" Jim asked him.

Madog shook his head, but half turned his horse and

pointed ahead along the road they had been following. He said something in the same liquid language that he and Dafydd had spoken together.

"Clearly," said Brian, "he waits for us to follow him."

Jim nodded. They put their horses into motion, the sumpter horse shrugging as she necessarily followed on her lead rope; and, behind the Drowned Land soldier, they went on their way, now at a trot instead of the walking pace they had been using before.

"Meseemeth," said Brian judiciously, "that this fellow is eager to discharge the duty Dafydd laid upon him and get back to others more familiar."

"I wouldn't doubt it," answered Jim.

They followed Madog in silence for perhaps half an hour; and though the landscape on each side of the road continued much the same, they began to see, along the horizon ahead, either rugged hills or distant mountains. Shortly, they also saw a whiteness ahead but off to their left; and as they moved on, it resolved itself into a city, its buildings—some of them of surprising height—apparently constructed of some marble-like material. A little later the wide road they were on divided, sending another route, equally wide, off in the direction of the city.

Madog, however, continued to lead them straight on for some distance, then branched off onto a narrow road to their right. Jim looked ahead with some surprise. It did not seem that they had covered so much distance, but now the mountains ahead were a great deal closer.

As they went on, their new road narrowed; more so when the ground began to slope upward into the flanks of the nearest mountains. Shortly, it had dwindled to little more than a bridle path on which it was only just possible for two to travel side by side.

They were higher up now, and the mountain was beginning to live up to that name. Under the horses' hooves earth had given way to rock, loose chips of reddish white stone on which the metal of horseshoes slipped; and uneven surfaces of the same rock, unbroken. The sumpter horse, not usually taken far from Malencontri, had not been considered worth horseshoeing, and was having an easier time of it. So, Jim noticed, was the horse of the royal guardsman up ahead. Of course, he told himself, the Drowned Land must almost certainly have sunk beneath the waves long before the medieval invention of the horseshoe.

"James!" said Brian in a low voice, behind him.

Jim turned his head. Brian was reining Blanchard close in beside him as they climbed; and Jim could hear the hard breathing of the warhorse.

"What is it?" he asked in an equally low voice, for Brian was clearly not trusting to the soldier's claim that he could not understand English.

"Have you noticed?" Brian said. "The shadow. Does it not seem to you to be going along with us?"

Jim, deep in his own thoughts, had not. But now he looked up at the sky, clear and blue save for a few puffy clouds on the northern horizon; and at the mountainside, brightly lit in the afternoon light, with its wealth of dry stone riverbeds and spires. No visible shadow showed; but he knew what Brian meant. Now that he gave it his attention, he felt its presence—the darkness they had noticed in the Great Hall. There was no doubt.

"Yes," he said.

"It is watching us, you think?"

"Maybe," said Jim, "but also maybe it seems to follow everyone who knows it's there."

"I think it follows us, especially," said Brian. He reached for the hilt of his sword and loosened it in its scabbard. "I would counsel that we be alert for attack."

"I wouldn't think—since we're only just into the Drowned Land, not Lyonesse—" began Jim, then checked himself. "But maybe you're right."

Now that he had taken notice of this shadow of the Dark Powers, he felt the same instinct to be wary that was moving Brian. Half unconsciously, he reached for the hilt of his own sword; and followed Brian's example by breaking the tightness that riding and gravity had brought it to in his scabbard.

"Darkness . . . and mist," he said to Brian. "Remember the mist that held about the marsh and the Loathly Tower before Carolinus showed up with his staff to hold it back so we could fight what they sent against us. We might watch for any sign of mist or fog."

"No sign of such, yet," muttered Brian. He scanned the peaceful sky overhead. "But you say well, James. From now on let us be on watch—though our guide does not seem concerned about it."

He frowned at the back of the soldier ahead.

"If our way grows much steeper," he added, "we will have to dismount and walk, leading the horses."

This was correct, Jim realized now. The soldier was not sparing his own horse, or acting as if he was about to. But just then they entered a cleft running upward in the rock; and when at last they emerged from this into the open again, the way they were following had struck a long downward slope that continued until a belt of trees could be seen. The soldier broke into a gallop.

"Hold!" shouted Brian furiously, reining in Blanchard. "Damn your bones and guts! Fellow! Come back here!"

The language might be unintelligible to the rider ahead, but the tone of Brian's voice was not. The other pulled his horse to a stop and turned in his saddle.

"Come back here!" roared Brian, beckoning him with full arm movements. The soldier turned his horse and rode back up to them.

"Are there no wits at all in that wooden head of yours?" exploded Brian. "Do you think I'd risk the legs of a warhorse the worth of Blanchard by galloping down a slope like that—just because you don't give a damn if you break the neck of that screw you're riding? By all the Saints in the Calendar, I'll see you in Hell and roasting first! We go down as carefully as we came up, or you can . . ."

Brian's language became very colorful indeed. Once more, the words in which they were uttered might mean nothing to the soldier, but Brian's obvious anger, reinforced by emphatic gestures at his mount and the rock underfoot, could not be misunderstood. The expression on the soldier's face hardly changed. Only his mouth tightened. Without a word he turned his horse downslope once more and walked it forward.

Jim and Brian followed at the same pace. Brian, deprived of a target for his outrage, snorted and grumbled for several minutes to Jim, gradually bleeding off what was left of his fury.

"It could be," said Jim diplomatically, when his friend finally fell silent, "his horse is used to a pace like that on such a slope."

"Bloody fool, anyway!" muttered Brian. "But you may be right, James. He may not have thought it a danger any more for us than it was for him."

With that, the fit of anger, like all such with Brian, was gone, and already half-forgotten.

They reached the trees in a very short time, after all. Distance seemed strangely foreshortened here in the Drowned Land, thought Jim. Perhaps that was part of its innate magic for those who had chosen to stay with it—to have a kingdom larger than it seemed.

Now that he had noticed it, he was not surprised when, after traveling for only a short time through the trees, they came out on a grassy plain. In the apparent distance there was another green band of trees, stretching as far ahead of them as Jim could see; and in no way different from the trees they had just passed through.

Here, however, their guide reined in his horse. When they rode up level with him, he waved his hand forward, almost as if shooing them onward, and turned his own horse around as if to ride back.

"He can't mean that is Lyonesse ahead there," said Brian. "James, I am going to have a word with Dafydd when this is all over. The same sun, shining on the same sort of forest? That's not what I remember from the moonlit, black-and-silver country we visited before. Can you not find some way to speak to this—this maggot?"

"Madog," said Jim; and the soldier, hearing his name pronounced in approximately recognizable fashion, looked at him.

"Lyonesse?" asked Jim, pointing his finger forward and sweeping it from left to right across the grassy plain and the trees beyond it.

Madog said something in his own language.

"Lyonesse?" Jim repeated, still pointing.

Madog nodded his head vigorously, rode forward no more than a dozen feet out onto the plain, dismounted, and, holding the ends of his reins, stepped forward a cautious step, followed by no more than half a step, even more cautiously. He stopped, and swept his own pointing finger right and left as Jim had, above the grass of the plain.

"I doubt him," said Brian coldly. "It does not look like Lyonesse, it does not feel like Lyonesse. There is something amiss here, James, and it begins with this one. I no longer trust him."

"But we don't have much choice," said Jim, "unless we want to turn around and go back. I can't believe Dafydd would send us with a guide who couldn't or wouldn't show us where we wanted to go."

"There is that," said Brian slowly, running his forefinger across the stiff blond bristles of an upper lip unshaven since the day before. His eyes went to the soldier. "Harkee, maggot! If thou hast played us false, and I live, I will bring thee to due reward for it!"

Madog looked back at him fearlessly, but otherwise with no expression at all, remounted his horse, and left them at a good pace, back up the side of the mountain they had just come down.

Brian, for his part, looked over at Jim.

"There being small choice, then," he said, "let us go on."

"Just a minute," said Jim, dismounting. "I want to check on something. Brian, if I disappear, it'll only be for a short while. Stay exactly where you are. Don't go either forward or back."

"It's just three more steps on, m'Lord!" piped up a small voice behind him; and both Jim and Brian turned to see Hob's head poking out from under the cover of their belongings on the back of the sumpter horse.

Hob had been completely quiet from the moment they had left Malencontri, possibly taking no chance that Jim might get annoyed with him and send him home by magic, after all. But now his face was one wide smile. Jim had actually forgotten he was with them; and he suspected Brian had also.

"Lyonesse, you mean?" Jim said.

"Yes, my Lord. The edge of it, that is."

"How do you know?"

"I can see it, my Lord."

"How can you see it?"

Hob's smile turned into an expression of puzzlement.

"I don't know, m'Lord."

"Well, it doesn't matter." Undoubtedly, Jim reminded himself, this must be another of the unconscious magics that various Naturals possessed. Of course Hob couldn't explain it, any more than he could have explained how he could ride long distances on a brief waft of smoke.

Jim turned. He took a step forward across the grassy plain toward the farther band of trees, bright in the sunlight. Then a second step . . . and a third—

With the last, the warm sun was no longer overhead. There was no distant line of trees, but black, heavy trunks with black, twisted limbs loomed close about him, under an oversized, white sun or moon shedding a light that was bright, but showed no color anywhere, in ground or trees; and the sky was a pale white like the horizon just before moonrise.

Jim turned about and looked behind him. Brian was gone, along with the normal sun and the rising ground to the mountain they had just crossed. Where those had been was a small glen, or treeless patch, with only colorless grass sparse upon the black soil. All shadows were sharp-edged and impenetrable in their darkness.

He took a long step back the way he had come—and there was sunlight, blue sky, green vegetation, Brian, and the horses.

"Stay where you are a moment, Brian," he said. "It's

Lyonesse, all right. I just have to check on something else. Be back in just a few moments.''

He visualized KinetetE's sitting room and felt his magic work. He was there; and KinetetE was in the same chair he had seen her in before, but this time apparently reading from the rolled parchment of a manuscript. She looked up at him, over the top edge of it.

''Well?'' she said. ''What's it this time?''

''We've reached the border between the Drowned Land and Lyonesse,'' said Jim. ''But not at the entrance to the Gnarlyland caves. I just wanted to check with you as to whether this was a safe place to cross over.''

''I haven't the slightest idea,'' she said.

''But I haven't described where we are to you, yet—''

''Not necessary. Scrying glasses are toys for a magickian's childhood in magick. I can see where you and Brian are.''

''Oh,'' said Jim. ''Dafydd had to leave us to go to the King of the Drowned Land—''

''I know. What else do you want to tell me that I already know?''

''Well, for one thing . . .'' he said. He was becoming so used to KinetetE's sharp-tongued manner that it hardly registered on him anymore. It was simply a different version of Carolinus's short-tempered way of expressing himself. Perhaps all Mages developed something of the sort with time. ''Well, for one thing, Brian and I and Hob—''

''Jim, you let that pesky little devil have anything he wants—''

''Now you're telling me things I already know,'' said Jim; in spite of the tolerance he had achieved toward her, he found himself enjoying the chance to interrupt her. ''As I was about to say, Brian, Hob, and I are headed across the border. I can feel the magic you gave me. Will I also be able to feel it in Lyonesse?''

''Can you feel magick directed against you?''

''I don't know,'' said Jim, suddenly baffled. ''I don't know if I ever had—''

''Oh, you've had. Obviously, that's something you've still

got to learn. To answer you, I don't know whether you'll be able to feel what I lent you, once you're in Lyonesse. It depends on you—and on Lyonesse."

"And when you told me," Jim continued, "I'd have to leave Lyonesse to get it again; did that mean that whoever there took it from me wouldn't be able to destroy it, or keep it for themselves?"

"No one," said KinetetE severely, "can *destroy* magick. As for anyone keeping it for her or his own, that is not possible, even in a place like Lyonesse. No, once you're outside, it will automatically come back to you as the magickian it belongs with."

"Good," said Jim. He took a deep, relieved breath.

"Now," he said, "one last question. Have you any advice, any instructions, warnings . . . anything at all to tell me?"

"I have not."

"I suppose there's no point in my asking about Carolinus?"

"He's resting," said KinetetE. "But it may be some time before you see him. He has a tendency to get overexcited when you're around; I should never have let him go to that last dinner of yours where you celebrated by getting drunk, for instance."

"I did not celebrate by getting drunk!" said Jim. "It was an accident—"

"If you say so," said KinetetE in a tone of utter disbelief. "Is that the end of your questions?"

"It is," said Jim stiffly.

"Farewell."

"Farewell."

"Oh, there you are," said Brian. "I brought the horses up to where you disappeared."

"Thanks." Jim climbed into the saddle on Gorp's back. "Ready, Brian?"

"I have been ready some little time now. What is that strange sort of armor you've put on your nose?"

"They're called glasses," said Jim shortly. "Both magic and necessary. Pay no attention to them. Here we go."

Together they rode into the silver-and-black land.

Chapter 8

They rode through the black-and-white land in silence for a while. In too much silence. The dense, black-appearing grass below them absorbed the sound of hoof-falls from their horses. No air stirred other sound to life in the branches above them. All was either in bright sunlight or utterly black shadow; and there was no path for them to follow.

But the thick-trunked trees stood a distance apart, as they might have in the world above where the shade of leaves overhead had killed off nearly all undergrowth. Here, too, the trees were miserly, with scant leaves, but their heavy trunks and thick branches hid the ground from the white sun, painting it with a pattern of utter darkness.

It was all no different than it had been the time they had ridden through this same sort of forest under this same unnatural sun; but Jim had forgotten the feel of it until now. Glancing over at Brian, he saw his friend's face was set and expressionless; and guessed Brian had forgotten, also.

There was no indication of the way they should go—except straight ahead. But, unless this part of Lyonesse was different from that they had passed through on an earlier trip, they would come eventually to some person, creature, or sign that would give them an idea in which way they might head.

But silence like this on Brian's part was not like him. Jim glanced at his friend out of the corners of his eyes. Brian was riding along, frowning at Blanchard's ears, now. That was better. It was not Brian's nature to be impressed with any gloomy emotion for long—and, as if Blanchard knew this—he was wonderfully sensitive to Brian's moods—the horse was finding his own way softly over the dark growth carpeting the ground between the trees.

Jim opened his mouth to say something to rouse Brian, but before he could speak, Brian spoke.

"Hold, James," he said, reining in. "Something is bothering Blanchard's right leg. Ho, now, lad—stand you still!"

He swung down out of his saddle and expertly lifted his destrier's right leg, bending it up backward at the knee to look at the surface of the hoof.

"As I thought, a small stone. . . ." While he spoke, he was prying the source of irritation out, using his eating knife to do so. No knight in his right mind would dull his carefully sharpened and pointed poignard or other dagger in that sort of task. "Underfoot growth like this often hides such. . . ."

Sitting Gorp and waiting, Jim was suddenly aware, from the edge of his vision, of a branch bending down as a small, dark form ran down it and leaped fairly onto the pommel of his saddle. It stared at him. He stared at it. A squirrel—gray at guess, if he had been able to see it in color. It looked at him completely unafraid, its jaws a little open—almost as if it was about to laugh at him. Then it leaped to the ground and was gone.

". . . For all that," Brian was going on as he remounted, "we should be in a sad contretemps in this foreign land, if either of our horses need shoeing." He settled himself and picked up his reins. They moved forward. "—But you know, James, it may be I misjudged that fellow Dafydd gave us for a guide."

"Language difficulties," offered Jim.

"Ah, you think so?" said Brian, brightening at once; and Jim, with a sinking feeling inside him, realized that the knight had not understood his answer at all; but had taken it as an explanation that completely relieved him of any need to feel he had been unkind. "Still, that is the way things are nowadays, James. A hard time to be alive and live as a gentleman should."

There was no point in trying to correct him now. Jim nodded.

"Could you ever have imagined any times like ours?" went on Brian; and, without waiting for an answer, he began to pour forth words. "One never knows how a fellow like that—a foreigner, poor lad, of course; not a word of English—will react to the simplest order; and it's not as if he was an equal one could call to account for his attitude or tone of voice. All a piece of the same thing nowadays—three pence a day for extra men at harvest time, ever since the plague began! Our fathers and our fathers' fathers lived in paradise by comparison. Who could expect so much change in one generation? In their time, life was at least as a man might expect it to be: if they were faithful to Holy Church and lived as men ought, they could expect things to go as they should from birth to grave."

"Well . . ." began Jim, but Brian poured on.

"Oh, there might be an occasional short harvest and a somewhat heavy winter—hunger in cot and hall. Raiders from the sea might foray inland upon them from time to time; and a few other ordinary difficulties might arise. But if they went on much as their forefathers had, they knew that life would go as all men were used to it."

"Every generation—" Jim made another attempt, but was still thwarted.

"Of course!" Brian was going on. "True, they knew nothing of the larger world. Unless they went on Crusade, they never set foot in the Holy Land. They wore armor of no more than naked chain mail—and you know yourself, James, that while chain mail without plates at vulnerable spots—I am not speaking of those rich suits all of plate—plain chain mail, I say, may stop a sword point or edge from cutting the flesh; yet the force of the blow alone may well break the bones beneath the chain. And old-fashioned helms such as our guide wore—"

"Brian," said Jim, with determination to get a word in edgewise, "in every time and place, people think no other time could match theirs for troubles and accomplishments. But half a century later their great-grandchildren are singing the same song."

" 'Singing,' James . . . ?"

"I meant 'saying.' "

"Then their great-grandchildren must be greatly ignorant."

"That's precisely it. Just as Angie and I were of this—" Jim caught himself just in time. "The point is they *are* ignorant; because they never lived through their great-grandparents' time and only knew a few small facts about it. Beyond those facts, they tended to assume it had all the advantages of *their* time and none of its drawbacks. They would probably assume, for example, that knights of this time wore full plate armor."

"But that is exactly what I am telling you, James! Such would think that the small things they knew and endured must be the best and worst of all that could happen—that none could ever struggle as they did, or endured what they were enduring! Would it not open their eyes to live in the times we do now?"

"It certainly did . . . I mean would—" Jim caught himself just in time. But Brian, in full cry after his argument now, did not hear.

"They would be amazed at what we could do and have done; but think the Earth was about to be called to justice, when they learned of the plagues, the assaults, the wars, the crushing taxes—"

"Well, now, the taxes—"

"—the evil abroad everywhere in men. The plague, as I mentioned, the weakness of our kings—now, Edward the First of glorious memory was a man and a king! Whereas our present Edward—and his taxes are piled upon taxes until we are stripped to the bone. I tell you, James . . . hark, hold up a moment! Do you hear what I hear?"

Brian had pulled Blanchard to a halt. Jim stopped Gorp beside the other horse and listened. Now that neither of them were talking, he could clearly hear what Brian had mentioned, though it was at some little distance. It was someone crying, although the sound was not that of a child in tears. Possibly a woman.

"Come," said Brian, and started Blanchard through the trees off to their left. Jim caught up with him, after being stopped short by the need to catch the lead rope of the sumpter horse, which Brian had summarily cut loose from Blanchard's saddle.

The sumpter horse, in fact, had taken advantage of their pause to crop some of the dark vegetation underhoof; and it looked at Jim with a disgusted "What now?" expression as it had to follow once more.

"I just hope that stuff growing here doesn't poison you," Jim said to it.

"James?" Brian looked back over his shoulder.

"Nothing," said Jim. "Keep going."

Brian did; and scarcely a minute later they came out into a little glade, lit by the white moon (or sun) through a rare opening in the forest canopy overhead. On a mossy bank there was what looked like a girl in her teens, dressed in a long white gown, with a filmy scarf, also white, adorning rather than hiding her long, black hair.

Brian spurred to her, and reined Blanchard in sharply just before her.

"My Lady," he said, "is help needed? Because if it is I am at your command."

She wept a few more tears.

"Oh, kind knight," she said, "I seek my father, who has been carried off by cruel enemies, who live further in this wood. But a dear little creature of these wild lands, who by some miracle was able to speak to me, did just now tell me in words I understood that those same enemies are lying in wait for me, a round dozen of them. They wait to take me, in ambush, only a little further on. So I dare not go on; and yet I must go on. Oh, was ever a maiden in such a trouble as this!"

She began to weep more heavily, into a tiny white handkerchief that should by this time be too sodden to be of any use; but at this moment seemed as dry as if it had never absorbed a tear.

"Brian," said Jim uneasily, looking at that handkerchief. But Brian paid no attention.

"I pray you, sorrow no more, fair lady," he was saying. "I and my friend will escort you forward; and I promise it, you may fear none of those who lie in wait for us."

"Brian—" began Jim more strongly; but before he could say anything else, the blackness of the grass below him seemed to flow up about him, wrapping itself around him like a tight, heavy blanket, immobilizing and stifling him, so that he could not breathe. He felt himself suffocating, slipping away so that he plunged into unconsciousness.

He came to groggily at first, but his head cleared rapidly. He was in what was clearly a castle, remindful of some of the older ones he had seen in England, since its walls were of rough-faced cut stone. But the arched doorway and ceiling gave a different feel to the building. Brian was not with him.

The room was large and the ceiling high. A few straight chairs stood around the walls; and one, with carved armrests and a tall back with what looked like a snake cut into it, sat alone on a dais at the far end of the room. Immediately before him was the maiden they had seen, but grown suddenly taller, and older—with all the helplessness gone out of her.

She was a tall woman now; and her dress, while still white, was a delicate thing of lace and a shimmering fabric like silk. But her hair was the color of utter lightlessness and her eyes so dark it was impossible to say what their original color might have been.

She was incredibly beautiful, but there was a hardness and imperiousness about her that was the extreme opposite of the helplessness he and Brian had looked upon earlier.

"So," she said, "you are recovered. You understand me now, do you not, my rash young intruder? What made you think you could intrude on my domain, as if these lands were free of passage to anyone—"

She broke off and sniffed at him.

"Aha!" she said. "I smell magick on you. So you know something of the Art and that is what made you think you could trespass here—and you have a little ward, as well—no doubt with your filthy little magick inside. How did one so young even think he could learn enough to face me?"

No answer came to Jim, offhand. This was all too much like a very old-fashioned melodrama, with the villain twirling his black mustache and saying to the heroine: *"Hah, me proud beauty! So you dared to come plead with me yourself? . . . etc."*

He stood wordless, staring at her.

"—Well, I'll just strip that ward from you and see what pitiful little power you do possess. . . ."

Her hand came toward him as she spoke, but before it touched him, a little flare like miniature lightning leaped from Jim's chest to meet her oncoming fingers; and she snatched her hand back, crying out.

"Poisoned!" She spit the word out. "Poisoned against me, personally! Who dares do that?"

Jim's lips parted without his willing it; but the voice that came out of him was not his, though it had become a very familiar one lately.

"I am KinetetE."

"Kin . . . what sort of unpronounceable name is that? I never heard of you. You must have some small holding of magick to poison the ward about this young lout here—let alone poison it against me! Did you realize who you were offending when you did that to Queen Morgan le Fay?"

"Oh, I had you clearly in mind at the time, I promise you, Morgan."

"Why you insufferable cow! How dare you address me by my given name?"

"We Mages speak to all lesser ones so."

"Lesser! I am not lesser! All are lesser than I! I just told you—I am Morgan le Fay, Queen of Gore! And in this land, there is none who does not feel fear at my name!"

"There are two who don't."

"What two? I tell you there are none such! What two?"

"Why, I'm one and the young magickian who stands before you in my ward is the other."

"I don't like her," Hob was muttering between Jim's shoulder blades, barely loud enough for Jim to hear. For the first time Jim realized that the little hobgoblin must have crept into his favorite hiding place there under Jim's clothing, without his noticing it.

"There's one other, at least, come to think of it," added KinetetE's voice, thoughtfully.

"Name her to me!"

"He, in this case. Merlin."

There was a moment in which nothing in the vaulted room moved—even the air about Jim refused to enter his lungs. Then Morgan le Fay spoke.

"Merlin is locked in a tree forevermore. I am unchallenged in Lyonesse."

"Time is greater than you think, Morgan," said KinetetE. "Not that I think Merlin would have ever considered dealing with you as anything of a challenge."

"You tire me," said Morgan le Fay. "It is time I was rid of you." She pointed a finger at Jim. "Come to me, here, Kin—whatever your name is! Now!"

The finger stayed there. Nothing happened.

"As I've been trying to make clear to you, Morgan," said KinetetE, "you vastly overrate yourself—and most vastly underrate me. You can't move me unless I let you. But if you really want to try yourself against what I know, come to where I am."

"You are Elsewhere, in the world where Lyonesse was once," the Queen said. "None of us who lived there in its past may go back again. You know that much, at least. What has been cannot be changed."

"I can move you here, if you really want to come. Just say so."

"I will not let you take me against the Time, to break its Laws. Nor can you bring me there against my will."

"Frankly," said KinetetE, "you're right. No, I can't."

"So!" Morgan's voice was triumphant. "You admit a weakness!"

"Which you don't; and which is the reason I know more than you do and keep on learning more. The Knight-Dragon will take care of you eventually, no doubt. But for now he must be tired, standing there and listening to us talk. I suggest you put him back carefully as he was; and don't bother him or anyone with him, from now on. I may not be able to get us together, but there are sendings I can direct your way; and I can promise there won't be one of them you like."

"Sendings cannot touch me."

"These can. But as I say, enough of this. Send Jim back now while I'm still watching."

"Jim? Knight-Dragon? What is he? Both or which? What's his name?"

"Don't you wish you knew? As far as your other question goes, he's the Knight-Dragon because he can be either knight or dragon—even in Lyonesse."

"Nonsense! But I'm glad to be rid of you both. Go, Knight-Dragon; and your name and bodies with you!"

Jim was back, sitting on Gorp—who gave a grunt of surprise at the sudden weight returned to his saddle.

Jim came close to giving a grunt of surprise himself. He, Gorp, and the sumpter horse were back in the forest of Lyonesse, but not in the glade where they had been when the shadows snatched him away from Brian and the weeping maiden.

Morgan le Fay's voice spoke out of the air beside him, savagely.

"Very well, my Knight-Dragon! I have done what your friend asked, but just because I couldn't lift your ward doesn't mean you aren't going to lose it along the way—and then you will be one to find what it means to anger Queen Morgan le Fay. I've just sent you and your beasts to the Forest Dedale. May you enjoy yourself there!"

Jim got a sudden, very clear impression that Morgan le Fay had now abandoned him.

"Hell!" he said. He leaned back to make sure that the sumpter horse's lead rope was securely tied to his saddle, then put them all in motion. He was moving at random, possibly in the wrong direction, but it helped him to feel he was attacking the situation rather than sitting baffled and helpless.

This was a fine start for three heroes who had gone off to perform a rescue. Dafydd left behind in another Kingdom entirely, Brian almost surely tricked into going off on a rescue that was probably a trap even he couldn't fight himself out of—and Jim, himself, having already found an enemy in the most powerful magician still active in Lyonesse; and not even knowing where he was.

The Forest Dedale?

The name ''Dedale'' baffled him—though it had a familiar ring, as if he ought to know it. It sounded something like a French word, but what did it mean? He had an uncomfortable feeling about it. Morgan le Fay would not have sent him here if it was a pleasant or happy place to be. But the meaning of the name, if any, eluded him; though there was a faint tickle in the back of his mind . . . if only he could pin it down to some specific meaning . . .

''Dedale . . . Dedale . . .'' He said it out loud, and Gorp looked back at him curiously. The sumpter horse ignored him completely and thought about grazing on the ground cover. Hopefully it would not turn out to be poisonous to horses. Jim went on thinking.

French, of course, was a latinate language, so there should be an ancestor of that word familiar to Romans—or even ancient Greeks. He knew Latin to some extent; but this did not sound as if it could be twisted into a word in that tongue. More likely the ancestor was a classic Greek one—he had it!

Daedalus, of course! It all came back to him suddenly. The man, according to legend, who created the Labyrinth in Crete, to contain the Minotaur, the manlike monster with the head of a bull. Theseus was the name of the hero who finally killed it—and Daedalus died when the daughters of King Cocalus poured boiling water over him as he sat in his bath. They really liked gruesome endings in those early legends—come to think of it, so they did in this other time he had chosen to live in.

''Of course!'' said Jim out loud. ''A maze! That's what it is!''

''What's a maze, m'Lord?'' asked Hob in his right ear. The little hobgoblin had moved out onto Jim's shoulder.

''A puzzle. A place that someone made deliberately hard to find your way out of,'' said Jim. ''That's what this Forest Dedale is—this place Morgan le Fay's landed us in.''

''Is it a bad place, then?''

''I don't suppose,'' said Jim, ''that it's any worse than any other location in Lyonesse—except that it's like a closed box with only one hole in it. I'll just have to find that hole so we can get out."

"If it's a box with only one hole," said Hob, "I can find the way out for us in no time at all, my Lord."

"You?"

"Yes, my Lord. All you have to do is light a fire."

"Just light a fire?"

"Oh, yes," said Hob. "If you make me some smoke, I can ride it to find the hole. If there's a way out of any kind of box, smoke will find it."

Jim hauled on the reins; Gorp stopped, and the sumpter horse had to check abruptly to keep from running into the stallion's hindquarters, with the danger of automatically being kicked.

It glared at Jim's back. *Now what?* it was clearly saying. Jim, used to the sumpter horse and its ways, ignored it.

"Hob," he said, "you're a genius."

"Oh, thank you, m'Lord!" said Hob; and hesitated. "Er—my Lord, is it good or bad to be a genius?"

"It's good, very good," grunted Jim, now bent over, scanning the ground from his saddle for twigs and other small burnables to start a fire with.

"Oh, thank you, m'Lord! Why am I a genius?"

"Because you thought of using smoke to find our way out. I know about how you ride smoke, but it just never occurred to me to use it here."

He dismounted as he spoke, to gather some twigs and dry grass; and began to struggle with flint and steel to get a spark. He had finally learned how to use the two for that purpose, but use still did not come easy. After several ineffective strikes of the one against the other, a spark did jump, the dry, dead ground cover he had piled in a small heap for tinder began to smolder—and seconds later a small flame wavered upward.

"Oh, good!" said Hob happily, leaping on the first thin waft of smoke that lifted from the flames. "Be right back, m'Lord."

He zipped off, out of sight in an instant between the black

trees. Jim sat back, cross-legged on the ground, wondering how soon "right back" might be. After a few minutes, it occurred to him that in such a position he might be at a disadvantage if he was faced with a sudden attack by man, beast, or whatever. He climbed back onto Gorp; and, sitting there, lost himself in trying to think of a really popular fourteenth-century song that ended with everybody happy.

"Here I am!" sang Hob, bringing him back abruptly. "I found the way out, m'Lord." He hovered in the air on his waft of smoke a foot or so in front of Jim's eyes. "It's easy. First you go right, then you go left, then you go left again, then you go right, and then left and another right and another right—"

"Hold it," said Jim. "Why don't you just show me the way, instead of telling me?"

"Of course, my Lord. This way, then."

Hob started off between the trees to Jim's left and disappeared again. "Sorry, m'Lord," he said, reappearing. I'll keep just ahead of you."

"Yes," said Jim. "That'll be better."

They started, Jim riding and leading the sumpter horse, and Hob riding his waft of smoke, more or less level with Jim himself but slightly ahead and on the left.

"Now right, my Lord," he said, turning for no apparent reason between two of the big trees. "That's right. Now go right again . . . now left . . . now left . . . now right, and right again—"

"Whoa! Stop! Come back here!" called Jim, pulling his two horses to a stop. Hob turned and rode his waft back, looking apologetic.

"Pray forgiveness, my Lord. I didn't mean to get ahead—"

"It's not that, so much; though I'd like you to stay level with me. The horses and I keep trying to catch up with you. Stay beside me, if you can. But what I wanted to say was there can't be this many turns! It doesn't make sense. Are you sure this is the only way to get out of the Dedale Forest?"

"Oh yes, m'Lord. If we went any other way we'd just

come to a great wall of stone like the face of a cliff, or a bottomless pit or a deadly marsh."

"Well," said Jim, "if you say so."

"We do run into some people on the way, m'Lord."

"We do? Well, we'll deal with them as we reach them. Lead on."

Hob turned his waft of smoke forward once more, and they went on together.

"—And now left," Hob was saying, for what seemed to Jim to be the thousandth time; Jim's mind was elsewhere again, considering whether he should use the magic inside his ward once he was out of the Forest, to find Brian. Brian might have run into serious trouble by now—if not something worse. Jim told himself not to think about anything worse. Brian must remain unkillable, in Jim's mind at least.

But also, there was the unhappy feeling that the first time he dared open his ward to use magic, Morgan le Fay would know of it; would pounce on him, gaining some advantage that could end with her managing to take it from him, or working out something disastrous with the Dark Powers—or something else to put him and Brian in trouble.

"And now right . . . and there he is, my Lord."

"Brian?" said Jim, startled back to his surroundings. "Where?"

"No, my Lord," said Hob. "The first of the people I said we'd meet with."

Jim stared ahead. They had come out into a large opening in the trees, a space big enough to hold a castle in the farther distance; and, closer, a pavilion before which stood another young maiden with a very sorrowful, pale face. An armed retainer with a sword stood on each side of her. Before her and these others a large knight, fully armored and weaponed, sat waiting.

Chapter 9

Jim checked Gorp.

"Is something wrong, m'Lord?" whispered Hob, in the air beside him.

"Have you any idea who that is out there?"

Hob looked earnestly through the thin screen of the last trees that hid them from the seated man.

"I think . . . he's a knight, m'Lord."

"Do you? Well, that helps."

"It's nothing, my Lord." Hob glowed with pleasure. "Nothing any genius couldn't do."

Jim sighed. Irony was wasted on Hob. He lifted the reins of Gorp and rode into the clearing. The knight jumped to his feet at the sight of him.

"Ah!" he cried. "Long have I waited here! And now ye shall die, unless ye save your life by a foul deed."

"Foul deed?" echoed Jim, reining Gorp in hard. "What's all this?"

"It is my curse—fetch my horse and forget not the lance," he added to the closest of the armed servitors, who ran back into the pavilion. "I had a curse laid on me that I should never have wife nor children, though I would always be able to find a maiden I loved. But once I had, I must fight with the first knight who came this way. If I won, the knight I fought might have his life spared only by one act. He must strike off the head of the maiden I loved. Only if the passing knight overcame me and showed me mercy would I be free to marry and know happiness and family."

"Well," said Jim, and ran out of words, his mind busily hunting for a way to get out of this situation. He was only too aware of how little skill he had with the lance, or any other weapons—in spite of Brian's efforts to teach him. Furthermore, he was enough of a magician to know how complicated a curse like that would be, and how much magical energy would have to be invested in making it.

More likely, he thought, the knight was given to delusions. So it would not be possible to simply talk him out of believing as he did. An excuse in his own terms was the only thing that would work.

"What a sad shame it is, then," said Jim, "that I've only this one lance I ride with. It is consecrated; to be used only against a certain, especially foul foe. A knight who has committed so great a sin it cannot be named. But don't worry. Someone's bound to come along who can beat you."

"Never!" said the knight; and to Jim's embarrassment, he saw that the other had begun to shed tears. "For another part of my curse is that no one but a man who was never born on earth can best me. But joust you must, for fight I must; and I have no lack of spears."

He turned his head.

"Bring another lance!" he shouted into the pavilion.

"Hob," said Jim in a low voice, "if I made some smoke in a hurry, could you carry me past this place?"

"Not when you're wearing all that armor and weapons, m'Lord. You're too heavy. Er—m'Lord, with your grace—I think I'll wait for now on the sumpter horse."

"You might as well," said Jim gloomily. He reached down to untie the sumpter horse's lead rope, and simply let it fall to the ground. Where were his brains? There had to be some way of avoiding this nonsense.

The retainer came out with two lances under one arm and leading a saddled and bridled warhorse, the color of pale mist over a black swamp on a cloud-dark, early morning.

The knight wiped his eyes with a large forefinger, shook the wetness off the finger, and took one of the lances. He climbed into the saddle of the mist-colored horse. The retainer brought the other lance to Jim, took Jim's lance carefully from its socket on the right side of his saddle, and laid it reverently on the grass.

Jim balanced the lance he now held. It felt strange, for it was a good deal lighter than those Brian had trained him with. It was, in fact, little more than a pole with a steel point on its end. Untypically at a loss to think of any further excuse, Jim turned with the long weapon balanced in his hand, to face the knight of the pavilion.

It was well he did. Without any further challenge or warning, the knight had already put his horse in motion and was coming at him.

Belatedly, Jim got Gorp moving. He did not have time to bring his horse up to full gallop; but, fortunately, just as the lance he had been given had turned out to be lighter than what he was used to, so the knight's mount was both smaller and lighter than Gorp. Jim found himself approaching the knight with their combined speeds at slightly better than ten miles an hour.

Jim was doing his best to hold the spear loosely until the moment of impact, as Brian had taught him; but looking along its length at the foe thundering toward him, his spearpoint seemed to be wavering and bobbing all over the landscape. He tried to hold it more on target, but without tightening up. It was no use—and now the knight was upon him.

At the last second Jim, for the first time without being reminded of it by Brian, remembered what his friend had tried to hammer into him—*slant your shield!* Holding the heavy shield high to cover his head as well as his upper body, he angled the face of it to the left.

There was a sickening impact, and the point of the knight's lance shot past him on his left. Gorp collided with the other horse and knocked the lighter animal to the ground, with its rider still in the saddle.

The knight pulled himself loose from his steed just in time to avoid being pinned as it fell, staggered to his feet looking dazed, and pulled his sword by what must have been more reflex than anything else.

The collision had brought Gorp to a standstill, however, and Jim had profited by the time that gave him to get his own sword out first. From the advantage of the height of Gorp's saddle, he hesitated for only a fraction of a second before, wincing but desperate, he brought the edge of it down with all his strength—again as Brian had taught him—on the side of the knight's simple, old-fashioned helm, which had only a steel nasal bar to protect his face.

The steel head covering was proof against the edge of Jim's sword; but the padding between helm and head in the era this armor came from was nothing to write home about. The knight dropped.

He came to within seconds. But Jim was already off Gorp's back and had the point of his weapon at the other's throat.

"Yield, damme you!" he panted, without stopping to think that this was hardly the chivalrous way to ask a fellow knight to surrender.

The knight made a sudden, convulsive move to squirm sideways from under the sword point, but by that time, Jim was on his knees, this time with the sword edge against his opponent's throat.

"I yield me, gentle knight," said the other. "Never in all my life have I been bested—nor thought I could be—so swiftly. You are one of great prowess. Though, if my steed had not fallen, perhaps—but such talk is idle. I pray your mercy; which I have never given any knight in no such work of arms, myself, and which you will refuse, of course."

"That need not be," said Jim, now remembering the proper way to talk in such situations, "for you on your part are better than anyone else I have ever met in such a wayside bicker as this. I grant you your life—on one condition only. That is that you swear upon your honor to immediately take to wife that maiden I see yonder, if indeed she it is whom you love."

"That will I, and gladly," said the knight. "For this day sees the hope fulfilled which I had given up long since. Yet do I repent me that fought so poorly as to be defeated."

"Don't blame yourself," said Jim. "It just chances that of all knights now alive, I happen to be the only one who was not born on this earth."

"And is this so?" The knight leaped up. His sword was still in his hand, but he threw it from him and clasped Jim in a rib-threatening embrace. "Then my curse is broken and I will be a happy man all the rest of my days. Ye are my savior and I and my family-to-be will never cease from blessing your name. Pray tell it me."

Jim felt the cold hand of a reasonless caution on the back of his neck. Certainly it ought to do no harm to mention his name. Still, he hesitated.

"Alas," he said, "I'm forbidden to tell anyone that. But you can think of me as the Knight-Dragon—and now I've got to keep going."

"Farewell and Godspeed, then, Sir Knight-Dragon," said the knight, turning to hurry to the maiden, who—seeing him come—began to hurry to him. Jim picked up his own lance and remounted Gorp, and felt a sudden small pressure at his back.

"I am with you again, my Lord," Hob said.

"Welcome back," said Jim. He looked over his shoulder as he rode off with the sumpter horse nodding along behind him at the end of the lead rope again. The knight and the maiden were entwined in each other's arms; and it looked to Jim as if both of them were now weeping—happily, he trusted.

It was not until they were lost to sight behind him in the forest that it occurred to Jim why he had been right in avoiding the telling of his name. Any magic-maker gained a certain amount of power over another simply by discovering that one's right name; and Morgan le Fay, who could be watching him in the Lyonesse equivalent of a scrying glass, right now, was most certainly a magic-maker who, by simply knowing he was in Lyonesse and a beginning magician, knew too much about him already.

His thoughts moved to different possible dangers.

"Hob," he said, "you mentioned other people we'd meet on our way out of this wood. How many more of them do we still have to run into; and what are they like?"

"Oh, just two, my Lord. That is, only two important people. One will be a great black horse; and he will have a bad-tempered little man with him. The other is a poor little bird tied to the limb of a tree; and with her a plant that squeaks and squawks so loudly you can hear it a long way before you see it. It says it knows you, m'Lord. It has big, drooping green leaves; and it said it had told you its name, but you were impolite and didn't tell it yours. It wanted me to tell it what your name was; but it commanded me to tell, instead of just asking, so I wouldn't."

"Good," said Jim. He realized that he should have thought of this before. "Don't tell anyone my name, Hob, while we're here. Will you remember not to do that?"

"Oh, yes, my Lord. I never forget anything."

They rode on. That is to say, Jim rode on, Hob flew on, Gorp and the sumpter horse paced forward. Jim, however, was not thinking of those with him. His mind was occupied with the fact that he had been extraordinarily lucky to come out safe and sound from his combat with the knight—to say nothing of winning. It had been that one piece of advice from Brian on fourteenth-century weapon-handling, plus the advantage of Gorp's size and weight, that had brought him through it unharmed.

He must do some thinking, he told himself, about how to avoid such fights from now on. This Forest Dedale seemed to be a place of adventures right out of the original legends about King Arthur and his Knights. Almost anyone else he encountered most likely would not only be thoroughly trained in using weapons, but powerful with them, as a result of frequent use. In a fair and even combat with an opponent like that, he probably wouldn't stand a chance of coming out alive.

If he could only stay alive long enough to find Brian, he might stand more of a chance. Meanwhile, what he was going to need was an all-purpose good excuse for not fighting. . . .

"There they are, m'Lord!" chirped Hob at his right ear.

"Already?" They had just reached the open fringe of trees bordering a clear area on the side of what could be called either a large stream or a small river. The remarkable thing about this stream, however, was that its waters seemed to be racing along at a speed Jim guessed to be around thirty miles an hour. In level country, how could it have built up such a speed—the race of a high mountain stream throwing itself down a precipitous slope?

Magic again! thought Jim, with immediate suspicion—but a second thought reminded him that the magic energy required to move such a volume of water continuously had to be mind-boggling. One way would be to remodel the countryside to create a high altitude farther up the river; but for such a speed, that higher ground would have to be very high, and very near. But he could see no sign of a hill or mountain upstream, looming over the treetops there.

Something else was at work here besides magic—figure that out later.

Now that he took his attention off the rushing stream, what caught his gaze was a very flimsy-looking, floating bridge crossing it. At the near end of the bridge a small tent was pitched; and outside the tent, apparently untethered, stood what might be the largest horse he had ever seen, a horse the color of the black water of a swamp just before the sun's rise. It was standing equipped with saddle, saddle-clothes, and bridle of the same color.

Jim reined up. He leaned forward in his saddle to get a better look through the thin screen of branches. "Where's that little man you talked about?"

"I think he must be in the tent, my Lord."

"What're he and the horse doing—guarding that bridge?"

"I don't know, my Lord. The man seemed to think I was some kind of bird. He waved his hands and shooed me away."

"Well, here we go, then," said Jim, starting Gorp forward at a walk. The sumpter horse followed sulkily.

The black horse paid no attention to them as they came clear of the woods.

Jim kept Gorp at a slow walk.

"Hob?" he said.

"Yes, my Lord?" came the little creature's voice, now from between his shoulder blades. Jim noticed that the little hobgoblin had been enunciating "my Lord," recently, rather than slurring it to "m'Lord," as was customary at Malencontri. He wondered if that might be some reaction to their being in Lyonesse.

"Good," said Jim, "you're still there. Stay there for the moment and don't say anything or make a noise. I'll give you a chance to leave me without being noticed, if you want that. I'll tell you when it's safe to go."

The closer he got to the tent, which appeared half black, half white—seeming black where the shadow of a great tree on the other side of the rushing water fell on it, and pure white in the part that was in the sun—the more puzzled he was. No one came out of the tent to challenge his presence, though he was close enough now for the creak and jingle of his horses' harnesses to be heard. The black horse himself did not look in Jim's direction, though horses were usually curious about the approach of others of their kind, and stallions particularly watchful for other stallions.

It was as if he and his two animals were not there at all.

"What is it, my Lord?" asked the muted voice of Hob in his ear.

"Just sit tight and be quiet," whispered Jim. He turned Gorp around, caught a disgusted make-up-your-mind look briefly from the sumpter horse, and led the way back toward the forest edge.

Once far enough inside it so that he would be more or less out of sight from the tent, but able to see it and everything else in the clearing from between the tree trunks, Jim pulled Gorp to a halt, turned around once more, and looked back at the scene they had just left.

"Hob," he said, "you can see that black horse, can't you? Of course you can, because you told me about seeing it earlier."

"That's right, my Lord. And I can see him now."

"But you're a Natural and I'm a human—"

"Pray pardon, my Lord, but what does a Knight or magickian have to do to become a human?"

"They're both human to begin with," said Jim. "All people are human."

"It isn't a special name, got for doing something brave?"

"No," said Jim. "Unfortunately."

"Oh. But, my Lord—"

"Not now, Hob," said Jim. "We've got other things to think about. We both see the black horse. He's paying no attention to us. If he was just a magic illusion, though, an animal wouldn't see him, because magic won't work on them. The horses could tell us—our horses—if they were able to talk. They don't act like they see it at all; and it doesn't act as if it sees them. I wish horses could talk."

"Are you through saying what you were saying, my Lord?" asked Hob timidly.

"For the moment. Did you have something to tell me?"

"Just—horses can do a sort of talking. But most of it's twitching their ears and baring their teeth, and things like that. If they think something that goes into words, sometimes I can understand them. But I don't know if they'd understand a question, or if when they answered I could understand them; and then, of course, you never know. Sometimes they just don't answer."

"I was afraid of something like that," said Jim. "But I still can't believe they're seeing him, or smelling him. The sumpter horse might ignore him; but for Gorp to ignore another stallion—I wish I could look at what's there through their eyes."

Of course, no sooner had he said it than he realized he could—or at least look at the horse through nonhuman eyes; and without risking using any of the magic inside his ward.

He had used his dragon-vision often before now, to get a good look at objects in the distance; but, of course, a dragon was actually not an animal—but also, for that matter, neither a Natural nor a human. They were a breed apart. But maybe it was worth trying. He visualized himself with the eyesight of a dragon, and felt the bulging sensation below his forehead that went along with the enlarged eye structure. He looked at the scene by the tent.

The black horse had not moved. No one had come out of the tent. There was no visible difference in the scene.

He returned his eyesight to human. That was that, he thought—but then it occurred to him his dragon-changing ability offered another possibility of help. If he could see with dragon-sight, as he had just done, he could as well fly with dragon-wings—all without once cracking his ward.

"Hob," he said, "if I changed to my dragon body, you could ride on me, couldn't you?"

"Yes, my Lord."

"Then, if I flew where you told me, could you show me from the air the way to where we can get out of this forest?"

"Oh, certainly, my Lord. But I don't think we could get out even if we got to it."

"Why not?"

"Well . . ." Hob sounded embarrassed. "I tried myself, my Lord, when the smoke took me to it—and the way out disappeared. The smoke had to find it again, in the new place it'd gone to."

"I see," said Jim grimly. A movable exit. Indeed, he told himself, he should have suspected that, himself. A brand-new Apprentice at magic should have.

If there was supposed to be only one way out, then the resident magic in a place like this Forest Dedale would have means of preventing any escape by cheating. Hob's finding the exit had not been cheating because it was part of hobgoblin nature to be able to ride smoke; and smoke had a right to find its way to any exit because that was a natural attribute of smoke. But Jim's going around and over when an ordinary escapee would not be able to without encountering the dangers set up along the way, would be blocked.

"—Besides, my Lord," Hob was saying, "aren't the horses too heavy for you to fly them anywhere?"

Of course, that was true, too. True, and so obvious he should have thought of it before he spoke.

Think again. Think thoroughly, this time.

He was not meant to escape from here so he could hunt for Brian, except by the established method and route. That was fact one. Following that, it was almost certain Morgan le Fay's magic was limited in that she could use it to do no more than just dump him in a place from which it was hard, but not impossible, for him to get out. That was not yet a proven fact; but it was the next thing to it. If she had planned something beyond his possible escape from the Forest Dedale, what would it be?

She had said, just before KinetetE joined the conversation, that she would strip away his ward, because she wanted to see how much pitiful power he really had.

She had not found out, of course—thanks to KinetetE. She had not even discovered his name.

This Dedale encounter could be set up to make him reveal as much other information about himself as possible.

The encounter with the knight who could never marry might have been a way to find out something about him. About his magic? No, there had been no magic involved to test Jim's. On the other hand, maybe Morgan was simply collecting as much knowledge of him generally as she could—since he had turned out to have KinetetE for an ally.

In fact, that last encounter had been more like a test of his courage and knightly skill than a simple attempt to make him use his magic—which would mean opening his ward and making himself vulnerable to her. Would she have realized how much of his success in the lance-running had been because of the difference between the ancient warhorses and armor of Lyonesse and that of the fourteenth century? Possibly not. Never mind—call that a test of him as a person.

But there certainly was magic at work with both the strange horse and the racing waterway. More so, if the black horse was not really there.

So, the black horse at least, if not the tent, the dwarf Hob had spoken of seeing, and the river, could all be part of a different test set up by Morgan le Fay to measure something else about him. Perhaps an attempt to force or tempt him to crack his ward instinctively, in panic or absentmindedness? So that Morgan could measure his self-control as an opponent?

Well, if she had mistaken him for a bold and skillful knight after his meeting with the Unwed Knight, she was in for another mistake. Most magicians from the land above had magic and nothing else. What she couldn't know or guess was that the greater part of his dangerousness to her was his knowledge that came from being born hundreds of years in the future.

He would go back to the tent and the river, and feel his way, this time, bearing in mind that the black horse could be an illusion.

"Hob," he said, "leave me and hide under the cover of the load on the sumpter horse."

The slight pressure against his spine that was Hob was abruptly gone. He lifted Gorp's reins and rode back to the tent by the river.

Chapter 10

As before, the black stallion paid no attention to their approach, and Jim's horses acted as if he was not there. But this time, when Jim was within a few horse-strides of the tent, the little man Hob had spoken of came out. There was nothing distorted about him physically, Jim noted. But the lines around his mouth and eyes made it seem as if he sneered, staring at Jim.

"Messire!" he said; and something about his high-pitched, thin voice matched the implication of his stare.

"Master Manikin!" replied Jim, falling back on the abrupt manners he had learned from observation of other knights dealing with inferiors in this age. "Will your bridge bear the weight of two horses, both laden? Answer me briefly, yea or nay."

"Not even one horse, unladen," said the manikin; and it seemed that he sneered even more by answering with other words than the ones Jim had ordered him to use. "It floats upon the water, messire, and with that much weight would sink deep enough below the water's top so that the current would sweep your horses off their hooves."

"Hmm," said Jim, deliberately ignoring the attitude of the other, who was now staring at Jim in an even more offensive way; as if any child would have understood what he had just said without being told. ''Dumb insolence'' the British armed forces had called that, a few hundred years before Jim's birth in his own world.

''Well,'' said Jim, ''I guess in that case we'll swim it.''

''I would not advise Messire to do that,'' said the manikin, lifting his head with his upper lip twisted unpleasantly. ''The current of the river is very strong; and no ordinary beast can swim it without being swept away and drowned. Only my Cloud Courser has the strength to stem its power. I will rent him to Messire for four gold pieces of value; and then whistle him back to me once Messire is on the other side.''

''Your price is a thought high, Manikin,'' said Jim, still playing his knightly part, since the other seemed determined to go on playing his, ''and your manner ill likes me. My horses will swim across.''

''Do not mistake . . . Messire,'' said the manikin. ''Look at the horse ye ride, and then at Cloud Courser. Has your horse such size and thews?''

Jim glanced briefly at the other horse, which had still neither moved nor made a sound. He was saddled and bridled, as if merely waiting for a rider. But it was true, Jim saw, now that the two were side by side, with only a small distance between them. The little man's animal was taller, heavier boned and muscled than Gorp by a noticeable margin—Gorp, whom he had never seen, until now, matched in size and obvious strength, except by Brian's Blanchard.

He looked again at the river. The broken limb of a tree shot toward them along the water's surface, caught for a moment on the edge of the floating bridge, and then was pushed underneath it by the current; to reappear a second later on the other side and shoot with equal rapidity on downstream, to where its above-water outline, like a sketch of itself in soft, dark pencil, was lost to sight in the greater uniform darkness of the surrounding forest.

The current was definitely traveling at the speed of a river throwing itself down the steep side of a mountain. No horse could live in that. It would be a miracle—or magic—if the black horse could.

Well, there was always the knightly way of dealing with this problem. Thankfully, he had seen enough of those called knights and gentlemen in this time and world to realize that men like Brian and Chandos were not typical of those who wore armor. This was a spot where being like most of the pack would work better for him.

"Churl!" he said, drawing his sword. "Not even that horse of yours could carry me across. You seek to slay me for some purpose of your own; and the loss of your horse is a cheap price to pay for the death of a knight! With four gold pieces of worth you could buy yourself ten such horses!"

The results were remarkably gratifying.

The manikin ducked and cowered back as the blade of Jim's sword gleamed like silver upheld in the white light. His face contorted.

"Not so, messire—my Lord!" he cried. "Not all the gold in the world could buy another like him! I swear on my soul he can take you safely across—take you, and pull your two horses with him on lead ropes as he goes!"

Jim lowered his sword, but did not resheathe it.

"Then you will make good those words!" he roared, beginning to be somewhat carried away by his knightly role. "You, yourself, will mount your stallion and ride him across the water. Now! While I watch. Do you hear me?"

"Yes, yes, my Lord!" The manikin edged around Gorp's rear hooves to get to his own steed. "But, my Lord—my four pieces of gold—"

"You dare speak to me of pay when I suspect you of tricking me to my death?" Jim roared. He reined Gorp half around to face the little man and lifted his sword once more in the air. "You'll get your pay if and when I choose to give it to you. Now ride!"

The manikin scrambled into the saddle of his stallion. He picked up the reins and the motionless animal came to life. Together they rode to the brink of the rushing water, just below the floating bridge, and plunged in.

Jim put his sword away, and frowned at the two of them. The manikin seemed to have no doubt of the horse and his horse no fear of the racing water. They quickly reached the other side, the big black horse swimming powerfully until it could put its front hooves on the farther bank and heave its body up out of the water. The manikin reined its head around to face Jim from across the racing current.

"You see, my Lord?" he called triumphantly.

"Now, ride him back across the bridge!" shouted Jim.

"But, my Lord—"

Jim flourished his sword again.

The manikin bowed his head and put the stallion in motion, reining him around. At the horse's first step on it, the bridge sank below the surface of the water.

By the time they were halfway back, the rushing stream plucking and pushing like powerful hands against the animal's legs as high as his hocks, Jim was sure that the running water would carry the legs from under any other horse; but this one came on without pausing to the near side of the stream, successfully stepping out at last and striding up to where Jim sat on Gorp. The horse still looked past Jim, rather than at him.

"You see, my Lord?" cried the manikin triumphantly.

Jim saw, all right. What he had just watched being done was physically impossible. The black horse might be able to swim that current; but there was no way, walking on that bridge, that he could keep it from pulling him off balance. The stallion had to have accomplished what he had just done by magic—there was no other answer.

If Morgan le Fay was behind this—and Jim was feeling more and more sure she was—then it was her magic making this possible. So, if the fight with the accursed, wifeless knight had been an attempt to test Jim's fighting ability and courage, it appeared more obvious all the time that this was an attempt to force him to use the black horse, for some reason.

Well, if that was what she wanted, she was not going to get it, he told himself.

The manikin must be in on it on her side. In fact, he, the stallion, the tent, and the river might all be her creatures or things. Unless they were all illusions—and Jim himself was enough of a magician to know they were not, now that he was close to them.

So, rule out illusions. What else was left?

"—Well, my most puissant Lord?" the manikin was saying, sneering once more and halting the still-wet stallion in front of Jim.

Jim stared at him, a long, wordless stare; and the sneer faded as the manikin's face grew pale.

"My Lord, my Lord . . ." he said shakily, "if I have said aught amiss—"

"I do not care what you say," said Jim, slowly and distinctly. "So, your animal can stem the river current. That doesn't mean he can tow my horses safely across as well; and I'm not about to risk them just to find out. Prove to me you can do that and I will think on it."

"How can I prove—" the manikin began, wringing his hands. But then he stopped suddenly and the touch of a sly look crept onto his face. "But why does your Lordship not ride him across yourself, and see how strong he is? He has strength to lead both your horses and to spare. You will see."

Jim hesitated. If the horse tried to throw him off and drown him in the river, he could always save himself, of course; but that would mean using his magic. And since the name of the game here had become avoiding any such use that Morgan le Fay might be able to observe . . .

Still, he had to go forward somehow. He could not stay on this side of the river indefinitely. He could, if he had to, try riding the stallion and see what developed. Besides, one of the few things that Brian-types and the kind of ordinary medieval gentleman-knight Jim was pretending to be had in common was that they never turned away from a challenge.

"I will ride the beast," he said, and waved in his best disdainful fashion at the little man. "Fetch a clean cloth and wipe the saddle."

"Yes, my Lord. Immediately, my Lord!" The manikin ran into the tent and came out with a cloth that seemed to gleam brightly silver in the Lyonesse sunlight. He carefully wiped the saddle and stood back from it.

"My Lord—"

Jim dismounted, Gorp looking back over his shoulder at his customary rider curiously. Putting his left foot into the stirrup of the black horse, Jim swung himself up onto its back. Under his weight and to his touch, the animal seemed as solid as any real horse could be.

Not only that, but he showed himself marvelously obedient to his rider's intentions. Almost without Jim's laying the right-hand rein against that side of the black neck, he turned about and angled toward the river just below the bridge. As he reached the edge and plunged in, Jim braced himself for the touch of icy waters, like those from high on a mountainside.

But the water was almost warm. Jim frowned. They were in midstream already and he tightened his legs around the barrel of the horse's massive chest—

—And like a soap bubble popping in midair, the horse was gone. He had simply ceased to be; and Jim found himself being whirled on by the racing stream, frantically trying to swim enough to keep his head above the water against the weight of his sword and armor.

In spite of his efforts, his head began to dip, and dip again, under the liquid surface. *"All right, you idiot!"* he told himself, *"you had to walk right into it . . ."* He could not keep up this struggle to stay afloat in his armor; and there was no way to shed any of his armor or even his sword without going straight to the bottom of the river.

This was it. Only magic would get him out of this—and once he cracked his ward, Morgan would have him.

Water filled his mouth and despair mounted in his chest. Brian and Dafydd—God knows he needed them, but they needed him. If Morgan took him out of the situation now, his friends would be lucky to escape Lyonesse alive; and Brian, damn chivalrous fool that he was, would probably consider it his duty to stay and do what he could alone. If so, Dafydd might well feel that he could not leave; and both of them might die.

Better to lose his magic and hold on to life a little longer. Maybe, even without magic, he could frustrate Morgan somehow . . .

His strength was going. The water closed over his head. He heard a roaring in his ears and felt the toes of his shoes dragging on the bottom of the river. Panic took him. He tried to push himself off from that surface and reach the air; and to his astonishment he bobbed up with his face barely above the water.

He gulped air for a wonderful moment, to get what he could into his lungs before he went down again—and then, to his dawning astonishment, he realized he was not going down again. He was floating on the surface, being rushed along by the galloping speed of the water. It was a miracle.

Or was it?

He suddenly realized he was no longer in his human body. He was in his dragon shape. Morgan had now gotten a good look at his instinctive shape-changing ability—and as far as Jim knew, there were no resident dragons in Lyonesse.

But wait a minute—dragons were supposed to be heavier than water—that was why Smrgol and all the other dragons of the Cliffside Eyrie had thought him a reckless fool for flying about at night. Why, in the darkness, a dragon could fly right into a lake, where he would sink and drown.

But he was not sinking—for some strange but welcome reason. He heaved a sigh of relief . . . and immediately began to sink. He was aware of his half-spread wings under water making rowing motions, trying to push him up that way.

Hastily he inhaled again, filling his lungs; and once more his body rose to ride high in the water.

So much for dragon beliefs that they would drown if they fell into any water that they could not scramble out of. Certainly the dragon body—as a body—was heavier than water. But dragon lungs were enormous. That was why dragons had the pouter-pigeon chests they did. The lungs had to pump an incredible amount of oxygen to the dragon body while it was taking off, flying almost straight up.

But still, he had changed his shape; and if Morgan was watching closely, she had discovered more than he had wanted to show her.

He had to have done it unconsciously. He had been a dragon often enough to know how, as a dragon, he had an entirely different set of instincts. When he changed shape, he not only appeared as a dragon, he *became* a dragon—emotionally, reflexively, as well as consciously. As a man he did not enjoy fighting—the way Brian and a surprising number of other knights, both good and bad, seemed to. But as a dragon, he could get emotionally caught up in a fight and think only of destroying his opponent.

So it was not surprising, really, that by this time he was almost as much of a dragon as a man. It would not have occurred to the dragon part of him that he could use magic to escape—though at the cost of letting Morgan le Fay know of it. The dragon-Jim would have been thinking only that he was at the bottom of a river and drowning.

At any rate, he had not had to crack his ward.

In his dragon body, he was now able to hold all of his head above water, when as a man he could not have. Even as he thought this, he was making plans. All he had to do now was scramble ashore—both wings and feet would help with that—and he could go quietly back through the woods, or even through the air—

He inhaled deeply, held his breath, lifted his wings out of the water, and spread them to their full, enormous width as a preliminary to taking himself back to solid land—and suddenly recognized that, ridiculous as it seemed, he was being carried back into the same clearing the river had whisked him away from.

Yes, there it was, the clearing, the bridge, and the tent. The manikin was staring with a horrified face at a completely unexpected dragon. Gorp and the sumpter horse, who had seen dragons before—and probably recognized this one even at a distance—were calmly watching. The black horse was standing immovable and unmoved, exactly where Jim had seen him at first glance.

At that moment, the river sucked him under the floating bridge. He came to the surface beyond it and was whirled past and out of their sight again, as the clearing ended and the river curved into the forest. He had pulled his wings back to his body just in time to keep them from possibly being damaged on the bridge—or, for that matter, since they stretched far enough, and the trees were close enough, on the massive, upstanding tree trunks on either side of the water where the forest started.

But he was breathing comfortably now; and he had instinctively begun to look forward, again. He would have to wait for some open stretch to risk trying to get out of the stream; then, he would have to pull himself ashore swiftly before the river took him into thick forest once more.

He had a few moments, at least, in which to think and plan—on second thought, he could take almost as much time as he wanted. The river might run fast but he would be far faster, once in the air. He could fly back to his horses in minutes.

The horses—there was still the problem of getting them across the river. No dragon could fly while carrying anything close to the weight of even an adult human. A dragon's powerful muscles could deal bone-breaking blows with his wings, as he himself had done when battling a thirty-foot sea serpent on land; but flying the horses across the river was out of the question.

So, how to bring them over?

He did not have time to answer himself. He had been riding the current in the middle of the stream, his eyes watching for a clearing that would allow him to spread his wings and get up into the air. Just at that moment he saw one.

But it was not the kind of clearing he had in mind. This one had a tent in it, a floating bridge across the river, and a black stallion—to say nothing of a Gorp and a sumpter horse with an identical load roped on its back.

Clearly—crazy as it seemed—it was the same clearing and

he was being carried into it once more. But the heavy trunks of the forest trees were still too close on either side for him to spread his wings at full stretch and literally fly out of the water. Cautiously, with the clearing he had originally left getting closer every second now, he tried half extending his wings; and made a great effort to move himself close to the bank.

He just managed it, half scrambling, half flying to the side of the river, the same one on which the tent and horses stood, ahead. There, he told himself; that took care of things for the present. He could get back in the river and be carried to the horses when he was ready. But first he wanted to unravel the puzzle of a river that raced in its shallow bed, but ended up going nowhere but back to the same point.

If he could only get up in the air, he could see the route he had followed and solve that puzzle. He looked around himself at the trees. First, he had to find the clearing he needed, large enough to spread his wings fully. Then, a short burst of his top takeoff speed, and he would be above the treetops.

Even as he thought this, he made out more than one—in fact, there were three such spaces visible, now that his eyes were above river level—deeper in the forest. He waddled to the nearest, cast a cautious eye upward to make sure the higher branches would not bar an ascent, and launched himself upward on an explosion of energy.

He did not need to go much higher than the treetops to see the secret of the river—what there was of it. As things like this nearly always turned out to be, there was nothing really marvelous about its galloping rush with no slope to account for it. The fact was, it was no real river at all.

Clearly, it was no more than a sort of very long, circular ditch. The warmth of the water, and its shallowness, should have been enough to make him suspect what he now saw. His knowledge of how magic could be used now made the whole matter an entirely possible creation. A trench like this could be created by magic—though human hands digging it would be cheaper if you had command of enough hands to do that much work for you.

Importing the water would take a chunk of magic, of course, but not an impossible amount if there was a lake or river lying not too far off; and he had to guess that Morgan le Fay might have as much magical energy at her disposal as any AAA magician in the world above. Given that, there was only the extra energy required to keep the water circulating whenever someone you wanted stopped reached it. It would still not be cheap to do, but well within the resources of an AAA individual.

On the other hand, Morgan might not be bound by the magical pattern he was familiar with in the world above. She might have a different kind of magic, and have it to burn; but just be a tightwad with it. Both Carolinus and KinetetE had shown some tightwad tendencies at times; and he had a strong suspicion that Charles Barron, the third of the upper world's only three AAA+ magicians, might show the same tendency, though he had had little to do with him.

But at any rate, he now knew the river was not the impassible barrier it had seemed to be. The manikin must know, too, of course, but squeezing him for more information would probably just be a waste of time. Chances were he knew nothing useful; and any effort to make him tell would only alert Morgan to the fact Jim was learning things—he was still convinced she was watching him.

No, the best way was to go back into the river as if he had never escaped it, then climb out, and go on playing the bully knight who was possibly not too bright.

Jim returned to the river and plunged in, still a dragon. The current snatched him quickly to the clearing; where his own two horses and the manikin stood looking at him, while the black stallion continued ignoring everything.

He made sure he stayed on top of the water, and came bang up against the floating bridge, which stopped him. Happily, it did not break under the impact of his weight, with the push of the current behind him. He used the claws on his upper legs to pull himself along it to the bank where the tent stood.

The manikin was still staring, standing as if frozen, as Jim climbed up onto solid ground. The sumpter horse, recognizing him in dragon shape, began grazing again. But Gorp, always glad to see him—either as human or as dragon—came heavily toward him.

Jim changed back into his human shape again, complete with his sword and armor. The manikin stared, then shrank back as Jim gave him a long, steady look. Jim deliberately said nothing more. With as ominous a look on his face as possible, Jim put his left foot into its stirrup and mounted Gorp.

"Hah!" he said, staring at the manikin. The manikin cowered even more. Without another word, Jim rode off along the river in the direction he had just come from, the sumpter horse following automatically at the end of her tether.

"Hob?" He glanced back over his shoulder, once he was in the woods out of sight and hearing of the manikin.

He looked back at the covering over the load on the sumpter horse.

"Yes, my Lord?" said Hob, emerging from under the cover.

"You can come back up with me, if you want, now."

"Yes, m'Lord!" said Hob happily, leaping the distance between the two horses. Jim felt the slight impact of the small body against his shoulder. "What're we going to do now, my Lord?"

"Ride around the river," said Jim.

"*Around* the river?"

"That's right," said Jim. "We'll have to go a little away from the direct route to the exit you and the smoke found. But we'll come back to it later. Do you think you'll recognize the way out when we cross it again?"

"Oh, yes, my Lord. But, how do we get over that river?"

"Never mind that," said Jim. "We're just going to follow the river until you tell me we're in line with the escape spot."

"The river goes to it? Well, of course, my Lord, if you say so. But—"

Jim suddenly realized he was taking a mean pleasure from the puzzled note in Hob's voice.

"It goes around almost in a circle, you see. We just go outside the circle," he said.

"Oh."

"Yes."

"I understand now, my Lord."

"I was sure you would," said Jim.

"Of course, my Lord. I'm used to magick."

"I was counting on that."

"*Very* used to magick."

"I know," said Jim. "I know you are."

They rode on together, Jim's conscience still bothering him slightly; but not enough to make him explain to Hob. Both of them were satisfied, but for distinctly different reasons.

"And we'll only have to stop a moment to rescue the poor little bird. Then we'll all be free!" said Hob happily.

Chapter 11

"Bird?" said Jim. "Bird—what bird?"

"The last of the people I said you'd meet, m'Lord—remember—Oh! There it is, there it is! Through the trees there on our right!" Hob was almost jumping up and down on Jim's shoulder. "This is just where the smoke went, away straight off into those woods, there!"

"You don't have to shout!" said Jim sourly. "Particularly when you're right beside my ear!"

"Oh, beg the grace of your forgiveness, my Lord. But this is it—what you wanted me to watch for."

"I gathered that much."

"But the river? We're still beside it. You know, m'Lord, it's strange I don't remember seeing that river when I rode the smoke to the exit—and how can we be past it if we're still going along the same side of it?"

"Magic," said Jim shortly, not feeling like making any greater explanation. His ear was still ringing.

"But—"

"Hob," said Jim, "it doesn't matter. Be still a moment."

"Yes, my Lord."

After a moment Hob added, a little timidly, "You're a great magickian, my Lord."

"Thanks," said Jim grimly.

But as he rode on the ringing faded; and it crept in on him that he had been a little hard on Hob. There was indeed a clearing plainly ahead, as Hob had said; and he found he was not looking forward to another talk with the singing dieffenbachia plant—the one that had told Hob he had met Jim had to be the same one he had met at KinetetE's—and what was it doing with a small bird, anyway?

Probably better not to ask Hob. Better to wait and see when they got there—they were already out of sight of the river.

"You know, Hob," said Jim, to change the subject, "I've been thinking. Even once we're out, I won't know how to start finding Brian, wherever he is now."—*If he's still alive, that is,* he added silently to himself.

"I need help. But the only person I know from that first time here is the younger Sir Dinedan. He may be the direct descendent of the knight of that name among the original Knights of the Round Table; but he didn't strike me as someone very useful in a case like this. Then there's the Questing Beast you mentioned back at Malencontri. He seemed to know everybody. But how to find him . . . ?"

Jim had ended up talking to himself, almost inaudibly. Nonetheless, his voice in his own ears was enough to cover the sound of Hob beginning to speak. Jim just caught the end of what he was saying.

". . . we could ask them."

"Who them? What them?" asked Jim.

"I could ask the trees, m'Lord, as I was saying," Hob told him. "Everything here seems to know the QB; they might even be able to learn from other trees where he is now.''

''How would you ask a tree anything?''

''Just ask them, my Lord.'' Hob looked at all the heavy trunks and thick branches about them. ''Trees, where is the QB right now?''

He fell silent. He listened. Jim listened. There was no sound, not even that of a breeze in the branches.

''They didn't say anything,'' said Hob, at last.

''I noticed,'' Jim said.

''Maybe it's because they don't know us?'' said Hob. ''We could have the horses ask them.''

''Horses?''

''Well, yes, my Lord. We're plainly strangers. But horses are horses—I mean they belong everywhere, if I'm saying it right, m'Lord. But you know what I mean.''

''Yes. But what I meant was—'' Jim broke off. There was no point getting into a discussion over it. ''Sure. Go ahead, have the horses ask them, then. We've got nothing to lose by trying.''

''Well, actually, m'Lord, I don't know how to ask the horses anything; but I thought you, with your magick . . .''

''Me?'' said Jim heavily.

Of course, he might have known Hob's inspiration would have been leading that way. Jim had never talked to a horse in his life—with any hope of being understood, that is. What good could magic—

The thought came to a sudden halt. Carolinus could talk to animals and be understood; and Jim had gotten the impression that this was at least possible. Carolinus had turned a huge boar into a warhorse capable of carrying a massive troll, magically armored to look like a knight for a joust at the Earl of Somerset's Christmas party.

That had taken not only shape-changing, but getting the boar to act like a horse, and to know what a horse was supposed to do in a joust. Carolinus had said he *talked* to the boar. Jim could at least try—but it would have to be non-magically, to avoid cracking his ward.

He half closed his eyes and concentrated on thinking like

a horse. If he could think in horse-thoughts, then simply visualizing the horse he had picked to talk to as hearing the message that was intended might help . . . simple words, of course—no horse would see any sense in unnecessary verbiage.

He thought.

"*Ask trees,*" he visualized in his best-imagined equivalent of a horse snuffling at his belt in strong hopes of finding there a chunk of fresh, sweet apple, "*how find QB?*"

He aimed the question at Gorp. Gorp snorted.

"*What? What?*" Gorp's snort wrote itself on the mental slate of his visualization.

"*I said—*" Jim was beginning again.

"*Stallions stupid,*" sniffed the sumpter horse unexpectedly. "*I say. You, tree—where QB?*"

Jim neither heard nor visualized an answer this time. But the tips of the lower branches of the tree—a splendid yew—that the sumpter horse's head was pointing at leaned down toward it.

"Did you hear it say anything?" Jim asked Hob softly.

Hob shook his head.

"The carrying horse is still waiting," he said in a whisper. "You know what, m'Lord? It's supposed to help with trees if you hug them."

"Hug a tree?" Jim turned his head to stare at the hobgoblin. Hob nodded solemnly. "You can't mean that. A horse can't hug a tree."

Hob twisted his limber body uncomfortably.

"You can, my Lord."

"Me?" Jim stared at the tree. "Why not you?"

"It might seem stronger . . . coming from you, my Lord," said Hob, looking down.

Jim looked at the yew, its branch ends still bent down toward the sumpter horse. The whole process was ridiculous, here in these strange and empty woods. It was unthinkable. Still . . . if it got results. The sumpter horse went back to cropping on the ground cover.

Slowly Jim swung down from his saddle. He felt embarrassed even by the eyes of Hob and the horses on him. Thank heaven there were no other humans to see him—particularly some of his friends. They would think him wounded, sick, perhaps insane—or the most laughable object they had ever seen in their lives.

He could imagine the incident being repeated down the ages on this world: "*. . . and did you ever hear the story of how the magickal and most valorous Dragon Knight fell in love with a tree?*" (roars of laughter from those listening; and the speaker urged to tell the story over again several times in succession).

He stepped over to the yew tree. Close up, it did not seem to have so much of the strange, alien look that the forest had as a whole. He stopped in front of it, hesitated, gritted his teeth, and put his arms around it.

He hugged it. Actually, though it was not in any sense warm to his touch, and its bark was somewhat rough, the tree also had a strangely friendly feel—as if it and Jim were old acquaintances. It was a well-meaning, good-natured tree, he could feel that now, solid and deep-rooted—

"*Over there,*" spoke the tree, voicelessly inside him.

Jim heard a faint rustle overhead and looked up, letting go of the tree trunk in time to see its outermost twigs lifting and withdrawing. He turned back to Hob, now sitting on Gorp's crupper.

"Over there?" he said to the hobgoblin, as he swung himself back up into the saddle. "That's what it said to me."

Hob nodded; and the sumpter horse gave a snort that could have been agreement.

"I heard this time, m'Lord," said Hob proudly.

"And what're those directions supposed to mean?" demanded Jim. "Over where? Over in what direction—and how far?"

"Can't you tell by magick, m'Lord?"

"Hob," said Jim, "you're a good friend and I like having you with me. But there's one thing you have to get straight, once and for all. Magic can't do everything . . . not just any thing you happen to want . . ." His voice ran down and became thoughtful. ". . . hmm."

"Hmm, m'Lord?" echoed Hob.

It wouldn't hurt to try, Jim was thinking. He could visualize himself in—and transport himself to—a place he did not know only if he could clearly visualize someone he knew as being there. In that case the operative command was—only it wasn't a command; that stage of magic was long behind him—the *visualization* was of him together with the individual he had thought of, wherever that individual might be. He had a clear, sharp memory of the Questing Beast, from passing through Lyonesse before.

At any rate, visualization had worked that way in the upper world, for him. Whether it would also work in this magic-laden land—which really seemed to be full of magic, drenched in magic—maybe more magic than reality . . .

No, he decided. He would have to crack open his ward even to do a visualization transfer; and he dared not do that for fear a watching Morgan le Fay might immediately take advantage of his being unprotected.

Of course, Morgan might have grown tired of watching him by this time—no, not when he still hadn't won free of the Forest Dedale.

And he still had the dieffenbachia and the bird to pass.

He swung himself back up onto Gorp.

"Hob," he said, "you were talking about the singing plant and the little bird right ahead of us there where we can see there's a clearing. But I don't hear anything."

"No, m'Lord," said Hob. "I don't either."

Of course, it was just at that minute that they did hear something—the sweet trill of ascending notes from a bird, followed by a saw-edged, high-pitched voice trying to climb the same musical scale.

"Well, here we go," said Jim; for the sounds came from the clearing just visible through the trees ahead of them. It revealed itself as a very small clearing indeed, but one admitting enough sunlight so that in its center an oak sapling about a dozen feet in height was daring to stretch out its skinny limbs almost parallel to the ground, just like its ancient relatives around it; with small twigs and sparse leaves on them.

On one of the lower limbs perched the small shape of a bird. Before it stood the *Dieffenbachia cantans*.

"Ah, there you are, Mage," said the dieffenbachia, without turning around.

Jim had no idea how the dieffenbachia saw—with the surfaces of its large leaves, perhaps? If so, it would be able to see all around itself at once. He put the question aside.

He also decided not to bother correcting the address of "Mage" which the plant had just used. He had grown weary of explaining that he was not qualified for that title. Those he told always listened, nodded, smiled—and went right on using it. If he was a magickian, he had to be a Mage—it stood to reason.

But he had reached the plant by this time. He halted Gorp, and the sumpter horse also stopped.

"Did you hear me exercising just now?" went on the dieffenbachia, before Jim could say anything. "She said I'd get steadily better, and I am!"

"She?" said Jim.

"The great Witch Queen, Morgan le Fay!" replied the dieffenbachia proudly, but in a decidedly rusty voice. "Didn't you notice the difference?"

"I didn't hear you sing exercises the last time I saw you."

"Well, take my word for it. With the great Queen's magick and that nightingale there glued to the tree by magick, I'm almost as good as I ever was. Perhaps better. Yes—almost better. In fact, so much better, I really don't need that bird anymore."

"Turn it loose, then," said Hob.

"Hob—" began Jim; but the plant was already answering what had come out from Hob almost as a command.

"Oh, I couldn't do that. The great Queen herself put it there. Once she finds my voice is back, she'll come turn it loose. Probably."

"Ha!" said Hob.

"Ha?"

"Hob!" said Jim sternly. "Don't do anything—please. Let me handle this. Clearly, *Dieffenbachia cantans*, you know nothing of hobs."

"Well, no," said the plant. "I never heard of them until now."

"I thought as much. Otherwise you might be shaking with fear. I call this one 'Hob' for short, but the truth is he's a HobGOBLIN!"

"I've never heard of them, either."

"And well for you, you haven't. Lyonesse clearly doesn't have any. But there's a whole kingdom of Goblins, much feared in the land above—and of all the varieties of them, there is only one variety among them shunned by all the rest—the HobGOBLINS."

"Are they"—the dieffenbachia's leaves had indeed begun to tremble slightly—"more fearful than the rest, then?"

"No one knows, from moment to moment," said Jim in the most low-toned and ominous voice he could manage, "what a HobGOBLIN may do. No one wants to risk finding out. They cannot stand being denied what they want. Hob, here, now has set his heart on seeing your bird set free; and woe betide—"

"I can't. I might need it. In any case, it's fixed there by the magick of the great Queen! I can't turn it loose!" cried the dieffenbachia.

"That is false!" shouted Hob, in a voice that unfortunately was somewhat shrill for a fearful HobGOBLIN. "Magick only works on people and Naturals. That's why your Queen couldn't just point a finger at you and cure your voice. All Creatures—birds and beasts—can't be touched by it and can't be helped by it."

"That's not true!" said the dieffenbachia, getting a little shrill himself. "If the great Queen's magick wasn't keeping it there for me, why did the bird stay?"

"Because nightingales are wonderful, gentle, and kind!" retorted Hob. "They feel the pain of others—Creatures and people alike! They feel it very much! But they need freedom.

Your Queen must have told this nightingale about your trouble and it let her put it there with you. Ever since, it could have left any time; but it thought you needed it here. It'll starve before it leaves if you selfishly go on wishing it to stay here!''

''I don't believe the great Queen can't cure me. Nobody else could—''

The nightingale burst into a sudden brief but beautiful fountain of song.

They all looked at it.

''What did it say?'' Jim asked Hob in an undertone.

''It?'' said Hob. ''That's easy, m'Lord. It said I was right and magick wouldn't cure the plant's voice.''

''You're all against me. Nobody wants to help.''

''Ha!'' said Hob again—the most hard-hearted exclamation Jim could remember hearing from him.

The leaves of the dieffenbachia began to tremble seriously.

''But I'm better already—listen, Mage!''

It burst into song—if song was what it could be called. Actually, Jim thought, its voice wasn't quite as bad as it had been when he had heard it at KinetetE's and as they were coming to this clearing.

''How's that?'' asked the dieffenbachia. ''Aren't I better?''

''Well, it's certainly different than I heard it earlier,'' said Jim.

''See, HobGOBLIN? I'm much better. Almost cured. I probably don't even need the nightingale anymore. It can go.''

The nightingale left its branch and flew to perch on Hob's shoulder. Jim picked up the reins of Gorp.

''Where are you going?'' asked the dieffenbachia.

''Out of this forest,'' Jim said; and the horses began to move.

''Wait—'' said the dieffenbachia, ''I'll go, too.''

They moved out together, the nightingale still riding on Hob's shoulder, Hob riding on the pack of the sumpter horse, Jim on Gorp, and the dieffenbachia travelling beside him—gliding along in some strange fashion, possibly on its root ends; but however it moved was hidden from Jim by the large green leaves of its upper person.

"Mi, mi, mi, mi . . ." he was chanting in a low voice to himself, running up a scale of notes and hitting about half of them very flat indeed.

And suddenly the forest about them was different. How different, it was impossible to say—but undeniably no longer what it had been. It was as if the atmosphere around them had changed.

"You know," said Jim, his conscience beginning to trouble him, "KinetetE was not able to help your voice. Morgan le Fay may not have been, either." He held up a hand before the plant could object in more than a startled squawk.

"But," he went on, "this land you live in, Lyonesse, is the most magical place in the world. And that magic is in the earth, the trees, and all the Creatures and everything else in it together. And it's a magic you've got as much a part of as anyone else. That could mean I can't fix your voice. KinetetE can't, Morgan le Fay can't—but it's just possible *you* can, using that magic that's always surrounded you. Believe in the song you sing long enough and you'll sing it as it ought to be heard."

The dieffenbachia's leaves rustled, all for a moment lifting toward Jim. Then they dropped, turning away again.

"No. No . . ." said the dieffenbachia. "The great Queen has almost cured me. I'll be back in full voice in just a day or so—I'll have to leave you now."

And it glided away between the trees, dwindling swiftly with distance, until the surrounding trunks hid it from view.

The nightingale sang two notes, took off from Hob's shoulder, and disappeared in the opposite direction.

"It's happy now, m'Lord," said Hob in a confidential tone of voice.

"Yes," said Jim, still thinking of the dieffenbachia—which was after all a thinking, feeling being—going off still unhappily wrapped in his self-delusion that Morgan would be his savior.

He shook himself out of that. The important thing now was

to find a local guide and counselor. Almost without thinking, he pulled on the lead rope. The sumpter horse did not protest but came up close beside Gorp, though with her head no farther forward than Gorp's shoulder. Then she resisted going any farther. The only other equine Gorp would allow ahead of him was Blanchard—and not even always Blanchard.

"Speak to the trees," Jim asked. "Ask them which way we go now to find the Questing Beast."

"You need not find me, Sir James," said a voice. "I am here."

And so were they all—still in Lyonesse. Still in a forested part of that land. But not where they had been a moment before.

Chapter 12

Jim now found himself looking at a small stream running through an open glade; beside which stood the Questing Beast, with his snaky neck outstretched, drinking from the clear, running water. As Jim watched, the Beast—or "QB," as he had asked to be called the last time Jim had been in Lyonesse—lifted his head and looked at Jim with no appearance of surprise at all.

"Forgive me," said Jim. "I didn't mean to startle you."

"You did not startle me, Sir James," said the QB in its pleasant tenor speaking voice, which at first seemed so unlikely coming from its snake's head. "After the first few centuries in Lyonesse, none of us startle. Things happen, people come and go—but, if you'll excuse me a moment . . . I was just moistening my hunting voice—"

He lifted his head; and from his serpent mouth suddenly came the sound of thirty couples of hounds questing. The sudden change in volume was enough to make Jim stiffen in his saddle. A few of the hound voices, moreover, sounded a little as if they were gargling.

The QB frowned. Jim was intrigued. He had never imagined a snake face being able to frown. How was the QB doing it? He had no eyebrows.

"—Crave a moment's pardon, Sir James," the QB was saying, even as Jim thought this. "But this won't do. I'll try it again . . ."

This time the thirty couples of hounds questing almost blew Jim out of the saddle; but every voice was clear and pure.

"Much better," said the QB. "You were looking for me? The trees told me that, so I brought you to me. Faster that way."

"The trees talk to you?" Jim asked.

"Yes, it was one of the two great gifts Merlin was good enough to give me, once. The other was to be able to become a black-and-white staghound when needed."

Jim opened his mouth to ask why becoming a staghound was such a great gift—then closed it again. The matter at hand was finding Brian. "Well," he said, "it doesn't matter now. We're here."

"In a sense," corrected the QB, a little severely. "Actually, you are not Here, you're There."

"There?" Jim stared at him.

"Look for yourself, Sir James." The QB pointed with his nose.

Jim looked down and saw his legs, but no horse between them. Nor was the sumpter horse to be seen.

"Hob!" he said, in sudden alarm.

"Yes, m'Lord?" Jim turned his head. But no hobgoblin was to be seen on his shoulder.

"You see," said the QB, "you're really still back there where you hugged the tree."

"Oh, you know about me and the tree?"

"The word as it was passed on to me was that you must have a noble heart to hug so well."

Caught between embarrassment and the need to say something modest in reply, Jim stammered a little. He regretted the somewhat stupid words, once they were out of his mouth.

"Well, I'm a Baron, of course."

"Indeed, it shows," said the QB. "But even kings, sometimes, have failed to have noble hearts. Not all are like our great King, Arthur Pendragon. Which reminds me. Whence do you come; and why are you here this time?"

"I'm down from the land above—my home's named Malencontri, in Somerset. England." The QB bowed with beautiful snaky grace, inclining his head and upper body. Jim bowed back in as courtly a fashion as he had yet learned to do. "But you know," Jim went on, "I'd like my horses with me."

"Then you shall have them," said the QB. "Follow me, Sir."

He headed off into the woods. Jim followed him, riding on invisibility and feeling very strange now that he knew he was doing it. But they went only a little distance before the QB halted again and turned back to face him.

"Stop!" he said. Jim pulled hard on his reins and stopped moving. "Now, turn your horses completely around." Jim could have sworn he heard the sumpter horse nearby, grumbling something.

"Is this what you mean?" he asked, when he had reined to the right until he was facing back the way he had come.

"Almost. A few feet to your left . . . there. So, there you are now; all together in one place."

Jim looked down, and saw himself. He also saw Gorp and the sumpter horse; and, turning his head, saw Hob on his shoulder. He did not understand it; but that did not matter.

"Were we that close to you and didn't know it?" he said.

"Oh, no," said the QB. "I was nearly half of Lyonesse away from the Forest Dedale, from which you must have escaped. But you've actually been here all the time; and it happens I'm able to move very swiftly if I want to."

"I see," said Jim. "And to take others with you, I see, also."

"We all have our little gifts," said the QB deprecatingly. "But in this case, I took you and yours nowhere; because you were really here all the time."

Jim coughed.

"Forgotten that," he said.

"An easy, small matter to forget," replied the QB. "Now, Sir James, how may I be of service to you?"

Jim hesitated, not sure how to ask someone like this politely for help.

"Let me ask you a question, first," he said. "How much do you know about the reasons that brought me here?"

"Nothing at all. I know only that you passed through Lyonesse once before, on your way to the Gnarly Kingdom. By the by, I hope your visit there was a pleasant one?"

"It was successful."

"Ah, that kind of visit. I also know that Queen Morgan le Fay of Gore had a dispute concerning you with a person of great magic from the land above; and that as a result she was forced to let you go, and sent you to the Forest Dedale. There was something said by the *Dieffenbachia cantans* who lost his voice—and therefore the honor of singing before the Original Knights of the Table Round at time of war—to the effect that you, yourself, are of strength in magic; and that is the reason Morgan le Fay was so incensed against you. Also, you came here with another from the land above; but he is not with you now."

"That's a lot," said Jim. "Actually, my friend's name is Sir Brian Neville-Smythe; and it's about him I was looking for help from you."

"I do not know the noble Knight, I'm afraid."

"No, of course not," said Jim. "But he was one of those with me when we came here before; and is a close Companion of mine, and my best friend. He's been captured by someone, I'm afraid. I thought someone who knew Lyonesse as well as you could help me find him."

Slowly, regretfully, in wide sweeping movements, the QB shook his head.

"Forgive me," said Jim, a little stiffly. He had not expected so quick and flat a refusal to help. "It was just a thought."

"A good thought, Sir James," said the QB. "An admirable thought. Pray don't think me unwilling. I just may not be able to help."

"Oh," said Jim.

"You must understand. I am of Lyonesse, and one of the Lords of Lyonesse, by virtue of being enshrined in the Legends of our great King and the Table Round. I know all there is to know about Lyonesse and what is within it; excepting that which is deliberately kept from me. I did not know your friend had been lost to you, therefore that knowledge must have been hidden from me. So I can neither know nor guess where he could be now."

Jim nodded slowly.

"I understand," he said. "But at least you know Lyonesse."

"Yes, Sir James."

"I don't. Can't you give me some kind of idea about where to look, or how to at least start looking?"

The QB looked at him with steady snaky eyes.

"At a guess—he must have been captured by someone or something of power. First to mind for that would be the Queen Morgan le Fay. But I have no way of knowing that, or finding where Sir Brian would be hidden."

"Well, give me the whole list; and I'll check them one by one."

The QB's head came up.

"Sir James," he said strongly, "you sound like a true Knight indeed; one well fit to tread the soil of Lyonesse. I will help you to my utmost. But a full list is not possible. It would have no end. From the Old Magick upwards, there are many, many magicks in Lyonesse. They are in all things here, and in almost all who live here—"

Jim nodded. He was beginning to understand. His own upbringing, from more than half a millennium later in time, led him to suspect patterns in everything. There could be one for the magicks here.

"—For example," the QB was going on, "there are those unskilled in magick, but with one magick talent. Recall how Gawain, having forced a fight with Sir Lancelot close to the time of our Great King's passing, made use of his gift of waxing in strength from morning to noon, to the strength of seven men; but Lancelot withstood him and won over him after the noontide.''

Jim would have sworn that his memory of the King Arthur legends had been buried and all but lost since his earliest years of reading. Now, though, with the QB's words, Jim found an image rising to his mind.

It was a mental picture of Gawain—but by a strange sort of double vision of the imagination, it was Brian at the same time—lying wounded and unable to get up, and shouting at Lancelot to come back and fight until one of them was dead, or Gawain/Brian would one day force him to fight again; and Lancelot's unforgettable words in Malory's account, just before he turned and left, saying ''*I woll no more do than I have done. For whan I se you on foote I woll do batayle uppon you all the whyle I se you stand uppon youre feete; but to smyte a wounded man that may nat stande, God defend me from such a shame!*''

For a second, to Jim it was all as clear in his mind's eye as if it was taking place before him.

He shook his head. No. Men could go crazy with hate or fury. But Brian—like Lancelot, not like Gawain, to judge from Malory—was too caught up in the ideals of chivalry. He would never act like Gawain. He would wait to heal himself and then go hunting for his enemy.

''Well,'' Jim said, ''give me the list anyway. I'll start with Morgan le Fay, then, and see where I go from there.''

''No,'' said the QB. ''You deserve better from me than that. I have considered. Clearly, you are brave enough to be taken where I can take you. If you choose, I will carry you to Merlin in the dark of the sky—which is soon, now.''

''Soon?'' Jim looked to his right, above the trees; and sure enough, the white sun was now almost low enough to be lost in the upper branches of the surrounding trees. ''It does set, then? How long is nighttime?''

''But a short time,'' answered the QB. ''Long enough only for you to ask Merlin's help—if he chooses to give it you; and if you do not fear to speak to him.''

''Fear? Why should I be afraid?''

"He is very powerful," the QB said. "He was always so; and he is still so."

"But wasn't he spell-locked inside a tree by Nimue?"

"He was. Nimue or Vivien—call her what you wish; that will make no difference to his talking with you—if he will. But only in the dark can you come to him; for he is also in the dark, as he has been, these long centuries."

Jim felt a coldness on the back of his neck; but shook it off.

"Take me to him," he said.

"Wait," answered the QB.

They waited in silence as Lyonesse's daystar sank with increasing swiftness as it neared the bulge of the earth. A scribbling of black branch tops crept up over its face first, then the light dimmed more swiftly as the heavier limbs below joined them. Quickly, no more could be seen of it although its white light, more and more feebly, continued to reflect from the sky until—suddenly—this, too, went; and they were prisoners of a total dark.

"Now we go, Sir James," said the QB's voice out of that darkness. "Do not try to move. I will move us."

Jim sat still on Gorp; and for a space of time nothing seemed to happen. Then he felt moving air on his face, as if he was leaning out the open window of a travelling car. The breeze stopped abruptly.

"We are here," said the voice of the QB. "Dismount."

In the total darkness, Jim swung out of Gorp's saddle with the familiarity of habit; and felt the heel of his foot jar against an earthen-soft surface a little before he had expected it. He took his other foot from the stirrup and stood by Gorp, holding on to the reins and the pommel of the horse's saddle. Gorp stood rock-still, as a well-trained warhorse should.

"I will be back to get you just before the light rises again," the QB's voice came. "But Merlin will hear you now if you speak to him."

Jim stood for a moment. In spite of the indifference he thought he had toward dark places, the coolness on the back of his neck was back again; and he felt a stiffening of the little hairs on the back of his neck.

"Merlin?" he asked.

His voice seemed strangely loud, but flat—as if lacking all normal echoes. There was no answer. Stubbornness lifted its head in him. He had come to get information.

"Merlin?" he said again—more loudly.

"Who calls?" The voice was powerful, not at all like the voice of an old man.

"Sir James Eckert, de Malencontri," said Jim, strongly enough in his turn, although he was feeling a strange dizziness—unnatural enough that he spoke with medieval formality. "I come to ask your help in finding my friend, Sir Brian Neville-Smythe, whom someone in Lyonesse has hidden from me."

Having said these words, however, he found himself feeling they had been both weak and pompous.

"Jim, eh?" said the voice on a more conversational level. "Carolinus's little Apprentice. That Carol-lad was always out to get himself in too deep, unless he looked out first—which he wasn't likely to do."

The shock was considerable. It was like being in a foreign country, face-to-face with a native; and addressing him with great effort in a halting and clumsy version of the local language—only to have the native reply instantly in fluent, colloquial English.

"Carolinus isn't too well right now," said Jim defensively.

"He'll survive."

"We hope so."

"I SAY SO." The voice had abruptly become powerful again, more powerful than before. "DO YOU DOUBT ME?"

Jim's memory awoke suddenly. Merlin's greatest ability, according to the legends, had been to see the future.

"No, Mage," said Jim hastily. "I didn't mean it to sound that way."

"And don't call me 'Mage'!" The voice, however, had gone back to the lower, more familiar level. "They can title themselves all they want; but I alone am MERLIN."

"Yes, Merlin."

"Well, Sir Knight Jim, why should I help you?"

"Because both Sir Brian and I came to Lyonesse to help it—but you probably know about that, too, Merlin."

"As a matter of fact, I do. In itself it's commendable. Well, I won't deliver him for you, but I can tell you where he's held. How badly do you want to rescue him?"

"I couldn't want to any more than I do now," said Jim. "Not only that, but Sir Brian would want to be free himself, more than anything in existence."

"Anything in existence?" said Merlin. "That's a strong reason to give, Jim. Are you sure your friend would use just those words if he were here?"

"Yes," said Jim, seeing Brian in his mind's eyes. "I believe he would. He'd stop short of pledging his soul, but that'd be about all."

"Very well, then," said Merlin. "Know that he is held in thrall by the Lady of the Knight More Bright Than Day. The QB will carry you to her castle."

"Thanks," said Jim. He looked into the dark about him for the QB, but of course saw nothing.

"Stay," said Merlin, "while I tell you one more thing. If you had not told me what you did, I would not have revealed where he's now kept; for if he is left there, he'll suffer a while, but live. However, if you find and free him, he may face a sorrowful death from which I fear no one, even you, can save him."

"What sorrowful death? Why do you say *even I* wouldn't be able to save him?" Jim stared through the blackness in the direction of Merlin's voice.

There was no answer.

Jim asked again. Silence.

"Merlin," said Jim grimly. "You may not be saying anything; but I bet you can hear me. All right, I won't ask for answers to what I just asked you. But I've got another question I came determined to ask you. Are all the magics in Lyonesse one magic?"

There was an extended silence. Even the dark about Jim

seemed to hold its breath. Then Merlin's voice came back, strangely hollow and distored, like someone speaking through a long tube or corridor from a great distance.

"In all the ages since I came here," it said, "not once have I ever replied, once I had said my last word. But perhaps Carolinus saw more than I gave him credit for, and you as well. This once will I give further answer. All magic and all else. Yes."

"Thank you," said Jim.

No other word answered. No sound.

Chapter 13

"Come, Sir James," said the voice of the QB, suddenly at his side, "you'll hear no more on this visit. Come. It will be light again, shortly, and we must be away from here."

Jim took a deep breath.

"All right," he said. He remounted Gorp by feel in the darkness; and again there was that sensation of a small wind blowing in his face for a short time.

Once more it stopped abruptly. Almost as it did so, there were the dim shapes of trees to be made out around them; and within seconds thereafter the light brightened in the opposite side of the sky from which Jim had seen it disappear; it became plain they were back at the place where they had started. The QB was still with him; and by the little hesitation as Gorp stepped out, Jim knew that the sumpter horse was still at the end of the lead rope tied to his saddle.

"You heard what Merlin said to me?" Jim asked.

"Only the last few words, of where your friend is."

"You'll take me to this Bright Knight, then?"

"Yes, Sir James."

"Will it be dangerous to you to do it?"

"No. To be correct, I'll be taking you to the castle of his lady. For the castle is hers, not his. But it is him you must fight to free your friend. Come this way . . ."

The QB led off among the trees, at the same easy, but swift, loping speed, with his leopard belly strangely close to the ground, that Jim had seen him show on his earlier visit to Lyonesse.

Jim and the horses followed.

"Why is it hers? Aren't they a pair?" he asked.

"A pair?" QB considered the word for a moment. "Yes, and no. They are man and leman, though not man and wife, because the Lady of the Bright Knight—she has no other name, by the by—is tainted with magick, and therefore cannot wed in the eyes of Holy Church. She was a damosel of Morgan le Fay; and won her freedom from service in some way only the two of them and Merlin might know. But, strange to say, there remained a kindness between her and Morgan; so that the Queen gave her this castle and lands."

"Where does the Knight come in, then?"

"Later, they say, the Knight came by and the two fell in love; and the lady went back to Morgan le Fay and begged a protection for him. For now he would be defending the castle and her against all comers—else all would have called him a false Knight. It was Morgan le Fay that gave the Knight the gift of such brightness as you will find to dazzle your eyes."

"Hmm," said Jim.

"You are not afraid, now that you have heard?"

"Afraid?" said Jim, questioning himself. "No. I'm a magician myself. But I'm married."

"Could it be you were married before you touched magick?"

"Why should that make a difference?" Jim asked.

"Unmarried, you would not be forbidden to the use of magick. But if chance brought you to marriage after you were accepted and the great magickians of the land above did not then strip you of its use, you could be both married and a maker of magick."

"That's what happened, I guess," said Jim. "Anyway, I'm both now."

"So, now we approach the castle, the Knight, and the lady."

"Good," said Jim.

The QB was leading the way at that same deceptively ground-covering speed he had used before, Jim thought. But there was little to see, and his mind began to consider a new problem.

He would probably have to do combat with an experienced knight if he hoped to free Brian. Plain luck and Gorp's weight—nothing else—had made him victorious over the knight who had been doomed never to marry. It was too much to expect another such result. His mind spun, trying to come up with a means of getting out of the fight itself.

His mind's motion produced no means to that end. Geared up though he was, he told himself, perhaps he was also dull-witted from lack of sleep. He had not slept, now he came to think of it, since he had left Malencontri; a day and a night—if the recent dark he had just been through could be considered a full night.

But he felt clearheaded and alert. He felt no need for sleep or rest at all. More of the general magic of this place? And what had Merlin meant by "all else?" The talking trees?

They came, after what seemed almost no distance at all, to a large, open, grassy area with a clean-looking castle of white stone at the far end of it. The area did not look as if it had been deliberately cleared, as was normally done around castles for defensive purposes; yet the trees of Lyonesse all stood back some distance from it, as if they did not want to be associated with it.

It had the usual water-filled moat around it, and a drawbridge over the water. But the tall and wide double doors at the inner end of the drawbridge were closed tight.

The QB halted, and so did Jim, as they emerged into the open space.

"You must sound your horn, Sir James," said the QB.

"I don't—" Jim caught himself just in time. "As it happens, my horn isn't with me at the moment."

"So!" said the QB. "Then pray display your shield and your arms upon it."

Jim reached for his shield—which in this unknown land was riding close at hand on his back—slung it around in front of him, lifted its strap off his neck, and held it up in the air, facing the castle. A touch of vengeful joy stirred in him. For several years now he had been struggling to memorize dozens of coats of arms which it seemed every village child over four could recognize without thinking. Now, in this kingdom where all the armorial bearings of those entitled to them should be immediately recognizable, they would be looking at one they had never seen before.

Jim and the QB waited. Nothing stirred at the castle. Jim's arm began to get tired; and he let the shield drop until its lowest point rested against the pommel of his saddle.

"Maybe the Bright Knight's not here at the moment," he said.

"I do not believe he would be gone," said the QB seriously.

Suddenly, everything happened at once. A long white pennant with what looked like a jagged black lightning bolt painted on it suddenly appeared and blew free at the top of the Castle's main tower. Several horns together sounded a chorded note; and a small door in one of the big, closed entrance gates opened.

"Ah! From this point on, Sir James, you will be able to handle matters yourself," said the QB; and vanished.

What looked like a teenaged girl dressed all in white came out of the door. She ran at remarkable speed across the drawbridge and the open space beyond, toward Jim. He gazed at her with admiration. Though he was used to Angie, who was surprisingly fast on her feet, this one was sprinting like an Olympic contender. She ran all the way to where he sat on Gorp, took only a couple of deep, quick breaths, and spoke.

"Sir Knight—" she said, "we do not know your arms. I am sent to find your name and purpose in coming here."

It was time to behave himself in pure medieval style. Jim stiffened a little in his saddle.

"What place is this, that does not know the Knight-Dragon?" he said as harshly as he could manage. "He who is known in the land above and all the lands below?"

"Pray forgiveness, my Lord Dragon," said the messenger. "I am but an ignorant servant of those who dwell in yonder castle and only ask what I am sent to say. Would you of your grace tell me of your purpose in coming here, that I may carry word of it back to my masters?"

"I am here," said Jim, slowly, and as terribly as he knew how to be, "to loose a pure and worthy knight I have heard is held captive in your castle—Sir Brian Neville-Smythe. To that end I will meet and destroy any who would fail to yield up that brave gentleman at once. I have in my time battled ogres, sea serpents, and demons—and vanquished them all. Let none think I will hesitate to do the same to any who would keep Sir Brian Neville-Smythe from me!"

He paused to see how, if at all, his words had impressed. Sometimes bombast like this just bounced off its hearer—sometimes it terrified them. You never could tell.

This time, the only change he noticed was that the flush on her face—in this colorless land, it had appeared only as a darker tone of gray—that had come from running had faded somewhat; but it was doubtful if she had actually paled.

"Then," she said, "I am sent to say to you, Sir Knight, that in this castle lives the Knight More Bright Than Day, who has overthrown and made prisoner or slain all who have come against him. You are warned to withdraw!"

There was no help for it. This called for the ultimate of knightly gestures.

"Withdraw!" shouted Jim furiously, drawing his sword and heaving it up as if he was about to cut the messenger in two.

She dodged—probably a well-conditioned reflex—and ran with surprising speed back once more to the castle, where the small door opened for her as she pelted in over the drawbridge.

Jim waited. The pennon waved from the tower.

"Are they going to take all day?" growled Jim to himself.

He was keyed up and finding it hard to sit still.

A boy of about twelve, dressed in what seemed to be black-and-white livery, emerged from the small door and began walking sedately and importantly across the grass toward Jim.

"Sir Knight," he said in a high treble, when he had come within a few yards of Jim, "know you that the Knight As Bright As Day does not fight with just any who comes. You must show some proof of what you claim to be."

"What kind of proof?" snarled Jim.

"That is for you to decide."

Jim snatched the glasses from his nose and held them out toward the boy, who shrank back.

"Do you know what this is?" roared Jim.

"No, m'Lord," squeaked the boy, all the importance gone out of him.

"I'll hope your Lord isn't as ignorant as you are! These are the Valorous Spectacles; and none has ever worn them who has not been named to wear them!"

"I'll tell him, byyourGracem'Lord—" The last words were slurred together in the boy's eagerness to get away.

"Stop!"

The boy froze, already half-turned. "It is for me to make conditions, now. I must know that the brave knight I came to rescue is safe and well. He must be brought out here, close enough to me so I can make sure he's all right. Otherwise I will not deign to match lances with your Lord. Bring him first—then I'll fight. You hear me?"

"Yes, yes, m'Lord . . ." And the boy was off and running.

Again, Jim and the silent Hob waited, along with the patient horses. But what happened next surprised Jim. One of the two large leaves on the drawbridge entrance opened just enough to let out a horse with a rider on its back; and the rider was Brian—in full armor and on Blanchard. Brian looked around the open space, saw Jim, and put Blanchard into an immediate gallop toward him.

Jim's heart lifted on a sudden hope. Could it be that the Castle's people had decided that giving up Brian was smarter than fighting someone with Jim's credentials?

Earlier, Jim had felt no real desire for combat with the defender of the castle. Possibly it was his victory over the first knight he had opposed; but he had felt an unusual sensation of confidence at the thought of dealing with this particular foe—maybe it was his interview with Merlin that had filled him with such self-confidence.

On the other hand, the practical side of his mind hurried to point out, nothing could be ruled out when it came to a matter of lances or swords, no matter how confident a fighter might be. A foot might slip, a strap might break—the man or his horse could be not quite set at the crucial moment of contact. A sword blow or lance thrust could land just that little off-target that made them harmless.

"Hah!" said Brian, sharply reining in as he reached Jim. He wound his reins around the pommel of his saddle and lifted both arms. There was a circle of iron about each of his wrists and about a foot and a half of metal chain between them.

"Didn't trust me!" he said. "Damn fools! Because chained or not, now I'm free to tell you of this gentleman you are to engage—and how to handle him. Seemingly, that never came to their minds; only the vainglory of pretending you could have me back, since they trusted you to fail in your meeting."

"Is this Bright Knight that good?" asked Jim, feeling the touch of coldness in him for the first time since he had come within sight of the Castle.

"Good? Well . . ." Brian looked away; and Jim stared. It was rare to see his friend embarrassed. The cold feeling in him increased. "I would say—but the fact is, James—" added Brian with a sudden rush of words, "I was lifted off Blanchard's back before I was well able to see him closely. Not to excuse myself—it is a man's own fault if he is set down—but let me say, first, he is indeed Bright, James; very, very Bright."

"Well, then . . ." Jim hesitated, hunting for a way to put the question that was foremost in his mind without hurting Brian's feelings. "I suppose you had trouble picking up the fine points of his lance work—"

"Oh, I was not as helpless as all that, James! I could hear the approach of his horse; and clearly, it was no trained and gifted warhorse such as Blanchard. More than that, his beast was uncomfortable. He was either sitting too far back in his saddle—a mark of a rider with little skill, as I have remarked to you before this—or holding his weapon too tightly, trying to aim with it; another fault of squires in particular and knights without real practice. But that brings me exactly to what I wish to suggest to you."

"What's that?"

"He will be too Bright to see clearly—so do you deliberately ride wide of him on your first essay against him—miss him, in short. They may cry coward at you, but the advantage is that I, watching from the side here, may see better how he does what he does, so warn you before your second pass, and give you the victory when you tilt next."

And Brian sat back in his saddle, literally beaming at Jim.

"I see," said Jim. His thoughts were racing furiously in half a dozen different directions at once. "You think I'll be able to win against him if you can tell me some things about him? You've never thought too much of my lance work."

"To be frank, James, I have not. But unless my ears deceived me, from the sound of his horse's hoofbeats, his own panting and grunting when he was close upon me, and the angle at which his spearpoint struck what might as well have been a blind man opposing him—" Brian halted the rush of words to smile at Jim.

"—and lo!" He beamed. "You behold me essentially unhurt! I was unhorsed, that much is true; but with such advantage he should have taken me in the helm and broken my neck, rather than at the base of my shield and merely pushed me out of the saddle. It is also true," he added, with a touch of darker tone suddenly showing in his face, "that I did not have my feet as firmly in the stirrups as I might have . . . because of the unusualness of his Brightness. Else he would never have taken me out of the saddle at all. But all this is not the point."

"Of course not," said Jim.

"The point is, he is as poor a man with a lance as—as any I've seen; and watching from the side where his light should not blind me so, I will be able to tell you how to meet him. Trust me, James—with very little skill you will unhorse him. Then down you to the ground; and it is a matter of swords, with which I know you to be . . ." Brian coughed a little, embarrassed once again. "More fit to win."

Jim grunted noncommittally. He knew only too well he was only slightly better with the sword than he was with the lance—and that made him among the worst of knights with both. On the other hand, he knew Brian was just the opposite: a demon with a lance, a wizard with a sword. He had no doubt at all that Brian could tell him what to do, faced with the Bright Knight. The only question would be then—could he do it? What had Brian not thought to tell him?

Like most masters of an art or skill, Brian tended to forget that what was obvious to him now, with his years of long and weary practice, was not necessarily so to someone else who had no such experience. Brian had not prepared Jim for this moment.

A crowd of what Jim took to be retainers had come out of the small door in the castle entrance, undoubtedly to see the show. Another female figure in white was just now emerging and joining them. Jim peered at the crowd through the lower half of his spectacle lenses; then realized what he was doing and snatched them off his nose, putting them in their case at his belt. It was not that he did not see as well through them, but he needed no unnecessary irritations at a time like this. He was aware of the strong beating of his heart in his chest.

Trumpets sounded from the castle. Both great doors swung wide. A figure on horseback emerged and rode out over the drawbridge.

Involuntarily, Jim's hands jerked in an attempt to come up and shield his eyes. For he could make out no detail of man or horse. The man himself was the center of a blinding glare of light. Trying to see him was, indeed, like attempting to look directly at the unyielding white sun of Lyonesse.

Chapter 14

But there was no mystery to it, Jim realized almost at once. The white sun of Lyonesse in its morning position was well clear of the trees directly behind him; and the armor his opponent was wearing was as reflective, if not more so, than the finest glass mirror. Magic was at work here, again; and undoubtedly it was some of it that was now focusing the reflection from the armor directly into his eyes.

He tried moving his head. Sure enough, the blaze of reflected light seemed to move with him. There would be no avoiding its blinding effect. It was far more powerful than any such thing he might have expected to encounter here. To safely ride past the other knight without crossing lances with him, Jim would have to ride a good ten or fifteen feet to one side of the direct path.

Nor had Brian been speaking idly about the spectators crying "Coward!" if he rode so. From what he had seen of tournaments, and other warlike exercises, those who watched would not be slow to make their feelings known. It was no matter to Brian, who—once convinced he was in the right—would not care if the whole world cried "Coward!" at him. But Jim had grown up being responsive to the reactions of others.

He became conscious that already the glare was making his eyes water. Jim rubbed them clear with the heels of his hands, temporarily shutting out the light—and with the feel of the hands against his closed eyelids, understanding dawned in him. He had not only been blinded, but unthinking . . . "Look for the front hooves of his horse. With luck you can see him coming," he heard Brian saying, in a tone of encouragement, beside him.

"It's all right, Brian," he said, still covering his eyes with one hand. With the other he felt for the case holding the glasses, found them and fished them out. "I've got something of my own, here—"

His first thought had been to alter the glasses slightly to make them a perfect foil for the glare. Then he was nagged once more by the recollection that he dared use none of his magic if Morgan le Fay was watching—as she probably was.

The glasses would have to serve as best they could without any changes. Still keeping his eyes shielded, he sneaked the spectacles up on his nose and hooked the temples over his ears.

Cautiously, he took his hand from his eyes and looked in the direction of the Bright Knight; and the spectacles needed no adjusting. They worked excellently. The glare was gone. The upper half of the lenses wiped it out, leaving all else plain to be seen. He found himself looking at the shape of a knight in armor, a shape that was perfectly featureless. The blackness of him was so solid and lightless it was as if his shape was a hole into a starless infinity, cut into the scene before the castle.

"These things I just put on my nose," he said, low-voiced, to Brian, "are magic engines. It's all right. I can see him clearly, now."

"Can you so?" But there was no doubt in Brian's voice. The magic word *magic* had taken care of any disbelief there might have been in Brian. "Still, James, I would counsel you to pass him untouched on the first essay; and on the second, follow my advice."

"Be glad to," said Jim. He was about to pull down the newfangled visor he had recently talked the castle blacksmith into adding to his helmet, when he realized this would knock the glasses off his face.

For the ride-by it wouldn't matter; and he might be able to figure out something before he had to ride directly at the man. A gust of irritation moved him. Damn all magic things, anyway—there was always a limitation, either to the magic itself, or to whatever was necessary to make it work.

A trumpet pealed. Jim, looking, saw the young boy in livery he had met earlier, taking a long, straight horn of silver from his lips.

"He starts!" said Brian; and Jim saw that the Bright Knight already had his horse at a trot, working up to the gallop that he and Jim should both be at when they came together.

There was no more time for thought; and Jim was just as glad there was none. He lifted his reins, leaned forward. Gorp in his turn broke into a trot, understanding immediately what he and Jim were up to and snorting an eagerness to be at the oncoming horse.

The Bright Knight came at him more swiftly as their speeds inceased. Jim saw he was indeed sitting too far back, as far as the high cantle of his saddle behind him would allow. The point of his lance, already leveled in Jim's direction, was wavering around in the air—a certain proof he was, as Brian had suggested, holding it too tightly and trying to aim for Jim too early, instead of merely balancing the long weapon in his grasp until the last possible moment. Only in that last second should he be seizing it with all his strength, to direct it at an opponent already upon him.

Temptation stirred in Jim. In sharp contrast to Brian, Jim secretly hated jousting. Privately, to Angie, he had called it "an invitation to a train wreck." He had steadily avoided having a bout with lances with Sir Giles de Mer at the Earl of Somerset's Christmas party the year before; in spite of the fact that Giles had come all the way from Northumberland in hopes of matching lances with both Brian and Jim. Brian, in fact, had taken for granted Jim would agree to meet Giles under Brian's critical eye, so that he could better instruct the two of them—and he had been puzzled as to how the chance to do this never worked out.

Now, however, for the first time in his experience, Jim was tempted to deliberately engage in one of the train wrecks. For the first time, he realized he was looking at a knight who might be no better with the lance than he was—indeed, the more he looked the more confident he felt. The feeling was outside all his experience—but the temptation was real.

He could explain to Brian, saying he had meant to pass by the Bright Knight, but blundered against him in the confusion of getting close—sanity returned to him just in time. Brian might believe anything linked with the name of magic, without question; but, with his experience in interpreting every move of a horse and rider, he would see through Jim's excuse in a flash. And facing Brian's shock on being lied to by his closest friend in that transparent, almost childish fashion, would be more than Jim himself could face—particularly if the Bright Knight had managed to unhorse him, after all.

No. He must do what Brian had told him to do.

But even while he had been thinking this, the combined speed of the two, now galloping, destriers had almost brought them together; and, to his surprise, Jim now saw the tight-held lance of his opponent swinging away from him, out to one side. After a sudden blink of bafflement, understanding flashed on him.

The other thought, Jim realized, that beyond doubt this stranger he faced, like all his other opponents up until now, was so light-dazzled he could not see what was happening.

The reason for the unusually tight grip on the lance, then, was that the Bright Knight had never had any intention of winning with the point of it. Instead—and even as he realized this, Jim saw the length of the other's lance being swung out to bar his path. He had just time to jerk Gorp's head to the side, throwing the big horse off-stride but turning him out far enough so that only the very tip of that lance scored a short path across the left edge of Jim's shield.

Snorting and tossing his head—now in deep annoyance at his rider—Gorp however let himself be steered back to Brian.

"A foul hit! A craven's strike!" fumed Brian as Jim halted beside him. "The ditch-born bastard! He would have struck you a sweeping blow had you not turned just in time. Let me see your shield—yes, there stands the proof for all to see; the scratch of his point on your shield. And to think it was the way he must have struck me, also, from my saddle—I thought I felt a blow on that side. But I was dazed from the fall; and, taking him for a gentleman, never suspected. James, cannot you by magick let me seem like you and ride this next time in your place? I would make him to learn what one who knows his lance work can do with such a one as he!''

''I'm afraid not,'' said Jim, suddenly finding reason for blessing the fact he could not use his magic here. ''This is Lyonesse, remember; where I may not do much I know.''

''Forgive me, James! Of course!'' said Brian. ''Yet it comes hard—nonetheless, I will put it from mind. Now, it is you who must ride against him in a moment. Let me quickly tell you what to do.''

''Yes. What?''

''You remember how I have been at pains, James, to teach you the art of tilting your shield from a foe's point to make it glance off? This time I would have you use it in a new way.''

Brian paused.

''Right—I mean, I shall!'' said Jim, correcting himself hastily—remembering his medieval role as a pupil, he knew Brian was waiting to hear his promise.

''Very good. This time, then, when you meet him—perhaps even a moment before because you are not yet as practiced with the shield as might be; and because he will be so sure of his sweeping blow that he will not be ready to adjust to another—you must crouch low in your saddle.''

Another pause on Brian's part.

''I shall do so,'' said Jim.

''Good. Cover yourself as largely as may be with your shield, and at the last moment swing it out to protect your left side, with its bottom point against the armor fringe there at the bottom of Gorp's saddle. So that you and he shall take the shock of the blow together. You understand?''

''I do,'' said Jim.

''Very well. Remember, be sure your head is down below the top edge of your shield, with no more than a small part of the top of your helm showing above. There is no shame in doing this, James, for you know there are no rules in way-side encounters such as this.''

"I shall so perform!" said Jim, doing his best to commit Brian's every word to memory.

"Wait. One last word, for I see him making ready to come at you again. The blow of his lance sweep, if unsuccessful, will unsteady him in his saddle; and if you, yourself, hit him at the same time with a sweep of your own lance—hitting him in the back, James, in the back!—it cannot fail to topple him from his saddle. In a tournament this would be disgraceful beyond belief—but here, against such a foe, it is perfectly justified. Then quickly get you down and your sword at his face. He will yield—and now time is out. You must go."

"Right!" said Jim, forgetting himself completely. He hastily poked his spectacles back into their proper position—they had slid down his nose while he was talking with Brian—lifted Gorp's reins, and rode.

The Bright Knight was already into his trot, holding what seemed through the spectacles to be a pure white, but otherwise a perfectly normal if somewhat light, lance. As Jim rode, his opponent broke into a canter, and a moment later Gorp followed suit on his own initiative.

Suddenly it was all too real. The fear of the meeting at arms was utterly gone from Jim; and with it the temptation to compete with his own skill against a rider no more skillful than he. What was left was a surge of adrenaline all through him, and the realization that this land was solid as any earth he had walked or ridden on—and lance sweep or not, the aim of the Bright Knight was to kill him, either after he had been knocked out of the saddle or once he had been conquered and made prisoner.

He and his opponent drew together at what seemed a much faster pace than before. When he saw the white lance shaft of the other swinging out sideways, he crouched behind his shield, holding it as Brian had told him; and, blindly, swung his own lance. It struck something so solidly that his hand quivered and stung as if he had tried to catch and hold the moving part of an engine.

He almost dropped the lance, but not quite. As he pulled Gorp to a skidding stop and turned the horse about, he saw the Bright Knight lying motionless on the grass. His horse, evidently as untrained as the knight himself, was running off toward the castle.

He took Gorp back to the fallen man and dismounted, tossing his reins ahead to the ground. Gorp instantly stood still. The Bright Knight still lay unmoving, his eyes shut, his face pale. Jim felt a sudden emptiness inside him; had he killed the other—no, the knight was still breathing, steadily. Just knocked out, probably.

Jim dropped to one knee to loosen the wide, padded collar of chain mail that protected the Bright Knight's throat, to make it easier for him to breathe—and at that moment became aware of a tumult of voices and an approaching pounding of feet. He looked up to see all those who had been watching running toward him.

"James! Out sword!" cried Brian's voice in his ear; and a manacled hand, its chain stretched tight to the other manacle, reached swiftly to pull out the sword still in the fallen knight's sheath.

Jim drew his sword and stood ready against the onrush. Brian had said there were no rules in these wayside adventures.

The retainers' lives and livelihoods, he remembered, would be invested in their overlord. Knightly honor was for knights—it was beside the point if swarming over a knight on foot and knifing him to death—even if half a dozen of them were killed or crippled in the doing—would save their Lord or master. As Brian had pointed out, this was no tournament field with an audience watching closely for any violation of honor or manners. It was a private fight and practicality ruled.

But a high voice overrode the other shouts—a high voice on a note of command. The shouting stopped, the rush of retainers stopped; and the woman in the elaborate white dress came forward alone. She ran to kneel at the side of the fallen warrior.

Jim, seeing her alone, had returned to unlacing the neck armor. Just then it came loose and fell away, as did the helm;

and for the first time Jim took a good look at the face of the man before him.

Having done so, he stared, for the face he saw under a thick thatch of black hair was the beardless face of a boy just turning the corner into manhood—probably not yet out of his early teens. No wonder he had been as inexpert as Jim, in a time when most squires could be seasoned fighters, with a number of different weapons.

It was an incongruous face to see above the large and powerful-looking body. Jim's stare was suddenly interrupted by what seemed an avalanche of white, filmy cloth, as the lady kneeling on the Bright Knight's other side threw herself across the still figure—between the fallen man and Jim.

"Do not kill him—oh, do not kill him!" she cried. "If you must kill someone, kill me! I was the one who sent him against you. He will yield to you. I promise he will yield to you. Have pity. Wait but until he can speak. Spare him!"

Now she was the one Jim stared at. It came to him, admittedly a little late, that she had assumed he had taken off the Bright Knight's neck armor so that he could cut the other's head off.

"I didn't—" he began; and suddenly realized he could be stepping into a trap. If he admitted to having no intention of killing his opponent, then from the practical point of view of this lady and the retainers, the Bright Knight had not lost the fight at all. Once he was revived, he and the retainers could still take care of Jim and Brian.

Jim swallowed. He stared at her.

He had assumed she was the Lady of the castle. But only now did he appreciate how expensive, in cut and quality, was what she was wearing—like a Witch Queen, herself. The fabric of the dress he looked at was many-layered, of some fine, thin material; and there was a silver chain around her neck, with what seemed to be an enormous pearl at its lowest point—a pearl a good three inches in diameter.

Her hands were long and slender, with smoothly tapered fingers; and she was not merely good-looking, she was beautiful. Nor was her beauty spoiled now by the tears running down her face—rather the opposite. Everything about her spoke of rank and power. Jim felt an unexpected sweep of sympathy for her within him; and all his instincts cried out for him to reassure her that the unconscious man was in no danger.

But caution came quickly to check this. Several years now in a medieval environment had taught Jim that a pitiful face could change expressions like lightning. Jim had seen fourteenth-century ladies make the shift from helpless waif to Valkyrie just that swiftly, on occasion.

"Pray, Sir Knight!" she began now. "I pray you—"

Brian, Jim saw, was standing close by, looking at Jim with a strangely concerned expression.

"Stay!" said Jim to her, as sternly as he could. "I must first see if all has been well with my friend here whom you held captive!"

With that excuse he got to his feet, and left her, still pouring tears; and now stroking the unconscious face of the Bright Knight. Jim stepped aside with Brian.

"Brian . . ." he began in a low voice.

"What's amiss!" broke in Brian, almost angrily, not bothering to keep his voice down. "Will you let this woman charm you into sparing one who has no knightly honor, fights with a magic advantage, breaks all the rules of fair lance work—and he is not even married to her, is no more than her leman!"

"He is not my leman!" choked the Lady. "The world has called him so; and for his safety I have let them think it. But he is my son, my only child!"

Now Jim really did stare at her. She looked hardly more than in her early twenties, herself. But in this era, girls could be married off at nine years of age, or even younger, and bear a child a year or two later.

"Bah!" said Brian to her now. "Rather the other way about!"

"I will swear it!" cried the Lady. "Bring me a Holy Cross and I will swear to it. Oh, my Lords, I have kept him safe, lo these many years, by a spell granted me by my great Mistress, Morgan le Fay—but alack! Neither of us suspected there might come someone like yourself, so skillful with the lance. I pray you, spare him! Perhaps you have a son of your own and can understand . . .''

Her words continued to pour forth.

Jim risked a glance at Brian, who was staring at her in outrage. He moved the same outraged look to Jim.

''James,'' he said, stiffly, but low-voiced enough so only Jim could hear, ''I hope you are not taking to heart any of what we are now hearing. '. . . *one so skillful with the lance!*' indeed! I wonder you did not wish to hide your face on hearing it. By Saint James—your name Saint, doubtless—flattery has its limits; and this demoiselle far exceeds them!''

Jim scrambled in his mind for an answer that would placate Brian and at that same time deal with what indeed was an outrageous buttering-up by the Lady. But, as it happened, she was still talking—now back on her feet.

''. . . a lad of twelve, to die so young—'' she was now saying to Jim in a choked voice.

''Twelve!'' said Jim and Brian at the same time, staring at the six-foot figure on the ground.

''He is big for his age. All were astonished at how he grew. But then his father was full seven feet in height—''

Now Brian and Jim looked at each other. Men seven feet tall were not unknown in these times—though inevitably they were well known when they happened. Harold Hardradda—Harold the Third of Norway, Jim remembered from his future life—had been mentioned in the *Heimskringla* as being some seven feet tall. He also had one eyebrow higher than the other, according to a more contemporary historian—for some reason that detail, too, had stuck in Jim's mind. Then there had been France's King Charlemagne . . .

''—but rather I will die myself. If you will not slay me yourself, then suffer me to throw myself on your sword, for I will not outlive him, in Mary's name—'' And she made a snatch at Jim's sword.

He tightened his grip on it just in time—some of these women of the gentry were as able with weapons as men—

and he was surprised by the strength he had to use to keep her from taking it.

But by this time, the Bright Knight had recovered consciousness. His voice boomed at them from the ground.

"Will you stay out of this, Mother? I'm a knight. If he cannot grant me mercy, I must die as a knight!"

"Never!" shouted the Lady. "Before you kill him, you must kill me first!" And with that she threw herself once more on top of the young man, child, or whoever he was; literally interposing her body between him and any weapon—and, incidentally, effectively muffling whatever he might be trying to say from beneath her.

Both Jim and Brian looked at each other. Then Brian beckoned Jim.

"If by your courtesy you would step aside with me for a moment?" he said.

They walked several steps farther away from the pair on the ground and Brian lowered his voice once more.

"James."

"Yes, Brian?"

"I do not know exactly how the words of your vows went, of course, when you were knighted. Doubtless there was some difference from mine. But you must have had the part about rescuing and protecting women and children?"

Jim hated to lie to Brian, but of course his imaginary knighthood would have had equally imaginary vows, if either of them had existed at all before his necessary protective lie on his first meeting with Brian.

"Yes," he said.

Brian coughed.

"Well, it seems we may have something of a conflict here, James. My vows were quite clear on the subject, and I will imagine yours were so as well."

"I imagine so."

"That leaves it as a problem for us—for you, I might say, but I feel an obligation, since it was to rescue me you engaged in this spear-running. The words of our vows ill rest beside your slaying not only a child of possibly twelve years—if such a child boy he is indeed. But can we take upon our souls the chance of breaking vows made before the altar?—by compassing not only his, but the sin of his mother's death as well? It might well be a great double sin, James. Against my own inclinations I feel I must crave your indulgence by counseling you to grant them both mercy."

Jim's heart lightened amazingly.

"Well, perhaps you're right. I guess so," said Jim. "I suppose there's no hope of doing anything else?"

"No hope at all, alas, that I can see."

"That's it, then," said Jim.

He turned and walked back to where the Lady still lay covering a good area of the Bright Knight and glaring up at Jim. He looked past her at the one eye and ear of the Bright Knight that was visible.

"I grant you mercy," he said.

Chapter 15

"Let us all to the castle, then," said the Lady, now on her feet, tears magically gone, all smiles and a sweeping curtsy, with the Bright Knight on his feet also, hulking behind her—his brightness no longer blinding them, however—"so that we can celebrate this day of deliverance!"

"Better perhaps out here under the trees," said the QB, suddenly reappearing. Was it Jim's imagination, or had the Lady's face suddenly turned a shade paler? But she laughed merrily, and clapped her hands at the servants. They were too far away for the sound to be heard by any except those with the keenest ears; but evidently the mere sight of her hands in action brought them all running to her.

"A pavilion! A table! Meats! Wine!" she ordered. "Strike the irons from this other good knight"—she pointed at Brian—"and return his weapons!" They raced to obey; and most hurried back toward the castle as she turned once more to face Brian and Jim.

"Sirs," she said, "I am the Lady Annis of the White Castle, that Keep you see behind me; all of which is now at your disposal. May I crave your pardon, Sir Brian, for any discomfort you might have encountered while you were prisoner in my home?"

"You have it," said Brian, deep in his throat and without a smile. "Though I have slept more comfortably before this."

"We will endeavor to make you amends for that, Sir."

"And you," said Brian, speaking over her head to the Bright Knight, "I was never made acquainted with your name. But if you are in any way disappointed with my showing against you, it will be my pleasure to remove that disappointment any time you wish to meet me once more with the lance—or any other weapon, for that matter."

"Sir, my name is Sir Boy; and I join my Lady in hoping that your stay with us was not too burdensome upon you."

"I minded it not."

Some of the retainers now returned with a blacksmith, who quickly cut off Brian's manacles; and this was speedily followed by the return of his equipment and arms, and the erection of a pavilion, and its furnishing with table, tablecloth, wine cups, platters, wine, and food—it all would undoubtedly have been faster if they had been conjured up by magic—but not by much.

"To your great healths, my Lords," said the Lady, once they were all seated, downing a nearly full cup of wine, unmixed—as far as Jim could see—with water.

Jim thanked her graciously. Politeness had now automatically laid its hand on all of them. Even Brian, Jim noticed, was relaxing now that he had drained a cup of wine—a little greater swallow than usual on his normal company manners—after that first prickly verbal exchange with Lady Annis and Sir Boy. His spine was still stiff, however, and his face unsmiling.

Both Brian and the QB seemed unusually alert, on guard with their hosts. The QB, apparently taking his inclusion in the party for granted, was standing now at one end of the table in the pavilion, the serpentlike forward part of his body curving above its surface on a level with their own.

One odd thing, Jim recognized suddenly, was that—while he could have sworn no trees were close enough to where the pavilion had been pitched to do any such thing—now the shadows of branches could be seen on the cloth roof over his head. They lay dark above the table's end occupied by Brian and himself, while above Sir Boy and Lady Annis at their end, the cloth showed bright with unshadowed sunlight.

"What do you in Lyonesse, Messires?" asked Annis. "For I see by your armor and weapons that you are from elsewhere."

"Just passing through," answered Jim. He was trying to think of some way of learning more about her connection with Brian's capture—Boy was clearly of minor importance.

Undoubtedly it had been Morgan le Fay behind Brian's capture; but there must have been some reason it was this Annis of the White Castle who had been chosen to do it.

That reason—and possibly other useful information—might be extracted from Annis if he could be clever enough in questioning her, thought Jim. But he doubted he was that clever—particularly if she was determined not to talk. Her swift and easy switch to the role of genial hostess, and her skill in playing the social part involved, was as good as a preemptive strike. As long as the assumption was that he and Brian were now guests, pinning her down with any obviously hard questions had become socially difficult.

Had Morgan wanted Brian just as bait to catch Jim again, perhaps? No, Morgan could never have arranged for the QB and Merlin to work as a team to feed him the information on where Brian was being held.

Of course not—and one puzzle at a time. He would get further by finding out more about Annis herself. For a beginning, she had certainly managed to at least obscure the question of whether Boy was her lover or her son. But she certainly—he searched for the word he wanted—had seemed *disappointed,* at least, at not being able to get both Brian and Jim inside their castle.

Meanwhile, the QB, since his reappearance, had been acting very much as if he was on his guard, suggesting they sit down outside, rather than following Annis under her roof. Jim found himself wishing for an excuse to move the QB and himself out of her hearing, so he could question this one friend he and Brian had here, about this situation.

But nothing came to mind that would sound natural. Only, why hadn't Annis objected to sitting down with them out here; and insisted on their going to the castle? Of course, obviously the appearance of the QB had been a shock to her. Any such insistence under these conditions probably would have sounded suspicious.

Clearly, if Morgan le Fay was the cause of all that was happening to both Jim and Brian, there seemed to be something more than just a Queenly annoyance involved.

As Queen of Gore, she was too important, here in Lyonesse, to go to this much trouble over the minor irritation Jim and KinetetE had caused her. Almost certainly the Queen had little doubt she could deal with KinetetE with one hand tied behind her back, if she only had KinetetE here.

It was an opinion, Jim was fairly sure, that would be very badly wrong. He would bet on KinetetE any day. But Morgan—used to having most things her way here on her home grounds—would have to learn better the hard way before she would believe. Meanwhile, it was annoying that he and Brian could not be about the work they had come to Lyonesse to do, because of this chance side issue—

A wild thought struck him suddenly. Surely, Morgan le Fay—independent, all-powerful here in magic with Merlin out of the ring—could not have been recruited or brought to be an ally of the Dark Powers in their attempt to take over this land!

Or could she?

There was some evidence that the forces involved here had already started to line up on opposite sides. The QB was on their side; and Merlin, the one individual possibly more powerful in magic than Morgan, had pretty well declared himself out of the contest. But the trees were helping; as they had been ready to help on the Gnarly trip, by reaching down and strangling the black-furred giants the QB had ordered to leave Brian and Jim alone.

How in the name of this crazy world could a takeover of Lyonesse by the Dark Powers be to Morgan's advantage? For that matter, how could it be to the advantage of the Dark Powers? The Powers might be able to win it; but they couldn't occupy it without physical servants to hold it at their orders. And Jim could not see Morgan voluntarily becoming the servant of anyone or anything.

But that wasn't the situation. None of this made sense. Morgan's siding with the Dark Powers did not make sense. Moreover, this was the first time, Jim realized, that he might have encountered someone who could be considered to have evil in her bones—so to speak—instead of being merely human—or animal, or Natural—and seduced into evil by greed for wealth or power. He found her and all those around her, like Annis, hard to understand . . .

While he had been thinking all this, however, Annis had continued talking, keeping up an easy flow of unimportant conversation. He came back to sharp attention suddenly, though, when he heard her saying "—and it would pleasure us deeply if the two of you would guest with us for a few days."

"I regret," said Brian, without waiting for Jim to answer.

"Yes, I'm afraid we've got matters that'll have to take us away from here," said Jim with almost equal quickness.

"Sir Boy would be so glad to learn what knights like yourself could tell him of the finer uses of weapons, and no doubt as well of the many adventures you both have had."

"*Sir* Boy—," began Brian harshly—then checked himself, coughed, and buried his nose in his wine cup.

"It's too bad; but as we say, we have to move on," added Jim, for he could feel Brian's temperature beginning to rise once more. To Brian the situation here must be intolerable: Sir Boy, if truly twelve years old, in Brian's eyes could in no real sense be called a knight—a member of a highly trained profession. He could never have been dubbed—unless he was someone like a king's son, in which case knighting could come ridiculously early. No way could he be both knight and boy at once.

The danger of an explosion of outrage was still fizzing under Brian's barely polite surface; and a word could set him off.

"Perhaps," Jim added hastily, "you can help us on our way."

"Anything at all I can do to aid you both, my Lords."

"You, having been one of the demoiselles of Queen Morgan le Fay, undoubtedly can tell us something of her. Is she at all alarmed by the attempt upon Lyonesse now being made?"

"You speak most knowingly of a matter no one has ever mentioned to me. What makes you think I have served the great Queen?"

"A man in a tree told me about it"—and Jim, this time without question, saw her face pale—"but is she alarmed by the Dark Powers?"

"The—" Annis stared at him for a second, then laughed ringingly. "You must forgive me, my Lord. I have never heard of those Powers you speak of. What did you call them—the Dark . . ."

"Dark Powers," said Jim. "So, you never heard anything of them from her?"

"Oh, but my Lord! I was only one of her demoiselles, by your admittance. It is not likely she would speak to me except to give me orders."

"Still, even if you don't know, she must have. Are you sure you never heard her speaking of them, perhaps to others? Particularly when all Lyonesse is in great danger from them?"

Annis laughed merrily once more.

"Now, I ask you, my Lord," she said. "Who could a simple demoiselle like myself overhear her speaking to?"

Jim's memory of the Arthurian legends had been coming back steadily as his time stretched out in Lyonesse.

"Oh, perhaps one of the other three great Witch Queens," he said. "The Queen of Northgales, the Queen of Eastland, or the Queen of the Out Isles. I understand they're often in her company; and you'd think all three would be equally concerned with her. You must have seen her with them, many times."

Annis's eyes had been fixed on him; but then their focus shifted, looking upward toward the cloth roof—and Jim also looked up, to see the white fabric over the heads of Annis and Sir Boy now also darkened by the shadows of heavy tree limbs; and the sides as well as the front of the tent darkened likewise.

More than that, the broad, rough, black bark of an enormous tree trunk could now be seen blocking the space between the two flaps of the tent that gave entrance and exit.

"It would be well if you answered the good knight about the Dark Powers," said the QB unexpectedly, "and answered truthfully. The Old Magic in the forests of Lyonesse is concerned; and the time of battle is coming, not to be avoided."

Annis turned to stare at him—then suddenly, and so swiftly that none of them could have stopped her even if they had not had a table in the way, she tore the great pearl-like globe from its chain around her neck and threw it down onto the tabletop. It burst, sending up a momentary waft of white smoke or vapor.

"My Queen!" she cried to the ceiling of the tent. "They seek to use me against you! Help me! Help me!"

Her words rang in the tent, were gone; and silence flowed back. She lowered her eyes to glare at them.

"It was to no avail," said the QB. "The forest is all around you now. The leaves will drink up the magic in the ball you broke. The trees will carry your words back and forth across all Lyonesse, until they are so worn and tattered that they will be less than a whisper and bring no sense to any ears that can finally hear them—even if those are the ears of Morgan le Fay. Are you desperate enough to think that she will challenge the Old Magic of this land—for you and yours?"

Sir Boy shot up from his chair, drawing his sword. He advanced on Jim and Brian; who both also jumped up and drew theirs.

"You leave her alone!" Boy shouted. But he checked, looking around at Annis. "I'm not Bright!" he said.

"Of course not," said the QB. "There is no sun inside this tent to make your magic work."

Boy turned back.

"I don't need to be Bright!" he growled, advancing toward Jim, who still held his sword and was closer to him than Brian. Brian was already putting his sword back into its scabbard. He was being courteous, giving Jim first chance at the single foe—a hell of a time for politeness, thought Jim!

This was an instance in which Boy's inexpertness might be compensated for by other factors. They had all left their shields outside the tent with the horses, so it would be sword against sword only; and Boy, though probably as poor a swordsman as he was a jouster, was slightly taller and a good deal heavier and thicker-boned than Jim. In sheer muscle strength he had the advantage—and he certainly was willing to fight. He bulked large in this confined space . . .

"My great thanks to you, Brian," said Jim, putting the best face he could on his situation.

"Boy, you fool!" cut in the sharp voice of Annis. "Come back here! These men have each been trained for more than your lifetime—" *If she only knew the truth about me,* thought Jim. "—Either one can kill you easily. Come back, I say!"

She literally stamped her foot on the carpeting that had been laid down around the table.

Reluctantly, scowling, still holding his sword, Boy backed to his chair and sat down in it. He did not resheathe his sword, but laid it before him on the table. Annis sat down and looked at Jim and Brian, still on their feet, with a suddenly pitiful face.

"What can I do? Oh, what can I do?" she said. "Ask what you will; and I will tell."

"All right then," said Jim. "You can start by telling me about Morgan's meetings with the other three Witch Queens I mentioned."

"But I know nothing of them! How should I know—"

"Come on, now," said Jim, "people who live in a castle

know everything about each other. I should know. I live in a castle myself—" *And if I catch any of our servants listening outside the door of our Solar one more time . . .* The stray thought wandered in before he could shut it out. "As I say, I know from experience that you'd know. So, answer me—" He had a sudden inspiration. A shot in the dark—but she could hardly deny it, since it was something all the gentry did. "After all," he added, "the four of them get together regularly. Everyone knows that."

"Perhaps! I do not. I know only what concerns me, such as my duties, attendance on the Queen—"

"And on her guests of rank, when there are such," said Jim. "Northgales, Eastland, and the Out Isles would hardly bring their complete retinues on so frequent visits. Those who served at the Castle would be called upon to do duty for the visitors. Tell me that never happened to you!"

She twisted in her chair. She was a powerfully persuasive actor. Jim forced himself to remember that her appearance of helplessness could change just as quickly as had her earlier one of gracious hospitality.

"Of course, there were occasions—"

"At one time or another you would have been chosen to serve one of the three Witch Queens; and by now you have been, perhaps, demoiselle to all three, at some time?"

"No. Yes, I suppose I could have. But I would never know who they were. Only I took orders and obeyed them."

"There was a reason, of course, for such frequent getting-together," said Jim. "What did the servants in the castle think it was?"

"I do not talk to common servants!"

"Of course you do. Everyone talks to servants. Even I," said Jim, seeing an opportunity to hint at a higher importance than she probably thought he had, "have talked to servants. I've talked to blacksmiths, to cooks; I've even talked to common soldiers and serfs. Why, I've even talked to Apprentices."

Her eyes grew round and dark. For the first time, Jim thought he might be seeing an honest reaction. Then he remembered that there had been no Apprentices mentioned—that he could remember, anyway—in the Arthurian legends.

"Apprentices?"

"Certainly. Apprentices, the scum of the earth, lower even than pirates, which I've also talked to, to say nothing of kings and—but we aren't talking about me. Answer me now, what did the people think brought the other three so often to meet your Queen?"

"Well, of course . . ." She looked down at the table. Her fingertips were trembling, ever so slightly. "My Queen must lead among them. For of all four, she is by far the most powerful, and they dare not offend or cross her."

Jim's mind was beginning to click, as it usually did when he got his teeth into a situation.

"So, most of the time she was calling them to her to hear what she wanted them to do?"

"I do not know that! I do not know it at all!"

"It strikes me," said Jim slowly, "that your promise to tell whatever I should ask was a false promise. That being so—" He reached for the pommel of his sword.

"No, no, my Lord!" It was literally a cry of fear this time. "I'll speak. I'll tell you what you want to know. It is indeed of the Dark Powers that my Queen and the others talk now. My Queen feels that Lyonesse would be better off under those Powers—she does not deign to tell the others why. None but she knows. She has told them their only choice is to join the Powers now, while they can; for the Powers will be stronger than the Old Magic, which has always been a threat to the four of them!"

There was a moment of utter silence in the pavilion.

"It is false," said the QB. "No power is greater than that of the Old Magic. We have Merlin's word on that."

Annis laughed unhappily.

"Merlin is tree-bound," she said, in a bitter voice. "Shut up and made helpless by a demoiselle little more than a child. Men are ever more persuaded by the child in women."

"You know nothing of it," said the QB. "Merlin is wiser than us all; and it was not because he was in his dotage and bemused by a woman-child alone that he ended in the tree."

"Hah!" said Annis. She tossed back her long hair, which had fallen forward when she looked down at the table. She looked squarely at the three of them. "Well, Messires? You have what you came for. Go."

"We were planning to," said Jim.

"There is no reason not to," said Annis. "Sir Brian is returned. You have your answer and there is nothing more I can tell you, though you question me for a twelvemonth. Leave us in peace."

"Lady, it was you who chose to trouble them," said the QB. "But yes," he went on, "I believe you have told all you know. Sir James, Sir Brian?"

Jim nodded. This was awkward. He felt he should say something; but there was nothing more to be said.

"Good-bye," he said, anyway. She looked at him, but did not answer.

"Get that lad to someone who can teach him lance and sword," said Brian unexpectedly as they turned to go, "if you hope to keep him. Magick is a chancy staff to lean on for those of us not magickians. Some skill may save his life someday."

Her eyes moved to Brian; but she still did not answer. The tree trunk blocking the pavilion entrance was gone now, and the canvas flap of the entrance fell shut behind them, cutting off sight of her and Sir Boy. It was only then that Jim realized the limb shadows he had seen cast on the pavilion roof had been gone for some unknown time.

"Hah!" said Brian, mounting Blanchard. "It is a great relief to be free and have weapons to hand once more. Again, we must thank you . . . er . . . Sir QB."

"I am one of the Lords of Lyonesse," the QB answered. "But it pleases me that all just call me QB. It is a pleasure to me to see you free."

"Nonetheless," said Brian, "if my help can ever be of use to you, you have earned it most certainly. You will remember?"

"I shall, and thank you, Sir Brian."

"Good. Harkye, James; I believe yon Sir Boy was no lad at all—or at least no lad as the word is meant to mean. I think he was silly."

"Silly?" Jim made the connection quickly, but not quickly enough to stop himself before he got that question out. Of course, *silly*, as Brian knew and used the word, meant Boy was not as mentally adult as someone his size normally would be.

"Yes," Brian was saying, "and while I cannot say I have much love for Lady Annis after a night in her dungeon, I do believe her to be not lacking in courage. Only her love for her son—and it could be he is her son, though she seems passing young for such a large lad. Only that, methinks, made her tell you what you wanted to hear. Courage is to be admired in whoso has it."

"Yes," said Jim. "And I think the way you do about Sir Boy. It occurred to me, too. He may not be a very large child at all—more like twenty-four; but with the mind of not even a fourteen-year-old. What do you think, QB?"

"I do not know," said the QB. "Repute all has it that the Bright Knight is her leman. Merlin would know, but I cannot ask him."

"Either way, it is a shameful mock of knighthood to put such a one in armor and set him to carrying a lance—yet he, too, did not seem to lack courage, when he thought her threatened. It will be a blessing if she takes my advice and gives him some training, setting aside this unfair magick he uses."

"Even with training, he's probably just going to get himself killed, if he doesn't have what it takes to think quickly in a fight, Brian."

"But he would die honorably—by the by, James, where are we headed now?"

Jim reined Gorp to a sudden stop. Brian halted Blanchard beside him, and QB, running a little ahead of them, stopped and turned back, inquiringly.

"Hell!" Jim said. "I don't know!"

Chapter 16

The sumpter horse had necessarily also stopped. Hob stuck his head out from under the cover of the goods on that horse's back, startling Jim slightly. Hob had been out of sight and quiet so long he had again forgotten the hobgoblin was with him. The QB turned and trotted back to sit down on his leopard haunches.

"What is it you seek now, here in Lyonesse, Sir James?" he asked.

"Sir Brian and I both came to help Lyonesse as much as we can against the Dark Powers, who seem to want to take it over."

"Why did you not say so before?" The QB shook his serpent head. "When you were here before, you were only travelling to the Kingdom of the Gnarlies. It was but natural I should think you once more bound elsewhere, on some errand of your own; particularly since I heard you tell the Lady Annis that you were merely 'passing through.' " The snake-like head shook from side to side once more.

"If you will forgive me," he continued, "I will point out that since you have freed Sir Brian, you have been riding off in a direction directly away from the great cliff wherein is the entrance to that underground land."

"I just rode. I wasn't thinking," said Jim. "I beg the grace of your pardon, QB. I'd taken it for granted anyone here would know what the Dark Powers were trying to do. So I also, I guess, took it for granted you'd know what we'd come for. Is it a fact only a few people here like the Witch Queens with their people, and Merlin I suppose—as well as yourself—know about this Dark Powers business? I really thought everyone would know."

"All know. People, trees, Creatures, the very winds themselves. Everything knows. And now we are learning that you, too, know—a thing Queen Morgan, plainly, was aware of all along."

"Why do you say Queen Morgan knew all along?"

"Surely it was her knowing you were here to help Lyonesse that earned her enmity."

"Right!" Jim said. "I've been wondering why she was so hostile to us. But how can she be on the side of the Dark Powers, when she belongs to Lyonesse herself?"

"She alone knows," said the QB, in a deeper tone of voice than Jim had ever heard from him before.

There was a moment of awkward silence.

"Well," said Brian, "things like that will happen, damn it all! Now that we all know we know, mayhap we can together set about being useful."

"Brian's right, of course," said Jim to the QB. "Do you have any suggestions about what we should do next?"

"Return whence you came, perhaps? Lyonesse is accustomed to dealing with her own difficulties."

"By Saint Peter, that we will not!" said Brian. "We did not come this distance to turn back with no thing done. Only point us to where these Dark Powers are."

"They are in no particular place, Sir Brian," said the QB. "They are everywhere in Lyonesse."

"I should have explained that to you, Brian," said Jim. "Forgive me."

"Hah!" said Brian—that useful sound which took care of every situation for which there were no ready words. "Well then, QB, there is another point on which you can inform us. These Witch Queens. If it be that they are with the Dark Powers, what forces do they field?"

"Forces?" said the QB.

"I think Brian means how many and what sort of armed men can they put in the field if it should come to a battle between our strength and theirs," said Jim.

"Why, none."

"None?" exploded Brian.

"Oh, they may each have a few knights of less than good repute, some men-at-arms of like kidney and common men of such; but all, more for courtesy and show than any other reason. This is Lyonesse, Sir Brian. If it comes to battles, they will be fought in happenings of magick and other ways, but not with armies, not since the days of the great Arthur, himself—we have none such now to lead us.''

Brian sat on Blanchard, shaking his head.

''Can this be true?'' he asked Jim.

''I think we can believe it if the QB says so,'' said Jim grimly. ''But you know the Dark Powers as well as I do, Brian. They're not beings or Creatures in their own right. They have to use others—like the Hollow Men—or make monstrous things to fight for Them, like ogres and that Worm you fought for hours at the Loathly Tower.''

''I have never heard of this Loathly Tower,'' said the QB suddenly; ''though monsters are possible anywhere. But do I understand what I have just heard? The two of you have had rencontres with the Dark Powers before this?''

''Certainly,'' responded Brian, a little curtly; just as Jim spoke.

''I'm sorry, QB,'' Jim said. ''This is something else we should have talked about before—in fact, I should have told you the minute I met you this time. Brian and I have had more than one''—he remembered to use the knightly term—''brush with them. It was because of our experience we came.''

''Also, there are knightly obligations,'' said Brian.

''But then you are triply welcome to Lyonesse at this time!'' There was a new note in the QB's voice. ''I had no thought this might be so. Of course, if you have faced Their strength before, and particularly if you then overcame Them, you may be of help to us now. Would you of your favor and grace tell me somewhat of these brushes you have had with Them?''

''Sir James would entertain you in that way better than I,'' said Brian. ''More important, would you tell us, then, with what kind of magick you of Lyonesse plan to defend yourselves?''

''Alas,'' said the QB, ''I know not. That is all in the

hands—though there are no hands involved, of course—of the Old Magic. Only if we have solid enemies to fight can we act; and then, of course, the Knights of Arthur will fight as they have always fought. But may I venture to you that it may be of help to you with others here, if you will tell me of some of these brushes with the Dark Powers."

"I believe the Lord QB is right, Brian," said Jim.

"Hah! Well," said Brian, "it can be done shortly enough. The first time it was the betrothed of Sir James stolen away to the Loathly Tower by a dragon of ill repute ensorceled by the Dark Powers there. We, with a few friends, went to the Tower and got her back. The next was a matter of a Mage, a magickian of high rank ensorceled by the same evil forces, who had stolen our Prince, the eldest son of his Majesty King Edward. We got him back . . ."

As Brian had promised, the telling as he told it could be done, and was done, shortly enough.

"I understand now," said QB when he finished. "You are not of the common sort of visitor to Lyonesse; and I crave pardon for having misjudged you. But these matters, nobly as you and your friends handled them, were not so great a thing as a threat to Lyonesse. I cannot believe it will be with Worms, ogres, or stolen princes that these Powers will try to wrest from us our land; and necessarily overcome the forests, the earth, and the Old Magic, itself."

"No." Jim shook his head. "And we don't either. I was just hoping you might have some idea of how they'd have to go about it."

"I do not. Nor does any I know, except perhaps Merlin; and for centuries now he has remained silent and apart from all that happens. But you say the Dark Powers must work through living men or other beings?"

"They might be able to do damage by Themselves; but They're forces, not flesh. They could help people or things conquer those here in Lyonesse, but it would do Them no good unless They could hold and use it; and They could never hope to do that without living bodies to occupy it. Look at all History and its greatest conquerors. Rome only held its greatest size some hundred years, before its power was gone."

For a moment Jim had forgotten he was in a magical land in a strange world of a different universe. He was back in Riveroak, in his own future time, striding deep into an argument at an academic get-together.

"Rome wanted tribute from Arthur, but he refused them," the QB said.

"Quite right!" added Brian. "Any Englishman worthy of the name would do the same. Nerve of those Romans! Tribute! You'd think they didn't know where they were!"

"This is Lyonesse, of course," said the QB delicately.

"Arthur was an English King!"

"In any case," said Jim, to head off any discussion that might be brewing, "what you just told us about the Witch Queens—their not having any private armies of their own to act for the Dark Powers—raises the problem of how they're going to be helping the enemy after all. Also, there's that question of what Morgan le Fay stands to gain by doing it. Probably the first thing we ought to find out is if all of the Witch Queens are involved with the Dark Powers, and what they stand to gain by helping."

He looked directly at the QB.

"Which of the other, lesser, Witch Queens would you suggest we check on first? Who'd be the easiest to get to? Hopefully without letting her know why we're doing it?"

"The Queen of Northgales, most surely. But I would not advise that you call her a *lesser* Witch Queen, at least where she may hear you."

"I'll watch it," said Jim. "But let's head toward wherever she is, then."

"I can carry you there in moments," offered the QB.

He did so. Once more, after they seemed to have covered no more than a hundred yards of forest distance, they emerged into a scrub-grassy, cleared circle around another castle, this one built entirely of a hard-looking, dull white stone, rising into many towers topped by heavy battlements.

It was all but windowless and lacked even as many arrow

slits as might have been expected. It had a heartless, touch-me-not look about it. A steady moan of small, cold breezes circulated among the embrasures—the openings between the cops, as the raised sections of the battlements were called—reaching down to chill Jim and Brian even in their armor.

"In faith!" said Brian, "there seems little welcome here. We had best hammer on their gates, even to let them know we are come."

But there was no need of that—nor need for Jim to display his shield with the arms upon it. They had barely entered into the cleared area, when one of the gates opened and a powerful figure in full armor rode out on a horse of the size to bear him, heading straight for them.

This was no Sir Boy. Just the opposite. He was the largest man Jim had seen so far in Lyonesse, fully as big as Sir Herrac de Mer, the Northumbrian knight who was the father of Sir Giles de Mer, Jim's friend and Brian's. But where Sir Herrac, though stern, had been kindly enough—unless his wrath was stirred—there was no kindness to be seen in the man now riding toward them.

Under his helm with its single nasal projecting down to protect his face, the expression of this man was as bleak and remote as the castle from which he had come. He had no beard; but both his eyebrows and the narrow trimmed mustache above his upper lip mixed white hairs with black. His eyes were also black as the stone of the castle where shadow fell across it. Their unyielding gaze and his straight mouth brought no light to the weather-darkened face, curving shield-like down to a square jaw.

"James!" said Brian in a low voice, but urgently, riding Blanchard to close on Jim. "This man must be mine!"

Jim would have given a great deal to agree. The man riding toward him looked more like death approaching on horseback than anyone he could ever have imagined. But it was at him the man was looking; and he was the one who had suggested they come here.

It was foolish; but he found himself being operated on by

the standards of the world he had come to live in, rather than by the common sense he had grown up with.

"I can't—"

"James," said Brian, understanding perfectly. "I beg this grace as a gift from you. I must wash from my mind the taste of my defeat by that Bright Boy, back at the last place we were."

Jim hesitated. The excuse was a good one; but the trouble was, both he and Brian knew it was an excuse to save him. He shook his head. "Brian, I'm sorry, but you know—"

However, the knight was now almost upon them. Brian, taking matters into his own hands, rode ahead to meet him.

"Hold!" he said, reining Blanchard sideways like a barrier across the other knight's path. "Before you speak to Sir James, you must answer to me, Sir!"

The large knight halted. His expression did not change; but he looked down—a long, long way down—at Brian.

"You are young," he said; "later, you will learn that you will have enough of fighting without seeking beyond your own causes. I will pass, by you or through you."

"Sir, I challenge you to break a spear with me, since you lightly me in that fashion."

"So be it," said the knight. He turned his horse and began riding back toward the castle, far enough so that he and Brian would have time to bring their horses up to full gallop before they crossed lances.

"How dare you!" cried a shrill, high-pitched little voice.

The large knight checked his horse, looked back over his shoulder, and stared. He turned the animal and rode back toward Brian, pointing at a small, sharp-featured face that had now lifted up the edge of the rain cover over the goods on the sumpter horse and was staring at him.

"What is that?" he asked.

"That?" said Brian, hesitating and looking at Jim.

"It's all right," said Jim hastily. "It's just my hob-goblin—"

"Goblin!" The large knight stiffened in his saddle. "Here in Lyonesse?"

"*Hob*goblin!" Hob thrust his face farther out from under the rain cover. His eyes were blazing and his tiny jaw was set. "Rash knight, dare not to speak of we of the Hob in the same breath with whatever Goblin-called Creatures you may know!"

He erupted completely out from under the rain cover, to stand tall at his full fourteen inches of height; and he stamped one small foot noiselessly on the neck of the sumpter horse, who turned her head to look at him in mild surprise.

"You have not answered me!" he shouted. He was clearly beside himself with anger—the first time Jim had ever seen him so. His voice had gone up a good three notes, and rang with a strange, artificial rhythm.

"How dare you," Hob continued, "threaten Sir James and bar his entrance to the castle of the Queen of Northgales, when he has come this great distance to talk to her? Lo, he is no mere knight like yourself; but a great Magickian, come to speak privily with your Queen. How dare such as you offer to fight him—the most manly man in armor to abide—and scorn Sir Brian, the Paladin who rides with him? I pray you, show him some of your terrible magick, my Lord, that his ignorance may be informed!"

It was a very peculiar speech to come from Hob; and it threatened to put Jim on the spot. Happily, however, he had been through this sort of thing before—a well-meaning ally, without warning, demanding a demonstration of Jim's powers. There was always one trick available because of his first appearance in this world having taken place in the body of a presently living dragon.

It was the bit of instinctive magic that had been, effectively, a gift to him, completely apart from all else he had learned since he met Carolinus. It could be used without breaking his ward, and he could turn it on or off. But otherwise he had no control over it. It was exactly the same as the innate magic of Naturals, such as the troll-light of the trolls, and Hob's ability to ride a waft of smoke to other places halfway around this world.

He swung down from his saddle—and turned himself into a dragon.

The large knight was evidently not given to making noises, jumping, or otherwise showing alarm; but he became very still where he sat on his horse, lance in hand; and remained that way without sound or movement for so long that Jim was beginning to get concerned—when the man abruptly broke into movement, wheeling his horse brutally around and galloping for the gate to the castle.

It opened for him and immediately shut behind him.

Jim turned himself back into his human form, armor and all.

"Hob—" he began sternly, turning to the hobgoblin. But Hob, still standing on the neck of the horse, thin shoulders squared and arms folded adamantly, interrupted.

"Damme, m'Lord!" he said, looking down at Jim from the height of his own stand on the back of the sumpter horse, "are we to brook such insults from any man in armor, who has not even the courtesy to name himself before offering battle to you, who are so far above him? I say, NO!"

Jim stared. Off to the side, he could see Brian staring also. Hob's language had suddenly become as extravagant and ornate as could be imagined even among the actual knights of this time in the land above. These words and phrases were more than high fashion; they were an exaggeration and burlesque.

That last thought brought a possible explanation for this startling change in his hobgoblin.

"Hob," he said, "has someone been telling you stories?"

"One has, my Lord, indeed," Hob said, with a graceful bow. But then he relaxed and his voice became natural again—and confidential. "The ballad singer who came to the castle has been giving me lessons on how to speak with the gentry."

"What ballad singer?"

"You remember, m'Lord. The ballad singer who came to Malencontri at the time we were just about to bring the summer in. He gives me a lesson twice a week, and m'Lady has been teaching me things, too. I can sign my name—'H-O-B'—just like that. . . . *no other Hob in all the land can do the things that I can do. Not only do I understand the way to polish swords—*"

The light of complete understanding broke in on Jim. In his last sentence, Hob had begun to misquote *The Knight Whose Armor Didn't Squeak*, a poem by E. E. Milne, the writer of the Pooh stories—a poem that no ballad maker in the fourteenth century could possibly know. Hob had to have learned that from Angie. What had gotten into her?

But Hob was already explaining that.

"—M'Lady said I could tell the children stories, now, to keep them quiet at banquets, instead of making faces, twisting myself about and standing on my head, getting them all excited the way I did at the great feast after Mage Carolinus was rescued."

Well, there was the explanation for Angie's involvement. He could hardly say anything to Hob about that. But the other influence was still not as it should be.

"Are you telling me that ballad singer who came at midsummer's stayed with us at Malencontri ever since then?" He glared at Hob, who was maintaining his pose on the sumpter horse's back. "How could he have been in the castle all this time—"

Jim broke off. He did not need an answer to that. The castle servants, if they wanted—and when they all wanted something, they went after it as effectively as the most powerful labor union—they could keep an elephant in the castle for years and he would never see or hear anything to suggest it was there. For the first time he wondered what else they had hiding down in their ground-level servants' quarters.

A sound of trumpets took his eyes and his thoughts back to the castle. Both the great doors in its curtain wall not only opened but were thrown back, now. The large knight on his large horse came back outside, with all his arms and armor, but did not approach them. He sat his horse to one side of the gate, while a half-dozen figures in white-and-gray livery laid out a black carpet from inside the curtain wall out over the drawbridge.

"We are all at once honored guests, James," murmurred Brian. He had ridden back to sit Blanchard side by side with Gorp, turned toward the castle.

"Yes," said Jim, and remounted; and began to feel a touch of uneasiness. What would the Queen of Northgales expect of him, after this kind of a welcome? But he was forgetting Hob.

"Hob," he said, without turning his head.

"Yes, m'Lord?"

"You evidently said just the right thing at just the right time."

"I kiss your feet in gratitude, my Lord."

"No you don't," said Jim. "Not now or ever. Forget everything that ballad maker's been teaching you—for the moment, anyway. Just talk like yourself. Besides, from here on in I'll do the talking."

"Yes, m'Lord." There was a moment of silence, and then a very meek voice. "Are you angry with me, m'Lord?"

"No," said Jim. "It's just that you were lucky once, but we don't want to stretch that luck too far."

"Oh."

"Yes."

"I won't say anything unless you tell me to, m'Lord—my Lord."

"Good."

The carpet was laid now and the knight was riding toward them, no slower or faster than he had come out originally, but with a certain stiffness in the way he sat his saddle that signaled a formal rather than a punitive approach.

"My Lady the Queen of Northgales requires your presence. Messires, would you of your grace follow me? I will lead you to the presence of our Queen."

Jim nodded. Neither he nor Brian said a word. Formality was catching. The knight turned back toward the castle and they followed him, Jim pondering whether his quick acceptance of this invitation would help or hinder him with Northgales.

Beyond the great doors, there was the expected courtyard, with more fire-prone wooden utility buildings—cookhouse, blacksmith shop, and the like—than would have been trusted in the fourteenth-century lands above Lyonesse. He thought there was a certain slovenliness about not only the buildings and the courtyard but the people, all clad as if for deep winter, who could be seen standing or lounging about. Jim suddenly became conscious that the QB was once more no longer with them.

Jim looked at the knight. That armored figure was half a dozen horse-strides ahead of them.

"Hob," Jim said, out of the corner of his mouth, in a low voice, "when did the QB leave us?"

There was a slight pause before the answer came, also in a hushed voice.

"Forgive me, m'Lord, I didn't notice when he went. I didn't miss him until you mentioned him just now."

"Probably didn't want to go with us inside this castle," Jim muttered to himself. For a moment he found himself wondering if the QB was like Aargh in not wanting to be enclosed. But Jim was becoming adjusted to the QB's abrupt coming and going. After all, he was the only one of his kind in existence, and had undoubtedly ended up making his own rules of conduct. No doubt he would be showing up again before long.

Even as Jim thought these things, the large knight led them through the arched stone entrance to the castle proper; and this was as clean and high-ceilinged as the courtyard with its service buildings and staring servants had been slovenly. But there was something about it that was as chilled, bleak, and unwelcoming as the outer walls of the castle had appeared from the outside.

Chapter 17

Jim's first thought was that the place was unusually cold. But he was used to cold castles now. They were all cold, unless you were standing less than ten feet from a fire in a fireplace in midsummer.

But it was not that. This was a different kind of cold; as if the very spirit, the identity of the place, had no warmth.

Now on foot and leading their horses, they had stepped directly into what seemed to be a large formal hall, furnished not with tables—or the trestles that could be covered with boards and tablecloths to set up as tables—but merely a few great torches that burned with unnatural white flames and lit up the arching stone walls that came to a meeting far overhead. Only, in that torchlight, there could be seen a dais at the far end of the chamber, with a tall throne on it that looked as if it had been carved out of a single block of ice.

"You will wait here, my Lord, Messire," said the knight, also leading his horse and having brought them to the edge of the platform. He turned away. He and his horse literally vanished.

"James . . . ," said Brian, in a low, but troubled voice.

"It's all right," said Jim, making no effort to keep his own voice down; and his words came back to him, repeated out of order and all tangled with each other, from different reflecting areas of the upcurving walls. "I think I'm supposed to be impressed."

He turned himself once more into a dragon. The echoes all stopped suddenly, as if they were part of a public address system which had just been switched off.

Jim turned back into a knight again. In the stone wall behind the throne a small door that had not been visible before opened suddenly; and a tall young woman, not unlike the one who had run out to question them at the castle of the Bright Knight, emerged and curtsied.

"If you will follow me, my Lords?"

She led them through the door from which she had come. This was high and wide enough to let them tow the horses through also. They did so, following her into a room that, by contrast with the one they were leaving, was bright with illumination. But that illumination turned out to be nothing more than the brightness of Lyonesse's outdoors. It was the room itself that was startling.

It was not so much a room as—impossibly—a section of Lyonesse itself, seen as if from above a range of snow-crowned mountains, somewhat inland from the stony seashore. It was spread out, miles of it, underneath them, forest and plain, as if they looked down from several thousand feet of altitude; but there seemed nothing holding them up. They looked down, without any feeling of height, from this apparently unbelievable altitude; and Jim's first thought—*A glass floor!*—was instantly rejected. A sheet of glass this size, of necessary thickness and clearness, was not manufactured anywhere in the fourteenth-century world—let alone in Arthurian times.

Part of the impossibility was the fact that neither Brian nor any of the horses seemed bothered by finding themselves standing on nothing but air. Brian might simply be dismissing it as magick—which made anything possible. But what made the horses indifferent was unanswerable; unless it was that they could neither smell nor hear anything from the landscape below, so dismissed it as unimportant.

"Well, my Lord Dragon," said a woman's sharp voice, "you find me overseeing and guarding my realm. What brings you to beg audience with me?"

Jim took his eyes off the scene below him, and saw a thin, rather elderly-looking woman, sitting in a smaller version of the ice-colored throne he had seen in the great room they had just left. About her was all the clutter of a bedroom that was lived in as much as it was a place for sleep; a bed with tall curtains half pulled back, showing rumpled bedclothes, three small padded chairs without arms, and some small tables, all loaded either with plates and decanters or carelessly tossed clothing—all white in color.

Their young guide had already vanished, and with her, evidently, any pretense that the visitors had a right to speak as equals or near equals with this lady.

"Punch holes in them first, then go in with the crusher!" Jim had continually been advised by his high school debating coach—who had also taught boxing.

Accordingly, Jim now waved a hand, indifferently.

"Why, nothing of importance, now that I see you at your duties," he said lightly. "You seem to be handling them pretty well, yes—pretty well, everything considered. I guess there's nothing I should feel concerned about here."

"My duties!" she exploded. "It is my pleasure to rule Northgales and all that doth pertain to it! What impertinence is this, that you might pass judgment or concern yourself with me and mine?"

"Come, come," said Jim cheerfully, "when was concern for another of the Craft an impertinence? We must stand together as even a family does, when an enemy approaches."

"Enemy?" The word came out scornfully enough; but Jim felt she delayed a little too long in answering, as if to see if he would enlarge upon what he had just said. "There is no enemy. No enemy would dare approach Northgales."

"Indeed! You had not heard, then?"

"Heard? Of course I've heard—everything there is to be heard in my realm. There is no thing amiss."

"Ah, well," said Jim sadly. "I see I can be of no help, after all." He turned to Brian. "You were right, Brian."

"Right?" Brian stared at Jim.

"Yes. We should have gone to the Queen of the Out Isles first, since time presses. But seeing we had the Dark Powers for foe again, I was so sure this great ruler of Northgales . . ." Jim let his voice trail off.

"Sure of me? How might you be sure of me? What is this of Out Isles, and your pretence of having some sorts of Powers as foes?"

"Oh, as it happens, Sir Brian and I have met Them several

times; and conquered each time. This is known by all those of''—Jim made an effort to sound as much as possible like a fourteenth-century individual in his pronunciation of the word, for once—''*Magick* in the upper world, where the war to keep the Powers from disrupting History and Chance is ever active. Our experience with Them has made us more aware when They're close. But, there is no point to talking about this if you don't know Them and haven't felt Them yet. Brian, we must to Out Isles, right away.''

He started to turn around.

''Show me not your back if you would keep it whole! You came at your pleasure, you will stay now until I let you go! I—'' Northgales checked the tone of her voice abruptly. ''That is to say, I do so entreat you, my Lord and Messire. I am always glad to speak with any of the Craft, particularly those of your experience with these—what did you call them? Black Powers? And you have warred with them?''

Jim turned back.

''Mere bickers, only,'' put in Brian, probably out of sheer social reflex. But then he clamped his mouth shut and looked at Jim with a question in his eyes.

''How well you put it, Brian,'' said Jim. ''Those were mere bickers, indeed, compared to the Rape of Lyonesse which the Dark Powers contemplate now.''

''The Rape of Lyonesse. What nonsense! If any Powers had any such in mind, I would have known.''

Jim decided to follow the example of Carolinus and KinetetE, who always talked down to nonmagicians, no matter what their worldly rank.

''Of course you would. Come now,'' he said, ''let's not play children's games. I happen to know you've known it for some time. It'd be impossible for someone like you not to know.''

''That's what I said!''

''Exactly. So you do know, and you know Their proper name—the Dark Powers. I'll bet you believed whoever told you you'd be an exception to Their conquest of Lyonesse;

that Northgales would remain untouched and all yours, as it always has been?''

Northgales snorted. She did not sniff, she snorted.

''Hah! My Dragon Knight, don't think you can cozen me with such nonsense! I would trust no such words as those you speak!''

''Then how do you know what I say is nonsense?''

''Because,'' said the Queen, ''I have the truth on an authority you know not of.''

''You could be wrong about that, too,'' said Jim. ''But never mind. No doubt you trust whoever told you utterly, enough to put your life in her hands. However, if that's so, you're already in danger. For among the first changes the Dark Powers always make happen is to turn sister against sister, brother against brother, friend against friend. But, clearly, I take it you're sure you can defend Northgales without our help. In that case, we really must be on our way. You can't keep such as us here if we really want to leave, you know.''

''Hah!'' said Northgales. ''But, on second thought, I find you tiresome. You may go.''

Jim smiled at her.

''Well, since you understand matters and have things so well in hand here,'' said Jim, ''there are others I must be talking to. Give you good day, my Queen, and all luck attend you on your way.''

He felt a little proud of the way he had followed his debating coach's advice and put in the crusher. In this case, he thought he had hit just exactly the right note of regretful pity for the Queen in his last few words.

He smiled confidently once more at the Queen. She stared coldly back at him. His self-congratulations began to evaporate like the last skim of water in a pan over a blazing fire.

''Come, Brian,'' he said; and started to turn away.

''Hold! I command you! Since you are here,'' said Northgales, ''there is no reason I should not make use of you to measure what you claim to know about these so-called Dark Powers. Have you ever seen them?''

Jim turned back.

"How could I when They have no form, no substance? But at the Loathly Tower the first time we met Them, Brian and I saw Their creatures—the Worm and the Ogre, not to mention their Harpies—"

"Harpies?"

"Come, come. I'm sure you know what I'm talking about. Flying creatures with women's faces and a bite that is deadly poisonous—though it's true one of our number, the greatest Master Bowman of all worlds, refused to die of such a bite once he discovered he was loved, and with the help of that love threw off the poison—"

"There are no such creatures here in Lyonesse."

"There will be soon, then."

"Absolute nonsense! There're no such things."

"You may also see ogres and Worms."

"No such things."

"But the worst part," Jim said slowly and impressively, "is, the last person you would think let herself be a creature of the Dark Powers will turn out to be this one you will have been trusting all this time; and who has been betraying you into their power as well—or to destruction!"

He stopped speaking. She sat still on the throne, not saying a word.

"Well, farewell, as I said earlier." Jim turned around, beginning to move toward the small door that had let them into this curious chamber.

"Did I not say 'Hold'?" she cried, behind him. "Come, help me up."

He looked back over his shoulder. The expression on her face had not changed. Abruptly Jim remembered how Morgan le Fay had reacted when she had reached out to strip his ward from him—as if her fingers had touched hot acid. This Queen of Northgales might not yet have sensed his ward. If not, then it was best she did not learn about it while he could keep the information from her. It might tell her more about him than he could want her to know.

"I suggest you call one of your servitors, my Queen," he

said—more confident now that she did not really want them to leave. "You seem to have many to serve you. Excuse Sir Brian and myself."

"Neither of you will help me up?" She was looking directly at Brian now. "If there were others I could ask, do you believe I would ask you? Of your kindness, the edge of this seat always presses into my legs, and before I realize, they have gone numb. I am as one crippled. Will no one help me—no one?"

But Brian had picked up on Jim's wariness.

"I regret," he said.

"No one—no one at all—will help!" It was a cry of such real-sounding despair and unhappiness that Jim almost had to check himself from stepping forward, after all.

"Oh! Yes!" cried a high little voice. "I will!" There was a soft thud behind Jim; and Hob ran past him toward the Queen.

"You?" she said, looking down at him. "Whatever you are—you would not make more than a spoonful. Or do you, too, have magick?"

"Only in that I can ride the smoke, your Royalty," said Hob. He had reached her throne and stepped close beside it. Now he turned around to face back toward Jim and Brian. "But I'm really strong. Just put your hand on my shoulder and lean your weight on me. Go ahead. Just push down on me and lift yourself up. It'll be easy."

"Hob!" said Jim. "Come back here. That's an order!"

"I can't, m'Lord." Hob turned an agonized small face toward him. "She needs me!" He looked back at the Queen. "Go ahead! It'll work. You'll see."

"Very well," said the Queen. She reached out a long arm and took a grip of Hob's nearest shoulder. Pressing heavily on him, she levered herself upright.

"See," said Hob . . . but his voice had gone suddenly weak. As the Queen let go of him, he started back toward Jim, but wavered as he got closer, as if he was dizzy. His knees gave with each step, and his steps came slowly and more uncertainly. Jim ran to him; but before he could catch him, Hob fell; and Jim, looking down at him, saw that the whole of his small body had gone white and shrunken.

Jim scooped the feather-light figure up in his arms. Hob's eyes were closed now; and he seemed unconscious, but he was shivering convulsively. Jim held him close to his chest as he turned back toward Brian and the horses.

"Brian!" he said urgently. "Get clothes, blankets, anything warm there is to put around him, from the sumpter horse! Wrap them about both of us—Hob and me!"

"What is all this?" demanded the Queen, now standing tall beside her throne. "No doubt the creature was useful to you in making your magick, but it is not as if I cannot and will not replace it. I will get you another just as good. It was too small, that's all. One of you two would have been all right—oh, perhaps a little chilled for a while. I have been cold all my life. Anyone who touches me must give up heat to me."

Jim ignored her.

She stamped her foot.

"I tell you it is no good anymore! Throw it away! You insult me with all this to-do about it. Did I not tell you clearly I would replace it?"

"My Queen," said Brian, hard-voiced, not pausing in his task of pulling cloth of all kinds out from under the rain cover on the back of the sumpter horse. His eyes were like the points of two spears aimed at her. "May God's Justice find some kindness for you; for I would give you none!"

"Wrap us both up together," Jim was saying, still paying no attention to the Queen.

His mind was made up. It would mean breaking his ward; and while the cloths around them would hide him from physical sight, Morgan le Fay's magic might well see through them for the instant his guard was down. But that did not matter in this moment.

If his own body heat and any magic that was within his power could do it, Hob would live.

It grew darker around Jim as the layers of clothing and other material closed around him and Hob; but he paid little attention. All his concentration was focused on the ice-cold little body in his arms, now shivering so weakly that he could barely feel it. Then there was no light about them—only utter darkness.

So much the better, he thought. Maybe Morgan le Fay would not be able to see after all. He opened his ward and pressed Hob against his chest, closing the ward immediately again around both of them, so that even if Morgan had seen, perhaps the opening would have been too brief for her to gain any advantage.

It made no difference to the feel of Hob against his chest; but now he could use his magic. And with all his will, he concentrated on funneling the warmth of his own body into the one he held. It was merely another version of the first aid given, when nothing else was available, to a person who had been deathly chilled, as by falling through the ice into winter-cold waters—which was to strip the victim, strip yourself, and take the freezing person into a sleeping bag with you, so that your own body heat would replace what the other had lost.

There had been no time to strip himself, but with magic he could do away with the clothing that might act as a barrier between him and the hobgoblin. He concentrated on that and the flow of heat from him to Hob.

He could feel the warmth going from him, but Hob did not seem to respond. The moments slipped by; and he conjured up a fever temperature within himself—cursing himself for not thinking of that in the first place.

But then, gradually, gradually, the faint shivering of Hob's body became stronger; and stronger yet. Slowly, but definitely, Jim's feverish body was beginning to feel a gradual increase of warmth in Hob's.

He shut everything else out of his mind, concentrating only on that transfer of heat; and after what seemed like a long while, a thin voice spoke.

"M'Lord?"

"Hob! Are you warming up? How do you feel?"

"Sleepy . . ." Hob answered after a long moment. "Why

do I—what are we doing, m'Lord? What happened?"

"Tell you later. How do you feel now?"

"I feel good . . . I think. I'm not so sleepy after all. Passing strange . . . Hobs never sleep. But you're all hot yourself, m'Lord."

Jim cancelled the fever.

"I'll cool down," he said. "Are you chilly at all?"

"Oh, no. I'm very good and awake. Isn't it time for me to wake up now, m'Lord?"

"Yes. I guess it is."

Removing Hob from the ward was not the danger that putting him in it had been. That had been a matter of opening the ward, and then holding it open long enough to enclose Hob with him before closing it. Now, however, since Hob was already inside it, Jim could simply let him melt out through the ward, so that there was no gap around him as Hob left. He went like a drop of water through a thin, loosely woven cloth.

"Brian!" shouted Jim into the blanket end covering his mouth. "Unwrap us, will you?"

Nothing happened for a moment. Then Jim felt the outer layer being unwound from around him. Light showed through, and suddenly, the cloths that were left simply dropped to his ankles. Brian picked them up and piled them, like a small mountain, on top of the rain cover worn by the sumpter horse, who looked at Jim curiously.

"Where are we?" said Jim.

For they were no longer in the castle of the Witch Queen of Northgales. Nor were they just outside it. They were out among the great trunks of old trees, with the white sun of Lyonesse shining through their high branches and black leaves. Trees everywhere. No castles. No Witch Queens.

Chapter 18

"How did we get here?" Jim asked Brian, who was beside him, but looking bewildered. Brian shook his head, wordlessly. Hob, who was out of Jim's grasp now, ran to the sumpter horse.

"Are you all right?" he asked anxiously. "All the things you're carrying are out from under cover, all over your back and on the ground, here."

The sumpter horse looked at him disgustedly. Human or hobgoblin, as far as she was concerned they were all the same thing—nuisances. Everyone not a horse was the same thing; and now that she stopped to think of it, she could not think of a single horse that was any better. Oh, those two stallions over there might have their points if she was interested. But she wasn't.

"I think it was the Old Magic that brought you out," said the voice of the Questing Beast; and Jim looked to his left to see the QB also beside him there. "My Lady Queen almost had you prisoner at her pleasure. You took a great chance matching words with her as you did. Look at the trees, Sir James."

Jim looked, and saw each one in view was stretching out its lower branches, downward and toward him. He looked further around him, turning completely about.

"Oh, m'Lord!" said Hob, staring at the trees, now. "They're all honoring you."

"Why?" Jim turned to the QB.

"We can never be sure," said that individual. "You have either done something noble, or have proved to be noble in some way."

"But I haven't!" said Jim.

"The forest is never wrong," said the QB in a slightly frosty tone. "There is magick in *all* trees. In Lyonesse there are three powerful magicks. One is the Old Magic. The trees are the second, and the beasts the third."

Jim stared at him.

"But people cut down trees and burn them for firewood," he said. "And the beasts, the deer and others particularly, are hunted by people, kept, killed, and eaten."

"People also kill each other. Knights fight. Old trees overshadow and starve young trees for sunlight so they die. The beasts prey upon and eat each other. Yet, as a kind, like unto like, they feel together. What is the difference, except the difference of feeling in one way of magick from another's?"

"Well . . ." said Jim; and found that he had no words ready to his tongue.

"Of course," went on the QB, "in magick there is also one more, who is Merlin. But he no longer uses his magick now; and would not, I think, even to save Lyonesse. But the trees altogether are not to be thought less of. When our great Arthur was a boy, his royal lineage a secret even from him, the trees would reach down to him as he passed; and if he stood before a fire, the smoke would curve toward him before going upward."

"You see there, my Lord?" said Hob. "The smoke's never wrong. It never makes a mistake!"

"James," said Brian, deeply and solemnly, "it is like you to so hide your true nobility that you do not realize it yourself. I have always been impressed by that in you."

There was no point in explaining how wrong they all were, thought Jim hopelessly. He would never convince them, anyway.

"Well, on other subjects," he said, to get them all on to something else, "I'm very grateful to the trees if they're the ones who rescued us from Northgales's castle just now. How can I thank them?"

"They are already thanked by your thinking of it," said the QB. "But I, also, am glad you are safely away from there and from any other of the Witch Queens, who are each very dangerous and unpredictable—even to each other. It is strange, but the Old Magic has never seemed to set limits upon them."

"Trees, and the Old Magic—how do they divide up their powers between them? I mean—which has what power?"

"There is always power in trees and growing things, the running waters, the earth and rock, Sir James. The Old Magic is apart from those others and all that to them belong; but in its own way it fits with and works with them."

"But you think," said Jim, "it wasn't the Old Magic but the trees that got us out of that castle just now?"

"Does it matter?" asked the QB.

"Yes, it does matter," said Jim. "Brian and I came here hoping to join whoever might be willing to fight the Dark Powers. But we can't seem to find any."

"Do not think of the Old Magic as an ally, then. Accept its presence, only," said the QB.

"You're not helping," said Jim.

"It is better," said the QB, "to know you are unholpen, than hope for help when there is none. But perhaps I can be of more aid if we talk further. What did you think to gain from the Queen of Northgales?"

"You'd said earlier none of the Queens had forces of fighting men. I wanted to find out how they were able to keep their power without them."

"Lyonesse lives because Arthur lived and because he and his Knights live on here, unforgotten. To this the Old Magic is agreed, and the trees and creatures also. Each in their own place. If fighting is to be done, it is the Knights' part to defend their ground; which is the ground of creatures and trees as well."

"Seems a little one-sided to me," said Jim.

"Have you never known a time when your last friend had been slain beside you; and you found yourself alone?"

"I don't think so. No," said Jim cautiously.

"I have," said Brian unexpectedly.

"When someday you do—as I think all must, Sir James," said the QB, "you may be surprised. You will feel naked, and perhaps a certainty of life's end; but, strangely, also a great relief such as you never felt before. For death and all things now are in your hands, alone. Come what may, all decision is yours at last, and none can take it from you."

"By all things good!" said Brian. "It is true, James!"

Jim turned to look at him. Brian's eyes were shining.

"You never told me," he said.

Brian opened his mouth, hesitated, closed it again.

"Someday," he said. "Not now. Mayhap it shall not be for some years yet, or until after you have known it for yourself. Then we may talk together, each of his own moment—but without that in common how will we know our words speak of the same thing?"

There was a little silence. Brian broke it.

"Ah, well," he said. "We could have saved ourselves a visit to Northgales by asking the Lord QB here instead. But we did not know that—and, indeed, I cannot quarrel with his words that Arthur's Knights should defend the land they hold. But that they should do so alone, though surrounded by magick that can, however, not fight by their side . . . it seems neither fair nor right."

"It seems as if that's how things are, here," said Jim. "But I wanted to see Northgales, anyway, to see what other Witch Queens were like."

"I must confess I wanted that, too—and damned odd this one was! But we missed an interesting lance meeting with that champion of hers."

"Just as well we missed him," answered Jim. "But I admit it was the talk I wanted most. Only, I also wanted the Queen to want it as much as I did."

"James, you should have told me."

"I know I should, Brian; but there wasn't a chance." And just as well there hadn't been, thought Jim. Brian was the last person to play a part successfully. His instinctive habit of being straightforward about everything would give him away every time.

"But after all, we learned nothing from her."

"Not exactly," Jim said. "I learned something about the Queen, herself. She let us in, hoping to learn what we knew about the Dark Powers; not only to check on what Morgan le Fay must have told her, but gambling she'd pick up something that would give her an edge over Morgan and the other Queens."

"How can you be sure of that, Sir James?" asked the QB.

"The fact that she really didn't want us to leave, even when she told us to go. That's how I could force her to order us to stay. Once she did that, she'd effectively admitted she was interested in what we could tell her about the Powers. When I didn't give her much, she got ready to play rough. She was hoping one of us would help her up and be weakened enough by her heat-stealing so she'd have an excuse to keep us with her in the castle and work on us some more. She misjudged the way we stand by Hob."

"Certainly, her request for aid from you in her own house was unlikely enough," said the QB. "Perhaps she thinks you have a magick which will work against that of the Dark Powers?"

Jim became aware he was frowning; and stopped doing it.

"Oh, I don't think she does," he said, sounding as confident as he could. "I don't believe the Dark Powers have any magic at all—in the sense we use the word. But also I have to think They're immune to magic, as we know it. Our magickians in the world above have always fought Them off by guile, or by defeating Their creatures, instead of any other way. If magic worked against the Powers, I'm sure the Collegiate of Magickians would have used it before this. No, our magic can't touch Them; but Their magic won't touch us directly, either. They've got to use Their monsters or human allies to take anything by physical force."

"Then you are telling me they must have fighters to take our Lyonesse?" said the QB.

"That's right. They'll have to have a fighting force, men of some kind. I suppose Morgan could contribute the knight I met in the Dedale Woods—and some others; and Northgales could contribute that knight who was ready to fight me, and perhaps others, but that's not putting together much of a force compared to Arthur's Knights and their male Descendants. It beats me how the Powers are planning to do it.''

''Sir Dinedan—the current Descendant of *the* Sir Dinedan, that is—who we met the first time through Lyonesse—'' volunteered Brian, ''seemed a goodly knight to oppose villains . . . though somewhat given to fits of weakness and falling from his saddle.''

''But why fighting *men,* especially?'' said the QB dubiously.

''How else?'' exploded Brian impatiently. ''Only we can hold what we win. Ogres could not. Worms could not. Harpies could not. It takes unending wit and effort to hold. *Le fort main*, our Norman forebears called it when they came to England—'the strong hand'—it is continually needed to keep what you have gained against the rising of those conquered, or attempts by others to wrest it from you!''

''I must bow to your superior wisdom,'' said the QB unhappily. ''And if that is so, we have the Knights and their families—those that have them. And seemingly the Dark Powers have none. But then, why the attention to you by the Witch Queens? Why then your concern over the Dark Powers here in Lyonesse at all?''

''Perhaps the Queens think we know where the Powers are going to get the army that's needed, and they don't,'' said Jim. ''As for our concern, the Powers have never been known to show up or try to influence anything unless They had some way of getting what They wanted—''

''Army,'' echoed the QB. ''You are speaking then of a host of foemen?''

''Yes.'' Jim was aware of a sudden chill in the back of his mind. If what he had just said always held true, why had the Dark Powers appeared at Malencontri as They had? To frighten him and his friends off from helping Dafydd and getting involved in Lyonesse? If so, it hadn't worked.

Because Jim, Brian, and Dafydd had won against Them before? Unanswerable questions. The Powers did not think like humans—if They thought in any real sense at all. They might be merely a great, complicated bundle of reflexes.

Think about that later, he told himself firmly. The QB was talking again.

"—for Lyonesse, we can add to the Original Knights not merely their Descendants, knights themselves, like King Pellinore's three famous sons, but as well many of the good creatures that live in our land. True, opposing them could be some of villainous breed from the borderlands between us and the Drowned Land—like those giant, black-furred, club-carrying creatures you were about to be assaulted by on your first visit here, had I not come by in time to order them back. But it is hard for me to believe that magick . . . particularly the Old Magick . . ."

His voice trailed off.

". . . But I must take your advice on it," he went on, after a second, "since you are those who have fought and won against the Dark Powers before. But I must confess the idea of a host to oppose our Knights and conquer Lyonesse like some ordinary kingdom never occurred to me. How would such a host come here—and without our knowing of it?"

"That's a question," said Jim. "But I've been thinking about it; and there'd be one way, at least: Remember when the Gnarly King that was had captured my young ward, he was hand in glove with Agatha Falon, half sister to my ward and someone out to get rid of the boy so that she, not he, could inherit the family wealth."

"What has that to do with this, James?" Brian frowned at him.

"Just that Gnarly messengers went back and forth between Agatha at Windsor Court and the Gnarly King. I saw one of them in a dungeon at Court. He'd come, apparently, by digging a tunnel to the dungeon from Gnarlyland—they're great diggers . . ."

"That is true," said the QB. "We know that much of them."

"All right," went on Jim. "So this one supposedly tunneled from Gnarlyland to the Court. But anyone with any knowledge of magic at all knows neither the Drowned Land nor Gnarlyland, nor Lyonesse, can be simply *dug to* from our land above. Somewhere along that tunnel, and probably not too far along, there had to be magic involved to make the far end come out in a place that otherwise couldn't be reached."

"But is there indeed such magick?" said the QB. "In some hundreds of years I have never heard any, Merlin or other, speak of it."

"There is," said Jim. "There's something called a Witches' Gate—you remember, Brian, how I mentioned that when we went from the sea into the Drowned Land?"

"You did, James. But you said it was nothing of concern—something simple, I believe you called it, for witches only."

"Right. It was developed by witches originally to let them into the houses of other people they wanted to reach. It's simply a little spell that can turn things inside out; so that the witch, instead of being outside the wall of a house, is then inside it. But it could be used just as well to move to such places as Gnarlyland, or the Drowned Land—to some spot inside them."

"James, is this indeed true? For I have never heard of it happening to any man, woman, house, nor other what-have-you."

"It is, Brian. Believe me. It's just that for some centuries now it's been all but forgotten; because any who hold to a faith, who suspect witchery coming against them, are able—by wearing or putting the symbol of their faith between them and the witch—to bar that small piece of magic from working. Any faith honestly held, any true symbol of it, blocks the powers of a witch as effectively as a shield blocks the spear strike or sword blow."

"But could it be used to bring in many men against us?" asked the QB.

"I think it could," said Jim. "But whether it could bring a large number in all at once, or just keep importing one or two at a time, I don't know. I'm only an Apprentice magician, remember, and I've only picked up a few scraps of knowledge about Witchery. But an accomplished practitioner in the Art ought to be able to set up such a thing; and once set up in a particular spot, keep it in operation there, bringing in their men as they need. And certainly Morgan le Fay is accomplished, after all these hundreds of years of being a Witch Queen.''

The QB was wagging his snake's head slowly.

''And where might we look for such a Gate?''

''Somewhere in Lyonesse—or perhaps in the Drowned Land—those men will be gathering. The Gate itself would be camouflaged—hidden—of course, if only so that those who came through it wouldn't be tempted to use it in spite of being ordered not to. But it will be somewhere near where the men are. We'd be wise to look around for such a gathering place.''

The QB shook his head again.

''It does seem wise, as you say,'' he said. ''I can ask both the trees and the animals. But time means nothing to them outside of the present moment. We might not hear back from them for weeks, after it is found. But in any case, Queen Morgan le Fay may already know of such a host to use this strong hand you spoke of; and if she does, she is already before us. But how she found them I cannot guess.''

''I don't think Morgan would have gathered them,'' said Jim; ''though she may have helped whoever did. Most likely, the Dark Powers were hand-in-hand with whoever did it. The danger is, though, that they're already here.''

''These Powers ordered these men here?''

''No. They can't directly control humans. The best They can do is offer someone bait, or a bribe of one kind or another, to get whoever it is to work for Them; then he—or she—locates men who will work without caring about the consequences. That's why I think their bait-taker in this case is Morgan. Who else could call together an army to Lyonesse?''

''No one,'' said the QB promptly. ''No one but our great King Arthur. But he would never raise a host to fight against his own Knights and this land. In any case he is not here—if he were, all Lyonesse would know it.''

Jim shook his head at this.

''It doesn't make sense,'' he said. ''The people of the Drowned Land, a land next door that Lyonesse ordinarily has nothing to do with, knew the Dark Powers were trying this. Even our own magicians in the land above know about it—that's why we're here, Brian and I. The Dark Powers just have to have that host, someplace; and someone in Lyonesse has to know where they are and how they were gathered. If it's not Morgan who's gathering one for the Powers, then who?"

He looked hard at the QB.

"It's true—I can think of none other," the QB said. "But it may be that answer to the whole matter is beyond us. It may be that the time of fire is on Lyonesse, when it will sink forever back deep under the sea, to be known no more. But it has always been believed that day would only come when Arthur and all of us who knew him are forgotten by those in the world above, where History lives." He stopped for a moment, then went on.

"But I would caution you, Sir James, about asking such questions as you have just asked, here in Lyonesse. You, Sir Brian, and the small hobgoblin, I think, know nothing of how you escaped from the Queen of Northgales's castle. Best, perhaps, I tell you, after all. I did not plan to, since speaking of the Old Magic too much can be perilous."

There had been a change in his tone of voice as he spoke; and he was looking very steadily and hard at Jim.

"I am right, am I not. You do not know?"

"No," said Jim.

"Then I will tell you, whether it brings us all good or ill. Look at the sky of Lyonesse. Have you ever seen a cloud in it?"

Jim looked up, instinctively. So did Brian and Hob—and so, startlingly, did the horses.

"I don't remember ever seeing one," said Jim.

"It would be strange if you had, for centuries have gone by, without one appearing. But there was one came into view above the castle of Northgales, but a short time ago; and when such a cloud comes, if it covers the sun, then for the time that the sun is hidden, darkness holds Lyonesse—a dark as of the night in which you spoke to Merlin."

There was no good reason why a shiver should run down Jim's spine, but one did; and he found himself chilling all over as he had chilled holding Hob and warming him back to life.

"When that cloud came, and covered the sun, there was the darkness I speak of—and in that particular darkness you, Sir Brian, the Hob, your horses, and all they carried left the castle in less than the thought of a breath, to find yourself here where you are now."

Jim shook off the shiver.

"Why tell us this just because I wondered who else besides Morgan le Fay could raise an army?" he asked.

"I tell you to remind you that the Old Magic is powerful beyond imagining; and always with us. I said it only to warn you, because such a cloud is not likely to be seen again in your lifetime . . ."

His sibilant voice died. He lifted his slit-pupiled eyes once more to the sky. The rest of them looked with him.

A small, harmless-looking, fluffy cloud was over their heads, moving toward Lyonesse's sun. As they watched, it touched that white star, eating into it as the moon eats away the sun during an eclipse of earth's star. Rapidly, the light dimmed; until suddenly it was gone completely and each of them stood isolated in blackness.

Just as suddenly, it was bright day again.

"—But this is not Lyonesse!" cried the QB.

Chapter 19

No more it was. A yellow sun beamed down past a few errant clouds, warming them with a summer warmth where they stood at the edge of a wood, on an extended plain covered with long green grass. No breeze was stirring. A large tent—almost more pavilion than tent—had been set up not more than fifty yards away; and a group of tall, lean men, half of them with unstrung bows hanging from their shoulders and long quivers full of arrows dependent from their broad leather belts, stood in a group.

They were dressed in tunics and tight leather leggings such as Jim and Brian were used to seeing Dafydd wear, each man in solid blue, green, or brown clothing, their talking now interrupted by discovery of the presence of Jim and the others. They stared at Jim and these other new arrivals; and Jim, his own eyes all but blinded by the comparative brilliance of the green of the grass, the blue of the sky, and the gold of the sun overhead, stared back at them. But one among them stared only briefly before starting with long strides toward the newcomers; and he was Dafydd.

"It's all right . . . all right . . ." Jim heard Hob's small, high voice behind him saying; and he looked over his shoulder to see the tiny hobgoblin stroking the scaly neck of the QB. The latter seemed to have grown half again as large as usual, suddenly, as people and many higher mammals do when ready to fight—drawing themselves up, expanding their lungs, and bristling whatever hair they possessed.

Hob went on talking softly, steadily, to the QB, stroking the long neck over and over again; while the QB, seemingly unaware of the hobgoblin, arched that same neck, his narrow tongue flickering in and out of his half-open mouth, which now showed wickedly curved fangs.

"It is wrong for me to be here . . ." the QB was hissing. "Only one villainously against the Legends would come to this place . . ."

"James! Brian!" said Dafydd sharply, stopping in front of them. This was the other Dafydd speaking—the one who was a Prince in this Drowned Land, rather than the ordinary archer of the land above. He was still the friend they knew, but everything—including his way of speaking—was different, more formal, commanding. "What do you here—and with this—"

He broke off suddenly.

"QB!" he said. "You? Here in—" He broke off; and—being recognized, the QB abruptly recognized Dafydd from his last time in Lyonesse, on the trip with Jim and Brian. His back flattened somewhat, his fangs became less prominent. "I crave your indulgence, my Lord Questing Beast," Dafydd went on, "—if I may call you so?"

"You may, of course." The QB was still not fully at ease. He still had a tendency to hiss the letter *s* when he spoke. "I am indeed a Lord of Lyonesse by virtue of my being mentioned in the Legends of our King."

The hissing faded out, however, as he spoke. He had gone back almost to his ordinary size and tone of voice, and with the closing of his mouth the wicked fangs now disappeared; but he was still tense.

"However, all call me the QB, and I prefer it so."

"Then with your indulgence I will do so—indeed, it makes matters somewhat easier. And James and Brian, will you both forgive me if I also address you before our people here simply as Sir James? Here in the Drowned Land, the title of Lord is only for our King—except in such instance as the QB here, who is a special case. Many of our people recognize a word or two of English; and in a moment I must name you to my cousins and friends; and to our new young King, the one surviving son of our King who has now died. The boy is young to take the throne, but there can be no other choice."

"Was it not said of that King we saw you with on our last trip, all his children were dead?" Brian said.

"All but this youngest. He has been kept safely hidden. His death was announced, for that he was so young and there has been dissension between the Colors. Come, let me take you to him. I am his Regent. I and the other loyal Leaders have met here urgently to decide what to do next—I have much to tell you, but no time to do it now. I must also make you known to the Leaders-of-Colors—there is no word for their authority in English—none even in Wales in the land above. Think of them as each speaking for something like a clan where all wear a certain color to their clothes."

This last sentence came out of Dafydd in a clear, carrying voice. It was obvious to Jim that he had said it as much for the information of the men with him, who understood English, as to Brian and Jim. For once, it was Brian who answered first to deal with the situation.

"This is your land," Brian said. "We are visitors. Your ways shall be our ways while we are here."

"Then I will now name you to my cousins and friends; and to our new young King, for whom I am Regent," Dafydd went on, in the same carrying tones. He lowered his voice abruptly to a level for Jim's and Brian's ears alone. "All the Leaders here are of clans loyal to him; and we are met to decide what to do next; for—"

He raised his voice once more. "—our land is at war with itself over who shall sit on the throne in this dangerous time."

Jim, Brian, and the QB were all silent. Even Hob had stopped murmuring comforting words to the QB and stood motionless, with the motionless horses.

"So, James, Brian, QB—may I beg your indulgence to follow me back to the gathering and stand with me; and that there you stay silent, unless it is necessary to declare yourself one way or another? In that case, I would hope that you would follow me in all I say and do. Is that agreeable to you?"

Brian looked at Jim. Hob looked at Jim. To his surprise, even the QB looked at him, waiting.

"Count on us," said Jim, out of a throat that had become a bit tense in recent minutes, itself. He did not like blind promises; and if it had not been Dafydd ap Hywel who was asking now, his instinct would have been to refuse.

Dafydd turned and strode off, back toward the waiting group of men before the tent. The rest of them followed.

"Gentlemen!" he said, in a short, sharp voice Jim had never heard him use before. All those standing there, who had been gazing at the sudden new arrivals, turned their attention back to the tall man in sky-blue.

But now Dafydd, back with the Drowned Landers, was giving all his attention to a boy among them, who seemed no more than thirteen years old, and had been unnoticed by Jim among the grown men surrounding him. He wore the same kind of clothes as the others, but his were colored all the shades Jim could see on the men present, as well as some shades not otherwise represented. Black and white both—for two—were not there.

"Sire," said Dafydd to the boy, in English, "may I name to you Sir James Eckert, Baron de Malencontri, and Sir Brian Neville-Smythe of Castle Smythe, both from the land above? Both blooded friends of mine, and trustworthy as knights are said to be, but seldom are. Also, may I name to you the Lord Questing Beast of our neighboring land of Lyonesse, also a friend. He is one at arms with us and these two knights in the matter of the shadows of the Dark Powers we have been feeling over our lands; and which some of us here have blamed for the unhappy time that has come upon our own kingdom."

"I am pleasured to know them," answered the young King—unexpectedly, also in fluent English.

"Now," said Dafydd, "I will tell those with us in our own language what the Lord King and I said in yours."

He turned to those watching, and spoke. Dafydd had always had a soft, lilting way of speaking, to Jim's ear. But when he spoke the ancient tongue of his ancestors now, it became different. The lilt was still there, but it was as if each word had been edged with steel. But that difference could be thought about later. The important matter was that Jim did not understand a word of it.

Oh, fine, he thought; then instantly realized that there was no problem, since he was no longer in Lyonesse. Morgan le Fay could neither see nor touch him here. He could safely work his magic inside his ward, and then open the ward to let that out to be effective in this land. He had learned the magical trick to understanding strange languages sometime since—concepting what he could hear—not the words spoken, but the meaning in the words just before they were uttered.

He made it so now; and started understanding.

The tight group of men listened with noncommittal eyes as Dafydd continued to speak, only occasionally turning to stare at the QB, Jim, and Brian—but with something less than welcome . . . but Jim became conscious he was missing the thread of Dafydd's speech.

"—The small Natural upon their horse of baggage," wound up Dafydd, as Jim heard in translation, "is the hobgoblin of Sir James's castle; and for all his small size, courageous and of loyalty beyond testing."

They ignored Hob.

"You are welcome, messires," said the boy, himself speaking in the tongue of the Drowned Land, in a high, clear voice, looking at the men before them. "Welcome, Lord Questing Beast. You are all doubly welcome if you have come to aid our cause."

"I'm afraid, Sire," said Jim, in the only language available to him, and with the first words that came to his mind, "we came for a number of reasons. But without going into those, all else that concerns us most certainly can't succeed unless your cause does also; so our aim, like yours and that of these gentlemen here, is to make things safe and right once more, both here and in Lyonesse."

"Kindly said," answered the boy; this time back in English and with what struck Jim as remarkable composure for someone his age. But, having said that much, he spoke no more and looked up at Dafydd's tall form.

"Sire," said Dafydd, "it would probably be best if, in spite of the urgency of the moment, I should take a small time to discover the details of what brought my friends to us; and this will be best done if I and they step aside. It will be a short interruption, only, I promise you and these gentlemen, who have traveled both far and fast to be with you now. Let me ask those of you—"

He broke off and looked around at the circular group of men in the different colors of clothing.

"—Are there any who would wish to speak against my taking this time from our discussion?"

For a moment it seemed that none of those looking back at him would speak. Then one man wearing green, as tall as Dafydd, with a mustache and beard, both trimmed short and showing flecks of gray among their stiff, brown hairs, turned his eyes from the QB to the boy; and began to speak in the language of the Drowned Land—not to Dafydd, but directly to the young king.

"Sire, may I remind you that some of us here have left our own places suddenly, to come without delay to you; and we must return as soon as possible. Moreover, is not one of our great concerns the monsters growing in numbers daily in the Borderlands? And is not this Questing Beast only another such? But your Regent has asked us to accept him immediately as one of us in our privy planning!"

The youthful monarch, however, was equal to being put in the middle of the disagreement.

"It has been my particular wish," he said in his high voice, "that my Regent should, for my good and that of all my people, rule in such matters."

A silence followed this.

"Is there any other who would speak?" asked Dafydd.

"Yes, by Saint Gildas!" burst out one of the men in brown, speaking the local language. Noticeably among the tall figures around him, with blue or gray eyes, their brown hair cut short on their long-shaped heads, which had seemed to be standard for most of the Drowned Land people Jim had seen—this speaker, while also long-headed, had his brown hair cut only in front and wore it down to his shoulders in back. He was also dark-eyed and short, almost stocky. His face was either tanned or deeply flushed; and his voice was angry. He shoved his way forward among those around him.

"I do not like strange beasts from Lyonesse being pushed upon us. The matter between us and the Sea-Purple is bad enough, without nightmare creatures and unasked visitors from the land above joining in our speaking! I tell you this plainly!"

"Now," said Dafydd—and his voice had gone back to that cool, almost lazy, dangerous tone Jim had heard from him before when things got tense, "—you would not be questioning whether I am a good Regent for our King, are you, Gruffydd?"

But the boy stepped quickly in front of Dafydd, facing the man called Gruffydd.

"Our royal ancestors were of the sky-blue!" he shouted. "Dafydd ap Hywel is my blood cousin. Before he died, my father offered Dafydd to take the throne in my place. If he had done so, he would stand here now as your King and mine. But he refused. So now I am King and have chosen him as Regent. Am I your King, then, or am I not? If I am your King, he is your Regent—and I say then there shall be no more discussion of those who have just joined us, or of Dafydd speaking aside with them. *Am I your King?*"

For a bare second there was no movement. Then, all together, including the man in brown, they knelt before him on one knee and bowed their heads.

"Rise," said the boy-King; and turned his back on the men as they did so, to face Dafydd, Jim, and those with him. "My Regent, take what time you need. I shall stay here, so that our friends may not think you talk behind their back."

Dafydd bowed his head and shoulders.

"Thank you, Sire," he said. "The time will not be wasted." He switched back to English. "Sir James, Sir Brian, my Lord QB, will you, of your favor, accompany me?"

Amid the continued silence of all those with the King, Dafydd led Jim and the rest to the tent. The horses followed, the destriers by training and the sumpter horse because she was still on the lead rope; they were, however, left outside, though Dafydd's beckoning finger summoned Hob with the rest inside the tent. There was little enough there. Some branches had been thrown down and covered with bedding, in a corner. Outside of that, the only furnishings were a bare wooden slab on trestles, set up as a table, and a large leather container, half sack, half jug, and some cups.

"Dafydd, James!" exploded Brian, once they were seated and the leather container proved to contain a red wine.

Both the other men looked at him inquiringly.

"For the love of all the Saints!" Brian said. "Will you tell me what all that talk in foreign speech was about?"

"It was not foreign, you know, Sir Brian," said Dafydd mildly. "English is the foreign tongue here."

"English? Foreign?" said Brian, becoming even angrier. He got himself under control. "Anyway, it was damned discourteous to speak it before a gentleman who did not understand it. You tell me what was said, then, James!"

He looked at Jim, who understood. It was not that Brian expected Jim to suddenly have developed an understanding of the Drowned Land language. It was simply that since Jim was a magician, he must, in some occult way, have known what had been said.

"I think Dafydd is just about to explain that and more to the rest of us," said Jim peaceably.

"I, too," put in the QB, "would like to know what the speaking was about."

"You did not?" Dafydd looked at him with surprise.

"You must remember," the QB said, "that while some of your people in the Drowned Land have from time to time come to Lyonesse—though there is danger for them to do so—none of Lyonesse have ever come to this country of yours."

"Never?" Dafydd gazed at him.

"Never," answered the QB. "Why should they?"

"They are human, as we are."

"But all their existence, like Lyonesse itself, owes its being to the Legends of King Arthur. Like those, they are part of the Legends. In fact, I did not believe it possible for me to be here. I had thought that none of us from there could live beyond its borders. I am still amazed to find myself with you and still existing; and I can only think that some special effort of the Old Magic has made it possible."

It was a solemn speech; and it had its effect on the rest of them.

"However," said Jim, after a moment, "you *are* here."

"That cannot be argued."

"It is a wonder," said Dafydd, "but one we should seek to understand another time. You all probably saw that there were some who were not happy that I should go aside with you as I have. The shorter the time before we rejoin them, the better. Let me swiftly tell you of the situation here, and my own place in it."

"I had hoped you would be free by now, Dafydd," said Brian.

"I thank you for that hope," Dafydd said. "But, barring a miracle, it is not likely that I will be free to join you soon. The King needs me by his side. He is a remarkable lad, as you will discover—you may have felt some touch of his abilities in the way he spoke up, but a short time past. However, words will not solve all things. I, and those who wear the sky-blue, outnumber and are more than a match for any two or three other Colors. Add in those who follow the Throne and it needs be a strong gathering of other Colors to challenge us."

"Why the need for gatherings like this, then?" said Brian. "Send home those who are not with you. Let it be known you will be happy to face all comers, and go about business as usual."

"We are not knights, Sir Brian, here in the Drowned Land," said Dafydd, with the touch of a sad smile. "We do not take arms lightly, nor lives if we can avoid it, even those of men who oppose us."

"Neither do I," piped Hob.

"Hob," said Jim.

"Sorry, my Lord. I won't speak again, my Lord."

"When I say that, however," Dafydd went on, "I must also say there are some of us who do not fit that rule. It so happens that the Leader of the Sea-Purple, and those of certain other Colors who have joined with him, now cry out that with monsters and strangers increasing in numbers hourly in the Borderlands, we need more than a King so young to lead us."

"But harkee!" put in Brian. "Would it not be possible to challenge this man of the Sea-Purple to put all to test on a single combat and meet him yourself—or have a champion—I would not refuse a request to fill that office for you, myself. It might cost one life; but surely that is a cheap price to pay for unity. What does this Purple Leader look like?"

"You saw him outside the tent," said Dafydd. "It was he who spoke just now against my Lord QB and yourselves."

"That man was wearing brown!" said Jim.

"It was only because he came here under shelter, as guest of the Browns."

"You let your foremost enemy walk freely into one of your councils?" Brian stared. "Surely, Dafydd, that is not wise, or good?"

"As I have said," Dafydd answered, "we and our ways are different here, Sir Brian. He is on honor to act honestly as our guest, and we trust him in that; as he would trust me, were I amongst those who had joined them as they talked. It is all the Drowned Land that is threatened by what is happening in the Borderlands; not just we around the Throne."

"What exactly is happening in these Borderlands?" asked Jim. "And where is it?"

"It is a wild strip of forest between Lyonesse and the Drowned Land," said the QB. "You went through it the last time you were here—it was there I helped you against the tall, black-furred ones."

"It is only part in Lyonesse," said Dafydd. "Therefore we are responsible. It is like a finger of our land reaching into the earth of Lyonesse—so that you can be in Lyonesse one moment and, with little change in what is about you, pass into Drowned Land space for a moment—and then be once more in Lyonesse. So perhaps it is there that the poison of what the Dark Powers attempt in Lyonesse has seeped, finding a safe nest between our two peoples. Certainly, there is now a gathering there of strangely unlikely creatures, and men never born or raised in either of our lands—a strong force of them there."

"But if they're confined to the Borderlands—" Jim broke off. "—How far from here is this Borderland, anyway?"

"Close," said Dafydd. "Less than an English mile. But it was through the south corner of it that we passed before on our way to the entrance of the Gnarly Kingdom."

"Yet I thought we were still in Lyonesse at that time,"

said Brian. "And perhaps it was the Lady Agatha Falon who blinded me with arts witcherly, to lead us into her trap."

"Perhaps some of your Knights of Lyonesse, my Lord QB," said Dafydd, "could tell us more of what is afoot there?"

"Of your grace and pleasure," said the QB, lifting his narrow head almost regally to Dafydd, "I pray you again, that you address me simply as the QB. I am more used to it and prefer it—yes, we know the Borderland; but none of our people live close to it. A dark and friendless place."

Jim looked at the strange, legendary animal with sudden curiosity. If none of those belonging to the Arthurian Legends lived there, what had the QB himself been doing there—and how had he happened to show up just at the right moment to help them? Jim opened his mouth to ask, and then closed it again. It would be awkward to request an answer to those questions now; and in any case this was not the place to do so. However, probably not too surprisingly, Dafydd's thoughts seemed to have been running along the same line Jim's had.

"You must go there from time to time yourself," he said to the QB, "since you showed up when we needed you. Have you been there lately?"

"I have not," answered the QB.

"Then you knew not it had become a gathering ground for all such as I have just mentioned," Dafydd told him. "It is ill to have this coming upon us at this time, with our young King still some years from his full manhood; and when the Dark Forces are at work in your Lyonesse. Tell me your thoughts, QB. Do you think these powers have designs on the Drowned Land as well?"

"I know not," said the QB. "I could have asked Merlin, had I suspected it; but almost surely he would not have answered me. It is like him to know—but for his own reasons not to tell. But at least magick does not enter into the tangle of your people here."

"Does it not, James?" said Dafydd, looking at him.

"I'm afraid it does," said Jim. "Tell me, Dafydd. How old is your King right now?"

"He has fifteen years."

"He's older than he looks, then. I'd have guessed a year or so younger. But still he's more capable than I'd have expected for that age."

"He is one who will make a great King for us, if his life is spared," said Dafydd. "He has the wits of a grown man—and not just any grown man—perhaps one such as your friend Sir John Chandos, James, when he had the age of our lad."

"You're measuring the boy against an unusual man," said Jim. He smiled as he said it; but in fact, to his way of thinking, Chandos was the kind of individual who comes along only once in several centuries.

"You will see," said Dafydd. "But now, since time presses, will you tell me why and how you have come here?"

Jim looked at Brian and the QB, but neither said a word.

"Brian and I were both captured. He was led into the hands of the Lady Annis, a demoiselle of the Witch Queen Morgan le Fay—who captured me. You must have heard of the Queen."

Dafydd inclined his head, briefly.

"Morgan tried to get at me magically, but KinetetE stopped her; so Morgan turned me loose in the Forest of Dedale. I got out of there, met QB, and he took me to Merlin, who told me where Brian was being held. I went there, we got Brian loose, and went on to the castle of the Queen of Northgales, to try and find out what she knew of the Dark Powers, since she had been named to us as an ally of Morgan le Fay. We got nowhere with her, however. She seemed to want to hold us in her castle; but then, either the trees of Lyonesse or the Old Magic got us out when a cloud covered the sun and something—I think it was the Old Magic again—sent us to you—but none of us really know."

Jim took a drink of wine and a long breath. He had thought he could tell their story in one long sentence; but it had not turned out to be possible.

"Sent you to us? You think so?" Dafydd rubbed his chin,

gazing at Jim. "Could it not have been the Dark Powers instead that got you out of Northgales' Castle and sent you here?"

"No," said Jim, and hesitated. "It's hard to explain to anyone who hasn't worked with magic. You were with us in my Hall when the Dark Powers showed up there, and I told them to get out. Do you remember how you felt when They were there?"

"Yes," answered Dafydd. "I am not a fearful man, I think; but there was something then that touched the place where fear is in me, in that moment."

"All right," said Jim. "Well, to me—to any magician—that touch, once felt, is something to be recognized at once, if it's ever felt again. It's the way magic-workers of any kind get in touch with each other, if they're able to reach out far enough to feel for it. Morgan, and Northgales as well, could probably use it to find me anywhere, as long as I was in Lyonesse. Of course, once I'm here, I'm lost to them."

"You are?"

"Absolutely!" said Jim, with a strength that surprised him. He could not have said why he was so sure of that; but now that the words were out of his mouth, he had no doubt about the truth of them. No doubt at all.

"Then that would put a limit to what those Powers can do?"

"Yes," said Jim, with the same surprising certainty. "They found me at Malencontri only by following you to me."

"But you had had to do with them several times before. Surely they knew where was your castle?"

"I think," said Jim, choosing his words slowly, "that just as your ways in the Drowned Land are not the ways of Brian in the land above, so there are differences between people like us, and forces like these Dark ones. For one thing, I don't think they *see* the way we do. Earth and sky, tree, Creatures and humans—could be to Them only parts of a general swirl of energy—like the flames of a fire . . . or something like that—"

He broke off. On this he was no longer sure. He had let

Dafydd's questioning run away with his thoughts; and begun to talk about possibilities beyond what their medieval minds could imagine—he could see it in the faces of Brian and Dafydd because he knew them so well. Even the QB, he saw, had his snake's head cocked curiously on one side—saying nothing, watching him.

"But let's talk about your problem, Dafydd," Jim said. "It must be tied into ours, or else the Old Magic, or whatever, wouldn't have brought us here. You wanted to get this interview over quickly. We and you may be two parts of a puzzle that fit together, but we won't know until both of us have both parts. How does the threat—whatever it is—against the King tie in with the business of the gathering in the Borderlands?"

But he had delayed just a little too long. There was a sudden, alarmed shout from outside the tent, and a second later ugly, short, tearing noises, as things began to come through its cloth walls.

Jim, Brian, and Dafydd hit the earth floor of the tent at the same moment. The QB and Hob stayed upright, looking wonderingly about them.

The noises stopped. They had actually only sounded for a moment. Dafydd was immediately back on his feet, Jim and Brian only an instant behind him. Dafydd wrenched what looked like a short, thick arrow out of the tabletop.

"Quarrel!" he said grimly. "There are no crossbows in the Drowned Land—not the Drowned Land as we know it!"

He threw the shaft flat on the table, turned, and ran out through the entrance of the tent. Once again, Jim and Brian were right behind him and caught up with him as they went.

Outside, where the group of men had stood, two men lay on the ground. Another five stood upright, being bandaged by those around them. Some quarrels were sticking at an angle in the ground. But Dafydd ignored all this. It was at another small group, so tightly clustered about someone else that it was impossible to see, that he looked; and it was toward this group he ran.

"Is the lad hit?" he shouted as he went. "Is he hurt?"

Faces turned toward him, but he was breaking into their midst, with Jim and Brian following, before they had time to answer. Sure enough, the boy-King was on the ground, motionless, eyes closed; with one man in brown kneeling over him, pressing gently on his chest as if to invite him to breathe. He raised his pale face as Dafydd and Jim reached him. It was Gruffydd, the visitor from the Sea-Purple.

"There is no wound on him," he said. "But he breathes not; and I cannot hear his heart."

"Let me at him," said Jim. "I have wisdom with wounds."

"Sir James is a magickian, Gruffydd!" said Dafydd harshly. "Up, and stand aside."

Reluctantly, the brown-clad Leader of the Sea-Purple rose from his knees, his face dark now, and his lips pressed close together as he looked at Jim. He looked again at Dafydd.

Chapter 20

The Sea-Purple's Leader, now on his feet, took no more than half a step backward; not enough to give Jim room by the still figure.

"I'm just trying to help," said Jim to him in English, suddenly forced to remember what he had acquired by magic had been only an understanding of the Drowned Land language when others used it—not the voice-training to speak it.

Dafydd translated. Grudgingly, the man took another step back. Dismissing him from his mind, Jim knelt beside the boy. He felt for a pulse in one lax wrist.

There was none.

"None of the short arrows hit him," said a tall man in blue above Jim's head to Dafydd in the Drowned Land tongue. "It may be he has only swooned."

Jim held his palm over the King's mouth to feel for any warmth or moistness of exhaled air that would signal the lad was breathing. There was none.

He rolled back an eyelid, then the other one. The pupils underneath looked perfectly normal; neither was enlarged, or bulged outward. According to what Jim remembered of his first aid, the pupil of a dead person would be expanded to its full size, the muscles completely relaxed in death. If just one pupil had been enlarged and the other not, then the opposite side of the body could have been damaged. But neither eye showed as anything but normal.

Just to make sure, Jim reached down to pinch the inside of the left thigh of the King. The right eye reacted. Good, that was as it should be. Holding the eyes open, Jim turned the head to let the sun of the Drowned Land fall full upon them. The pupils shrank.

He sighed silently with relief. The boy was certainly not dead. But whether Jim could bring him out of whatever had caused this condition was another question.

He looked up at Dafydd.

"I think I can make him well," Jim said. "I have to try, because I think he has been attacked with magic; and the longer the magic is with him, the more damage it'll do to him. So I'll do my best; but your people'll have to understand I can't promise they'll see him completely well again."

Dafydd rattled off a small torrent of harsh words at those standing around. There was a moment of silence, and then an answering murmur of approval.

"How can we be sure—" Gruffydd began at the top of his voice; but the murmur rose in volume and became menacing. Those who had moved back from him earlier now began to move in to form a tight, inescapable ring around him. He drew himself up, looking back at them scornfully.

"James," said Dafydd, "do not hesitate, for the love of God!"

Jim was staring at the motionless young King. There was, as the man in blue had said, no sign of a wound. But a sudden suspicion woke in his mind.

He lifted his head and turned it. Taking advantage of the fact that most of those around him should not understand English, he snapped at Dafydd in that language.

"No one's to move!" he said. "Everyone stand still, just as they are. Then every one look about them for something the size of a small stick—not just some stray twig, but something shaped purposefully. It's most probably on the ground. But it may be hard to see, so look closely. Anyone finding something like that, bring it to me. Everyone else stay exactly where you are until I say you can move!"

A light weight landed on Jim's left shoulder.

"My Lord! Can I help find it? I'm good at finding things!"

"No, you can't, Hob," said Jim under his breath. "Get back under cover on the sumpter horse."

"Pray, m'Lord, can't I stay with you? Pray—"

"All right," muttered Jim. "But don't say or do anything unless I tell you to."

Dafydd was still passing on Jim's instructions, in a voice hard with authority. There was no sound for a moment, then a sudden grunt of pain from one of the men in green, standing to Jim's left and about twelve feet away.

"I've got something!" he called in the Drowned Land tongue.

"Bring it to me," said Jim.

Dafydd translated. The man walked to Jim, gingerly holding what looked like the back half of a quarrel, a broken shaft with only two feathers still showing on it. He carried it delicately by one of the feathers, between two fingers of his left hand. The fingers of his other hand were held out as if to be cooled by the air of his movement.

"I did not think it could be what was sought," he said to Dafydd, as he held out the stick to Jim. "But I picked it up, thinking it strange that it had broken so, and wondering where the rest of it was—"

"Lay it down on the ground beside me," said Jim, without waiting to hear the last words, or Dafydd's translation of the whole. "Carefully, now!"

Dafydd passed on the instruction. The man carefully laid the broken shaft down not more than six inches from Jim's right foot. Jim picked it up carefully by the same feather the man had been holding, and let it dangle from his fingers.

Something like the tingle of a mild electric current touched the fingers. Carefully, Jim took hold of the feather with the thumb and forefinger of his other hand and slid the original two holding fingers down the feather closer toward the shaft. Immediately, the tingle surged upwards in strength to become a burning pain.

"Warded!" said Jim, with grim satisfaction. "It's all right, the rest of you. You can move around now."

The tone of his voice was enough, even without Dafydd's translation. There was no movement, but a faint wave of relaxation that went through all those standing closely about; and something like a sigh of relief.

Jim turned to Dafydd.

"This stick was prepared ahead of time," he said. "It was magicked; and the magic was protected by a ward. It did not come here through the air. Someone here struck the King with it when the quarrels started falling. Who was standing closest to the boy?"

There was no answer. But a small, almost noiseless movement went through the men standing about, like a ripple on the surface of a pond; and everyone had moved away again slightly, so there was now a little space around Gruffydd.

"Here," said Jim in English, holding the piece of wood by its feathers and extending its further end toward Gruffydd.

"Take it!" said Dafydd harshly in the Drowned Land language.

"I will not," said Gruffydd. "Am I to obey the whim of any Saxon?"

"You will obey me," said Dafydd.

"Not even my Lord King, if he were so speaking," said Gruffydd, throwing back his long, brown hair in a wild, fierce movement, to stare up into Dafydd's face. "Who in any case is yet to be agreed upon by all the Colors, as our law demands!"

"Take it!" said Dafydd. "Or is it that you dare not?"

"Dare?" shouted Gruffydd. "I dare anything!"

He snatched the quarrel end from Jim, wrapping his hand around the shaft. Jim knew the others standing about could not be aware that the man was doing the equivalent of grasping a red-hot shaft of iron; but not as much as the twitch of a muscle in his face gave away the fact.

"Here, take it!" Gruffydd extended the shaft to Jim; but Jim had already gone back a step and was out of reach.

"Keep holding it a while longer," he said in a level voice. "It'll burn to the bones in a moment or two; and then you'll have nothing left but a claw for a hand."

The threat of being made one-handed got the result for which Jim had hoped. Gruffydd threw the stick at him; and as he did, his self-control broke. He grunted, waving the hand that had held the stick in the air, as if to cool it. A dark line could be seen running across his palm.

Once again, it was only Jim there who saw the mark as confirmation of what he had suspected. That line—very like a burn—was Gruffydd's body's reaction to the magic that was still animating the stick.

It was not for nothing Jim had been an AAA-rated volleyball player in the future from which he had come. With only a few feet between himself and the Sea-Purple Leader, he still easily sidestepped the thrown stick and caught it with his right thumb and forefinger, grasping one of the flight feathers, holding it harmlessly as he had before.

"Dafydd," he said, "tell them what I say."

"I will do that," said Dafydd.

"This I hold," said Jim, raising his voice, "is not the broken-off back of a crossbow shaft it seems. Let any man who doubts that try to find the front end of it, on or in the ground here. It is a made thing, touched with special magic, so that it may be safely held a certain way, to kill or make unconscious anyone touched with the broken end of it. Your King has been touched with it, none noticing, as the crossbow quarrels came down upon you. It is magic that has made him as he is now—but it may be magic that can be driven off. I'll try!"

He dropped onto his own knees beside the unmoving King. He still had the stick in his hand, held by one feather; and he looked at it closely.

He could safely open his ward to use his personal magic. That was no problem here. On the other hand, on their last trip through here to Gnarlyland, his magic had not worked. But—he remembered suddenly, that was before KinetetE sent him back down with her own double ward.

So, there was a way around the magic limitation, he knew now. He could envelope the boy with him *inside* his double ward—and work all his art within the special enclosure that made possible. No, getting the magic and the boy together was not the real problem. The problem was which way to cure the young King.

The obvious way was to strip it from him, as Morgan le Fay had intended to strip Jim's magic from him—if KinetetE had not booby-trapped his ward against anyone trying exactly that. This that held the King in thrall might well be booby-trapped, too; and the trap could be deadly. It could be a killing trap of the sort that could only be used in offense—that type of use which the Collegiate of Magickians, to which Carolinus and KinetetE belonged, had agreed never to use.

He could try to direct the magic elsewhere—but that meant he would be responsible for using its power offensively, if it did turn out to be a killer. He wondered why it had not killed the boy. Obviously, it must have been deliberately designed not to—but he could inquire into the why of that later.

A weighty, additional problem was that if he did any of these things that helped the King magically, whoever had designed this piece of wood to do its work would have to know another magician had countered it—and that this other magician had to be loose now in the Drowned Land.

Only as long as he did not use magic outside himself here would he be invisible to someone like Morgan le Fay. She would have to physically come, herself, into the Drowned Land, to use her magic against him, of course—but there was nothing to stop her doing that. The QB might have been doubtful if any of the legendary figures from Lyonesse could go on existing outside it; but Morgan would be under no such delusion. If she did come . . . magic for magic, she would be like a heavy warship compared to him as a weekend pleasure boat.

But how could he possibly remove magic from the boy without using magic? It was an impossibility—

No, it wasn't. His racing mind had stumbled over the answer and almost passed on without recognizing it. There was just the shadow of a possibility . . .

He had touched the King already to examine him; and nothing had happened. So the boy's body was safe to handle. He looked around himself and saw, at about fifty yards of distance, a grove of what looked like oak trees.

"Dafydd," he said, "can we carry the King carefully over to the nearest of those trees? I want one with a thick trunk."

"Yes," answered Dafydd; and switched to the Drowned Land tongue, calling to the crowd.

"My cousins! I need your help! Three of you—William, Thomas, and Rhys!"

Three of the tall men in sky-blue with bows on their shoulders came forward. Dafydd explained; and they, with him, picked up the lax figure and followed Jim. The rest of the crowd trailed behind.

Jim led them all to the largest tree trunk he could see.

"Put his Majesty down, sitting with his back against the tree," he said to Dafydd.

They did so. Happily, there was a space between two large exposed roots for the lad's hips to fit; so that he actually sat at a small distance from the trunk, and only his upper back and head leaned against it. The tree was broad enough so that his head did not roll back around either side of it. He held his position, once they had put him there.

Dafydd, however, hovered nearby in case the unconscious body should slip. The three men who had helped to carry the boy backed off; and the crowd that had been following formed a circle at a respectful distance from any magic that might be about to happen.

"It's all right, Dafydd," Jim said. "You can stand by if you want, but you'd better back off a few feet. The King won't slip. I'll use magic if necessary to keep him as he is."

Dafydd took two steps back.

"My Lord," whispered a small voice in Jim's left ear. "My Lord, can I—"

"Just sit tight," said Jim, almost voicelessly. "I'll have something for you to do in a minute."

Jim stepped a quarter of the way around the tree from the young King. Then he moved to the tree and put his arms as far as they would go in both directions around it, and laid his cheek against its rough bark. It seemed to him that, like the tree he had hugged in the Forest Dedale, there was a warmth and friendliness to the touch of the rough bark.

Turning his face away from those who watched the King, he thought the words he wanted to say but dared not risk saying out loud. There was one other way he might manage—a way the tree should hear, but not the people standing close by. He could feel the movement in his vocal cords as he tried it, subvocalizing his message.

"Dear tree," he subvocalized, "can you help this lad sitting against you? Or can you get in touch with the trees of Lyonesse and see if they can't take away whatever magic has him unconscious now? I think it is part of the alien magic that is trying to take over the land of Lyonesse, and now troubles matters here. I know the trees of Lyonesse are willing to help. Will you? I can't do it myself, or I would; and I'm afraid that if the magic isn't taken off him, his unconsciousness will give way to death."

He stopped. He could not hear or sense any response from the tree.

"Hob," he whispered out of the corner of his mouth. "Did the tree hear? Did you hear it say anything to me?"

"Oh yes, my Lord. It said the boy wouldn't die, but he would not wake up, either. That would mean the leaders of the Colors would have to choose someone else for King. No one, not even the man in brown you made hold the magick stick, dares to actually kill a king. But unless rescued, the boy will sleep forevermore; and there is no hope for the Drowned Land under a wrong king."

It was a long speech for Hob, Jim thought, even as he was turning the information over in his head.

"But will the tree—this tree, or the trees of the Drowned Land in general—help?" he asked finally.

"This tree says so, m'Lord—I mean, my Lord. Pray pardon for not telling you that first. This tree's going to take the magick holding the boy and push it out through every leaf, twig, or branch end it's got. He says any tree can do that much. Then the magick'll be split up into lots and lots of small parts, so that none of them will be big enough for whoever sent it to find; and many too many to be put together again. So no one can find how it never worked."

"Excellent!" said Jim, hugging the tree in sheer happiness. Then he let go of the trunk. "But why didn't I hear the tree say that? I heard the one in Lyonesse."

"The Lyonesse trees talk in a different place from the ones here—or back home."

"Place?" said Jim. "Place?"

"Yes—" Hob hopped off Jim's shoulder to stand remarkably balanced on a wartlike bulge of the tree trunk level with Jim's eyes. He held his two hands flat, palm to palm, one above the other, with their fingers parallel but with a space between them. Then he passed the two hands back and forth on their different levels, still one above the other.

"See, m'Lord?" he said. "When a tree in Lyonesse tries to talk to a tree in the Drowned Land, they miss each other. Neither one can hear the other. They miss."

Jim stared for a long moment. Then, suddenly, it made sense.

"You mean—they're on different wavelengths!"

"Wave? Oh no, m'Lord, it's just in the air, not on the water."

"Never mind," said Jim. There might be time later for him to work out a means of bringing the trees of the two countries to a single wavelength—or at least finding a magical way for him to hear any tree, anywhere. The important thing right now was to bring the King back to consciousness.

He embraced the tree again.

"Thank you, tree," he told it. "Will you do that, then?"

There was a sound like the faintest of rustling of the tree's leaves, though no breeze had come up to break the stillness of the warm air. The boy sitting against the tree opened his eyes slowly, stared about him, and then jumped to his feet before Dafydd could reach out an arm to stop him.

"What is this?" said the King. "One moment we are under attack, then we are—what happened?"

"My King," said Dafydd, dropping to one knee in front of him. "God be praised. You are restored and well!"

"Of course I am well! Why should I not be? I asked what had happened? Rise, Dafydd; and answer me!"

"You will learn all, my Lord King," said Dafydd, rising to his feet with his face darkening. He shouted over his shoulder to the cluster of men in their different colors, behind him. "Seize Gruffydd ap Howel and bring him here!"

There was a stir among the men, a stir that prolonged itself and finally, shamefacedly, settled into stillness. Gruffydd was not among them. He was nowhere to be found.

Chapter 21

Strangely, no one had missed him, let alone noticed his disappearance. Each of those in the group who had followed Jim to the tree, it turned out, had been thinking someone else would be keeping an eye on Gruffydd, while they looked for the magicked stick and then for the health of their king. But none had.

"As Aargh would tell us," said Dafydd grimly, "a cold trail. There will be no way to follow Gruffydd's going—or trace that tainted quarrel-piece back from where it came."

He looked at Jim.

"Unless magick can help us, Sir James?"

"I doubt it," said Jim. "I'll try to think about ways; but I don't know Gruffydd well enough to find him just from my memory of seeing him here."

The answer was a form of half-truth. The full reason was that the object or person to be found had to be *visualized* by the magician. Well enough with someone you had met and got to know to some extent. But Jim, who had been preoccupied with the matter of saving the young king, had only a general impression of a man, shorter than most in this land, with long hair and wearing brown clothing.

The tall leader in green, who had been the first to object to a welcome for Jim and those with him, came forward and dropped on one knee before the youngster.

"Sire," he said, "the life of our King is a sacred life, not even to be threatened. Of your grace grant me pardon for speaking against these strangers, one of whom has now saved you for us. I own my error of judgment and I entreat your forgiveness for that I doubted your Regent."

"There is nothing to forgive, Llewelyn," said the boy, now on his feet. "I know you spoke so from care for me. Rise!"

The man rose and stepped to Dafydd. Dafydd's right hand caught him by the elbow and held him up as he started to descend again.

"Leaders do not kneel to Leaders, Llewelyn," he said. "And the Regency is a temporary title. You spoke like an honest man and a fair one. I have forgotten what words you used, other than that."

"I will speak for the Greens, then," the man said. "We will trust these you have brought here as you do; and we will follow you as you may lead from now on, without further question. Let others say what they may."

But there arose a chorus of voices, as men in one Color or another pushed themselves to the front of the crowd to endorse what Llewelyn had said, for their own Colors.

"Then," said Dafydd, looking at the boy, "if our King agrees, there is no reason we should not continue our talk out here with all listening—unless there are still some who doubt the honesty of our visitors?"

No one spoke.

"Damndest chatter-chatter I ever heard!" muttered Brian in Jim's ear, once more obviously irked by the fact he could not understand the tongue of the Drowned Land. "All jostling together to do service—and one of them just magicked their king. Who's to say there's not another like him still among them? What's to keep one of them from lying about his feelings and running off to tell their enemies every word we say here?"

"Shh," said Jim, embarrassed. Brian's grumble in English was too low-pitched for anyone else to make out the words—even the King and Dafydd, who could have understood them. But the fact he had said something in Jim's ear was obvious to everybody. "Dafydd told you they do things differently here."

"Cut their own throats differently—" Brian closed his mouth. Happily, no one in the mass of faces Jim was looking at seemed to have suspected offense.

Dafydd's ears, however, may have been sharper than the others. He turned to Jim and Brian.

"How are your wishes in this, then, Sir Brian, Sir James, QB?"

The QB graciously fielded the fact of finding himself among those to be consulted.

"It may well all be for the best," he said.

"I wish us to find these people who may have been moving into your Borderland—find and deal with them!" said Brian.

"As long as we three aren't expected to make any firm commitments," said Jim, "I think that's probably the next order of business. We don't want to be bound, though, in case something unexpected arises."

"Sire, you will allow us then?"

"Oh, certainly. Certainly, Dafydd. As our forefathers would have done it."

"Then let the table in the tent be brought out here, so that our King and visitors may sit in your midst."

The first half-dozen men to reach the entrance to the tent disappeared within. The rest stood back. In moments, the King, Dafydd, and the visitors were seated all on one side of the table under the bright sun, with an audience of the men of Colors seated cross-legged on the ground in a semicircle before it. Those at the table spoke in English, their words translated by Dafydd for the men who did not understand.

"Sir James," Dafydd said now, "you, a magickian as well as a knight, have just seen what came upon us here. Magick is something of which our land has always been free; nor do we wish it now. What can such as we do against such as just struck down our King?"

Jim looked at the earnestly gazing faces of the men on the ground.

"To tell the truth," he said, "I don't know what you can do. It seems plain enough that, however the Dark Powers plan to gain control of Lyonesse, Their plan seems to involve the Drowned Land, too. But I can't think why They want to take you over—it doesn't make sense. Lyonesse is different. The Dark Powers are magic forces; and of course, Lyonesse is full of magic—so like might draw to like. There might be a connection there. No offense to you, QB—"

He glanced at the QB, beside him at the table, sitting on the ground with his snake-head well above its top.

"I do not take offense easily, Sir James," the QB answered, his tongue flicking out for a moment, startlingly thin and black in the bright, yellow sunlight. "But are you sure you cannot think of a reason these Powers and Their invaders would have to concern themselves with this land as well as my own?"

"Well, there's one—only one—" said Jim. "There's no Chance or History in Lyonesse. Its mold is set; and time, except for its minute-to-minute aspect, doesn't seem to exist. In other words, History is not moving forward there. But the Drowned Land has both History and Chance. Its own version of it, of course, compared to that in the land above—but History and Chance, nonetheless; and the Dark Powers exist for the destruction of either one of those two elements, wherever They can do that."

"But how—" began the young King.

"I don't know," said Jim. "It's a far-fetched bit of reasoning, but the best I can do right now. It could be the Powers are just using the Drowned Land because it's conveniently here for what they want to do. Didn't you and the QB tell me, Dafydd, that the Borderland could hold their invasion force?''

''Perhaps, James,'' said Brian unexpectedly, ''you might explain why Chance and History are so important to the Dark Powers. I swear England is full of gentlemen and ladies—not to mention those who swink and sweat all their lives for their living—who have never given a thought to either one. Must say it took me a little time to get my wits around it, myself!''

''Indeed! I think that a good idea of Sir Brian, Sir James,'' said Dafydd. ''Would you tell us, then?''

Jim looked across the table and around at the waiting, hopeful faces. How to explain the Dark Powers?

''I can't, really,'' he said. ''I don't understand them myself.''

Dafydd translated. Jim went on. The light of hope began to die in those he watched. Magicians were supposed to have answers.

''The best I can do,'' he said, ''is tell you what my Master-in-Magick''—he did his best this time to pronounce the word as those here said it—''told me of the Dark Powers. My Master's name is Carolinus, and he's one of the three most powerful magicians in the land above. Would you want to hear that?''

''Speak of it anyway in your own words, Sir James,'' said the King in English; and a few heads nodded in the half circle before them—obviously belonging to those who knew enough English to follow the talk so far—even as Dafydd translated for the others.

Jim looked at the half circle of faces, watching and waiting to hear what he would say. For a moment, in their stillness and unvarying attention, they reminded him of children—no, not children. Perhaps actors playing the parts of obedient children.

Perhaps they were indeed playing a part, he told himself. A part in a life-play of some kind. For a moment Jim found himself caught up in a dizzying sensation of unreality. Colors, Leaders, a sunlit land hundreds or thousands of feet under the ocean surface—another land of legend and magic, but like the first, one where people lived and could die. Talking trees, Old Magic, Dark Powers, Witch Queens . . .

His mind spun. Reality and unreality were all mixed up. For the first time since he and Angie had come to this world, Jim felt a piercing homesickness for the century of their birth. A time when there was no magic or strange powers, no archaic loyalties, obligations, and ways. He felt as if caught up in a whirlwind with nothing stable around him.

He longed for Angie. Once back with her, even this world would have a firm point—all else would fall into order. Safe within himself, protected by his ward, he had the magic to return to her in a moment. He could be back with her at Malencontri in no time at all.

But these were real people he would be leaving to their fate; and two—no, three, counting the QB now, were his friends. Still, the temptation to do so was almost a physical force taking over his body.

"What Carolinus told me was that the Dark Powers seek to either hold History back until it is motionless—in which case, all things stop; and what stops, eventually, dies—or to keep enlarging Chance until there is no more certainty in the world—when Chaos would rule: bits of earth, water, buildings, everything, mixed up and flying mindlessly through the air together, evermore—in which case there would be nothing left to live for; and therefore all people would have reached their end."

He could not bring himself to do it. A sense of duty as ancient as the land that surrounded him now—duties of friendship to Brian and Dafydd, even obligation to the QB, and the cantankerous, willful old man who was Carolinus—all these stopped him.

He paused. They were listening now—they were actually listening closely as Dafydd translated.

"So," he finished, "the Dark Powers must be opposed in all They do, if we wish to survive and progress. That is a duty on all men and women—and, indeed, it's the duty that brings Sir Brian, the QB, and me to you now. It does not matter who the Dark Powers attack, or where. Their attack has to be stopped each time.''

He finished speaking, and Dafydd's translation, which had almost been keeping pace with his words, ended also. Jim waited for someone to say something. But no one did. After some long seconds it dawned on him that somehow he had reached them. He had touched them. In some way, across the double barrier that was the difference in their lives from his, their language from his, they had come to feel the reality and dangerousness of the Dark Powers.

''Is there no defeating these Dark Powers for good, then, Sir James? Killing them, mayhap?'' said the King, at last.

''No, Sire,'' said Jim, ''because in a way They're''—he caught himself just about to say *''a product of the environment''*—''offspring of the natural battle between History and Chance. We humans are always trying to mark our History on time. A wise man once said, 'For every action there is an equal and opposite reaction.' Chaos is the reaction to History.''

The King frowned, trying to absorb this.

''Then, what can we do?''

''Try to stop them whenever they try to interfere with our lives, Sire. The Collegiate of Magickians in the land above, which I mentioned, has had some luck in backing certain people to oppose those men and women the Dark Powers use, to try to make the changes They want.''

''But how do we find such men and women?''

''They have to be here, somewhere, in the Drowned Land and in Lyonesse, since both lands are under the shadow of the Powers. They must be found, that's all.''

''But, again, how?''

''This is what Sir Brian, the QB, and I came here to try and find a way to do. The first step's to find out who the Powers are working through. One might be Morgan le Fay, a Witch Queen in Lyonesse. But who are they working through here—if they're actually working here as well?''

''That broken quarrel piece was magick,'' said the King. ''What more proof do we need?''

"And as for one working for them here," said Dafydd, "when I became Regent, I was told by our people that Morgan le Fay paid our land a visit but five weeks past."

"She did?" said the QB—it was the first time Jim had heard him sounding startled. Even their sudden, surprised appearance here in the Drowned Land had not brought that note to his sibilant voice.

The young King had looked quickly at Dafydd.

"I was not told!" he said.

"It was before your father's death; but when he was already into his last sickness. There seemed no reason then to disturb you with word of it. But clearly, from what Sir James says, our people and those of Lyonesse must help each other now—if those stiff necks in Lyonesse will allow help from us."

"I will speak to them. I am as much a king as any king among them."

"Perhaps, Sire, that might be good," said Dafydd. "But I would wish to look for other ways first. Sir James, Sir Brian, my Lord QB, have you any suggestions?"

Neither Brian nor the QB spoke.

"I think we can all make guesses," said Jim. "But it's not smart making decisions on guesses. Someone else besides Morgan le Fay could be an unwitting tool of the Dark Powers—it could be another person or persons completely. We need to find out all we can about the situation before heading in any particular direction. What was it, said just now, about the Borderlands; and about monsters and strangers there? Sir Brian and I—and the Lord QB if he will—had better go take a look at it."

Dafydd, who had continued to translate the English of this conversation for the benefit of those beyond the table, broke back into English.

"If you go there, I must needs go with you," he said—"with my King's permission, of course."

"You have it, Dafydd," said the King; and himself repeated Dafydd's request and his agreement to it to the audience in their own tongue.

"Thank you, my Lord King," said Dafydd in English.

The seated men rose and began to form in line—a line that was still stretching out even as the first of them came to one knee, as close before the King as the width of the table would allow. Dafydd spoke to them directly, almost harshly, in their own language.

"What was that now?" growled Brian into Jim's left ear. "What did he say?" For the line was now formed and the King was rising to lean forward across the table to a man in green, the first man to kneel before him.

"He said, *'You will keep and protect him as if I was here to tell you to!'* " Jim answered, suddenly realizing he had forgotten Brian was not understanding anything not said in English.

"That would be well," Brian said.

"—But he had to get the King's permission. The King gave it; but that meant he'd be doing without his Regent. Dafydd was just telling the others to watch out for the boy as if he was still there."

"Ah. What are they up to now, then?" The youthful King was stretching to reach across the not-narrow width of the table, to place his hand on the shoulder of the kneeling man—who then gave up his place to the man behind him. Much as Jim and Brian had seen in a similar situation during their earlier trip through the Drowned Land, the King was laying his hand for an instant not merely on the shoulder, but the head of each one.

"Some ceremony?"

"I think they're all pledging their loyalty personally—and possibly that of all those who wear the same Color—to him while Dafydd is gone."

"Very well. Properly done, then."

"You did hear the King say that Dafydd could go with us to the Borderland?"

"Of course!" There was a note of relief in Brian's tone now. "And I approve. A wise decision. Dafydd will be much more useful with us than nursemaiding that boy." Brian broke off on a sudden note of worry. "James, you don't suppose his Majesty could change his mind now?"

"No, not after this ceremony."

"Well, that's a relief. The King is a good lad, but still young; and these foreigners, you know—"

"Sir James, Sir Brian, QB," said the King to them, "Dafydd"—he reeled off the Drowned Land's unpronounceable—for Englishmen—rest of Dafydd's full name and title down here, *Prince of the Sea-Washed Mountains*—"will go with you to the Borderland, or where else you four may need to go. Keep good care of yourself for my sake, Dafydd."

"I will, my King," said Dafydd, kneeling to be touched on his head, in turn.

He stood up once more; suddenly again the tall woodsman and Master Bowman they had known in all their time before. "I will need to guide you. Let us go."

They mounted their horses and followed Dafydd—who was on foot—away from the tent and all those there, up the slope of a green hill in the near distance. They had ridden off at a walk. But as they reached the top of the hill, a thunder of hooves sounded behind them; and there was the tall man with the graying beard, riding up to them with a led horse, the reins of which he gave to Dafydd.

"Thank you, Llewelyn," said Dafydd, mounting. The other lifted his hand briefly in something between a wave and a twentieth-century-style salute, turned his own mount, and thundered away at full gallop back down the slope.

"They must break a lot of necks here, men and horses both," said Brian, but without any real rancor in his voice, as they reined in for a moment to wait for Dafydd. "By God, they can ride, though!"

"Our first horses were stolen from the Romans," said Dafydd, reaching them in time to pick up the words. They all moved on. "But we bred them lighter and faster; and we made our own way of riding."

"Is it far to the Borderland from where we were?" asked the QB.

They had all but forgotten him. But there he was beside

them, loping along as if he could keep up the pace all day.

''Just beyond the next hill,'' said Dafydd.

''It was in my mind to move us all there swiftly by means of the magick I own—but I remember now that, not being in Lyonesse, I do not have it here. Why do you not use Drowned Land magick to move us there quickly?''

''No,'' said Dafydd. ''There is no magick in the Drowned Land—or was not until today with Gruffydd and our King. Even the word is not one in good repute among us. Nor was I ever, or wished to be, a magickian. No, the King and I set our meeting place back there close to the edge of the Borderland for reason.''

''Hah!'' said Brian with satisfaction—he, as Jim knew, being the kind of person who wanted all things done for a definite reason, if they were to be done at all.

''Yes. It was in our minds, if everything else failed to make agreement among the Leaders—he and I might decide to enter the Borderland to see what was now to be found there. Those with us of the Colors could never have let us go alone, for shame. Then might we all have seen. It was a happy chance indeed, James, that you suggested we three—crave pardon, QB—we four should go alone; since that was our aim in any case.''

While they were talking, they had gone down into what was only a fold in the hills, and were halfway up the slope beyond. Within minutes they had reached the top of what Dafydd had called the ''next'' hill; and they looked down on an open hillside giving way to a forest as inviting as any Jim had seen in the Drowned Land, where the landscape as a whole was inviting.

But as they halted their horses at the top of the hill to let them breathe—and without making a particular point of it, let the QB himself catch his breath, in case he also needed it—it was only then that Jim, gazing at the trees—which here were elms, rather than oaks—and the greensward visible before and between them, got a feeling, a very definite feeling, of uneasiness.

Chapter 22

"Do any of you feel anything?" Jim asked the rest of them.

"No," said Brian. "Though I would say it is not the merriest ground in the world, ahead there—couldn't say why, though."

"Ware!" said the QB. "I feel it also—" And almost in the same instant Hob cried out.

"Ware, m'Lord! Ware! The trees are calling *'Ware'* to us!"

"Back!" said Brian, wheeling Blanchard. Jim turned Gorp sharply about; and they all galloped back down the slope they had just come up. The moment they were completely below the brow of the hill, the feeling disappeared.

Brian reined in. They all stopped.

"The edge between my land and Lyonesse moves back and forth sometimes in the Borderland," said Dafydd. "But I have never known it to be this far into ground that is ours. For this must be magick, unless—"

He broke off and looked at Jim.

"It's magic," said Jim grimly.

"The small one has it," said the QB. "It is the trees here giving warning; and since they do not know me in this land, it must be to the little one or you the warning comes."

"I wish I could hear them," said Jim. "I learned to hear the Gnarlies and the horses. I ought to be able—"

"It may never be that easy for you," said the QB. "The Gnarlies are Naturals, which are closer to you than trees. I am not learned in magick, nor am I gifted like Merlin, or even the Witch Queens. I only hear the trees and the animals because the Old Magic or the Legends made it so."

"Well, we cannot sit here all day through, talking about it," said Brian. "James, do we go forward, or not?"

"Forward," said Jim. He found his jaws were clenched tight. "If there's magic ahead, let me deal with it."

He made his jaw unclench as they went back up the slope and then down its farther side, toward the first few trees. These stood more or less in a row across the edge of the clear ground; and there was some distance between them and the next trees, which were the more obvious beginnings of the forest. The feeling of uneasiness grew as they went, until they reached level ground, now only twenty-five or thirty yards from the nearest trees. Then it held steady.

Jim led the way straight ahead, between the two largest trunks in the front row. The sun was at his back, and so the grass beyond those first trees was darker and more indistinct. No one said anything, no breeze stirred the leaves overhead. They rode in silence, and Gorp suddenly tossed his head, as if he found the bridle bit in his mouth uncomfortable.

It was only when the next step of Blanchard, who was leading, would have carried them on between these first sentinel trees that Dafydd stepped out from behind the thick trunk of the tall elm on their right.

The horses stopped immediately, without reins being touched. If Dafydd had not been beside him at that moment, Jim would have found it almost impossible to believe that the figure just before him was not the Prince-bowman he knew.

The new Dafydd said nothing. He only turned and swept out an arm, as if unveiling the space behind the trees—and as they all looked where he indicated, the ground there sagged, broke, and opened into a chasm across their way, its ends cutting a deep rift in the earth that ran away between the trees on either hand, out of sight.

The edge of this rift that they could see fell steeply below view, showing earth with broken stone protruding—stone that as you looked deeper into the cleft became blacker and more black, and bulged and creased into shapes. Shapes like the upper halves of human bodies, their lower parts buried in the stone itself, shapes like gargoyles and part-human figures, spitted on sharp outthrusts of the stone.

But the rift itself went down and down into darkness.

"Even if that was not there," said the second Dafydd, "I

would not let you pass. You must kill me to go by here, and you cannot do that.''

His voice was eerily like Dafydd's in timbre and rhythm, but his speech was without living warmth, almost mechanical.

''Indeed?'' said Brian, and picked up his reins.

Dafydd—their Dafydd—thrust out a hand to stop the knight, but checked himself before he actually touched Brian's armored upper arm.

''No, Brian,'' he said, ''it must be me.''

''Wait a minute,'' said Jim. ''Let's none of us rush into this without thinking. This is nothing natural for the Drowned Land, is it, Dafydd?''

''No,'' said Dafydd. ''That is why it must be I who meets him. He is a blemish, a false thing and a false place, desecrating our land!''

''Hold on, Dafydd, Brian,'' said Jim. ''As you said, Dafydd, this is a false thing. It doesn't belong in this land of yours, where there's no magic—but plainly it is magic. Let's take a second or two and think about it.''

The other two were patiently still. So was the QB. So was Hob on Jim's shoulders—even the other Dafydd was silent, waiting. Jim studied him—or, rather, it. The fake Dafydd stood, utterly unmoving, perfectly mirroring the real man, with no change of expression, evidently content to wait as long as they did. The perfect duplication, Jim told himself, was not a matter of importance, as long as magic was obviously at work. Once again, as with the false river, he was face to face with what seemed to be a massive work of magic.

Jim's mind searched for some other difference, some possible giveaway mistake in what had appeared before them. He did not know what he was looking for; but he had a strong feeling that if he kept searching, he would discover something. But over the shoulder of the second Dafydd, he could see the bottomless rift as plainly as ever.

All that came to mind was the fact that the river had turned out not to be a massive magical construct after all; but largely an artifact, to be turned on and off like a water faucet. The same could be true here—because if what he was looking at was real, the amount of magical energy required to make it was all out of proportion to the need to bar the way further.

"Come with me," he said to the rest of them, turning Gorp. They rode back the way they had come, and after some hundred yards he reined in and looked back over his shoulder. His companions stopped and looked with him. The second Dafydd stood as he had, the empty, tortured darkness still deep behind him, and still barring their path.

"Mayhap we may ride around that hole in the ground," said Brian. "Though it would sit very ill with me to let that imposter go unpunished."

"We may not have to," said Jim. "Come along." He turned Gorp to his left and led off along the front of the trees. A glance over his shoulder showed the second Dafydd still there, behind them, smaller with distance but still seemingly on guard; and when he looked between the trees they were now passing, he saw the dark mouth of the rift extending parallel with their progress, still.

"Wait for me a moment."

He turned and rode directly for the nearest trees. As he got closer, he could look down into the rift and see the stone of its far side, with its bulges and indentations. They none of them clearly showed tormented human shapes, but they pulled at his feelings nonetheless, making him imagine more, the more he looked.

And suddenly the second Dafydd was there, standing in his way once more.

"Bingo!" said Jim softly to himself.

"My Lord?" asked Hob, behind his head.

"Nothing. Just thinking out loud. It's all right."

"Yes, m'—my Lord."

Jim rode back out to his waiting friends.

"I think I'm beginning to understand this," he said. "There's no use our trying to go around that whatever-he-is there"—he nodded at the imitation Dafydd behind them—"or that hole in the ground. But let's ride out a ways and then back the way we came. I've got an idea."

"I feel I should be of more use here, James," said Dafydd. "After all, it is my land now being disturbed."

"Don't think of it that way, Dafydd," said Jim. "This is something I'm the only one equipped to do something about. In a word, for the rest of you, it could kill you, but you couldn't kill it. Now, let's get back to where we first saw that thing that looks like you."

They rode back along the front of the trees. Once more, they left the false Dafydd standing behind them; and once more he was there when they got to their original position.

"And you, James?" said Brian, breaking the silence of that ride and crossing himself as they halted at last to face the Dafydd image again. "Can he not kill you?"

"Not unless I let him," said Jim.

The answer was designed to reassure the others, and to obscure the fact that he did not yet have a clear understanding of what they faced. But a bottomless crack in the earth, stretching as far as they might try to ride in either direction, was ridiculous, in terms of the magical expense it would represent. If it was the real thing.

The first thing he needed was a close look at the rift from a safe distance. He changed to his dragon-sight.

"James!" said Brian, sounding a little sick. "Your eyes—"

"It's all right," said Jim. "I've part-changed them into the eyes I have when I'm a dragon, so I can see better—no different than looking out a couple of windows."

"Damned ugly windows."

Jim ignored the comment. From his present distance he was closely watching the false Dafydd. The advantage of high-flying birds like the falcons, the eagles, and others was not so much that they saw things on the ground larger than a human would see them; it was that they were very much better at picking up movements—even very small movements—from very great heights. That was one reason many small animals tended to *freeze* when such a predator appeared overhead.

Now he kept his eyes on the false Dafydd, looking for any

kind of movement, even the slightest. There was none. The guarding figure stood like a carved statue.

"Ah!" he said in satisfaction, returning to his normal human vision. But this time he spoke carefully to himself. He was tempted to tell the others what he had in mind; but experience with the people of this time and world told him that once the word *magic* was uttered, their eyes glazed over and you might as well have sung a lullaby to them as tried to explain yourself—what he was saying was plainly something too mysterious for them to understand. So they didn't.

Besides, they would—or at least Brian and Dafydd would—disturb his concentration with their concern—spoken or unspoken—that whatever he had in mind wouldn't work. They were too used to being the ones to take care of him in more ordinary troubles and tight places; but this was something too massive and too much beyond their experience for them to understand.

Jim swung down out of his saddle.

"Stand!" he said to Gorp—unnecessarily. Gorp had finally learned to stand if his rider ever left him with his reins dropped to the ground.

"James!" said Brian sharply. "What are you intending?"

"Sir James!" said Dafydd—and the more formal address emphasized the sense of responsibility in him. "I said this was my land, my duty."

Jim waved them back as they both rode toward him.

"There's nothing to it," he said. "This is just something I've been equipped to do; and neither of you have. Hob, hop back onto Gorp's saddle, and wait for me there. That's an order!"

"I'm not afraid, my Lord."

"That's not the point. Sir Brian and Master Bowman Dafydd ap Hywel aren't afraid, either, but they, too, have to let me do this alone. Hop!"

Jim had already stepped a couple of paces from Gorp. Hob hesitated a second, then made one of his remarkable leaps across a good six feet of space from Jim to the saddle.

"Be right back," said Jim, waving his hand to them all again, as he turned his back and started off toward the false Dafydd and the dark rift beyond.

He did not walk straight at the Dafydd figure, but on a path to pass close by it. Nonetheless, the figure did not move as he came closer.

He came on steadily, but as his vision became filled by what was before him and his friends were left invisible behind, tension began to mount in him. He reminded himself that he was surrounded by his ward, and that ward could not be penetrated by anything unless he allowed it—that he was a living being; while he had a strong doubt that the Dafydd figure before him also was.

So if the figure and the rift were, as he had guessed, merely another ward, untenanted, set up and left—like Carolinus's ward that could protect his frail cottage, pond, and flowers from unlimited armies, even though Carolinus himself was not there—then within the armor of his own ward he must be safe against what was here.

But a conclusion was not a certainty. Particularly not a certainty in his guts. He could be wrong. If he was wrong . . . he felt his body start to stiffen and became aware that his right hand had crossed his waist to close upon the hilt of his sword. So much of the fourteenth century had now, after all, become a part of him.

If he *was* wrong, the sword would be no more use to him than his empty hand; but it was warming to the chill that was growing inside him, in spite of his magical knowledge and experience. The false Dafydd was three steps away from him—he was two steps away—he was one . . .

Jim turned his head to make himself look straight into the calm face of the figure as he passed by it, and saw it suddenly distort and collapse, as if it were made of water pouring under gravity—but a gravity beside it instead of beneath its feet—pouring into him; or rather into the ward around him.

And in that ward it was lost, swallowed up, disintegrated. He *felt* it happen—as he had bet on it happening.

His hand dropped from his sword. He had been right. He went forward toward the rift. That was the bigger gamble, the greater unknown.

The closer he came to it, the more he saw into it; and the more it sickened him to look at it. Close up, the bulges and hollows in the stone sides that had merely appeared human-like in shape, seemed more and more clearly so; like the shapes of actual people caught and overwhelmed by a flow of molten stone. The growing chill he had felt, approaching the false Dafydd, came back on him, but far more strongly; for to finish what he had set out to do, he would need to walk forward as if the rift was not there—eventually even stepping out into the emptiness of the air between its sides. To fall—where?

His mind told him that since the figure had proved to be false, there was no doubt the rift was, too; but his body sweated anyway, and his right fist was once more gripping his useless sword. There was still much he had to learn about this sort of magic.

But he was a man of the later centuries, he reminded himself; a man of reasoning mind and willpower. And with his mind he drove himself forward, on to the very lip of the rift with his left foot; and, with a powerful effort, out over nothing with his right one.

His right foot touched nothing solid.

There was no sound; but the universe seemed to scream voicelessly around him, as the walls of the rift began to flow up and up on either side of him. He was falling.

No! He was not! *It* was rising!

Up into his ward—up into the small unbreakable space surrounding him, was now pouring all the massive structure of the rift, being eaten up—engulfed—destroyed by the suit of magic armor that was the ward KinetetE had given him—what he had guessed was a more skilled version of the double ward in which he had smuggled his magic back into the Gnarly Kingdom. Bless KinetetE's magic. He should have had faith it would be stronger than anything a magic-maker of these lands could put against it. Or bless the Laws of Magic that had made what was happening possible.

—Or bless both.

It did not matter—but as he faced that fact, he became conscious that the knowledge that the rift was being destroyed by his ward, rather than his by the rift's, was becoming harder and harder to hold to. Exhaustion was growing in him from the great effort it took to disregard all the evidences of his senses and hold to what his mind knew.

"I'm standing still. The rift is moving—" he told himself. *You lie! You lie!* screamed his eyes and all the evidences of his physical responses. *You're falling! Falling—deeper and deeper. You're lost!*

He fought it. The sensitivities magic had begun to build in him, these last few years, told him he must fight it. If he gave in, if he let that inner voice triumph, the balance could shift and the ward of the rift would win back everything it had lost, and him as well. But his strength was going.

There was a pressure, a flow of energy so massive and continuous against him that he was being made bound and helpless by it. In that helplessness he felt himself unbalancing, as if he had been standing on one foot. He fell over on one side, stiffly, as a one-legged toy falls; and still the other ward poured into his. It was like being buried by a rising volcano. He had to hold on.

He reached for something to cling to—and his mind went to Angie. Angie was the one part here of the world they had both come from. She was real. She was part of a reality that had nothing to do with magic. Everything like that here was a dream or illusion. As long as he could see Angie in his mind, he told himself, the rift could not take him.

—And, suddenly, it was over.

He got up, still facing into the wood with his back to Brian and Dafydd, still on their horses. He was soaked in sweat and his body was trembling. It was an effort to keep standing, rather than simply collapse where he stood. But the rift was gone.

"Easy!" he ordered his body under his breath, making it

a magic command. "Stop sweating. Stop stinking!"

The body obeyed. He turned and walked slowly back toward the others. He thought they all, even the horses, looked at him strangely.

Chapter 23

"James—?" said Brian, the sharp blue eyes on either side of his falcon nose keen upon Jim.

"I'm fine!" said Jim shortly, feeling an unreasonable irritation—probably a hangover from his experience with the cleft. He took hold of Gorp's reins and saddle and started to mount. It was almost more than he had strength to do. Brian reached out an arm and helped him up.

A light weight landed on his shoulder.

"Are you hurt, m'Lord?"

"I'm fine, Hob!"

"Drink deeply!" said Brian, holding his own saddle flask to Jim's lips.

"I'm all right, I said!"

"Drink!"

Jim drank, almost choking on the volume of red wine Brian poured into him. He pushed the flask upright and away from him.

"That's fixed it," he said—for otherwise Brian would never leave him alone. His ever-filled flask was not only Brian's first aid prescription for any problem—it was the prescription of his historic time and place. "I'm all right now."

"Good red wine!" said Brian, on a note of satisfaction, driving the leather-clad wooden stopper back into the neck of the flask with the heel of his hand. "Just the thing for a sudden blow. It was a magical blow of some sort, was it not, James? We saw you pass the creature that looked like Dafydd and make him disappear, then you took a few more steps, stood in mid-stride for a moment to destroy the hole beyond, and then fell over. A magical blow, I said to myself, at once.

He's had a magical blow—God send it did not kill him! But it had not, thanks to Him—and will not thanks to the good red wine."

"Thank you, Brian."

"Hah!" said Brian, embarrassed. "Well, shall we ride on?"

"Yes," said Jim. It was remarkable. His mind was clear as a bell, though it might become a bit foggy when that wine, swallowed in one sustained gulp, caught up with him. "Unless Dafydd—it's his country. Dafydd, what do you think? Also, where are we in this Borderland of yours, because I assume we entered it once we passed those trees behind us."

"We did," said Dafydd, "and I find it hard to call it my country anymore, with such magicks and pitfalls in our way. Somewhere in it, though, are those responsible for such things; and it is well we have come to see who and what and where they are. We are a little above the middle of the Borderlands, which stretch the length of our border with Lyonesse. The cliff you know, that was the entrance to the Land of the Gnarly King, is near the south end of the Border, which is to our right. I suggest we go straight across here, try north first, then south until we find what strangers are with us."

"Cannot you find them by magick, James?" said Brian. "Some swifter way?"

"I don't think so," said Jim. "If I knew someone among them, maybe; but . . ."

He let the sentence trail off. There was really nothing more to say.

"M'Lord—my Lord, I mean," said Hob timidly, "why don't you ask one of the trees?"

They all looked at the hobgoblin.

"The little one's right, of course," said the QB. "The obvious answer, and none of us thought of it for ourselves."

Realizing that they were now all looking at him approvingly, Hob glowed, radiating happiness down to his fingertips.

Jim was the first one to think a step further. A good deal of his first feeling of satisfaction with Hob's suggestion went down the drain as he realized Brian and Dafydd would be watching him doing the asking.

"QB," he said, "wouldn't it be a good idea if someone else were to be the one to ask the tree this time—Brian, say, or Dafydd? Get the trees used to them, too."

"No. No, I don't think so," said the QB. "You've already been in touch with one Drowned Land tree for the Land's young King—and in a good cause, a very good cause. Also, if the trees here are at all like ours in Lyonesse, other trees in this land will now know you the minute you put your arms around them."

"Of course," said Brian, clearing his throat, "I cannot believe it would be quite the right thing for a knight to do—I speak, of course, of a simple, ordinary knight—rather than a Mage . . ."

"I'm not a Mage!" said Jim. "You know that as well as I do. Just a C+-class Apprentice magician. I'm nowhere near a Mage. Anyway, there's no reason anybody couldn't do it."

"You're sure you would not be forswearing yourself, or anything of that nature, dealing with strange magicks?"

Jim found the unreasonable irritation that had followed his dealing with the rift threatening to rise in him again. He knew Brian too well. His friend was deliberately needling him, egging him on.

"Certainly not, Brian. Nothing of the sort. The QB made a good point. Of course I'll do it." He looked at the thick trunks around him. "Which tree?"

He looked at the QB.

"That is for you to decide," the QB said. "There is an oak right over there. Oaks are among the trustiest and kindliest of trees, in my experience."

He pointed with his snaky nose. Jim looked off to his left at an angle of some forty-five degrees; and saw a massive trunk with its lowest branches at least ten feet above the ground.

He walked to it. The others followed him. He wrapped his arms around the trunk, with Brian and Dafydd watching him with deep interest.

"I did not think to watch him when he saved the King," Jim heard Dafydd remarking to Brian. "I was watching only my King."

"This is the same," said Brian.

Jim shut their conversation out of his mind. He hesitated only a second before putting his cheek to the rough bark.

"How should I tell a tree what we're looking for, QB?" he asked.

"It is difficult for me to say," answered the QB, "since we don't know what they are. Perhaps just—*other strangers*?"

"I'll try it," said Jim. He rested his head against the tree once more, and thought, *"We're looking for other strangers, here in the Borderland. Not friendly strangers like us—whoops!"*

The last word, or rather sound, came out of him with a jerk. The kindly oak had not only located what they were seeking but taken them to it, as the trees in Lyonesse had taken him to the QB originally.

"A small token of thanks from the trees of the Drowned Land, the tree says," translated Hob.

"Never mind that!" said Brian. "We're in plain sight, with the nearest foe less than fifty yards away!"

Jim looked around. Dafydd was looking also. Now they stood near the foot of a tall yew tree—the only tree in a large, soup bowl–shaped meadow that was surrounded by the flanks of green hills clothed with distant trees above the rich green of Drowned Land grass. Before them, to the right and left, and behind them, were loose gatherings of men in half armor, or no armor at all—knights at leisure, and a few crossbowmen and foot-spearmen, generally without their warlike tools.

But all wore swords, however, or daggerlike sidearms too long and solid to be eating knives. Half-obscured by this strolling, talking crowd were the upper parts of some tents, less than clean and new, in the distance.

"The Saints be with us!" said Brian grimly. "We will stand out as if we were painted red to the first one who takes a good look at us!"

"Look you," said Dafydd, in his lazy, ready-for-action voice, "it may not be so, if we act as they do. I see no one here I know; and therefore none who knows me. Unless you, Sir James or Sir Brian, see some who know you?"

Jim and Brian both shook their heads, looking around them.

"Then I would suggest we simply walk among them, leading our horses as if we had somewhere to go in this place. They cannot all know each other. Even if we seem different, they are most like to take us for several who are part of their—but I was forgetting—" Dafydd broke off suddenly. "Our friend the QB is sure to attract attention—"

He again broke off suddenly, looking away to his left deep into the crowd. They turned to look in the same direction, but he looked back, shaking his head.

"A man of the Drowned Land—not wearing his color," said Dafydd. "I do not think he saw me. He was going even as I looked, and gone now."

"How did you know him if he was not wearing—" Brian began.

"It would be hard to explain," said Dafydd, smiling at him. "But I would know anyone of the Drowned Land, anywhere. It does not matter. He is gone, and I will be on watch for him or any other like him. Let us on."

He turned his eyes on the QB as he said this, and kept looking. Jim, Brian, and Hob turned to stare. Where the QB had been, a tall, short-haired, black-and-white hound was now standing.

" '. . . It's only me,' the Lord QB's saying, my Lord," spoke up Hob—and he continued to translate as the QB went on in a low growl, mixed with whimpers. " 'This is the other of the two gifts of which I told you earlier that Merlin gave me. It has been sometimes useful for me when I was with not only King Pellinore, but his pack of hounds as well—to not look like prey when we were on the hunt for roebuck or fallow deer. If you have a length of leather thong on your baggage horse, I suggest you tie a length around my neck, and one of you hold the far end.' "

Jim turned toward the sumpter horse; Brian, however, had

already seen his move and beaten him to it. He was already there and loosening the cover. It was probably just as well, Jim thought. Brian always knew where anything was among their baggage, and how to get it out without disturbing the other things there. He could also pack a horse in about a fifth of the time it took Jim to do it; and was inclined to get a bit testy at Jim's slow clumsiness.

The horses had all gone to nibbling on the grass, as they did any moment they were not being ridden or led. They would be a hundred pounds overweight apiece by the time they were brought back to Malencontri. Only for a moment had they paused to pay brief attention to the transformation of the QB. He now smelled like a dog to them, instead of smelling most noticeably of leopard and lion tail—the snake-like forward part of his normal form had little smell worth sniffing at more than once.

So they paid little attention to the change. Hounds were unimportant, unless they got underfoot.

"There!" said Brian, finishing the tying of some five feet of leather thong about the neck of the lurcher—as hounds of the QB's present shape and color were called. He passed the loose end to Jim, without a word, as if he was automatically in charge of anyone on a leash, turned away, and started to remount.

"I would think it better that we walk and lead the horses, as if we were taking them to some place to be tied up," said Dafydd. "Let us walk most easily; and if we are spoken to by anyone who speaks the language of my land, let me answer. I will explain you neither speak our tongue nor understand them."

They started off again, strolling rather than walking, and seeming to chat among themselves as the strangers about them were doing. The led horses and the hound on its leash lent some credence to them as people at home in this gathering—whose numbers were surprising to Jim—as their party mixed with the general crowd. They kept their voices low, and this, too, helped with their cover; for most of the other men walking around in clumps of two to half a dozen were doing the same thing, to keep some privacy to themselves while taking advantage of the open air.

The fall weather of the land above—from which these men had probably come, most of them, Jim thought—could have turned cold or rainy since he and his companions had left it. There would be more privacy, of course, in one of the tents ahead of them, at the far edge of the encampment—but a tent could be uncomfortably hot under the sun.

There was something of a sameness about all of those they passed, it seemed to Jim; though it was difficult to put his finger on exactly what that was. They were a raffish bunch, even the beswordedones, who should technically be knights. It was as if they were all adventurers or outlaws from America's Wild West days, in spite of their present good behavior. The only noisy ones were obviously drunk; and those were paying no attention to anyone but their immediate companions.

"I fear me," said Dafydd, in a voice even lower than he had been using up until now. "I had guessed these were mainly of our Drowned Land people and talking in the language of our country. But these people speak as all do in the land above."

Brian nodded, almost imperceptibly. They were deep into the crowd, now; and the tents were more visible. Behind them, it now appeared, there was a long picket line of horses, tethered and free of reins or saddle.

Beyond those, the slopes of the hills, topped by trees, that surrounded this open space on all sides.

"Hah!" said Brian triumphantly, but in almost a whisper. "The clean tents on the end will belong to those of importance—none less than knights of renown; and more like to be nobles of rank. If we can find an empty one and look around inside it, it will tell us much of who has it. Even a knight of small worth will carry his tablecloth and tableware—both of which should have his coat of arms on them—to say nothing of other stuff marked as his."

"If they are from across the narrow water to France and

beyond, will you know them by the arms you see, Sir Brian?" said Dafydd.

"French—some," said Brian; "but in any case, foreign arms will look foreign; and as I say, we may be able to tell more from other possessions there. We would have to see within a tent to know."

"And that is another question," said Dafydd. "How are we to part the flaps of a tent and look within without showing ourselves to anyone who chances to be there? We cannot tell even if the tent is empty without going in to look."

The hound on the leash in Jim's hand whimpered again.

Jim looked down at him, puzzled. The hound whimpered more emphatically, lifted his piebald head and sniffed energetically at the air, looked at Jim and whimpered yet once more. He looked toward the sumpter horse.

"What's he saying, Hob?" Jim asked.

"I don't know this time, my Lord," answered Hob's troubled voice from his place under the cover on the sumpter horse.

"What is it, QB?" Jim asked him in a voice calculated to reach only as far as the hound's ears. "Can't you talk so that Hob can understand you?"

The hound shook his head.

"Why not?" Impatiently, the hound lifted his right front paw and scratched at the underside of his throat.

"Because your throat's different? Your vocal cords . . . never mind," said Jim. "But it beats me how a wolf like Aargh can talk, and you can talk with a snake's head when you're yourself, and—"

QB growled briefly, shook his head violently, and made sniffing gestures at the air.

"He's angry because you don't understand, m'Lord," said Hob.

"Can you hear him talking?" asked Jim.

"No, m'Lord. I don't think he's talking. But I can feel he's angry you don't understand. He's trying to tell you something."

"He thinks we ought to sniff?"

Dafydd and Brian, intrigued, had drawn closer, so that—clustered together—they effectually hid the dog in their middle from the sight of those around. The hound growled once more and shook his head vigorously.

"He thinks *he* ought to sniff!" Hob said.

The hound nodded vigorously and gave a low-voiced bark of approval; as if to say *Good two-legs!* Jim resisted whatever impulse he might have had to wag his tail and lick the hound's nose.

"What were you thinking of sniffing at, QB?" he asked.

The hound pointed with his nose at the closed entrance to the nearest tent.

"Of course!" Dafydd, Brian, and Jim said, more or less at once. They broke up their tight grouping and began to stroll idly toward the nearest tent, Jim holding the leash and walking on the side closest to the tent row.

The hound pulled a little ahead, paused briefly to sniff at the closed flaps of the tent's entrance, then kept on going. They went on with him. In this manner they passed half a dozen tents, one of them so noisy with voices inside that they would have known to pass it up anyway. Some kind of drinking and dicing party seemed to be going on.

As they moved down the line, the angle at which the tents had been pitched slanted closer to the horse lines and the trees behind them. Also, the tents themselves were smaller and dingier. They came finally to one at which the hound first sniffed, then stuck his head in through the closed flaps.

"I had best take the horses around back out of sight," said Brian. "I can do it quietly."

It was true. Blanchard was likely to kick up a fuss on general principles if anyone but Brian tried to lead him about. Gorp and Dafydd's horse were easygoing and did not care. The sumpter horse was indifferent.

"You know," said Jim, once Brian had taken care of this small duty, "with all these tents occupied even in the daytime like this—nearly all these men we see moving around outside must sleep outside, too, with no shelter."

"Of course," said Brian.

He might have said more; but the hound had now pushed his way, all but his cheerfully wagging tail, into the tent.

As casually as possible, they followed him.

"Whew!" said Jim, as he came in; and indeed, the tent stank. *Smell* was too kind a word for it. The reek was that of mingled spilled and rotting food, wine gone sour, and dirty clothing.

"Hah! As I looked for in such a coil as this!" said Brian, diving past Jim to snatch up a shield leaning against a pair of saddles. "Your old enemy and mine, James. Sir Hugh du Bois de Malencontri!"

And indeed, Jim saw, it was the arm amputated just below the shoulder, slightly bent at the elbow and dripping three drops of black blood, against a gold background—in heraldry it would be called something like *A shield* or, *a naked arm embowed.* It was about as attractive a coat of arms as Sir Hugh had been a knight. He had owned Malencontri before he was driven out after an attempt to conquer Malvern Castle and marry Geronde, by force.

"He's alive still, after all then," said Jim.

"So it seems," replied Brian, his blue eyes gleaming. "God send he come my way."

Jim knew that Brian would like nothing better than to face Sir Hugh with any weapon at all, after what the man had done to Geronde, shortly after Jim and Angie had first come to this alternate world. But it had been Jim who had actually fought Hugh later, after the Malvinne episode—fought with great-swords and won. But Hugh had disappeared in the aftermath of the fight, when the King and Queen of the Dead had taken Malvinne, the renegade AAA magician.

Jim had thought then they had taken Hugh also.

Clearly not. It was a chilling thought that the man was still alive, active—and here. For one thing, he would recognize Jim and Brian on sight. If he had been among the men they had passed on the way to this tent . . . Jim shook the thought from him. Brian was still rummaging among the litter in one corner, and the hound was nosing at what looked like a pile of dirty clothes in another.

Brian looked up finally from his last investigation and dusted his hands.

"Since he is here, he may return at any moment—and he knows us," Brian said. "He may walk in here at any moment and there is no escape for us—"

"I am attending to that now, look you," said Dafydd; and indeed he was standing at the closed flaps of the tent entrance, with a few inches of it parted by the thumb and forefinger of each hand, peering through it. "I will warn if he comes."

"Well done!" said Brian. "And I will give us a way out."

He drew his dagger and slid the edge of its blade in a line from above his head almost to the bottom seam of the cloth wall of the tent's back, that faced the horse lines. Blanchard, smelling him on the other side of the slit, stuck his head forward against the tent back, as if to nuzzle his master. Brian pushed him back.

"QB," said Jim, "don't you think you might be better off, if trouble comes, if you change back to your ordinary shape?"

The hound shook its head. It whined.

"M'Lord," said Hob, seeing Jim frowning in puzzlement, "I think he means as a hound he might be overlooked."

"There's that," said Jim, nodding. "In his own shape he'd be inviting attack—

"Ah, now!" said Dafydd from the entrance of the tent. "Here comes this Sir Hugh de Bois; and some seven of his friends with him, loose-drunk, but not to the point where they are less dangerous than they would be sober. We must get away."

There was a brief, tearing noise behind Jim, even as Dafydd spoke; and Jim turned to find Brian holding the slit open.

"This way," he said.

The hound slipped out. Jim, following, found he had to turn sideways and bend almost double to get through the gap in the cloth; and saw Dafydd, coming after him, do the same. Brian, who had been holding the cut edges open, came last, then pulled the sides of the slit back together as much as they would go. The cloth fell back into almost its original shape, with no more than a slight gap in the middle where their bodies had pushed through.

"With luck," said Brian, "it should take them a few minutes to see the cut; and even then it may seem as if someone tried to enter so to find what he could steal, but was frightened off by the sound of their coming. We have some moments. Sir Hugh and one from the Drowned Land who would know Dafydd are two too much for our safety here. Let us ride!"

"No," said Dafydd. "Walk—toward the far end of the horse lines we can see down there. Lead the horses as if that was our goal. The hound can follow on its own."

But the hound was no longer in sight. Jim stared around unbelievingly. He had never thought of the QB as someone to desert companions who were in danger.

But Brian had taken Dafydd's advice and was leading Blanchard, Dafydd doing the same with his horse and Gorp. The sumpter horse, still chewing on her last mouthful of grass, followed where the lead line took her.

"Ho!" called a strong male voice from the horse lines, "Anton, Alan, Guiscard—come look at this white destrier! A horse worth a hundred pounds if he's worth a penny!"

"Keep walking," said Dafydd. "Anything else will attract attention to us."

Brian and Jim did so, but Brian spoke.

"If it comes to a pinch, we must mount and ride. Blanchard can most likely outrun any horse here; so I may get away and you two be taken. If so, know I'll be back for you."

"Better for the Drowned Land you make your escape and live to tell the King and others what is here!" said Dafydd in a low voice.

"My companions are my companions," said Brian in an equally low, but hard, voice. "After my duty to them, I will have time to think of other kingdoms. Your land, Dafydd, is not mine!"

Dafydd said no more, only continued leading his horse; but Jim felt the sudden coldness between his two friends as if it was a brick fence between them. His mind scrambled for some way of removing it. Maybe it would just evaporate of its own accord, with time . . . here, Dafydd was a Prince. Little by little the habit of giving orders was taking him over—and Brian was the last in the world to take orders easily.

They were no more than halfway to the end of the horse lines.

But now, not three but five men from among the steeds were running toward them. They wore the patched and ragged clothing of those who were servants to men little better off than themselves; and the tall man in the lead, leaving the others behind with his long legs, was closing swiftly on Brian, who, with Blanchard held close behind him, was ahead of the others.

"Who rides a steed like that?" he asked Brian, walking backward now in front of him, a lean man in an archer's coat of boiled leather, too small for him, and with black hair above a face much pitted from smallpox.

"Out of my way, fellow!" said Brian. "Stand aside."

"Oh!" cried the man, whipping off a stained green cloth hat, not unlike a beret, and holding it wide from his body in an exaggerated, sweeping gesture. "I beg the grace of your forgiveness, noble Knight! Pray grant me the mercy of putting aside my great pertness toward you, my Lord! I did not know you were Royalty itself. My eagerness to touch the hem of your garment overcame me. May I grovel in the dust before your Lordship?"

Brian, his face expressionless, walked directly on toward the man, as if he was not there. At the last moment the individual from the horse lines leaped back.

"You touch me at your peril!" he shouted. "We are on duty here on the horse lines; and no man is to order us without authority!"

There was a long, narrow knife in his hand, now; and his fellows from the horse lines had caught up with him, several producing knives of their own. One man had a heavy cudgel, cut from a young oak, with the curve and swelling of the tree's root forming an ugly knob at its far end.

Brian came on, the tall man retreated again; but now the

rest were forming a ring around the little party; and now there were shouts from the line of tents, behind them.

"Where?" cried one drunken voice behind them. "Where's a horse worth a hundred pounds?"

"You going to buy it, Dahmer, with what you've got left from last night's dice-playing?" called someone else; and there was a burst of laughter, growing as those laughing came closer.

"That, and ten more like it, after this eve's play," said the first voice. "Wherezit, I say?"

"Right ahead," said someone else. "Too many people around to see it clear—you knaves stand aside so knights can see! No horse is worth a hundred pounds!"

"That one is," said an approaching voice that made Jim's heart sink in his chest. "I know it and the man who owns it. He owes it me for past debts. Come, help me collect!"

From behind now rose the pounding sound of running feet, and Jim tugged at his sword; but he was barely able to get it out before it seemed that they were closely hemmed in by bodies. Blows rained in from all directions. There was no room to use his sword. He could feel himself being struck from all angles, and the sun seemed to spin around him. The knobby end of the cudgel he had seen flashed at his head. He felt himself going down.

Chapter 24

Jim came awake in utter darkness, to an aching head followed by awareness of other pains, in succession like the waves of an incoming tide. His shoulders ached and his arms had no feeling in them. He discovered it was because his wrists were tied behind him—he had been lying on his back with them underneath his body,

Rolling over on his stomach, he flexed his fingers—or tried to—but like his arms, they were too numb for him to tell if he was actually moving them. He kept at it, though, and gradually feeling came back. Feeling—and a heavy, deadening ache.

The ache gave way to more specific pains—the bindings around his wrists were cruelly tight; and—following with a rush—came messages from a host of other places on his body that had been bruised, or cut.

He was in darkness. A darkness that, by its smell, was just such another tent as they had explored to find the shield with the arms of Sir Hugh de Bois . . . with whatever further extension of his name he had presently, since Malencontri was no longer his. But where a certain amount of sunlight had made its way through the cloth walls of the earlier tent, to let them see what they were doing, there was no such light here. It must now be nighttime.

He could not think clearly with his head splitting; and a clear head was the first item on any action list. Inside the ward, he could use his magic safely on himself, if not on others. He did so now, banishing his headache and making use of his art further to repair other damages, like contusions. It was one of the things he had learned early from Carolinus—the possibility, not the way to do it—that magic could be used to repair wounds, but not cure sickness.

With a clearer head now, he looked around, trying to see through the darkness. But he could not even make out the uneven dirt floor he was lying on.

"Brian?" he said. "Dafydd?"

"James," said Brian, in so strong and ordinary a voice and so close to him that—if it had not been for his bonds—he would have started, "—all Saints be praised. You took no harm?"

"No," said Jim. "Dafydd?"

"I am well," said Dafydd's voice, a little farther off than Brian's had been. "It was you, James, we were concerned about. You have not answered for some time. But you are unharmed?"

Jim grimaced in the darkness. By fourteenth-century standards, his other bumps, bruises, or whatever they were, did not count. He spoke into the darkness.

"Hob?" he asked. "QB?"

No answer from either one.

"Mayhap, they were taken away with the horses," said Dafydd. "But, James, you have not answered me. You are unharmed?"

"I'm just fine," he said. His conscience chewed on him about the others. They had no magic to cure their headaches or other pains; but he could not help them unless they identified what was hurting them—and such minor things, he knew, neither would admit to. Besides, he could not act to help them without breaking his ward, dangerously.

Worse than that, his conscience reminded him, they thought he was enduring his own less-than-vital pains just as bravely.

"James," said Brian, "that bastard Hugh de Bois has my horse!"

"I know," said Jim. "We'll have to get him back."

He heard a faint breath in the darkness—not quite a sigh of relief, but meaningful enough for Jim. Brian's attachment to Blanchard was second only to his love for Geronde. But he would feel better now that Jim had promised the horse's return.

Brian had infinite trust in Jim's ability to deal with anything by magic; and neither he nor Dafydd knew Jim was inside the ward KinetetE had put around him—a ward Jim was beginning to feel more and more superstitious about breaking for any reason. Some hunch or instinct was at work inside him, insisting that to do so would expose him and those with him to something a lot worse than just Morgan le Fay's countermagic.

Maybe, he thought now, it had been reinforced by the fact that the false Dafydd and the cleft had been massive, major magic. It could have hardly been anyone less learned than she who set those two things up. Moreover, the false Dafydd alone was evidence it had been aimed primarily at Jim. She had been out to get Jim to break his ward there, just as she had tried repeatedly with his adventures in the Forest Dedale.

For some reason beyond what he knew now, his keeping his ward unbroken was of critical importance in this situation.

His early life in the future had taught him to be skeptical of indications without proofs. The fourteenth century—*this* fourteenth century—was a different ball game. It had taught him you gambled on your instincts as a necessary element in staying alive.

He decided to use his magic to heal also the smaller discomforts that had resulted from the rough handling he had been given. He would think more clearly without them; and since he was not free to cure Brian and Dafydd of theirs, he should feel no guilt over repairing only himself.

At least, so he told himself. The excuse did not wash as well with his conscience as he had hoped. Illogical damned things—consciences!

With an effort, he did his best to put everything else from his mind, to concentrate on ways by which they might get out of this situation. Magic would free them. It might even not be impossible using nonmagic means—how much of his magical energy should he hold back against a worse need?

He should try nonmagical efforts first, at least.

He, Brian, and Dafydd were bound only at wrists and ankles. But it was surprising how thoroughly, with his arms locked behind his back, he found himself helpless.

Maybe if he got back to back with Brian or Dafydd, they could untie each other's wrist bindings. Brian was closest; and possibly had the stronger fingers. But maybe Dafydd, being an archer, would have even stronger fingers, come to think of it—

But he had been too long getting around to thinking of it. There were voices outside, approaching; and a few seconds later the entrance flap was pushed aside. Sir Hugh de Bois came in, carrying a torch of twigs, apparently smeared with some kind of fat or resin, which smoked in the close air of the tent. It flared brightly, blinding Jim for a long moment, and stank abominably.

Hugh was in full armor, with both sword and poignard. The five who followed him in were likewise armed and armored.

"They could get some of those idle varlets to do this!"

muttered one of these; as, with the help of one other, he jerked Jim to his feet. "Belted knights are not—"

"Your wits are still in your wine, Croyon," said Sir Hugh. "Use common knaves and have the whole camp knowing by morning what might be done and said? My Lord knows better than that. That's why we're here. Cut the rope holding their legs and bring them along."

Two to a prisoner, and holding the bound men up half the time because their legs were cramped by being tied so long, they marched Jim, Brian, and Dafydd out into the night. The fresh air—it was surprisingly warm—outside was comforting to the lungs; but it was a black night, as if thickly clouded, and everything was a deep black, except the tents, which all glowed from the lights inside them, faintly illuminating small areas around each of them. Jim walked better as the muscles of his legs loosened, and he began to think about making a break for it, after all.

But he would have to signal to Brian and Dafydd, somehow, so they could all make the break together. They should certainly be able to outrun their guards, weighed down with armor as those were—he shook off the thought. He was still not thinking clearly. He had not been stripped of his own armor. Certainly that meant that Brian, too, would be similarly encumbered, although Dafydd had been wearing much less than the two knights.

"Brian," he whispered—but the men holding his arms cuffed him, ordering silence.

Jim considered. Of course his eyes, and those of his friends, had been adjusted to the darkness while inside their unlighted tent. But that slight advantage might now be gone; and in any case, they would none of them be able to run much better than these men around them, with their arms bound as they were.

Jim closed his eyes and let himself be led blindly, hoping that his night-sight would come back to him swiftly. Dafydd and Brian, farther back from the torch Hugh was using to find their way, would be better off—while the eyes of the guards would have become accustomed to looking almost at the torch.

The darkness, then, would help—but before he could think of a way to not only loose himself from his captors but free Brian and Dafydd also, they were shoved through a canvas flap into another tent—a large one, this time.

Inside, it was surprisingly bare. Evidently no one lived here. A tabletop was set up on trestles near the far end of the tent, and crosswise to its entrance, four tall candles alight upon it.

It took a moment for Jim to make out that there were two people at the table, for they were seated on its other side, and the candles between the two and Jim dazzled his eyes after the darkness outside.

As he and his friends were jerked to a halt again, a good eight feet from the table, Jim's vision began to adjust and clear; and he could make out that the two across the table were a woman and a man. The shadows of their bodies, exaggerated where they were thrown on the end wall of the tent, made a deep pool of shadow there; and Jim thought he could make out one more figure back there.

After peering into the shadow fruitlessly, he looked back at the first two figures again—and found that his eyes had adjusted better to the candle-glare. Seated some distance back from the table before them was Agatha Falon, the sister, and would-be murderer, of Jim's ward, her baby half brother, Robert Falon.

Next to her was a tall, burly, middle-aged man—almost as familiar, and also named Robert—but a very different sort of Robert.

This one had Plantagenet among his other names; and he was half brother to the King of England. He was also the Earl of Cumberland, a man used to a position of power and authority—and a man whom Jim and his friends had already thwarted several times, in his various plans. The Earl had no cause to forget Jim.

But now the nobleman was paying no attention to Jim, or Dafydd or Brian—any more, Jim thought, than he might have done to three chickens brought for his inspection before cooking.

"—All of you, except Sir Hugh!" he was saying. "Outside. Stay well away from this tent, and let no one else approach. Go!"

The hard hands gripping Jim's arms released. He heard the guards moving out of the tent behind him.

"Sir Hugh!" said the Earl, focusing now on the former owner of Malencontri, once the others had left the tent. "You're a fool. What made you bring them inside?"

"My Lord—I thought you said I should."

"I did not. You added that on your own. Mind it well, man, I do not care for those who play with my orders. We are not alone, here."

Jim looked again into the shadows at the end of the tent. His eyes had now made their best adjustment to the candlelight, and he could see now that there was a man standing in the shadows behind Cumberland and Agatha. He was wide-shouldered and powerful-looking, wearing a robe or coat of some dark material.

Jim tried to make out his face, hidden in shadow though it was. It seemed to be rectangular in shape, strong-boned, for there was some gleam of light off a high forehead and cheekbones. His head was held high, almost as if he was looking down his nose at all those in the tent; and the lower portion of his face was more deeply shadowed, as if he had a black, bushy mustache and goatee. But in spite of the forehead and bearing, there was something young about him. Fully adult, but young-adult.

"If I have been at fault, my Lord," said Hugh stiffly, "I freely acknowledge it; and crave your gentle mercy for transgressing."

The Earl grunted.

"Damned little mercy in me!" he said. "You'd do well to remember that, too. Well . . ." His eyes came to rest at last on Jim and the others. "Now that you've brought them here, what say you we should do with them?"

"I had not thought beyond whatever your Lordship might

intend,'' said Hugh. ''But hanging, drawing and quartering should make good warning for any others who come to spy on our camp, in especial with heads and limbs up on poles about our lines.''

But if Sir Hugh had hoped to see this cruel form of execution, in which the victim was choked *almost* to death, then gutted and divided into four parts—hopefully, while there was still some life in him to feel what was being done to him—he was mistaken. The scar that remained on Geronde's cheek, after her refusal—even at dagger-point—to marry him, was proof enough that Sir Hugh had more than a little of the sadist in him.

Possibly he had been guessing that Cumberland shared his tastes. But the Earl was intelligent for all his bully-boy appearance and actions; and, as a Plantagenet, perhaps considered himself above such petty pleasures. His upper lip took on an ugly twist.

''I said you were a fool!'' the Earl said. ''Damme, but you would make a poor counselor! I asked what use could be made of them—any witless country lout could suggest hanging, drawing and quartering.''

''My Lord,'' said Hugh, ''I—''

''No. Spare me more of your suggestions and afterbleatings for mercy.'' The Earl's gaze shifted at last to Jim. ''Well, mighty Mage! Where is your magick now, that you let yourself be taken so easily by this cowhead in armor, here?''

''Bingo!'' said a small, but always alert, part of Jim's mind. The Earl had just given something away. Exactly what, that part of Jim was not sure yet. But that question had rung either false or out of character.

''I still have it,'' said Jim, managing to get the words out in an amused tone of voice, in his best possible imitation of an answer to a stupid question.

''Then how is it we have you prisoner?'' Another slip. If the Earl was in command here, as he gave every appearance of being, then surely he would have said ''I'' rather than ''we''. Or was it a slip? The Earl had never made any secret of his willingness to be King. Was his involvement in this

Lyonesse situation somehow meant to lead him to England's throne—or some throne?

There was the possibility that he might use the word *we* instead of *I* in a careless use of the Royal *we*—the first-person plural used by kings when speaking for their whole country.

"—In any case it makes small difference," Cumberland went on without waiting for Jim to answer this time. "Hugh, take the other two out and hang, or do whatever you want with them. Leave this one here."

"If they go, I go, too," said Jim quickly.

"How? Unless you are unbound and permitted?"

"I can go," said Jim. Practically speaking, it was a lie. He could go with Brian and Dafydd only if he opened his ward. But he was hot on the scent of what he thought the Earl was trying to hide; and he did not think the Earl wanted to risk losing him.

"Let us humor him, Sir Hugh, my Lady," said the Earl, putting his elbow on the table and resting his chin in his hand. "Let them all stay, Hugh. You go."

"Why?" demanded Agatha Falon sharply, opening her mouth for the first time.

"Because I said so!" The Earl's voice soared upward; and his chin came off his hand with a sudden movement. "Who consulted you?"

"Oh, I thought you did, my Lord," said Agatha in a waspish voice.

He stared long at her.

"Perhaps," he said softly, "you would like to leave us, too?"

"Thank you. No."

"Next time I will make it much clearer when I mean to consult you."

Agatha looked directly back at him, saying nothing. After a moment, the Earl withdrew his eyes and looked at Jim once more.

"You still here, Hugh?" Cumberland said without looking up. "Outside the tent flaps with you and wait my call."

Jim heard Hugh go. Excitement was rising in him. He was

beginning to consider the possibility that the Earl was not altogether happy that Jim was in his hands.

After all, holding a live magician prisoner was a little like holding a stick of dynamite in your hand when you did not know if it was lit or not. Keeping your grip on it too long could lead to unhappy results.

Jim had given the Earl a very rough time when they had last met, using magic to create a hypnosis-like dream state in which that nobleman seemed to live through a future that ended very badly indeed—with *him* being condemned to being hung, drawn and quartered; and—infinitely worse, for a man just as sensitive as Brian of his knighthood and ancestry, though for entirely different reasons—being stripped of his name and his arms.

It had been that last vision that had completely broken a highly courageous, if thoroughly despicable, man. But he was a native of the fourteenth century; and he had no mental ground on which he could stand to disbelieve what he had dreamed.

He had obviously shaken off most of the effects; but there would be no way he could be sure that Jim, even bound and apparently helpless as he was now, could not put him through something just as bad, again.

Jim's *Bingo!* reaction had been on the mark after all, he realized now. Cumberland was really not happy to have him here, face to face again.

Now, the Earl was in a quandary. Jim *looked* helpless; but was he? Had he been telling the truth when he said he still had his magic? If his helplessness was real, anything might be done with him. But if it was not, then he had only allowed himself and those with him to be caught and brought to this tent for some purpose of his own. That purpose could only be a trap of some kind, aimed at the Earl. But without admitting his fear—to himself, if to no one else—Cumberland could not just turn his three prisoners loose.

Time to play a little poker. Jim's eyes deliberately sought and met the Earl's, and their gazes locked.

Jim smiled.

But Cumberland also was silent. Jim would have to prod him with further words. He had to force the other man to say something Jim could get hold of and use.

"Perhaps," he said, trying his best to sneer—it was not a practiced expression for him—"my Lord would prefer that we three leave also?"

"Why not?" Cumberland said; and he smiled now. "Let you be given the night to think on your sins." He raised his voice. "Sir Hugh! Put these men away again for now. Let them be kept safe and unhurt. I have plans for them on the morrow!"

Chapter 25

The tent they were taken to this time, their ankles trussed again—thick rope, Jim noted—and left to darkness in, was not the one they had been in earlier. But the darkness was the same, once their ankles were tied and the torch had left along with their guards. Only the smells were different; but even that difference was a small one.

Jim waited until the voices of those who had brought them here were gone before he spoke. He had been able to see where Brian and Dafydd had been thrown to the ground—he himself had not been treated so roughly, but that was the only difference. Neither of them was more than eight feet or so from him.

"Why don't we get together?" he said in an ordinary voice. "It'd make talking a little easier, not having to call out to each other."

Brian was not ordinarily slow to take a hint; but on occasion he could be as ear-blind as any other person.

"I have not been calling out before now," he said. "Why should I here? You hear me as we speak now, do you not?"

"I think, Sir Brian," said Dafydd, "Sir James wishes to tell us it would be somewhat more companionable for speech if we were closer to each other. Perhaps you and I could roll ourselves toward him, since I remember seeing him between us when the torch was here.''

Dafydd's use of the formal ''Sir'' toward both of them when they three were alone together, plus the bowman's slight emphasis on ''companionable,'' woke Brian now to the meaning of what Jim had said.

''Of course!'' he said. ''Well thought on, James!''

Jim heard noises in the blackness and then Brian's voice barely murmured in his ear.

''Have you a plan, James?''

''In a way,'' said Jim, equally quietly. ''But now that they've left us alone—Dafydd, are you there?''

''I am,'' said Dafydd's voice softly near Jim's other ear. He had made his move to Jim's side much more silently than Brian had.

''—Not a definite plan yet,'' Jim told them both. ''But I think as long as no one can see us, we ought to see if we can't get out of these ropes. I thought if we got back to back, maybe we could untie each other's wrists.''

''Why not, indeed!'' said Brian. ''I think . . . James, you will not be offended if I suggest that it is Dafydd and I who should try to untie each other first. You see, one must wait, in any way, and it may be that of the three of us, Dafydd and I may have somewhat greater finger and arm strength—''

''Oh, certainly, certainly!'' said Jim; although he had actually been taking for granted that he would be one of the first two to be untied. ''I'll just slide out from between both of you, here. Just a minute.''

''Why do you not stay as you are, James?'' said Dafydd. ''I have done things not unlike this moving over the ground with my hands and feet tied before; and I can be at Brian's back quickly.''

His low voice was altering its position, even as he spoke; and, a moment later, it was talking from Brian's side of Jim.

''If you would hold your wrists steady now, Brian. Again, from experience, I have found that work goes fastest on unmoving cords. If you have some practice in using the fingers so, they quickly come to know where to reach all they have touched before.''

Brian grunted.

Jim lay in the silent darkness, wishing he had some non-magical way of seeing how Dafydd's efforts to untie Brian's wrist ropes were going. But there was none; and neither Brian nor Dafydd was likely to make sounds that would let him know—Brian, out of a lifetime's training in ignoring discomfort, and Dafydd from probably close to a lifetime of training in doing such things without a sound.

After what seemed a long wait, broken only by a sort of soft shuffling noise outside and behind the tent, Dafydd's voice broke the silence.

''I am afraid,'' he said, ''I can do nothing. These knots were drawn tight by a man who had the use of his arm muscles to do so. Because my own wrists are tied, I cannot pull the strands apart to start a loosening. Forgive me for raising your hopes, only to fail you both.''

''Never think so, Dafydd,'' said Brian. ''If you cannot untie my knots, then none of us can. Though I will try, in case my good name Saint should favor me with a small miracle, if the two of you would wish it. Also it may be that your bonds are less tight—''

Dafydd hissed suddenly for silence. Brian broke off in mid-sentence and Jim held his breath. The shuffling noise had grown slightly louder, but also it seemed closer. As they listened, it stopped suddenly.

Utter soundlessness for a second.

Then, a soft, rubbing noise, very close to Jim, who was the farthest in from the door to the tent. The noise had come from the back wall of the tent, only feet behind him.

But before he could twist his body around and roll over so that he could at least face in that direction—even if he could see nothing—a rough, wet tongue licked his face; and there was a faint whimper that sounded familiar.

''QB?'' murmured Jim. ''Is that you?''

Another identical whimper.

"If you know where to get us some help, get it," said Jim. "Otherwise you'd better get out yourself—"

"It's all right, m'Lord," said a small, breathy voice in Jim's ear. "M'Lord QB's been leading me. In the dark we can walk right by these men and they never knew we were there."

Brian and Dafydd were silent, listening.

"But how—" Jim broke off. "What do you mean, *leading* you? Can he see in the dark?"

"Oh no, m'Lord, not in his own body or the hound body he's in now. He uses his nose."

"Oh," said Jim. Of course. Both wolves and domestic dogs—and dogs, for that matter, were actually wolves, only "socialized," as an academic friend who had studied them had once pointed out—saw the world around them only in black and white. But their remarkable power of scent allowed them to read the world in a whole spectrum of odors humans missed. Of course, a hound could make his way about a camp like this on a moonless night, with his nose giving him as good an awareness of nearby people and tents as daylight might to humans—except for colors, of course.

"We knew we'd get a chance to speak to you, finally," Hob was going on. "There's no one else around at all now. He just dug under the cloth of the tent. Now, we'll turn you all loose. He's chewing on the rope about your wrists now, m'Lord."

"I know," said Jim, who was being jerked one way and another as the hound alternately chewed on the ropes or set his teeth in one of them and tried to pull it loose. "How's he doing?"

But at that moment, Jim felt the ropes fall away.

"Good," he said, massaging his wrists and flexing his fingers. They did not hurt, what with his earlier antipain personal magic; but they felt a little numb. The ropes must have been tight. "Where's the QB now?" he asked the darkness.

"He's biting loose Sir Brian, m'Lord."

"Dafydd," said Jim. "Say something so I can find you. I can work on your ropes while the QB works on Brian's."

"I am a little toward the tent front and ahead of you, James."

Jim tried to get to his feet, and immediately fell over.

"My ankles are still tied!" he announced, as much to the QB and Hob as to Dafydd.

"Do you still have your little knife with you?" came the voice of Brian. Jim was glad of the darkness that hid what he was sure was a look of embarrassment. Outside of an eating knife, sword, and dagger, a knight was supposed to be above needing to carry any other weapons, particularly hidden ones. Brian, however, had disabused him of taking this commandment too literally. *What if you should encounter with some unknightly person?* he had pointed out quite reasonably.

Jim's visible weapons had, of course, been taken from him; but his little hideout knife was still tucked into its hidden pocket on the inside of his belt.

"I'll be right with you," he said to Dafydd, sawing on the ropes around his ankles with the small blade. The ropes parted; and he began to feel his way toward the archer.

"My thanks to you, James," said Dafydd, as his ropes were cut.

"Don't thank me," said Jim. "It's the QB who's turned us all loose. Brian? I can cut your ropes now."

"Needs not," said Brian with a grunt. "I have my own small knife in hand, now; and—there goes the last of my ankle bindings."

"Then best we leave this place as quickly as we can," said Dafydd.

"If I may say so," said the unexpected, normal voice of the QB, himself, "best that you hear what Hob and I have to tell you before we venture out. I will be a hound again in a moment: I just turned into myself so I could speak with you; and, I hope, lead you safely to your horses. But first you should listen—"

"The horses, yes!" said Brian. "Blanchard! I will not leave here without him. But our weapons, what of our weapons? We would travel naked—without them!"

"We found those, too," piped up Hob. "There was a dying

campfire in the open with no one around it; and I managed to get to it and ride off on a waft of its smoke, just as though I was going from a fireplace back at Malencontri. I went over the horse lines from end to end—Blanchard and the rest are at the end we were all going to when the men took you prisoner.''

''But our weapons!''

''Sir Hugh kept them, Sir Brian. It was all but certain he would,'' broke in the QB. ''Of your favor, Hob, I'd like to tell the important information first.''

''Important?'' said Brian. ''More important than Blanchard and our weapons . . . I crave pardon, my Lord QB, you were saying?''

''There is no need for any to crave my pardon. But it is important you know that after it grew to nightfall here, I stole back from where I had slipped off to, as a hound; and found that Hob had left his hiding place under the cloth covering the load of the sumpter horse as soon as the crowd of men who took you prisoner had carried you off. Unobserved, for twilight had already begun to fall, he was seeking the place where you had been taken.''

''Well done, Hob!'' said Brian.

''My humble thanks, Sir Brian!''

Jim could almost feel the warmth of the little creature, swelling with pride at the compliment. ''What did you think of my—'' Hob began.

''As I was about to say,'' interrupted the QB once more, ''together, we returned to the tent of Sir Hugh de Bois; but although my hound nose told me that you had been there recently, you were not there—though we found your weapons as I have said. But I followed your scent moving away from his tent, to a larger tent where you were talking to a lady and gentleman. That is the important matter; for with my hound's nose I smelled, from beneath a back wall of the tent, not only those two but another man hidden behind them—a man I knew.''

''Ah, the man I saw in the shadows,'' said Jim.

''It may be so.''

"Who is he?"

"Someone I never expected to see again. You may remember I said that in the past no one but our King Arthur could raise armies. I was wrong. There was one other: he who had in truth raised armies to fight against Arthur in our great King's old age—armies stiffened with those of Arthur's knights who fell away from him over the sins of which Guinevere was accused. It was his unluckily begotten son by another than Guinevere. His name is Modred."

"Modred," said both Jim and Brian—thoughtfully on Jim's part, but questioningly on the part of Brian. The QB had evidently heard the latter as well.

"Did you not know, Sir Brian," his voice said, "how Gawain, driven by hate for Lancelot, kept telling the King that Lancelot, overseas in his own domain, was raising great armies against him; and therefore, in the end, Arthur left his kingdom in the charge of Modred, and went with a great army of his own, but with a heavy heart, to France, to attack the lands of Lancelot?"

"Meseems to me now I did hear the tale of something like that," said Brian. "But it was when I was very young; and I do not remember well what came of it."

"Lancelot would not fight Arthur, and the King was loth to shed the blood of so many of his fellowship. Then, while all hung in the balance, came news from Arthur's realm that Modred, as Regent back in England, had claimed that the King had fallen in battle with Lancelot; and proclaimed himself King in Arthur's place. So Arthur came back and won one fierce battle at Dover against a larger force led by Modred. A treaty was agreed upon to fight no more, providing no man on either side drew his sword."

"It comes back to me now," said Brian's voice. "It was a knight of the King's side who was bitten in the foot by an adder, and drew his sword to kill it. Modred saw the flash of that sword and led his army against the King, so that at last the field was sown only with dead men—but the King saw Modred, and rushed at him with a spear—was not that the way of it?"

"It was. The spear pierced Modred through for half its length; and he, feeling his death-wound, thrust himself up the shaft of the spear with the life remaining in him, and struck his father with his sword, so that it pierced both helm and brainpan."

"So that he was wounded near to death," said Brian, almost in the same tone of voice, as if he was making a habit-engraved response in church, "and three Queens in a boat came to take him to the Vale of Avalon. Is that not how it went? But Modred, it comes to me now—Modred was ended by that spear blow."

"So he was," the QB said. "He fell down dead. I never expected to see him alive again; but in this latest trouble, many of those who died in the time of our legends have now returned—King Pellinore's two sons among them.

"Perhaps it is an act of the Old Magic which keeps our Originals, those Knights from the Table Round, still living—though their descendants bear their names and ride the Wood of Rencontres, where you first met me. But my hound's nose, which had smelled Modred at Arthur's Court aforetime, knew him," wound up the QB, "as I sniffed under the wall of the tent and you talked to the Lord and Lady at the table."

"Hadn't we better be going?" Jim said. "We can talk more when we're in a safer place."

"Indeed," said Dafydd. "And, more than that, I must be taking word of this back to my own King and people as swiftly as possible."

"While I must carry the same word to Lyonesse," said the QB, "and any other talking will have to be done with those who go with me. Will you come, James and Brian? After all, it was to help Lyonesse that you came, I understood."

"I think we must, James," said Brian. "But if you have other word . . ."

"No. We'd better go with the QB," said Jim.

"Then, once we are well out of this camp and into open country," said Dafydd, "none will be able to find or catch us. Trust me for that. We will part then."

"Yes," said Jim. "I'd hoped, after we came to the Drowned Land and found you again, we three'd be staying together for the rest of this mess. Things never go the way you think."

Chapter 26

"We are near the end of the horse lines, now," said the low voice.

Now that they were away from the dimly lit tents, the voice came out of an impenetrable darkness; as far as Jim knew, the QB might not have bothered to change back to his hound shape. If not, he had been leading just with his natural ability to read the scents about them; but he had been leading them all as surely as a seeing-eye dog. "This end of it is less than a rod's distance from us now; and I can smell your Blanchard, Sir Brian, clearly."

At less than sixteen and a half feet, Jim himself could now smell the horse lines. He could not, however, identify Blanchard's personal odor—the QB's normal nose might not equal his canine one, but clearly it was much better than a human's.

Beside Jim—in fact, holding to his sword belt, so as not to go astray; just as Jim was hanging on to Dafydd, who seemed able to follow the QB without hanging on—Brian gave a low, almost soundless, whistle.

Jim recognized it. It was one of the signals Brian had trained Blanchard to know: a warning not to greet his master with any sound. Jim had tried to train Gorp to the same response; but Gorp, who normally did not whinny at such times anyway, was not the student Blanchard had obviously been. He might just choose this moment to forget his training.

"Hob," said Jim, low-voiced, "could you go ahead of us and keep Gorp and the sumpter horse quiet—or could you get lost if you try?"

"A Hob never gets lost in the dark," said Hob's voice behind him. There was the faint scurry of small, shoeless feet out ahead—then silence. A moment later Jim literally walked into Gorp's wall-like side.

All the horses, of course, had been relieved of all they carried—saddles, bridles, and the sumpter horse's load.

"We must needs ride without gear and goods," said Brian wistfully. "But it were folly to go back and search for them at the risk of being retaken."

"Perhaps not," said the QB. "At least I can try. My hound nose is better than the one I was made with; but perhaps leopard's nose is all we need here—" They heard him sniff. "The whole encampment is asleep, except for those few tents still lit within. If we stay clear of such tents you may as well ride—and be ready to escape with speed if necessary. Your horses need only follow me. I will lead you to safety. Hob, can you tell Blanchard to follow me in the dark? I do not know this land, but I can still sense the trees and the spaces beween them."

"Blanchard won't listen to me," said Hob, startling Jim by speaking from behind him on Gorp's back. "But I can tell Gorp my Lord said so to do, and then Gorp will listen and follow."

"And Blanchard shall follow Gorp. My word on it!" said Brian's voice out of the darkness.

"And you, my Lord Regent," came the QB's voice, "will your horse also follow?"

"No," answered Dafydd's voice, sounding as if he were smiling. "But I will listen to the hoof-falls of your horses, and guide mine along with the rest of you."

"Then we go," said the QB; and go they did. There were a few moments of movement, then the QB stopped again. "We are close now—to what I assumed must be."

They went forward again. After another small distance, he slowed and stopped again.

"You cannot see it yet," he said in a low voice. "For that matter, neither can I. But this is the tent holding Sir Hugh de Bois's extra gear. I have followed my nose to the tarred cover on the load your sumpter horse carried. Now that I am close I can smell your saddles as well, along with other equipage that may belong to Sir Hugh, or perhaps to a number of knights. There is one man on duty inside it, as night guard."

"I will take care of him," said Dafydd.

"No. There is no need. He has drunk himself to sleep. Let us go softly; and each of you keep a hand on my back. We will go in and carry out what is yours."

They did so. With the QB's nose to guide them throuh the blackness of the tent's interior, it was a simple enough labor. They outfitted their horses, swung into their saddles, and were ready to ride.

Now that all the difficult work was over, the first paling of the morning sky announced that the night here, as short as that of Lyonesse, was all but over.

"The encampment still sleeps," said the QB. "Follow me now."

They followed. In no time at all they were surrounded by forest and trotting their horses behind a QB whose energy seemed limitless. They rode for what Jim judged to be almost a half hour. The sun was still not yet lifted above the tops of the surrounding trees, but overhead the sky was white with dawn, and at ground level they could see clearly where they were going.

"How much farther to Lyonesse?" Jim finally asked the QB.

"We have been there for some time," the latter answered, without turning his head. "Look where the first edge of the sun now rises between the thinner upper branches of the trees."

Startled, Jim looked up and to his right. It was a white sun now, and the upper branches through which the daystar's upper edge looked could not have been blacker. The bright color of the Drowned Land was gone. He reined in Gorp. The others also stopped.

"Just a moment," said Jim, searching at his belt for the case for his magic glasses. He put them on, just to make sure. No colors. With relief he put the glasses away again.

He was about to say something about going on once more, when Dafydd spoke up.

"Lyonesse it is indeed," he said, "and therefore I am going in the wrong direction. I must carry word to my King and that means I leave you now."

Without waiting for any answer from the rest, he reined his roan about and started off at a hand-gallop back the way they had just come.

"Wait, Dafydd!" Jim called after him, "you don't want to run the risk of running into that encampment!"

"There is no danger!" shouted Dafydd over his shoulder. "Now that the sun is up, I can find my way safely around it. This is my country!"

—And he was gone, out of sight among the farther trees.

There was a long moment of silence, which Brian finally broke.

"A proper sense of duty," he remarked. "Shall we on?"

They onned.

"I have been thinking how best to go about this," the QB broke the new silence after a little while. "The problem is that we here in Lyonesse have no king such as Arthur was, to whom news of that army on our border should go first. I would ordinarily believe that any evil chance for us in those gathered men would be small. They seem a force more prepared to take over the Drowned Land than Lyonesse. But with the Dark Powers looming over us as well, I have an uneasy feeling that our knights should indeed be warned."

"Why think you it may be small?" Brian looked curiously down at the loping leopard form.

"For more than one reason," said the QB. "Much more than Lyonesse, the Drowned Land is like to the land above, which these invaders are used to, full of people to be their servants and slaves; and finally, it is all but without magick. No matter what they may say, I believe that you people in the land above fear, but are used to living with, magick."

"With reason," said Brian, "if some of it is in evil hands."

"Yes, but in Lyonesse, with some few exceptions, magick is our friend. An old friend, as are the tree magick and the Old Magic, who together made a home for us when otherwise our stories might have been forgotten and lost forever."

"Such great stories are never lost!" said Brian. "Support me, James. Is that not true?"

"I can guarantee it," Jim said, "for another thousand years, at least. But QB, if you haven't got a king like Arthur to go to, where are we headed now?"

"To another king," said the QB. "Though his name is Pellinore, not Arthur. But he was one of the many at King Arthur's Round Table; and the only one whose strength was equal to or greater than that of Arthur himself. So much so, that once as they wrestled together in armor, Arthur's sword having broken, Pellinore overcame Arthur and would have slain him, but Merlin stopped him."

"I seem to recall some word of that tale, too . . . ," said Brian, frowning thoughtfully.

"King Pellinore is one of the Originals," went on the QB. "One of those Knights of the Legends who sit apart from their children's children's children nowadays. It is such as he who must be told of the danger in the Borderlands; for while our Knights can fight like no others can, I fear for them without Arthur. In Arthur was always victory—for his cause, for others, if never for himself . . . In some ways those of Lyonesse are ordinary men in spite of the Legends; and, lacking him, they lack something of what made them great—especially face-to-face with such greater numbers as those we have seen in the Borderland."

"Ordinary men may do unordinary things," said Brian.

"Yes, but . . . it is more than that. When Arthur went to war, the earth fought for him. The sky fought for him. All fought for him. You cannot understand what that means. You have not seen him as I have, his sword flashing like lightning in the melee! Had you, you would understand—" The QB's usually pleasant voice had taken on hoarseness not unlike that of a human who was close to tears. "I cannot explain! I cannot explain!"

"You don't need to, QB," said Jim. "Your word is good enough for us."

"Perhaps for you, Sir James and Sir Brian. But the Knights

of Lyonesse remember Arthur and will know what they lack—and in that is the greatest danger."

"There's help for them in Dafydd's people, too," said Jim. "Once those in the Drowned Land understand both kingdoms face a common danger, they'll be ready to join forces with Lyonesse—I can almost guarantee it!"

"Perhaps," said the QB.

"If Dafydd were still with us," observed Brian, "he might say that those of the Drowned Land have found little to love in Lyonesse as their neighbor. Remember, James, the stories he told us of Drowned Landers going into Lyonesse and being trapped there, lost and unable to come home?"

"But with a situation this dangerous, I can't see either the Knights or the Drowned Landers hesitating, Brian!"

"I hope you to be right, Sir James." The QB turned his head to look over his shoulder at Jim, without interrupting his smooth, swift running that kept the horses behind him at a fast trot. "But it must be put to the Original Knights as a question, since on their part they know that knighthood is unknown in the Drowned Land."

"Hah! If needs be, let me speak to them," said Brian. "It would be a foolish head that entertained the thought that Dafydd's lack of a knight's belt and golden spurs meant he also lacked warlike skills and the courage to fight; and I misdoubt there is any great lack of others in the Drowned Land like him."

"I do not hold him so, myself, certainly," said the QB, "and I will put it in just those words to King Pellinore. But the full problem must be put to him. A truce with you on this point, Sir Brian. We all have our own ways."

"Indeed"—Brian's voice dropped—"I should not have flown out at you so."

The QB halted suddenly. They reined in their horses sharply to keep from riding over him.

"I must call ahead," he said. They were in deep woods yet, with hills like small mountains all around them and no sign of buildings or people. But remembering how the QB had whisked him from one end of Lyonesse to another in almost no time at all, it struck Jim that they might have covered more ground than he would have thought since the sun came up.

But before he could start to guess where they were, there burst from the QB the sound of thirty couple of hounds, questing—and for the first time Jim was able to note that the sound came not from his serpent's mouth—but, as the legend had told it, from his belly.

After a moment a horn like that a hunter might use answered, followed by the yelping of other hounds—not thiry couple of them, but at least a dozen or so. The QB turned himself into his hound shape and put on speed, leaving them behind. Jim and Brian followed.

It could have been no more than seventy-five yards before they passed through a cluster of young trees and came out into a forest-encircled clearing. A large and long house of logs filled the far side of the clearing; with a sturdy bench next to its front door, made of half a log that had been split lengthwise, the bark still on its underside, the flat side on top, and eight thick legs fitted into it below, supporting it.

On the bench, in full armor, sat a clean-shaven, mature looking man who was one of the most tall and powerful looking individuals Jim had ever seen. He was not looking at them. From inside the closed door of the log building came occasional yelps like those they had heard before, to which the large man paid no attention at all.

The QB had halted at the edge of the clearing, still in his form as a hound. He looked back at them and whined in his dog voice.

"M'Lord," came the voice of Hob, "he wants to go ahead alone, first. Do you mind coming after him?"

"Not at all," said Jim, speaking quickly before Brian could say anything else.

The hound nodded and trotted toward the seated man. Jim and Brian gave him a head start of about half the length of their distance to the man, then rode out from among the small trees, directly toward him.

The man's eyes had been all on the hound from the moment he had appeared. It was only when it stopped some six feet from him and sat down on its haunches that the man looked beyond it, and stood up, seeing Brian and Jim.

"Who are you?" His voice was rusty with age, but as powerful-sounding as his body looked strong.

The hound turned suddenly back into the QB—and a chorus of dog voices burst out behind the closed door of the log house. The man turned his head toward the door.

"Silence."

—And silence it was. Sudden, almost shocking, silence. He turned back again to look at Jim and Brian, who had ridden up behind the QB, and drawn rein there.

"Sir Pellinore," said the QB, "these are my friends and yours—friends to all Lyonesse; and have travelled a long way to help us. May I name to you Sir James de Malencontri and Sir Brian of Castle Smythe, both from the land above? James, Brian, I have the honor to name to you King Pellinore, my friend and Original Knight of the Table Round."

Brian and Jim swung down from their horses and bowed. Pellinore inclined his head.

"In what should we need help?" he asked. His rusty voice was like a great drum booming in the wide cavern of his chest.

Jim found himself held by Pellinore's gaze. The King's heavy-boned face was expressionless and showed no wrinkles or lines of age; but his eyes were dark and deep under his black brows. They did not blink. The impression Jim got from him was one of tremendous strength and will—much more of both than he had expected. For some reason, possibly the way Sir Dinedan (a descendant, not the Original of that name) had spoken of him, Jim had got the idea of Pellinore as an almost comic knight.

He was anything but. Come to think of it, none of the Originals should be. Hamlet had his grave-digger in the play by Shakespeare. The Legends about King Arthur had no such character.

He found himself now in a staring match which he could do nothing but lose. He was about to give up and drop his eyes, when Pellinore looked once more at the QB.

"You did not answer me, old friend," he said.

"I was surprised you did not seem to know, King," said the QB. "Some evil forces, known as the Dark Powers and until now a trouble only to the land above, have made intent to perhaps try to take this land of Lyonesse for themselves, and for full evil purposes. Sir James and Sir Brian have encountered with these Powers before and bested them, not once but several times; and so they have come to do what they can to aid us of Lyonesse."

"In what shape do these Powers come, then?" said Pellinore's deep voice. "Surely there will be others besides me who will be willing to face them and send them away again?"

"In no shape, and with no face, King Pellinore. That is what makes them such terrible foes. Fighting them is like fighting the winter when it comes. Brave hearts, strong arms, and good weapon-work find nothing in them to strike at."

"This is hard to believe—yet I would never misbelieve you, QB," said Pellinore. His implacable eyes swung back to Jim and Brian.

"How then," he said, "can such as you help?"

"I am a magician," said Jim, speaking with all the fourteenth-century formality he had learned in the last few years; "and also, while the Dark Powers themselves are as hard to wound as ghosts or shadows—to take anything real, such as the ground we stand on, they make use of creatures that can be touched with weapons and killed."

"Creatures?"

"Harpies," put in Brian. "Like great bats, except that they have a woman's face and poison fangs. Worms, like giant lampreys, their circular mouths filled with rows of teeth. Ogres, giants four yards high, with bones so thick no mace or ax, let alone sword, can break them . . . and others."

"These I have never heard spoken of," said Pellinore.

"The Dark Powers may try to conquer Lyonesse with such as Sir Brian mentions," said Jim. "Perhaps with other sorts of creatures, too. But they will also come at you with those you had not expected to fight for them." He lifted a hand to indicate Brian.

"In the past," he went on, "Sir Brian and I have faced a rogue magician, a great army of sea serpents attacking us upon land, and a Demon from the Kingdom of Devils and Demons. Also those who were called the Hollow Men; and at another time the greatest and oldest deep-sea squid, a monster with a dream of conquering all the land above. Not only magicians are needed when the Powers attack; knights and any else who'll fight are needed to conquer their creatures."

King Pellinore's eyes watched Jim.

"You won these battles, I take it," he said. "Otherwise, you would not be with us now, if all you say is true."

Jim nodded.

"We won," he said; "but only because the rogue magician was defeated, the Hollow Men destroyed, the great squid finally made helpless by my Master-in-Magic—one much greater than myself."

"And what," said Pellinore, "if this time, the attack upon us calls for another, greater than you in magick?"

"There isn't any other to come and help," said Jim, his medieval formality begining to break down. "You're going to have to fight with what you've got now. Besides your own forces, I'm what you've got—Sir Brian and I. There're only two of us, but we've had experience with this enemy before. It's your Knights, us, and beyond that only the trees and the Old Magic."

"That is true," said the QB.

"Yes, it is true," said Pellinore. "But we do not command the trees or the Old Magic. We cannot even speak to them—we Knights cannot—I know you can talk to them, QB. But it may be they do not even decide a matter together as we do, who walk and talk beneath them. Who is to know whether they might aid us and how?"

"There's one," said Jim. "Merlin might know. I can ask him."

Not only Pellinore, but the QB stared at him without words. Jim was sud-denly embarrassed. It was all very well for him to talk of asking Merlin about something; but clearly neither QB nor the King had ever considered such a thing being done.

But then, as often happened with him, his own embarrassment made him angry, and anger made him stubborn. The words had just popped out; but he was not going to take them back now.

"However," he said to the QB, "I suppose you won't be able to take me to him until the next dark of the sun. The question here and now is what we can do with our strength other than magic."

"It will be dark soon," said the QB; and there was a hard note in his voice that Jim would not have imagined from the way the other had always spoken to him. "But you are right, Sir James, about our needing to count our strengths. For what use it will do, I will speak to the trees, of course—but King Pellinore is right. I have little hope of any direct help from them.

"As for the Old Magic, I know of no one who can speak to it at all—or if it has the ability to hear our words. But I believe it has a kindness for you, Sir James, and possibly could be your friend as well, because it helped you to escape the Queen of Northgales. Perhaps it will help, in its own way and time. But as to who may fight for us; and what they may hope to do—it is beyond me. That was why I ventured to bring these new friends to my oldest friend."

He looked at Pellinore.

Pellinore's eyes were looking past them, off at something in the distance.

"Never since Arthur left us for the Vale of Avilion," he said, as if he was speaking more to himself than them, "have all those here who once sat at the Round Table gathered together. I will go to them one by one and perhaps we can meet again. Be sure there will be none who dare not fight; but there may be some who for other reasons would stand aloof."

He stood up.

"Horse!" he said in a strong voice.

There was a whinny from beind the log cabin; and not more than a couple of minutes later, a tall horse, already saddled and bridled, and all white except for a black blaze on the muzzle and four black feet, came around a corner of the building and walked toward them, nodding with each step. It came to Pellinore and rubbed its head against the large man's chest.

Pellinore patted the white shoulder in an automatic gesture, took up the reins, and stepped into the near stirrup to swing himself lightly into the saddle.

"I will sound my horn when I have something to tell you," he said to the QB. "God's grace be with you, Sirs."

"And with you also, King Pellinore," said Brian.

The big man on the big horse rode off and was lost to sight among the trees.

"He seems a man of much strength and valor," said Brian, looking after him. "But at that pace, on that horse for all its long legs, we may have to wait months before he calls you with the word he has gotten from his fellow Knights."

"I pray you not to judge by appearances, Sir Brian. The Originals, as I can, may travel swiftly when they wish. If it would have taken a long time, he would have warned us of it."

"I doubt that not," said Brian, "now that you have told me about this matter of swift-going. I meant no slighting word. As I said, he seems a Knight valiant and of great power."

"He is indeed," said the QB. "And he had two pure and noble sons, as worthy in their own ways as himself. One was named Sir Percival and the other Sir Lamorack of Wales."

As he was speaking, the sky, the trees, the earth, and the building behind them all seemed to fade and to lose the sharp lines of their edges, as the day dimmed.

"Now comes the dark, Sir James," said the QB.

Chapter 27

The dark came swiftly.

"Sir Brian," said the QB, "I suggest you lead your horses with you to the bench and seat yourself there until we return. When the last of the light is gone, Sir James and I will be gone with it. But we will be back before the first light shows."

"I will await you," said the voice of a Brian already becoming a dim figure. "But I would I were going with you."

Jim swallowed. He had not forgotten what he had so unthinkingly said a little while past. But now, with the QB's last words, it had suddenly become immediate—and far too real.

"Face it," he told himself, *"you spoke up all right to Merlin the last time you saw him; but don't try to dodge the fact—Merlin chills you."*

Now that he had put the feeling into actual words, he realized how true it was. But the strangest part of what he felt was that even now he did not know why he should feel so. Merlin had not been threatening in any obvious way. The closest Jim could come to an explanation was to remember that in his first meeting with Carolinus he had been aware of a great deal of real power and strength in the older man—in spite of Carolinus's apparent ego and rather ridiculous cantankerousness. There had been a similar awareness—without the cantankerousness—at a much greater level when he spoke to Merlin.

But the QB was now speaking again.

"I pray you pardon me, Sir Brian. Merlin would not permit it."

"I should entreat your pardon," said Brian. "It is for him to say, of course."

Brian had already led the horses to the bench and seated himself. He was all but lost in the obscurity now. Surely, thought Jim, this was too soon for night to come again? Of course, this was Lyonesse and the last dark period had been in the Borderland, which was more or less in the Drowned Land.

But still, he had been assuming that the white sun above Lyonesse was the yellow daystar of the Drowned Land, only robbed of its color. But it could be they were different, as the kingdoms themselves were different—now the utter blackness of the dark period surrounded him.

"You need not move, Sir James." The QB's voice seemed to speak almost in Jim's ear.

"I wasn't planning to," Jim said, a little more sharply than he had meant to.

Once more, as on his earlier visit to Merlin, he felt a breeze in his face. It cooled his skin for a few minutes, then stopped abruptly. He waited. Then, without warning, he was hearing the QB's voice in what surely had to be the tail end of a conversation.

"—if in your kindness you will permit, Merlin."

"I will," came the same strong voice he had heard once previously. "He is a magickian of a different sort; and that makes him welcome when others would not be, so soon after his last visit. Beginning now, QB, you will hear, but not understand as we talk. We will be speaking of things it is not time for you to know."

"You know why I'm here?" Jim stopped his hand just before it went up in a ridiculous, instinctive effort to fan aside the darkness, as if it had been smoke or mist.

"That and many other things. Live as long as I have, Jim, and you will also know many things. You will also know that you know nothing—you are a babe just beginning to understand. But you do realize that simply by living, you are learning more each minute?"

"I hadn't thought of it that way," said Jim. Strange how Merlin pricked him to a kind of defensiveness. He was feeling the other's strong influence, but, as before, he found he could talk. "But if you want to include every bit of information, useless as well as useful, you've got to be right, I suppose."

"There is no such thing as useless information. You will learn that, too, someday. But there was a question you have come to me with."

"Yes," said Jim. "It was—"

"You did not know that I never answer a direct question. The time may come when you do not either."

"Then I've wasted your time and mine in coming," said Jim, a ready anger rising in him in reaction to the way he felt of Merlin's power.

"It is never a waste of time if the one you talk to wishes to talk. If you like, I will tell you a thing about yourself, instead."

"That'd be interesting," said Jim, holding on to his temper with a great effort. "But the question you won't let me ask needs an answer that's critical right now—more critical than anything—including what you might tell me about myself."

"How can you be so sure of that? So, you wish to hear nothing from me, then?"

Jim's *That's right!* was on the tip of his tongue, when, just in time, an instinctive caution stopped him from uttering it.

"No, of course I'll listen," he said. "Where there's life—I mean, where there're words, there's hope—or at least some information that can be useful."

"The first sensible thing you've said, so far," Merlin told him. "Carolinus said you had a sensible bone in your body. Just one; but that's more than the average individual has, by quite a bit."

"Have you talked to Carolinus recently?" Jim asked.

Silence.

"On the other hand," went on Merlin, "he also said you were always determined to do things your own way, so it was a waste of time trying to steer you in the right direction. But what you then do might be so remarkable it was worth gambling on you. Oh yes, he also said you had a good heart. I notice our trees back him up in that."

"I'd like to know how they think they know it," muttered Jim.

"So would I," said Merlin. "If you think that I know

everything, you're wrong. But to get back to what I was talking about, there are limits to what magick—as Carolinus and others pronounce it—can do—yes, I know you pronounce it another way, but your way makes a word that means something different to you than what Magick means to those like Carolinus.'' Jim found himself nodding, but Merlin was continuing.

''As I was saying,'' Merlin went on, ''the magick has its limits; and beyond them are further unknown territories where everything is different. Carolinus has gotten to the point where he can glimpse the unknown territories. But at the same time, and for the first time, he has also begun to doubt that he, himself, will ever reach them.''

''No!'' said Jim.

He had not had time to think before bursting out so sharply; but it had exploded inside him all at once that the Carolinus he knew—that sometimes-infuriating old man, apparently so jealous of his magical knowledge, and rarely seeming to exert himself for anything but his own ends—might also be, in his own eyes, stuck at the foot of a ladder he had always dreamed of climbing. Within, he could still be a serious young student yearning for something Jim himself could not even imagine; and in the process hiding inside himself—well, who knew what emotions?

''It is hard to suddenly see all we have overlooked before in others,'' said Merlin, as if he had been able to read Jim's mind in that moment.

''It's that bit about a promised land that gets me,'' said Jim, ''and your saying he'll never be able to cross over to it. Are you sure—I mean, it's hard to believe there's no way he could get there.''

''Perhaps you will show him the way,'' said Merlin.

''*I* might?''

''I will assume that was an expression of astonishment rather than a question,'' said Merlin. ''Why not? Stranger things have happened; and will go on happening forever—eternity being only a subdivision of possibility. At any rate, he hopes to see you get there yourself; and having seen how you did it, he may manage to follow you. So might I."

"You?"

Silence.

"But as regards your concern over this attempt by the Dark Powers to own Lyonesse. The QB was correct when he told you that Lyonesse cannot win unless a king leads the others. Arthur is gone. Lancelot also, to become a hermit for the rest of his days. Indeed, he may already have died. Could he be brought back he now would not lay hand to sword or lance again, even if he was as he used to be. But knowing you have done the best possible with Pellinore may give you some peace of mind."

"Forgive me," said Jim, "but what you say is pretty cold comfort."

"That is all the future ever certainly promises. I say that, whose work has always been with the future, not the present. Like the Old Magic and like you, I am not a magickian. I am a magician; but unlike you, my first concern is the future.

"I am a seer. That is why I do not answer questions and some other things. One whose study is the future must not only know the past, but avoid meddling with the present which will make it. I shall only tell you one thing with perfect certainty. In the end any battle is always between the selfish and the unselfish. The selfish often win in the short run. The unselfish always win in the long."

"But I've got to get some idea of where to go from here. I needed to find out from you whether the trees or the Old Magic would help us—and how they could."

"There!" said Merlin. "You have finally achieved a perfect example of what everyone should understand is meant by the word *communication*. It is perfectly possible to inform someone else of what you want to know, other than by thrusting it at him as a question."

"Thank you," said Jim.

"—And, incidentally, I am immune to irony. I will tell you some of what you would like to know. The trees do what they want; and no one can foresee what they will want. The animals share equally with we who are human and the land.

They have their own link with the Old Magic, one we have never understood—but we understand that Lyonesse is theirs as much as ours.'' He did not pause, but Jim felt a difference in the next words.

''The Old Magic, itself—note that I pronounce the word as you do,'' Merlin said, ''has its roots lost in the deep darkness of time; and is so different as to never be understood. I have looked as far down as I was able, to try and find why and how it does what it does—but the answer always lost itself in the ancient Dark.''

Jim was speechless.

''I can tell you only,'' the voice in the darkness continued, ''that the Old Magic is necessary to Lyonesse; and therefore necessary to the rest of us. In a very real sense the Old Magic's presence is necessary to keep us all living. Between our earth and our sky all belongs to Lyonesse alone, and from Witch Queen to gray squirrel we hold it in common; and if we lose it, we are lost indeed.''

''In other words,'' said Jim, ''there's no use looking to it for help—''

''There's no use *you* looking to it for help.''

''—As far as I'm concerned, I suppose I should have said. But perhaps the Old Magic is a part of Lyonesse that itself needs help.''

''I would not say so.''

''All right. But the Knights'll need it, the trees'll need it, if whoever invades wins. So it'll be a waste of time my trying to turn to either trees or Old Magic now.''

''Very good—and quite correct. But there are others who may help.''

''The Drowned Land people?''

Silence.

''But now the day comes,'' said Merlin, breaking it. ''You must be gone. I need no fellowship, here where I am.''

Jim breathed out a long breath.

''Good-bye then,'' he said, ''and thank you.''

''May God speed you as well,'' said Merlin. ''Thanks are unnecessary. No. Wait—''

Jim, who had been about to take an automatic step backward, checked himself.

"I will tell you one thing," said Merlin. "Even I do not understand it. The Old Magic has been active in some way, since the Dark Powers appeared over us. This can mean something that could be a help to you, or it could mean only some meaningless small thing like a change in our weather. We will have to wait and see."

Then Jim was back in final silence. The darkness seemed to wrap itself more tightly around him, alone.

"A moment only," said the welcome voice of the QB, "and we are on our way to our friends, Sir James."

Once more Jim felt the breeze in his face; and then the full darkness was no longer with them. The white sun of Lyonesse was not yet visible—indeed, it was probably still below the horizon which the surrounding trees hid; but the sky was beginning to lighten, enough so that he found himself looking at Brian, seated on the bench that was half a log and still holding the horses' reins in his hand.

The horses were eating, as usual. In fact, they had cropped a circle in the grass about the bench.

"James!" said Brian, starting to his feet, but still holding carefully to the reins. "You are back. I did not think you would be gone so long. Or else the dark seemed longer than I thought."

"Sir James was, in fact, longer than expected, Sir Brian. Even longer than I expected, who am familiar with Merlin and his ways." The QB looked at Jim. "Have you any good tidings for us, Sir James?"

Jim opened his mouth to say that Merlin had told him nothing important; and then remembered Merlin had, but mostly in matters that concerned him personally.

"He knows so much more than I do," he told the other two, instead. "I'll have to do a good deal of thinking about what he said. But the only thing he told me that might help was that Pellinore was a good choice to lead the rest, because he was a king. He also said something about every being in Lyonesse—human, animal, and tree—holding the Old Magic in common. He also said others might help us."

"What others, James?"

"I asked him. Unfortunately, he doesn't answer questions."

"A table dormant with empty plates and empty cups, that conversation of yours, then," said Brian. "Or perhaps he is not the Mage he is commonly claimed to be."

"Sir Brian—" began the QB, with sudden, unexpected fierceness.

"It's all right, QB," said Jim hastily. "It's all right. Brian, I give you my word as a knight and as your friend—Merlin is all they say and more. I'm not easily impressed by words alone—and it wasn't words alone, with him. I could *feel* his power; and you would have, too, if you'd been with me."

"Well, well," said Brian, recovering his usual good humor. "It could be common repute is right—it often is. I would much rather think of him as a great Mage, rather than otherwise. But what now, James, QB? Should we go in pursuit of King Pellinore, rather than waiting? Or somewhat else?"

"I do assure you he will be back at any minute, now," said the QB. "I give you my word. The word of a Questing Beast is not one that men are asked to take every day; but I promise you it is good—look, there he comes now!"

Jim and Brian looked where the QB was pointing with his serpent head, at the forest into which King Pellinore had ridden.

"Where?" asked Jim.

"By my faith," said Brian, "I do not see anyone."

"I forgot," said the QB. "Neither of you is used to looking from the bright day into the shadow of the trees as I am. Keep looking, though, and you will see him."

They stared for a full minute longer; and then Jim saw motion among the tree shadow, and then a shape that could be a man on a horse.

"So I do," said Brian. "You were right, QB. Our eyes are no match for yours."

"A matter of practise, only," said the QB.

They all watched as King Pellinore emerged from the

gloom and rode up to them, dismounting when he reached them. Without a word being said his horse walked off, around the same corner of the log building from which it had appeared. Jim and Brian watched it go with interest; but when they turned back to Pellinore, they saw his gaze was on the QB, rather than them.

"A marvel, QB," he said to the Questing Beast. "Balan and Balin are with us again. There is also word of others of the Table who fought against Arthur at that last great battle and were thought dead: but are also now back and repenting their falsity to him, saying that it was Modred who led them into such traitorous acts. Even Gawain himself—who, you remember, repented himself to Arthur on his deathbed—is back again and of a changed heart."

"I remember," said the QB. "He lamented to Arthur that he had been the cause of Arthur's unwilling war against Lancelot, and so of Modred's treason."

"So he did," answered Pellinore; and they both stood silent, possibly remembering things of a long time past.

It was not the kind of silence that strangers can feel comfortable interrupting. But Jim had been reminded of something, that now seemed as if it might be too important to go unasked.

"Tell me," he said. "You must both know what Modred looked like. Will you describe him for me?"

The two looked at him, then at each other. But, when the QB said nothing, King Pellinore answered.

"He was tall and well made," said Pellinore, "but not so great as his father, Arthur. Not an ill face, but neither what might be said to be a well-favored one. His shoulders were overwide for his height and his arms overlong, his hands large."

He turned to the QB.

"What else might you say of him?"

"He was young of face," said the QB. "Full-grown, but there was something of one almost too young for knighthood about it—though his years were enough and his skill with arms equal to those about him. But he was uneasy in company and preferred to drive the men he commanded, rather than leading them—just otherwise than did Arthur."

"For all that," said Pellinore, "there was no weakness of spirit in him."

"No," said the QB. "Indeed there was not."

"Tell me more about his face, his mustache, his beard," said Jim.

"He had neither mustache nor beard," answered the QB. "He was clean-shaven at all times, as much so as was Lancelot and Galahad."

"Then he couldn't have a bushy mustache and a chin-beard?"

"He could have, I am sure," said the QB. "But he did not care for such things; and also, such was not the fashion of the Knights at Arthur's court. Except for Arthur, who in his later years grew a noble beard."

"Why do you ask, James?" Brian's voice was curious.

"Remember, when the Earl of Cumberland and Agatha Falon had us in that large tent, there was a man behind them in the shadows? All I could make out was that he had a mustache and a goatee. But that was the man that the QB said was Modred, by his scent."

"I could not see him well," said Brian; "but mustaches and beards can be grown and shaved off again."

"Yes," said Jim, "and if Knights are being brought back to life again, Modred could have been brought back, too. Merlin told me the Old Magic had made some change, though he did not know what it was—that it could be something unimportant, but there was no telling. Perhaps this return of the Knights is part of that."

"Modred will find small welcome in Lyonesse," said Pellinore.

"I didn't think so," said Jim. "But there he was, behind the Earl of Cumberland and Agatha Falon."

"Who is this Earl and this Lady?" asked Pellinore.

"Old enemies of Sir Brian and myself," Jim said. "But I've never known them to be outside of the land above, before—wait! That's not true—I'd forgotten that Agatha appeared in Lyonesse to trick us into an ambush—you remember, QB, when you saved us from those giants."

"I recall, but I did not see her at that time," said the QB.

"No, she vanished once the trap had been sprung," Jim said.

"The Witch Queen, Morgan le Fay," said Brian. "She must have brought them."

"She shouldn't have the power to do that without help from the land above."

"James, you told me plainly that Agatha Falon was a witch."

"I didn't. I told you only that others said it. And KinetetE denied it, saying Agatha had only tried to learn Witchery and found it required more than she wanted to give it, in lifetime study and effort. But it's possible she picked up a bit of their art before giving up," said Jim.

But even as he said this, a thought came to him that he told himself he should have had before. A name or title could mean different things, depending on who said it. If someone had asked KinetetE, as little as a year before, whether he, Jim, was a Magickian, she would undoubtedly have snapped that he was nothing of the kind—yet! But by that time he actually had learned a number of things in the Art.

Still, by KinetetE's standards he would not have been qualified for the title.

But Jim had assumed from KinetetE's response to him that Agatha had left the witch-seminary without really learning anything. That might not have been true. There was the instance of the Witch-Gate, for example.

He stood, thinking a moment longer. Had KinetetE known about the invasion force in the Borderland, when he told her that he, Brian, and Dafydd were going to the Drowned Land and Lyonesse?

"Maybe there's a way to find out," he said, more to himself than the others. He turned to Brian. "It would mean leaving you for a little while."

"I am hardly a child to be watched and guarded, James."

"Of course not, Brian. I didn't mean that. I meant—

anyway, we've yet to hear from King Pellinore about how the other Originals felt when he spoke to them."

They all turned to face the towering man, who now stood looking down on them like some iron statue from an earlier age—iron face, iron hands, as well as iron armor.

"I spoke to no more than twenty of the Originals, if that many. I did not keep count. They were the ones who should be told first. The word will spread. They think on you, Sir James, as like to Merlin in that you must be able to see the future; and therefore pray you to name who will lead them to battle. It is sad . . ."

The iron face softened for just a moment.

". . . but the younger ones are not like us, desire what they may. They will wish to fight also, of course. But they are not of the mold of we of older days."

"We met a younger Sir Dinedan, our first time through Lyonesse," said Brian, "and I had the honor of encountering him with lances. But he had the misfortune to swoon just as both our spears were about to touch. I gathered from what he said that it was a family weakness."

"If so, I do not know of it," said Pellinore. "The Original Sir Dinedan has never given sign of any such swooning. He is a Knight of good heart and strength, though perhaps over-sudden in his decisions. No, this is the sort of change that has crept into our children and their children. I thank Heaven that the two sons of my own body, Sir Percival and Sir Lamorack of Wales, were of an age to belong to the Round Table while it still existed—and showed no such weakness whatsoever."

He broke off suddenly, looking at Jim.

"But Sir James," he went on, "you have not told me who you choose to lead we who are the Original Knights. You must come with me and name him to them."

Jim was thinking fast. If neither the trees nor the Old Magic was going to be of help, then he needed to get busy on his own. The first thing was to find out what the Dark Powers had in the way of ogres, Worms, Harpies and such. He had no time to go and talk to Knights right now. What if he had to name himself as that leader, to go ahead and have to try to counter what magic he could?

"Look," he said to Pellinore, "I've got reasons for not wanting to announce my choice of someone to lead them right away. Magic is involved in this; and I've got to find out how powerful it is, first. I'd rather you just told them the name of the leader is something to be revealed hereafter. For now, only tell them that no common man shall lead them."

Pellinore looked grimly at him.

"Indeed, that promise could be a better one," he said. "For, providing all other virtues be equal, it is always best that he who leads is a king. But since I myself am a king, and I would not have it thought that I had, in some way, unseemly put myself forward, it should be you, Sir James, when the time comes, who tells them who it will be. Horse!"

But even as the tall white horse was still nodding his way around the corner of the house to come to Pellinore, the QB cried out.

"King! Wait! The trees are speaking to me of an urgent message for Sir James. One comes with it, but does not know how to find Sir James. I must go to meet him; and bring him here, so that he not wander the land of Lyonesse for years."

"Go, then," said Pellinore. "Let Sir James hear him, but do not delay after. I have said the other Originals must swiftly know the choice of a leader is forechosen, and beyond dispute."

Chapter 28

Whether it was a result of the somewhat testy tone of King Pellinore's last words, or not, would probably never be known; but it was a fact that the QB reappeared in what seemed like a minute and a half after vanishing into the gloom of the surrounding trees at a full lope—a black-and-white leopard blur.

Having reappeared, however, he came from the trees to

them at a more reasonable pace, to let the messenger he had spoken of trot his horse level with him. The messenger was young—surprisingly young, Jim thought, no more than fourteen years old. But he wore the clothing of the Drowned Land leaders, among which Dafydd and his Blues belonged. Also, there was a quiver at his side and an unstrung longbow at his back, stretching from above his head as he sat in the saddle, down to past the horse's withers. A bow Jim would have thought too long for him to pull.

His face was pale and drawn with fatigue, which gave him the look of being older than his plainly youthful years—and it was only then that Jim realized that he was once more looking at the young King of the Drowned Land—a very worn young king.

"Your Majesty!" he said, stepping forward to hold the stirrup as the King swung down from his saddle. "I hadn't thought—may I name to you King Pellinore, one of the Originals of the Legends that people this land of Lyonesse. As of course is the Questing Beast, whom you have met already. And Sir Brian you already know, also."

"Yes," said the boy-King.

"King Pellinore, may I name to you . . ." Jim ran out of words and turned to the Drowned Land monarch. "Forgive me, your Majesty, but I'm afraid I was never told the name by which you should be introduced."

"I am David."

". . . Name to you King David of the Drowned Land. But what brings you, out of all the other people in your land, to me, your Majesty?"

"I speak for my people," said the young King, lifting his head and squaring his shoulders. "We must have your help without delay, Sir James. Otherwise my people and my land are lost."

Pellinore said nothing immediately; though the words "without delay" must have triggered a powerful reaction in him. But Jim felt his presence acutely, standing there, towering over both him and the newcomer. Jim's mind raced; and he hurried to speak before Pellinore should.

"I'm afraid you're asking me that at a bad time," he said, as gently as he could. "I'm not free to leave Lyonesse right at the moment. What's been happening in the Drowned Land? And why did you come, instead of sending someone else, like Dafydd?"

"Dafydd ap Hywel, like all our best bowmen, is needed to defend our cities, which now hold all who belong to the Drowned Land. Even the people of the fields and forests have fled to them for shelter from the winged monsters."

"*Winged* monsters—" For a second, Jim's memory had jumped back to his first encounter with the creatures of the Dark Powers. "Didn't Dafydd call them something other than that?"

"He did. I do not remember what it was. You are right, he had a name for them. But I had no time to remember it, for the decision was that I must go and get you to save us; for the bite of the monsters is death."

"He called them Harpies, didn't he?"

"Yes. That was the name. You know of them?"

Jim nodded, and the image of them as they had attacked at the Loathly Tower was back in his mind's eye—like it or not. The white, staring faces of women, borne on short, bat-like bodies and great, naked-looking wings, their expressions frozen in some form of insanity, swooping down upon him, Brian, and the rest—and Dafydd, coolly shooting down each one that was closest with a single arrow, in the moment they appeared out of the thick, low-lying cloud overhead, level with the top of the tallest ruined spire of the Loathly Tower.

In the end, his arrows used up, a harpy had gotten though to Dafydd and bitten him; but when Danielle, who was not then his wife, told him she loved him, he had refused to die . . .

"I know them," he said, jerking himself back from memory of that time. "They're one of the kinds of creatures the Dark Powers make. But none of us except Dafydd could do anything against them. I'm no archer and never could be one like Dafydd; and it took him to aim and shoot fast enough to keep them from us. Besides, didn't you say your best archers are holding off the Harpies?''

''Only the Blues are great with the bow,'' said the young King. ''The other Colors know it from childhood, but without a Blue to captain each guarding force, some Harpies would get through; and those Blues must sleep sometime. But beyond that, Dafydd said to get you. He said that where you go the Dark Powers draw back; you find always some means to drive them away. We must have you with us, Sir James, and speedily! Even the minutes we spend here talking count against us!''

''He cannot go,'' said Pellinore, in a deep, hard voice. ''He is committed to Lyonesse now. After he is done here, he may help you. Cannot you understand that, bo—'' He broke off just in time and substituted the words ''—King David?''

The young King swung about to face Pellinore, and stood looking at him. They regarded each other as a small terrier and a heavy-shouldered mastiff of four times the size might do. Then David turned to Jim.

''Is this so?'' he said.

''Well, you see . . .'' Jim searched for words that were not there. They would not come. David swung back to face Pellinore.

''Then I challenge you!'' said David. ''I will fight you for possession of him.''

Pellinore stared down at him.

''You are mad,'' he said. ''Your worry for your people has driven all sense out of you. You are still a boy, far too young; and in any case, not a knight.''

David threw his head back.

''I was knighted by my father on my fifth birthday. After that, like all kings' sons in the Drowned Land, one of my studies was the use of sword and lance. Yield up Sir James or I call you a recreant knight!''

Pellinore, Jim, and Brian stared at each other. It was unbelievable. Ridiculous—not merely like a terrier and a mastiff, but more like a small puppy squeezing though the bars of a cage in a zoo, to challenge the male lion there.

In this case, thought Jim, looking at Pellinore, the male lion was looking unusually grim—which baffled Jim until he realized the grimness was part annoyance, part admiration. Brought up in a martial environment, the one thing that was admired was courage—even if it was foolish courage.

Pellinore could be not without a feeling of kindness toward the boy. But unfortunately he was trapped by what and who he was. As a Knight of the Round Table, let alone as a King, he had been threatened by the one word he could not overlook. A *recreant* knight was one who was willing to buy his life at any price; and the young King, although he was inexperienced and something like a quarter of a man—in terms of his age and experience—was still old enough to know what he was saying.

There was no way out for Pellinore. As for the young King—Jim looked at his pale face, his head still held high. There was no way out for him either, now, but to beg mercy from Pellinore. No hope of that.

"King Pellinore," burst out Brian suddenly, "I beg you accept me as the champion, to do battle for King David—"

"I will have no champion!" The boy's voice cut across Brian's. "I am a king. I choose to fight. I, myself, and no other for me!"

"You have neither weapons nor armor," said Pellinore gruffly to David, looking down at his challenger. "I remember when my sons were your age . . . come along with me. Perhaps some of their armor will fit you."

He led the boy in through the door of the log building, closing it behind him.

"Is the child mad?" said Brian to Jim. "Could it be he was bitten by a dying harpy without remembering it, and poisoned just enough to lose his wits?"

"I don't think so," said Jim. "I think it's a couple of things, working together. One is that it's hard to believe you can die when you're his age. He knows what he's up against, just by looking at King Pellinore; but I wouldn't be surprised if he thought there was a chance for him to get lucky and win. But he's also got guts and a sense of responsibility; and

I'd bet he's hoping that if he's killed trying to get me to help his people, I'll be so ashamed and impressed that I'll find some way to get free of Lyonesse and go to their rescue. I give him credit for brains as well as guts."

"There is something magickal you can do there, then, about the Harpies?"

"No," said Jim. "That's the thing. There isn't. If I had the use of my magic—" He broke off, lowered his voice, and looked around. No one but the horses—five of them now—was within hearing; and in normal horse fashion, there being nothing else to do at the moment, they were eating grass. "Brian, I've explained to you what a ward is, haven't I?"

"The magick protection?"

"That's it. I've got one around me now. I probably should have told you about it after we got away from Northgales, but . . ." He briefly explained about the ward KinetetE had put around him and that Morgan le Fay had burned her fingers on, trying to strip it from him.

". . . So you see," he wound up, "it's as if I don't have any magic at all, right now. To use it I'd have to open the ward; and I suspect Morgan herself, or someone or something, is ready, just waiting for the moment I crack it open—"

Jim broke off as the door to the building swung open, and both of them turned towards the sound of its opening. David came out, now in armor and with a sword scabbarded at his side—armor that was somewhat loose for him, but did not fit him badly enough to hamper his movements.

The suit of chain mail, however, did make him look bigger and more able. Unfortunately, he was followed out by Pellinore; and with his appearance, the illusion of added size and ability about David evaporated.

"You will have to use your own horse," Pellinore said to the young King. "I have no horses here that will allow anyone but me to ride them. But I will ride the weakest of mine so that there shall be as little difference between us as possible. Horse! Back to where you belong. Tallow!"

His white horse stopped eating and headed back around the corner of the building, passing as he did so an approaching, somewhat overweight mare, also white, but of a rather strange white—literally, in fact, about the color of tallow wax. Like Horse, she was already saddled and bridled. She grunted agreeably as Pellinore's weight descended onto her back.

David had already ridden his own horse—it appeared to be gray in the Lyonesse lighting, and was light-weight and bred for speed, rather than strength, as most of the Drowned Land equines seemed to be—some thirty yards off. Now he turned it about to face back the way they had come. He sat it quietly, waiting.

"This is crazy!" said Jim, suddenly overcome with a feeling of revulsion. "I can't just let the boy be killed like that!"

Brian's fingers closed like a metal clamp on Jim's arm.

"You can do nothing," he said. "James, *do not* open or break, or whatever you do with your ward, over this lad. I would help him, too, if I could. So would Pellinore, if I am any judge of knights—Round Table or not. But there is no way King Pellinore can do otherwise than if the lad was full-grown and skilled. If he does not fight, this boy will become a man someday; and the story will be told of how Pellinore yielded himself to him. What you see is King David's doing and no other. May God's mercy be upon him."

He crossed himself as Pellinore touched his spurs lightly to the mare; and the animal, clearly startled by what was perhaps highly unusual treatment, leaped forward. The young King, seeing this, put his own horse into an almost immediate gallop; and had covered more than half the distance between them by the time they met.

David's spear, correctly balanced loosely in his hand as he and Pellinore neared, was seized tightly only in the moment in which they came together. His actions could have been used as a perfect demonstration of all Brian had tried so hard to teach Jim. The point of David's spear touched Pellinore's shield first by a fraction of a second—touched and slid off the angled shield into air.

Oh, no! thought Jim. But in that same second, Pellinore

lifted his spearpoint away from the center of David's shield, to strike only on its upper edge; and the mare, who in spite of being smaller than Pellinore's white warhorse stood at least three hands taller and weighed proportionately more than David's horse, rode the young King's steed into the ground.

—And the boy flew from the saddle, to fall heavily to the ground and lie without moving.

"NO!" This time Jim shouted it, furious at himself for letting this thing happen. He was already running toward David. But there was someone before him. Pellinore was already off his Tallow horse, walking with great strides toward Jim, carrying the small, limp body in his arms.

"You are magick!" thundered Pellinore, laying the boy at Jim's feet. "He is like Lamorack, my son, at that age. Save him!"

Jim glared at Pellinore, the fury in him at himself finding in this command an excuse to turn itself on the Round Table Knight. Pellinore's face above him was hard and grim—nothing more.

But abruptly, what he had said about his son Lamorack got through to Jim, making him realize that Pellinore was perhaps incapable of showing much other emotion—that inside he might be suffering over what he had just done to this boy. Jim turned on Brian, who had run out just behind him.

"Will you get out of my light, Brian?" he all but shouted, as he knelt beside the unmoving David. "How can I see with you throwing your black shadow on him?"

"Grant me pardon, James," said Brian, and stepped aside. The white sun overhead flooded the white, unmoving face of the boy. The worn, tired look on it was gone.

Now that Jim had shouted at Brian, however, there was little else he could do. David was either unconscious or already dead. Jim's hand felt for the boy's jugular vein, hunting for a pulse; and discovered that he, himself, was holding his breath. He breathed again, as he felt the throb of moving blood against his fingertips.

Unconscious meant hope—but it also could mean death in a while, if nothing was done when the unconscious person had suffered a concussion. In fact, even as he knelt beside David, the thought came home to him, hard and fast, that if anything was to be done, it should be done *now.* Seconds could be precious.

The hell with it! He would have to work quickly, almost instantaneously, before his vulnerability could be taken advantage of. But maybe . . .

He broke open his ward, concentrating on the magic for the healing of wounds. It was done in almost the same moment, but when he tried to close the ward again—just as quickly—it would not close.

David's eyelids twitched. They opened.

"Sir James!" he said in a dreamy voice. His gaze went beyond Jim to Pellinore. "I admit myself vanquished, King Pellinore, and do crave your forgiveness for my trespasses against you."

"You are forgiven, lad," said Pellinore in a harsh voice. "You rode and fought in proper fashion. You have a good heart; and if sobeit you live, may well become a passing good knight. The armor and weapons you wear are now yours, by my gift."

He turned and walked away, the mare following like a dog.

"James!" said the voice of Brian; and Jim, still kneeling, with an effort looked up and behind him, to find Brian smiling down at him.

"Thank you, Brian," he said, meaning "Thank you for not resenting that I took my own upset out on you." But the words would not come out clearly, for some reason; and the ground, the sky, the trees—Brian himself, and the QB, who had also come to join them about David—were beginning to whirl around him, all their parts running into each other, everything being sucked down into darkness, like water whirlpooling into a drain.

He was sucked down into that same darkness; and he heard a woman's laugh—in a voice he knew.

Chapter 29

"Where am I?" said Jim.

"Where do you think?" said KinetetE, standing over him. "Does this look like some place in Lyonesse?"

It did not. Sunshine flooded the room from its one high, arched window. Yellow sunshine. WHEN THY SHOE IS ON THY FOOT, TREAD UPON THORNS still proclaimed itself from the sampler on the wall.

"I had to open my ward," said Jim. "I thought Morgan le Fay had got me."

"I got to you first." KinetetE sat down in a now green-and-white, newly slipcovered armchair, opposite the one he discovered he was sitting in. Curiously, the severely cut red—magickian's red—robe she was wearing did not clash with the other two colors, any more than white and red flowers, together with greenery, in a vase, would have clashed with each other.

"That was lucky!" said Jim gratefully.

"No luck to it at all. I had a watch on you."

"You did! Thank you."

"Merely protecting my investment."

"Oh. Of course," said Jim, agreeable to anything, now that he had turned out to be somewhere safe. "It just hadn't occurred to me you might. But what I meant by lucky was, I was pretty sure Morgan would be watching and waiting for me to make a slip; and even if both of you were watching at the same time, of course she'd be closer to me than . . ." Jim became conscious he was talking nonsense. Distance made no difference to magic.

"What I meant was, you managed to beat her to me; and I'm grateful. She's pretty powerful."

"Not bad. No slouch, of course," said KinetetE. "Possibly worth an AAA rating if she were up above and lived right. The trouble is, she thinks she's better than she is. She's a fool if she imagines she can work with the Dark Powers and not be used by Them, for example. But being in the position she's got down in Lyonesse, now that Merlin's shut up in the tree—by the way, you spoke to him a couple of times, didn't you? What did he tell you; aside from what you told Brian?"

"I'm not really sure," said Jim. "He doesn't answer questions and he talked to me mainly about myself. If you don't mind, I won't say anything—for now, at least."

"Why not?"

"Personal matters."

"Are you," said KinetetE, "making game of me?"

"No, no," said Jim hastily. "It's just a fact that I don't feel comfortable talking about what he said. Wouldn't you want me to hesitate about telling everything I heard from you—no matter who asked?"

"I would," she said. There was a short, not entirely comfortable, silence.

"But," said Jim, "there're a lot of things I haven't said to anyone else that I do want to talk to you about. In fact, I've been thinking of trying to get in touch with you."

"Oh?" said KinetetE, suddenly in a thoroughly fresh, friendly, interested tone. "I'm glad to hear it. Your view of matters down there is exactly what I've been hoping to hear from you; but I preferred to have you volunteer to tell me. By all means, tell me what you wanted to talk to me about, Jim."

"It'll help if you'll tell me first if you've been watching everything I've been doing and saying; or just checking on me occasionally."

"Not checking," said KinetetE. "I've got more to do in my twenty-four hours each day than I can get done, without adding your concerns to the rest. I set up a watch to let me know if you got into real trouble, that's all."

"Then," said Jim, "I'd better hit all the high spots. You probably know Morgan sent me to the Forest Dedale—"

KinetetE nodded.

"After I got out of there, we got in touch with the Questing Beast—you know him?"

KinetetE nodded again—with a touch of impatience this time.

"He helped me find Brian and he's been a great help ever since. He introduced me to Merlin—oh, you'll know that, too—anyway, one thing Merlin did tell me was that Brian was being held prisoner by the Lady of the Knight More Bright Than Day. We got him free and questioned the Lady—Annis is her name—and she seemed to confirm that Morgan was working with the other Witch Queens. So we all went to talk to the Queen of Northgales—"

"She's a caution," remarked KinetetE.

"Caution?" said Jim. "Oh, I see what you mean. Well, she almost captured us; but we only got free with the help of—the QB thought—either the trees or the Old Magic. That reminds me, I wanted to ask you about the Old Magic—"

"I can tell you nothing about the Old Magic," said KinetetE frostily. "I don't know everything."

"That's odd—Merlin said the same thing. Anyway—" Jim went on hastily, "from Northgales's castle, all of a sudden we found ourselves in the woods. And while the QB was talking about the Old Magic, there was another darkness, and when we came out of it, we were in the Drowned Land—"

"Interesting," said KinetetE, putting the tips of her fingers together.

"—to find a discussion going on among men from several different colors, gathered about their new, young King—and there was an attempt to either assassinate or disable him while we were there. A man of the Sea-Purple was maybe responsible. Dafydd, Brian, and I went to look in the Drowned Land's Borderland with Lyonesse; and found an army of fighting men from up here encamped there. And guess what?"

"I never guess."

"Well, they took us prisoner; it turned out the Earl of Cumberland—you remember him and Carolinus at Malencontri?"

"I knew," said KinetetE, "the Earl of Cumberland before you were—a long time before you did. Just tell me what happened to you in his hands."

''We escaped from them into Lyonesse—that's it, in short form—but I thought you'd want to hear about our seeing Agatha Falon with Cumberland—and Modred.''

''Modred?''

''Yes. All those Knights who died in the Legends have come back to life—still not enough to match the numbers of the men the Earl seems to have brought into the Borderland—and so, it appears, has Modred. At least, the Questing Beast says he smelled his scent; although the person I saw was wearing a mustache and beard, which no one remembers him wearing.''

''Never mind Modred. How did Cumberland get an army into Drowned Land territory? There's no entrance but by magick.''

''Agatha,'' said Jim. ''She was there with the Earl. I know you told me she wasn't a witch, and I believe you—but she could have picked up a simple spell or two. I thought of the Witches' Gate.''

''Did you, now?'' KinetetE stared hard at him. ''And what were you doing to find out about the Witches' Gate, yourself?''

''Well, there were all sorts of servants' tales about witches getting into houses where every door was locked with a crucifix or a blessing. I just figured out how it was most likely to be done, tried doing it once on the wall of an empty guest room at Malencontri—and it worked. Is there another name for what I did?''

''No,'' said KinetetE shortly. ''Did Carolinus give you leave to experiment like that?''

''He never told me not to.''

''Hmp!'' said KinetetE. ''Well, what did you learn about Modred, Agatha, and the Earl?''

''Just that they all seemed to be in it together—and I suspect Morgan le Fay might be the link working directly with the Dark Powers. That's as much as I can tell you. After that we escaped back into Lyonesse.''

''And you broke the ward I gave you, to save that young King of the Drowned Land,'' said KinetetE coldly. ''Luckily, at that moment I was checking on you. Why, may I ask—or was it mere sentiment?''

Jim had been ready for this question, expecting it and having time to think his answer over.

''He's unusually bright. I think he's what the Drowned Land needs, so I did what I had to to keep him alive.''

''And to hell with Lyonesse?'' said KinetetE.

''Not to hell with Lyonesse,'' answered Jim. ''I also think the young King has a part to play in keeping Lyonesse safe.''

''You'll have to explain how to me.''

''I can't,'' said Jim, looking at her squarely. ''I'm not sure why I think so myself. That's why I've been wanting to talk to you. There're two things I'm pretty sure of, but I may be dead wrong on. The first is, there's only so much magical energy in the world—am I right?''

''Of course you're right,'' said KinetetE. ''Carolinus must have told you this more than once—save your magickal energy, no matter how much of it you seem to have at the time. For one reason, there's always something turning up that will require a good deal of it—something unexpected. Don't tell me he didn't tell you.''

''He did, many times,'' said Jim. ''But he didn't explain it was because there was only so much available.''

''But what other reason could there be? The nonmagickal person thinks that the high price he has to pay a magickian is simply because the magickian can get away with asking it—like that old dragon who was the grand-uncle of the dragon body you were in, whatever his name was—''

''Smrgol.''

''Yes. The time Smrgol tried to hire Carolinus's help to get Angie back from the other dragon who'd stolen her—''

''Bryagh.''

''—for the Dark Powers at the Loathly Tower. You'll remember, they settled on a high price—I don't recall exactly how much, but—''

''Four pounds of gold, one of silver, and a large, flawed emerald.''

''James,'' said KinetetE in a terrible voice, ''outside of my own duty to join you in this battle against the Dark Powers, I have a real affection for you and Angie. But if you do not stop footnoting every third word I say, I will maroon you at World's End—which I believe Carolinus showed you once—with no one to talk to for nine hundred and ninety-seven years but that oversize hourglass, counting the seconds until the next Phoenix wakes up!"

"Sorry," said Jim.

"I should think so!" she said. "As I was trying hard to tell you, the ordinary person thinks the high price is because the magickian can ask it; actually it's because magick takes magical energy, and that has to be earned in other ways by the magickian—so it's not that easily replaceable!"

"I know," said Jim. "Like I did at the Loathly Tower."

"Except you weren't—still aren't—a magickian."

"I understand," Jim said. "But I wanted to be sure of the fact that there's only so much magic in the world. If so, then the Dark Powers don't have an unlimited supply of it, either. That means there's a limit to how much of their power they can spend on ogres, Worms, Harpies, and the like. Particularly Harpies, because the young King came for my help because his people are being attacked by Harpies. Dafydd, who learned with us at the Loathly Tower that arrows could stop them, and his Blue clan have been defending them, but they're beginning to get exhausted."

"Ah!" said KinetetE.

"But if the Dark Powers can only afford to lose so many Harpies, then maybe the Drowned Landers can get by without me. That's important because I had to tell the King that Lyonesse had first claim on me. But, as it turned out, even though he had only been five when it happened, he had been knighted; and he challenged King Pellinore for me—"

"He did *what*?"

"Challenged Pellinore—"

"Just a moment. Are we speaking of the same Pellinore? King Pellinore of the Legends?"

"That's right."

"The boy was insane. High fever, perhaps."

"I don't think so, unless being young is sort of like being in a high fever most of the time . . . anyway, the boy was nearly killed in a spear-running, in spite of Pellinore's taking it as easy on him as possible. He would have died if I hadn't cracked my ward so I could heal him magically."

"So that was it," said KinetetE, with an unusual gentleness in her voice. "I wouldn't have thought it of Pellinore—he *was* challenged, of course . . ."

"And he *is* Pellinore. He lent the boy the armor of one of his sons, and gave it to him afterwards. But I think if it had been the son himself at that age, who had challenged him, he would have felt he had to meet him."

They both sat in a little silence for a moment. Jim finally broke it.

"Tell me," he said, "do you happen to know how long it would take to make a new harpy to replace one who's been killed?"

"No," said KinetetE, "but I can find out. How long to create a new harpy, you?"

She was speaking directly not to any ordinary, invisible magician's tool, but to the sampler. As Jim looked, its message about treading on thorns vanished. A new message spelled itself out in large letters.

9 DAYS 3 HOURS 4 MINUTES

"That's good!" said Jim. "That's very good! If the rest of the Blues are even a patch on Dafydd, they could pretty well have stripped the Dark Powers of Harpies, by this time—oh, by the way, KinetetE, can you send me back to Lyonesse only a minute or so after you brought me here? The longer I'm away from there, the more chance there is of someone doing something to tangle things up."

"You should have learned to handle time yourself by now," said KinetetE. "Practice! That's the thing—oh, well, I guess I can manage it for you, once more."

"Thank you," said Jim. "Good of you to do this. I'll practice. Oh, and by the way, could you send me to Malencontri first—I just want to say a word or two to Angie—and then give me a command I can say that will send me back to Lyonesse; arriving, as I say, just a minute or two after I must have disappeared?''

KinetetE looked at him for a long moment, and he was sure she was about to cancel the promise she had just made. But instead, she turned to the sampler.

''All right,'' she said, ''back to regular duty.''

The Years, Months, and Days in their numbers disappeared; and the advice about shoes came back again.

''I think,'' she said, in a perfectly calm voice, ''you said there were two things you wanted to ask me about?''

''Yes. I wanted to be sure about something. Am I also right that, being Powers only, the Dark Powers might be able to conquer something solid like a territory, but there's no way they can hold it? They can't change or build anything. All they could do would be to stand over it forever, ready to act against anyone else who tried to use it—and if they concentrated on doing that, they couldn't use their abilities anywhere else?''

''Perfectly right,'' said KinetetE. ''How does that come to be important?''

''It struck me even before I came to Lyonesse this last time. They've always worked through some other party when there was something real to be done.''

''Yes,'' said KinetetE darkly.

''—and I'd just chased them out of Malencontri, but this was the first time it occurred to me that, like everyone and everything else, they had to have limitations.''

''They're not the kind of limitations any magickian has ever been able to take advantage of,'' KinetetE said.

''If they're limitations, there has to be something an advantage can be taken of.'' Jim discovered he had clamped his jaws tightly together. He unclamped them. ''I think they've realized this themselves, maybe a good time back; but that's why they're trying to gain Lyonesse, then—and the Drowned Land, too, for all I know. Though I don't think the Drowned

Land's that important to them—except as some means to an end.''

''Why?''

''Why?'' echoed Jim.

''Why do you think the Drowned Land's only a means to an end?''

''Because it's only Lyonesse they can really use. The Legendary human beings in Lyonesse are already partly made of magic, or else the original Round Table Knights wouldn't be still alive. They could hope to work, hope to get control of these men and their descendants, through that immaterial, magical element in them, where they wouldn't find anything to tie to in ordinary, mortal humans—unless the human already wanted to do something evil. They could never get flesh-and-blood people to do what they wanted done, only those twisted by greed, or hatred, or whatever made them temporarily useful in the past.''

He stopped talking. KinetetE did not reply immediately.

''Well, do you think I'm right about that?'' Jim asked finally.

''I may owe you an apology, Jim,'' she said at last. ''You may see some things more clearly than the rest of us. I will tell you something I've made it a practice never to tell anyone: I don't have any answer for you. I just don't know.''

''But it's possible?''

''Only if you could assume that they had a way of taking control through the magick connection; and also knew why the individuals couldn't just refuse to be taken over.''

''Maybe people like the Knights of Lyonesse can't refuse.''

''I doubt that,'' said KinetetE. ''In any case, what else can the Powers do but ask—ask and hold out some sort of bait? Isn't that the situation, Jim? Just ask? And how far will that get them, with anyone who can't be tempted or tricked into doing their will?''

Jim thought about it.

''What would you do ?'' KinetetE asked, ''if they asked you to go do what they wanted?''

''I'd refuse, of course.''

"And what if they asked your King Pellinore?"

Jim laughed. He couldn't help himself; and the laugh cleared his mind. He had a sudden, clear mental vision of the Dark Powers dimming the Lyonesse sky and saying in their most terrible voice *Will you now go forth and be an evil knight?* and Pellinore, all seven feet of him—no, he wasn't seven feet tall, but close enough—in full armor and weapons—simply looking back at them with grim disbelief on his iron face, even more pronounced than that Jim had seen there when David had challenged him.

"If asking is all they can do, you're right," he told KinetetE. "But it worries me to think they might even try this if they thought they had no other way around their problem."

"We've got two different theories, you and I," said KinetetE. "Go back down to Lyonesse and find out which—or neither—is right. I've put your ward back. Give my regards to Angie."

—And he was gone.

Chapter 30

He was back in their Solar bedroom; and there was Angie, doing something to their bed, with her back to him, right within reach.

"Angie!" he said, enfolding her in his arms—

She shrieked.

"What's the matter—" he began as she writhed around in his arms—amazing how strong she'd gotten these last few years—recognized him, and glared murderously at him.

"It's just me," he said. "Aren't you glad to see—"

"I've told you, and told you!" she said fiercely. "Told you, and *told* you and TOLD YOU! NOT to come out of nowhere like that when I think you're a thousand miles away, and I don't know what might have just happened to you!"

"Lyonesse isn't a thousand miles away. Maybe a couple of hundred—"

"Who cares if it's a hundred or a thousand? You're not supposed to do that!"

"Actually," said Jim, although he felt his rejoinder so far had been rather weak, "I wasn't even that far off. I was with KinetetE—"

"That makes it worse!"

Age and experience had taught Jim a few things—one being that this was one of those arguments he would never win if he argued until the end of eternity.

"I'm sorry," he said humbly.

"You ought to be!"

"I'll go away and come back again after warning you first."

"No, you won't," said Angie, wrapping her arms around him—she really had become *very* strong—and hugging him fiercely. "If you've got any time left between visiting Lyonesse and seeing KinetetE, you won't waste any of it going away and coming back again. You'll spend it all here."

"Of course," said Jim.

"—I actually couldn't let you know I was coming in advance, this time," he said, after they had sorted themselves out—which took a little while. "KinetetE was sending me back down to Lyonesse. She did the ward that protects me down there, you see, and I'd had to open it, so she had to do it over again. Also, I wanted to check on a few magical points with her—I love you, too—and I got her to send me to you on the way back. She sent her regards."

"Just as long as it was necessary. Regard her for me, the next time you see her. Have you eaten anything in the last twenty-four hours?"

"Oh, I think so," said Jim, trying to remember. "There's been so many things going on, I have to think. Yes, I'm sure I did."

"Brian never thinks of it unless it's under his nose; and then he eats like an ogre. He can get away with that, but when you're with him you try to keep up with him. I could have some food sent up here in minutes''.

''No, there really isn't time. Anyway, of course I ate. It's just that so much has been happening.''

''Sleep?''

''Yes, I definitely did sleep, last night in the Drowned Land,'' said Jim, thinking of waking in the darkness of the tent to find himself tied up, with Brian and Dafydd in the same situation.

''Why did you need KinetetE to send you back to Lyonesse? You could send yourself there, couldn't you?''

''Yes,'' said Jim, ''but she knows how to send me back to the minute after I left it, so no one there has any idea how long I've been gone. I still need to get back as soon as I can—magic-wise it's expensive to burn time this way—but I couldn't come up here without seeing you.''

''You could have stopped in on your way up.''

''Well, things made it impractical.''

''What things? Have you been having trouble and running yourself into all kinds of dangers? I thought you were only going down there to be a lucky rabbit's foot for Dafydd!''

''Well . . .''

''Well, yes. Hah!''

''Well, you knew it might amount to something more. But as a matter of fact, it's Dafydd and the new young Drowned Land King I've just come from being concerned with. Dafydd, being related to the old King, and well-thought-of, is Regent to the boy.''

''But you said you came from Lyonesse.''

''Well, we stepped over the border to have a look at the situation in Lyonesse, met the QB—the Questing Beast, I've told you about him—and some other people, including a couple of Witch Queens—Morgan le Fay of Gore and the Queen of Northgales. Oh, and we met the Original King Pellinore, too. I think you'd like him. Kind of like Brian, double-sized and just as stiff-backed about being a Knight. He was one of the Round Table, you know.''

''I've read about Pellinore.''

"Of course you have. But I think you'll still be surprised if you ever meet him. I was. But how about you? How've things been here?"

"What you'd expect. The Castle people have their work down to fine points now, you know. Everything goes off like clockwork. I could sleep until noon every day if I wanted to and never be missed."

"Doesn't sound like the Malencontri I know," said Jim. "Like clockwork? We never have even twenty-four hours go by without something jamming up the clockwork."

"Everything was handled without dropping a stitch, I promise you."

"Oh?" said Jim. He could not put his finger on what was bothering him. He looked at her carefully. There were no shadows under her eyes, but he had the feeling that there ought to be something like that showing on her. "How about you, then? How have you been eating?"

"Alone," said Angie. "That's how I've been eating." And he could have sworn that it was an unfortunate choice of words; that if the shadows under her eyes had been there, they would have deepened.

"Something's wrong," he said.

"Don't be foolish!"

"I'm not. Maybe I'd better have John Steward up here. He wouldn't dare lie to me."

"Now, don't do that, Jim!" said Angie. "You know how they are. If you make a fuss over this, they'll all decide to be scared to death. It's like telling children not to be afraid of the dark. That just makes them sure there must be something in the dark to be afraid of; otherwise, why would you bother to mention it? I'll tell you what happened."

"What?"

"Well, your friends and mine came back—the Dark Powers."

Jim suddenly saw nothing in the room but Angie.

"They came?"

"Yes. The Dark Powers—now, don't get excited, nothing happened. But they came back again—to the Great Hall. I was down there having breakfast by myself at the High Table; and suddenly I could feel them there again."

"They came back!" he said furiously. "I told them to go and they came back! I'll put an end to that! I'll throw a ward around the whole castle. They may be Powers, but they can't move through a ward that's set up to keep them out. And I'm going to find some way to make them pay for this and for the time before—"

"Be sensible, Jim! Putting a ward around the castle is just as bad as questioning John Steward about it. You'll scare everyone else in the castle to death. Anyway, John wasn't in the Hall at the time."

"Who was?"

"Nobody! Not even the servants, unless there were some out of sight but still in hearing."

"What happened?"

"I told the Dark Powers off. Sent them away. Used your words from the time before; and, just like when you spoke to them, they went. Jim, we may not have any power over them; but what power can they have directly over one of us who's got no use for them? You said that to me, long ago . . . remember?"

"Did I?" he said, cooling down, but still ready to kill Dark Powers. "If so, I'd forgotten. But I'm glad I did; and I'm glad you remembered it and ordered the Dark Powers out. Angie, you're a hero."

She hugged and kissed him.

"Thank you, Jim," she said. "But I'm really not. I'm just like any other rat. If you corner me, I'll fight!" She hugged him again.

"Now," she said, standing back, "I've told you the truth about here. You tell me the truth about things down there. How are things in the Drowned Land and Lyonesse?"

He slumped a little, and blew out a long breath.

"Not good, as a matter of fact," he said. "For Lyonesse and the Drowned Land both. But that young King of the Drowned Land is bright and brave, too." He went on to tell her in detail about the challenge King David had made to King Pellinore.

"David didn't have a chance, of course," Jim finished. "Even if he'd been as big and strong as Pellinore, he wouldn't have had a chance. I had to break the ward KinetetE put on me to heal the hurt he'd taken, to make sure he'd live. Otherwise—"

Jim suddenly realized he was about to put his foot in his mouth.

"—Morgan le Fay might have got at me if KinetetE hadn't picked me up in time."

"So, *she* pulled *you* out of Lyonesse. That was why you went to her first!" Angie checked herself. "But these wards of hers really do keep you safe down there?"

"As safe as the magic glasses you dreamed up are keeping me."

Angie beamed.

"I'll accept that," she said. They looked at each other. "Now what, then?"

"I'm going to try to organize the Knights—the Knights of the Legends—cross my fingers and hope for the best."

"I'm glad you told me about the wards," said Angie. "That much is certain, anyway. What was KinetetE's plan for fighting the Dark Powers?"

"She didn't have any. I don't think Carolinus would, either. But Merlin—I meant to tell you, Angie, I talked to Merlin. Talked to him just like we're talking right now."

"But he's dead! Or as good as dead. Shut up in a tree with his own magic by what's-her-name—"

"There's some disagreement, evidently, about which name she actually had," said Jim. "He's shut up in a tree all right, but it seems he likes it that way. A powerful man, Angie, a powerful magician. I tell you, after talking with him I can believe people like him and Arthur and Lancelot were bigger than life. Oh, there was something he said I wanted to tell you."

"What was it?"

"Well, he wouldn't answer any direct questions—I got the

impression he was sick and tired of people asking him to predict the future. Anyway, I'd gotten out of him that I'd done the right thing in letting Pellinore go talk to the other Originals—other Knights of the Arthurian Legends—since Pellinore was a King and Lyonesse could only hope to win if its forces were led by a king—and Arthur and Lancelot are both gone; and since Lancelot had become a hermit for the rest of his days, he would never pick up a weapon again."

"But you said there was something Merlin said to you, you were going to tell me. Something else than what you've just said?"

"Yes. I was just explaining how it came about. I'd been trying to nudge him into telling me something useful about how Lyonesse could be made to win. He wouldn't say. But he did come up with this other statement—and it's hung in my mind as if it ought to mean more than it sounds at first hearing. He said, *the selfish win in the short run. The unselfish nearly always win in the long run.* You know, I can believe he's right."

"That was all he said?" Angie looked at him oddly.

"On that subject." Jim found himself sounding defensive. "It sounds like some old granddaddy saying, some old saw, doesn't it? But the more I think of it, the more it seems it ought to tell me something. Does it suggest anything to you?"

"I don't know," answered Angie slowly. "Was he talking about a man or a woman?"

"Neither. Or both. He didn't specify."

"Well, it's certainly got a lot of truth in it. Someone who's selfish usually just bulls in and takes what she or he wants, and leaves it up to you to object, if you want to. An unselfish person tends to let them get away with it—so there's your short-term winner. But the unselfish person, who wasn't just cowardly, but was in the habit of expecting to give more than he or she got, might just let it go. And in time, people would notice the unselfish one was unselfish; and like her or him for it. So the unselfish one would end up with more friends and a happier life—so there's your long-term winner."

"That's been pretty much the way I was thinking about it

myself," said Jim. "But what you just came up with was a general statement; when you start trying to apply it to the ordinary world, it gets tricky. Who's selfish? And who's unselfish?"

"That's splitting hairs, isn't it?"

"Not if you try to stick to what Merlin said to begin with. My first thought was that the people in Lyonesse, especially the Originals, had to be the unselfish ones. But then I remembered, the Legends reported some of them as not doing all that much that was unselfish. Take Gawain. Arthur himself, when Gawain was dying, said, '*In you and Lancelot I took all my joy . . .*'—or words to that effect. But it was Gawain who answered it was he who was to blame for all Arthur's final battles, because of the hatred he had developed for Lancelot. But Gawain's hatred was because Lancelot slew his two brothers—though Lancelot didn't know they were two of those he'd had to fight to save himself."

"Well, at least the Dark Powers are certainly selfish!"

"But are they? Or are they just as much a victim of what they were created to be—as the humans who suffer because of the way they help them try to destroy History or make Chance everything?"

"Got you!" said Angie, pointing her right index finger like a pistol at him. "You said they were 'created to be.' Who or what created them? Whichever it was, wasn't that creator selfish in making something only designed to destroy?"

"I don't know," said Jim. "Somehow, though, it doesn't help to give me any ideas about how Lyonesse and the Drowned Land can rid themselves of the Dark Powers."

"No, I suppose it doesn't," said Angie.

"I wish Carolinus was well and could help."

"Carolinus isn't any more of a magician than KinetetE," said Angie, "and she's left it all to you. Maybe that's what Merlin was doing, too."

"You could be right—though I'd rather they helped." Jim shook his head. "Anyway, I've been around and around in my mind with Merlin's words and turned up nothing. The trouble is, Angie, Lyonesse hasn't really got that many people in it. Just the Originals and their descendants—if it comes to fighting anything like a war. The Drowned Land has people, but outside of the Blues and maybe a few others, none of them are fully armed, armored, or experienced in fighting."

He sighed and held out his arms.

"But I've got to be getting back down." They held on to each other for a long moment. "Look, if you ever need me, just call my name, out loud. I'm setting up magic so I'll hear it no matter where I am; and be right with you."

"I'll be all right here," said Angie, as they let go. "You just take care of yourself down there."

"Oh, I'll be fine. The ones in trouble are those two unlikely little lands and the ones that live in them. But don't you take anything from the Dark Powers if they show up at all again. Call me."

"I will," said Angie.

"See you in not too long a time, now."

"See you," she said.

He vanished. There was a little inrush of air where he had stood, as if the Solar was breathing.

"Oh, Jim . . ." said Angie, looking at the place where he had been.

Chapter 31

Jim popped back into being. He was back where he had started from, with Brian, the QB, King David—everyone there just as they had been, except for King Pellinore, who was just now closing the door of the log house as he went inside it.

But there also was Dafydd, who had just swung down from a horse that was still sweating and breathing hard.

"Dafydd!" said Jim.

"I called you, James, just as I was coming out of the woods, but you were already gone."

"Well, I'm back now—" Jim stopped and snapped his

fingers in exasperation. "I knew I'd forget something. Be back again in a minute!"

"But James—"

However, he was now back in KinetetE's sitting room; and, happily, she was still there. She was talking to the *Dieffenbachia cantans* he had met there before.

"It's no use, I tell you," she was telling the singing plant. "The disorder of your voice is a side effect of the presence of the Dark Powers in Lyonesse. Leave Lyonesse and I can help you. Or stay until the Dark Powers go—Jim, what are you doing here?"

"Just a quick question," said Jim.

"But—" began the dieffenbachia hoarsely.

"No but. Begone!" said KinetetE. The plant vanished. "If it's not one thing it's twenty! What's gone wrong now?"

"Nothing—for the moment," said Jim. "I just forgot to ask you something. Tell me: Morgan le Fay can always watch me whenever I'm in Lyonesse; I assume you can watch me all the time, too, or you wouldn't have been able to snatch me up a little while ago, before she got me for opening my ward. So you ought to know what her limits are. Can she see me if I'm in my dragon body?"

KinetetE frowned at him.

"I don't know," she said, after a moment of silence. "Turn into a dragon and I'll see."

"Er—" said Jim, looking around him, "this is a very nice little sitting room, but—"

"It is perfectly capable of making room for a dragon if I want," said KinetetE. "Be one."

Jim turned into a dragon. The room had expanded.

"I see you clearly and unmistakably," said KinetetE. "Whatever gave you the notion that I couldn't—ah, I see what you're trying to tell me. Being human, I can see you with unassisted eyesight. Fly out the window and around the building until you're out of my normal sight. Then fly back."

Jim looked at the window—which was not all that wide—and hesitated.

"It's a little small," he said.

"What did I just tell you about this room? That also holds true for a window in it."

Jim extended his wings—without trouble, although they were of the enormous length required to lift his heavy body into the air and allow it to soar. He flew off through the window, finding himself outside what seemed one turret of a many-turreted structure. As big as a castle, but not one.

He flew around the blind side of the tower and back in the window.

"Quite right!" said KinetetE. "You're absolutely quite right. Magically, I lost sight of you the second you moved out of my physical eyesight. Of course! It's a branch-off from the Law that magick can't touch animals. It's true dragons are something more than animals—like Naturals—but that just means some things magickal work with them, some don't."

"Good!" said Jim. "And can I take off the ward you put on me and use my magic when I'm in dragon body, then?"

"Not unless you know how to poison the ward you put back around you later, so Morgan can't strip it off you when you have gone back to being human," she said.

"I don't suppose you could show me—"

"I could not. You know better than that by this time. Magick cannot be taught, only learned. A magickian must teach herself—or himself. Your way of poisoning a ward wouldn't be achieved the same way I achieve it."

"Yes," said Jim. She was right, of course. That principle was one of the first things he had picked up from Carolinus. "Too bad. I could be a real help down there if I could just use my magic."

"That's life," said KinetetE. "Begone."

"Poor Dafydd just rode in—more ready for a bed than a battle, James," said Brian, an edge of reproach in his voice. King David and the QB were beside him.

Brian was standing, for all the world like a male emperor penguin Jim had once seen in an Antarctic photograph, that was balancing an egg on his two feet to keep it warm under a fold of his skin in a howling, snow-filled wind. But instead of an egg, Brian was supporting Dafydd, who was seated on the ground, using Brian's legs for a backrest and sleeping so heavily he was on the verge of snoring. Very unusual behavior for Dafydd.

He had probably been captaining a team of Drowned Land archers against the Harpies, around the clock, thought Jim, remembering what young King David had told.

"Though, damme," went on Brian thoughtfully, looking down at their motionless friend, "it might have been kinder to him if you had been even longer."

He leaned down and spoke loudly into Dafydd's left ear.

"Dafydd! Wake! He is with us again. WAKE, I say!"

Dafydd's eyelids fluttered, tried to stay closed, reluctantly opened. He stared around at David, QB, and Jim as if he recognized none of them. Then, abruptly his eyes were wide open and he was struggling to his feet. Brian gave him a hand up.

"Sir James!" he said thickly. "I saw you from the edge of the woods and called—"

"And I disappeared again. I'm just now back. Sorry, Dafydd; but it was necessary for all our sakes."

Dafydd ran the back of a hand across his lips.

"Is there water, anything, to drink about?" he said. "My mouth is dry as a land in drought."

"Here," said Brian. He stepped over to Blanchard, untied his saddle flask, and pulled out the stopper as he brought it back to Dafydd.

"My thanks, Sir Brian—"

"Drink, man! And be done with courtesy!"

Dafydd drank and choked.

"Wine!" he said, when he could speak. "Very good wine, Brian, but if I might just have some plain water first—"

"I will go ask the good King for some," said David. "He must have water within doors."

But Hob was already coming up to Dafydd, carefully pouring water from a flask, as he came, into a rather battered bronze mazer—both items retrieved from among the goods on the sumpter horse.

Hob handed the brimming mazer to Dafydd, who took it in both hands and poured its contents down his throat without stopping to breathe; although the mazer would have held more than a pint.

"Good," said Brian, watching him hand the empty mazer back to Hob. He passed his flask once more to Dafydd; who, to Jim's surprise—Dafydd was usually almost as abstemious as Jim, himself—drank heartily from it.

"Now I have my voice again," said Dafydd, handing the flask back to Brian. "My thanks to you, Brian, and James and Hob. I will remember this kindness so long as I live. But James"—he turned once more to Jim—"matters are desperate in the Drowned Land. Did our King not tell you?"

"Indeed, he did so," said Brian. "And on being told James was bespoke by Lyonesse and could not come, challenged for James's release King Pellinore, whom you do not know—"

"But I do, if only by legend and repute," said Dafydd. He stared at the young King. "You were fortunate indeed he did not take up your challenge, as he had every right to do."

"But Pellinore did," said Brian, "and King David did right nobly in their spear-running, though of course he was unhorsed and the wits knocked out of him. But Sir James made him well again with magick."

"Thank God! And thank you, James." Dafydd looked at David severely and shook his head. "What madness took you to make such a challenge to a knight—a Knight of the Round Table at that?"

"At the worst, Dafydd," said the King, "it seemed to me he might feel a sadness at having slain me; and from that sadness felt an obligation. So that he might, possibly with some others of Lyonesse, come sometime to our aid."

Dafydd only shook his head again.

"You are King," he said. "You owe it to all those in the Drowned Land to live and work for their good; rather than die for them. There are no lack of men to do that."

"Yet I thought it worth the trying," said David, "and it came out well. Beyond that: look you, Dafydd, if I am King, these decisions are mine to make."

"Yes, Sire," said Dafydd. There was an uncomfortable silence all around for a moment or two.

"But you came here for a reason, Prince Dafydd," said the QB.

"I am no Prince here," said Dafydd, "but a Master Archer, Bowyer and Fletcher; and would wish to be no other than that. But you are right, my Lord Questing Beast—may I continue to address you so?"

"That, or simply as QB."

"I shall speak to you as QB, then."

"James!" said Dafydd, turning to Jim with all the urgency that had been in his first words on waking. "We have desperate need of you. We have found some good bowmen among the other Colors, who can captain a group of archers and give us of the Blue a chance to sleep and eat. But there is a limit to how long we can hold out, nonetheless, and no limit to be seen of the Harpies that keep coming at the cities. So far none of them has gotten through—"

"As a matter of fact, there's a limit to the Harpies you can have coming at you," said Jim. "I spoke to Mage KinetetE about that. I can promise you that for the Dark Powers to send endless Harpies at you has to finally exhaust their magical powers. More than that, though, I think I've come up with a way of hitting back at the Harpies."

He turned into his dragon self.

The QB started at the suddenness of the change, moving backward a pace. David turned very pale indeed, but did not move an inch.

"It's all right, Sire," said Jim, his dragon voice booming forth. "It's just me, James. Turning into a dragon is one of the things I can do; and I did it just now because I think being a dragon may let me help your Drowned Land people against the Harpies—"

Behind him a door slammed, and a voice almost as powerful as his own roared.

"What is this? A dragon?" There was the slick, rasping sound of a sharp sword being drawn from a scabbard. "Horse!"

They all turned. Pellinore had come outside. There had not seemed any great difference in this last cry of his, but this time his tall white horse came around the end of the building toward him at as close to a gallop as the turn made possible. As it reached him, he leaped into the saddle, returned his sword to its scabbard, and seized the tall spear that stood upright in its boot beside the saddle.

He reined the white horse about to face Jim.

"It's all right!" called Jim, changing back, with the middle word, from being a dragon to a human. "I was just demonstrating something."

Pellinore's spear was still in his hand and leveled at Jim. He reined his horse back to a walk; but came on, his face still dangerous.

"Are you such a magickian as Holy Church would approve?" he demanded.

"Assuredly, he is!" said the QB, who had moved forward once more. "Would I have brought him to you otherwise? Also, the trees have spoken for him!"

"Well," said Pellinore. "If that is so, I will put up my spear." He did so. "But what was it you had been about to show these others—and I trust you had not forgotten that your first duty was here, in Lyonesse?"

Jim was trying to remember exactly what he had said that had bound him to Lyonesse first. It would not come to him. But of course, he told himself, Pellinore would undoubtedly take a very strict view of a knight's word. Nonetheless, it was time to look this King in the eye.

"I forget nothing," he said, trying to sound as close as he could to the way he thought Merlin would have said it.

"It's time," he went on, "for you to tell me some things. I want to meet with whoever'll be the leaders of the Original Knights of the Round Table here in Lyonesse. While you're arranging that, I must make some magical preparations for what I may have to do; and for that I may have to leave Lyonesse—because as long as I'm here, Morgan le Fay's going to know where I am. As it is, she can't touch me, for certain magical reasons—but on the other hand I can't use my own magic to help you. But if I can get out of her influence, maybe I can arrange things so I can help. Starting—I hope—with what comes from my meeting with the Originals. Now, can you arrange that?"

Pellinore slid his spear, upright and butt-down, almost absentmindedly back into its boot by his saddle.

"Now that you speak of this meeting," he said, "I cannot remember such a gathering, since Arthur left us. But if all are to come and that means all who once were, save Arthur and Lancelot, to be with us once more . . . it minds me . . . my two sons could be there."

His face had taken on a light as he talked. Not a great light, but as if the rocky face of a mountain had been touched for a moment with winter twilight. His gaze, which had slid aside as he talked, almost to himself, returned and sharpened on Jim.

"I will essay it," he said. "But mark me, Sir James, if there are some who will not come, I will not attempt to force them. We have long since ceased from fighting among ourselves—for any reason."

"I have a feeling," said Jim, "that they'll all come."

"If God is with us," said Pellinore. Turning, he rode off, away from them into the trees, as he had gone before.

Jim changed back into a dragon.

"Brian, Dafydd, your Majesty, QB—forgive me, all of you. I can't tell you why I'm leaving you, because of the danger of Morgan overhearing; it may be half an hour, or it may be as long as a full day or two, I don't know. But if you'll all stay here, where I can find you when I come back, it'll help more than anything. Can you all wait for me; or is there anyone who'll have to leave?"

"James," said Dafydd, "I do not know what dangers you will be going into. But I do know that our Drowned Land needs their King. Even I am needed in this evil time. We two must return to our own land."

"That's up to you, Dafydd," said Jim. "I can only say I'd like you both to stay. The serious battle's to be here. And think about something else. Harpies can fly. That's what makes their poison teeth so dangerous to any who can't. But dragons can fly, too."

With that he extended his great wings.

"James!" said Brian. "Am I to wait here and do nothing, then?"

Jim hesitated, already crouched for his upward spring.

"Not for long, Brian," he said. "A day and a night at the most—probably much less. But I must have someone to find my way back to. Pellinore should be back before long. Remember how little the time was he was gone before. I'm sure he'll invite you in, if it turns out I don't get back until tomorrow."

"Shelter was not my concern," said Brian, a little stiffly. "It was the need to ride and do." He thawed abruptly. "I will await you patiently, James."

"Thanks, Brian. I'll be as quick as I can; then there'll be plenty for both of us to do."

He leaped skyward, leaving them with the thunder of his going.

Chapter 32

As usual when he was in his dragon body, Jim's first action—indeed, the first instinct always of his dragon body—was to climb for as much altitude as he could without getting out of breath. Like all animals, including humans, dragons had both flight and fight reflexes. And in spite of their size and strength, there were times when instinct took over and they ran—just as there were times when they instinctively attacked. At all times, the direction in which a dragon preferred to run was straight up.

Almost as instinctively, when Jim reached a safe height and a river of air moving parallel to the ground in the general direction of the Drowned Land border, he gave over climbing. He extended his wings and began soaring like a hawk.

The border was closer than he had expected, believing that

the QB would have used his magiclike ability to make large distances in Lyonesse seem like small ones, when he had taken them to Pellinore. Even now, as Jim looked around and behind him from this altitude, Lyonesse appeared to stretch to a farther horizon, with only the top of a ridge above the treescape, that would be the rock cliff-face behind which lay the passage to the lands of the Gnarly.

Interestingly, he could see both suns in the sky from up here, the white sun of Lyonesse and that of the Drowned Land. They were far apart, but moving parallel to each other through the two different skies. Evidently time must be very much the same in both lands; though they seemed to have nothing in common otherwise.

He pulled himself out of these thoughts to find himself over the Drowned Land, and evidently some distance into it. His soaring, however, had inevitably moved him downward in the air current on which he was travelling, until he was now not more than a couple of hundred feet off the ground.

This did not fill in with his plans at all. From his previous experience with Harpies, he expected to find them flying at no great height above the ground.

He put his wings to work again, climbing until he could now see the dark shape of the Borderland camp to his far left, like a blotch on the horizon. But there were several glints between him and it that must be Drowned Land cities. He started a more shallow glide downward toward the nearest of these, searching as he went for a thermal updraft of warm air that would let him climb even higher.

He found it; and mounted the upward-flowing air in spirals until he could see, beyond the reflected light of the cities, a thin, dark line that would be the sea. Not a seashore, as would be normal, but the wall of water that would be the undersea, stretching up to the few small clouds like puffballs in the Drowned Land, here looking like large, softheaded pins, holding the wall erect and keeping the sea from flooding these two ocean-buried lands.

The thermal thinned and died beneath him as it cooled, rising. He abandoned it, extending his spirals to slow his descent and examining the cities as he went, to find the largest one. That would be the capital city of the Drowned Land—almost certainly the city from which David and Dafydd both had come to Pellinore, and the one most heavily under attack by Harpies.

It was not hard to pick out. It was the city with the tallest buildings; the one from which their Drowned Lander guide had most probably come for Dafydd when they had first arrived in this land.

He focused his dragon vision on an invisible line that marked the shortest point between the city and the nearest dark edge of Lyonesse.

His human eyes would have begun to water after minutes of such a steadily held gaze; particularly a gaze which was concentrating on seeing some tiny movement in the air along the shortest line of distance between the border of Lyonesse and the capital city. His dragon eyes did not.

And their ability was rewarded. After perhaps an hour, during which he had to climb twice more to maintain the height from which he intended to watch, he caught sight of what seemed no more than a close, moving clutter of dark objects, broken occasionally by a flash of white amid the dark. The whole was moving at a height of no more than four hundred feet; and slowly—it seemed from his point of view—toward the capital city, sitting in the warm Drowned Land afternoon light.

He used his wings, slowly but powerfully, to move toward what he was watching, but kept himself a good five to six hundred feet above them. As he approached, the black and white resolved itself into the shapes of eight Harpies, flying toward the capital. The black was the color of their bodies and wings—all of each of them—except their faces. The unnatural white of those faces showed with the effort of their wings from moment to moment, to make the flashes he had seen from a distance.

He had been right. They were both low and slow—compared to his winged dragon body.

He hesitated over his next move. But here in the Drowned

Land he was beyond Morgan le Fay's touch and also—what was important right now—out of her sight. He could afford one experiment.

He put himself into a glide to a point at which he would be only a few hundred feet above the Harpies. The air rushed past him, the earth below grew larger—it was startling the way the distant Harpies seemed to leap at him. He maneuvered to approach behind them.

Seen from above as he came within range of what he wanted to try, they were flying in a V-shaped formation like migrating geese, but with about the rate of wing-beat of crows. Theoretically, he told himself, they should not be able to fly at all, with that heavy, human head behind each white face.

Then, as he flew along above them, he began to understand more clearly that there was no heavy human head. What each had was only the naked-skinned, insane white face, spread out over what would normally be a bird's head and upper body—like a mask, or almost like something painted there, after all facial feathers had been plucked.

But there was no more time to waste in observation. It was time to try his experiment and then get out of here and do the more important things he had left Lyonesse to accomplish.

He turned downward; and the reflexes of his dragon body took over for him. Like a falcon stooping upon a pigeon, he plunged toward the last harpy in line. At least he could rid the Drowned Land archers of one of these.

He had imagined himself dropping in dead silence—but he was no more silent than a light plane with its motor off, diving earthward. The air whistled and sang about his body, the Harpies heard—and the one on the end saw him coming.

He had counted on their having little or nothing in the way of brains. They should be flesh, blood, and feather—little more—killing machines only, judging by the other creatures made by the Dark Powers, like the ogres and Worms he and Brian had fought in the past. But either they also had self-preservative instincts, or they were programmed to fight in the air. The last harpy immediately flipped over; and he found himself falling directly into the white face, the mouth open like that of an angry cat and the sharp teeth gleaming.

He banked almost without thinking, to sideslip past the creature—and almost made it. He felt something, a hard blow, halfway out along his right leading wingtip. Then he was below the Harpies and pulling out of his dive, too full of his own adrenalin for his dragon self to react in any way to the fact that he might have been fatally poisoned, even while his human mind was telling him he had been an idiot to attack as he had.

Then, as he steadied in level flight again, well away from the Harpies overhead, and easily able to outfly them—at least as long as life remained in him—he saw something dark, off to his right and tumbling toward the ground, falling be-low him.

It turned, falling, and it had a white face. Its bird body was crushed, almost cut in two in the middle, and the creature was either dying or already dead.

His mind refused to put two and two together for a moment; and then he remembered the blow he had felt against his wing. Plainly, it had been his contact with the now stricken harpy; and it had been too powerful and too brief for the creature to get its teeth into him, if the blow had come that far back from its mouth.

He had not been poisoned then, after all. The relief from realizing he had not been killed came so swiftly behind the realization of it that neither one really had time to register on him. He did not feel relieved, so much as he felt numb for a moment—no feeling at all.

The remaining Harpies were turning back, turning away from the city.

He exerted his powerful wings to leave them below and behind him; and flew off himself in another direction, toward the closest patch of trees he could see, less than a mile away. It was not a large patch, but the small forest was thick enough so that he could land out of the sight of either harpy or human. Most of the Drowned Land was arable open plain; but small forests, like this one, were to be seen scattered almost evenly about.

He landed, safely out of sight; and turned back into his human body to be out of his dragon one and get his mind working completely human-wise, and in the direction he had intended when he had decided to come here. There were no two ways about it. Being a dragon was advantageous, but it was not a body in which to do any deep thinking.

As a dragon, he was more adventurous; and therefore more thoughtless. As a human, he was prey to all sorts of worries that would never occur to his dragon self; but on the other hand he could think and plan more clearly. He had never thought of doing something mathematical, or playing a game of chess, or some such thing, when he was in his dragon body—just to see whether he handled those things as well as he did when human or not. He must try that, sometime.

Right now his greatest need was to be able to think. He thought he had something in mind that might do a great deal to change the balance of forces here; and he would bet it was something that would never have occurred to KinetetE or Carolinus, or anyone else dealing in either magic or magick. When in doubt, attack—some military notable had said once.

Of course, maybe it couldn't be done.

But the only way to find out was to try it.

He had now talked himself into a good humor; and he would have decided to stay being a human for a while, except that once he was, he must try accessing his magic while safely hidden on the ground.

But once safely on the ground with the trees hiding the empty landscape around him, human again and almost certainly free of watchers in any case, with the Harpies abroad, the first thing he did was to enlarge his ward so that it made a sort of small room, with about five feet of open space all around him. The next was to magically borrow the first small table he could think of, one in a storeroom back at Malencontri.

It appeared before him as commanded in the space he had made inside the ward, and he concentrated on its top, after blowing the dust off it. He wanted five different fruits.

"Apple," he said; and there was an apple—unfortunately rather small and green.

"Damn it! I meant a ripe, red apple, of course!" he snapped—and checked himself, suddenly reminded by the sound of his voice of the way Carolinus and KinetetE spoke to the Auditing Department. But who would have thought everything magical had to be spoken to or spelled out in the finest of detail each time something was wanted of it—he checked the short burst of bad temper; at any rate, this time he had gotten what he wanted. An undeniably ripe, undeniably red apple smiled placatingly up from the table at him.

"Everything ripe, now. Plum. Grape—just one—that's right. Pear. Banana—no, scrub the banana."

He was running out of fruits that could not give Morgan le Fay or anyone with her the idea that he was anything but an ordinary magickian from the land above. His first few choices were all growths that any English knight—if he could get them all in season at the same time—might be carrying. A banana was not that.

"Hell!" he said. "Make it one red grape and one white grape—seedless."

The one grape that had already appeared was a red grape. A white grape appeared between the red one and the pear.

They were lined up dutifully across the table.

"All right," he told the fruits. "Listen to me, all of you! If I take any one of you out and bite into you while I'm thinking of a magic command, the one I bite into will execute that command. I'm giving you all the power to do that. Do you understand? Jump up and down if you do."

None of them stirred a fraction of an inch.

"Hell!" he said again; and found himself suddenly aware of how his language degenerated when there was no one around to hear him. "I forgot. Now! I am now giving you the power to hear what I say to you—not just my magic commands—all right, let's see you all jump up and down, now!"

"—All right. *All right, I said!* You don't have to keep

jumping. Once up and once down will do . . . that's better. Now, I'm going to bring the ward in close around me, alone, once more. Then I'm going to put you in my purse''—he decreased the ward and started stuffing them into the large catchall bag hanging from his ordinary belt, a leather one that encircled him above the broad, weapon-supporting knight's belt—''and if I think a command at one of you while biting into whichever one of you it is, the magic in you will be liberated to execute it. Understood?''

The fruits already in his purse began to jump up and down. The apple, still in his hand, leaped clear out of it, back onto the table.

''Got you,'' said Jim, recapturing the apple and putting it safely away with the other fruits in his purse. Having done so, he remembered he had been going to try all this in his dragon body. Well, that part would have to wait.

Fruit pocketed—though ''bagged'' might have been a better word—and the ward closed up tight around him once more, he took off skyward; and once he had climbed to an altitude where he would not be flying into either incoming or exiting Harpies, he headed for a quick look from high up at what he had decided was the capital city.

He soared over it at a little above fifteen hundred feet. There were Harpies there, individually roaming its streets just below roof level of the buildings. Every so often, one of them would drop with an arrow through it. But from this height Jim could not make out where the arrows were coming from. All the windows were shuttered tight and there was no one to be seen in the streets.

Certainly, from here at least, the Drowned Land archers seemed to be more than holding their own.

Curiosity drew him down. He sideslipped lower and lower until he had the good luck with his dragon sight to catch the flicker of an arrow coming out from one of the shuttered windows; but he still could not see how.

Another hundred feet down and his dragon-sight was able to make out a small slit in the shutter. He pumped with his wings to lever himself up another story of the building and see if he could discover any other shutters with arrow slits in them—just as an arrow flickered through the air where he had been a second before.

It had not occurred to him that those in the buildings could be taking him for some other creature sent by the Dark Powers. Once more he found himself wishing that KinetetE had made his ward proof against weapons as well as magic. But it was clear he was simply going to have to take that lack into account in his plans.

He flew back to Lyonesse.

Somewhat to his pleased surprise, he found no one had left. Dafydd and David were still there, as was the QB. Hob was jumping up and down, possibly with excitement, as Jim came in for a landing and turned back into a human being.

"What happened to you?" he asked Brian, the first one to reach him. "You look different."

"Nothing happened. Dull, here. Unless you mean—" He ran a hand over the lower half of his face. "I am now shaven. King Pellinore was good enough to lend me his shaving knife. I did not bring with me a hone capable of putting a fine edge on any blade I have with me; and you may have noticed, James—I say, you *may* have noticed my beard grows somewhat swiftly. Outright nuisance! I remember I used to go two, or even three days without needing to shave—ah, your Highness! You wished to speak to Sir James?"

"What news, Sir James?" said David, pushing in between Brian and Jim. "What news? Have you any word of my poor land and people?"

"I don't think you need worry too much," Jim said. "I flew over your capital. Things may have been bad at the time you left; but everyone is under cover there now, with doors and shutters closed; and the Harpies are hunting around without much luck I could see. In fact, from time to time one of your archers, shooting through an arrow slit in a shutter, downed one; and it may be Sir Brian and I can do more about stopping any more coming, soon."

"James?" said Brian in a happy voice.

"Talk to you about that in a bit, Brian," said Jim. "But,

Sire, I was under the impression you and Dafydd were going back there."

"Indeed, Sir James, I came to a change of mind," said Dafydd. "With the countryside empty of people, the danger of bringing my King back to the capital across that much open ground and only myself to guard him from Harpies, seemed the worst choice. And then, by staying with you, we can be at your meeting with the Original Knights of Lyonesse; for it is my thought that we of the Drowned Land and they are together in this, and it would be well we should talk without delay of joining forces."

"Well, yes," said Jim. "It's been my thought, too—stop jumping up and down, Hob! I'll talk to you in a minute." For Hob was now standing on his right shoulder, going up and down like a magic fruit told to leap. "—My idea, too, that both lands should join forces. You've got plenty of people; but as I understand it, few armored knights. Lyonesse has a lot of them, but all together they don't add up to a very great army, since Lyonesse is sparsely populated forest, mostly. Am I right about that, QB?"

"Perfectly right," said the QB. "But I think Hob has something very important to suggest to you."

"He has? I'm sorry, Hob," said Jim. "I didn't realize what you wanted to talk about was that important. Sorry to make you wait."

"It was awful—I didn't mind at all, I mean—m'Lord," the blocked-off words came out of Hob in a rush, "but I've had this magnificent idea. None of you could do it—crave pardon, Master Dafydd, Sir Brian, m'Lords, and your Royal Majesty—I just mean because it's just something a hobgoblin is made so he can do. All I need is a waft of smoke here; and I can ride it back to where those villains are camped on the Borderland, and hide in the smokes of their fires, listening to their talk. I can probably learn everything they're going to do; and bring it back to you. It would be as easy as . . . as drinking milk."

"Hob . . ." began Jim, and checked himself. There were a number of reasons against Hob's doing what he had offered to do. But it would be tricky to phrase a refusal so that it did not make Hob useless and unhappy. He was fairly glowing with his idea.

Furthermore, Jim could not turn down Hob's suggestion in such a way as to seem particularly careful of the small Natural. Not with the others listening—all of whom were ready to risk their own lives, and would see no reason why Hob should not take outrageous chances with his, to gain information.

"It's a fine idea, Hob," he said; and Hob's face fell immediately at the tone of his Lord's voice, anticipating refusal. "The trouble is, though, that Queen Morgan le Fay is watching you and me all the time when we're here in Lyonesse. She'd notice immediately if you left me, and keep watching you to see where you went."

"I could wait until dark to go."

"How would you find your way to them in the dark?"

"Oh, that's easy, m'Lord. I'd watch the stars. I've done that before, nights out on the smoke."

"There are no stars here," put in Dafydd, "or in our Drowned Land. No moon in either one, either."

Hob stared at him for a second of silence; and then his face lit up again.

"I could take the QB with me on the smoke. He's heavy, but it isn't far. The smoke could manage him, too."

"I would be happy to go," put in the QB. "It is true, as you yourself know, Sir James, that I can easily go to where I wish, unobserved in the dark. I pray you will let Hob do what he suggests and take me with him, provided we wait until past sundown. I had thought there was nothing I could do to protect Lyonesse; but this would be useful; and I long to do it."

"No harm in letting the two go, James; and much mayhap to be gained. I counsel you do so," said Brian.

"I would give much to know," said King David, "when those in the Borderland plan to move; and in what direction. If it be toward the Drowned Land, we must beg the Knights and Kings of Lyonesse for assistance. We will give them as much as we have, if the attack is to be here.''

Dafydd said nothing; but Jim saw his friend was watching him closely.

''All right, Hob,'' said Jim, pointedly speaking directly to Hob and to none of the others. ''But I reserve the right to change my mind right up to the time you have to go. For one thing, QB—or any of you—has King Pellinore said when we might talk to the Originals? The sooner we meet with them, the better.''

''He said,'' answered the QB, ''that they are not all gathered together yet. Indeed, some may still be coming in by the time the issue of where battle might be is decided and the battle about to commence. Neither of his sons, Sir Percival or Sir Lamorack of Wales, have been heard of so far; and I know he yearns to see them. The battle will be nothing to him, compared to that.''

''He didn't say anything, then,'' Jim said, ''of just when a gathering of the Originals might take place?''

''He will make it happen,'' said the QB. ''But in any case most of the great King's Knights who decide to be here, will appear soon—and there would be no more time to wait now, in any case. The dark comes soon.''

''Again?'' Jim looked up at the sky and was startled to see the white sun once more low above the trees.

''Our sun was a gift to Lyonesse of the Old Magic,'' said the QB, ''and chooses its own way and time to come and go—and I think that its going so often, lately, is connected with our present peril. It goes now.''

Indeed it was. Even as Jim watched, its lower rim touched the tops of the black trees.

Chapter 33

Plainly, there were only minutes to go before it would be too lightless to see anything.

''We'd better tell King Pellinore. QB, perhaps you—'' Jim began hastily. He did not finish, however.

"You would tell me what?" said the deep voice; and Jim, looking, saw that Pellinore was with them again, having just ridden out of the trees toward his home.

"The Lord QB, I, Sir Brian, and the Hob are going to be gone for a while," said Jim; and as the sky dimmed relentlessly overhead, he talked fast to bring Pellinore up to date.

"Very well," said Pellinore. "I shall look for your return. When we are together again and it is light, we should go to the Gathering Place of the Original Knights. Meanwhile, I wish to invite and do so invite within, those of you who wish to stay. Candles will be lit; and food as well as drink prepared for those who wish it. While if those who are tired wish it, I can give you a bedded chamber apiece."

"Indeed," said Dafydd, "I am weary; and my King must be, also."

As he said this, Jim suddenly felt out on his feet. When had he last really slept? He could not remember; and the excitement of what had happened to him had kept him going. But there was no time for sleep now.

On the other hand, now that he had realized he had been without sleep, he was ready to fall over sideways to get it. But that would not do. He would need his wits about him to deal with things as they came up.

Reluctantly, he turned a little away from the others and fumbled in his purse for one of the grapes. *"Give me the equivalent of six hours' sleep in six seconds,"* he said to it under his breath, and ate it.

He blinked—and everything was exactly the same. But he was no longer desperate for slumber.

"—Come in then," Pellinore was saying. "QB, I know you do not sleep; and I have slept but little this last hundred years and more. I had hoped we could talk. It has been some time since we did. But the chance may come later."

The light faded ever more swiftly, even as he talked and opened the door, standing aside for Dafydd and the young King to enter. The candlelight within shone out around them in the almost total darkness as if it had the intensity of a searchlight; and as the door closed behind them, the last of the outside light went also; and those outside were apart and invisible in the dark.

"Hob," said Jim, "you're still on my shoulder."

"Yes, m'Lord," said the voice in his right ear. "I'd go to my Lord QB, but I can't see him now."

"Do not try to move, any of you. I will take us where we need to go," said the QB's voice, approaching Jim. "Hob"— and Hob's minute weight was suddenly gone—"I have you now. Sir James, Sir Brian, merely stand as you are."

For a few seconds there was that familiar feel of a slight breeze in Jim's face; and then the unrelieved blackness was suddenly invaded by the odors of the encampment. The next instant brought the sight of a string of tents stretching away ahead of them—all lit from within by candlelight or other illumination, showing through the cloth walls; so that with the ground invisible beneath them and no sky above nor anything else visible around them, the tents were like inhabited structures floating in space.

It was hard to think of them as the tents of dangerous enemies. Their interior lights seemed to give them a sort of glow—like a glow of warmth and welcome. Jim knew that the contrast of their brightness with the darkness hid all their dirt and threadbare patches, that daylight had so unsparingly shown.

But here they were again—there was no doubt about it.

"Sir James, Sir Brian," said the voice of the QB, "have no fear of speaking out. These cannot hear us, any more than they can see us. What is your wish? Do you stay here and wait for Hob and myself; or do you want to go elsewhere, without waiting?"

"We can't get anything done until we have light again," said Jim. "But what Brian and I are going to be after is the place where those Harpies come from. It would have to be in Lyonesse—the Dark Powers need a place that either has magic, or had it in the past, to make their creatures, Carolinus told me once. It can be as little and unimportant as the den of some Natural, who's used his or her instinctive magic in it. But there must have been some magic at that place. In one that never had magic—good or bad, black or white—the Dark Powers couldn't work."

"God send such a day when the whole world is so!" said the voice of Brian beside him.

"He may," said Jim, "in the long run. We'll see. But for now, QB, isn't that tent nearest to us, the big one, where the Earl and Agatha were, and Modred came?"

"I believe so," said the QB.

"I'd like to have a look inside it, if possible."

"I'll take you to it, Sir James. I suggest Hob can best be the one to look inside and tell us what he sees."

"I don't have any smoke!"—Hob's voice.

"There must be fires around a camp like this," said the QB. "Can't you smell them?"

"Oh, yes," said Hob. "But they're out where the men are sleeping on the ground—the ones not in tents. I could just go toward any one of them that's making smoke; but I'd probably walk on one or more of the sleeping men in the dark. Don't you smell the smoke?"

"Yes. I'll carry you to it. Would you wish the nearest one to us here?"

"Yes," said Hob, "and I can ride on your back to it?"

"Certainly," said the QB graciously. "As a Lord of Lyonesse, though I seldom make a point of it, I do not usually carry anyone on my back. But if a great magickian and Knight such as Sir James does not cavil at carrying you on his back, I cannot."

Silence fell. It stretched out.

"Tell me, QB—" began Brian's voice; then hesitated, waiting. There was no answer. "Ah, well. Gone already. James, what had you in mind—"

"Sir James, Sir Brian," said the QB's voice, beside them. "All has been dealt with. Hob is even now examining the large tent, which is not empty. I came to take you to it."

"Good," said Brian. "It's time we were doing something."

There was no sensation of movement, but suddenly they were facing the closed entry flaps of the large tent they had been in before. Enough light shone through the fabric that they could see its shape and dimensions.

"M'Lord! Sir Brian!" Hob's voice came to them in a half whisper. "Three of them. Look inside."

"We cannot," whispered back Brian. "If one of us steps within, we are revealed to whoever is there. Who are they?"

"The Lady Agatha and the Loud Lord."

"Cumberland?" Jim asked—they were all whispering. He was a little annoyed with himself for needing to ask, but he wanted to make sure. Hob had called Robert, Earl of Cumberland and, in this world, half brother to Edward the King of England, the "Loud Lord," ever since Cumberland had made his visit to Malencontri. "You only named two of them. Who's the other one?"

"A Lady."

"There isn't any man there with a bushy mustache and a bushy chin-beard?" Jim asked.

"No, m'Lord. Just the three."

"And this other one's a Lady, too? Not just some serving wench?" demanded Brian.

"Yes, Sir Brian. She was sitting at table with them."

That settled it, of course. A man of the gentry might sit at a table with a serving wench—but only where no one he knew would be likely to see him. But none would sit so if there were a legitimate Lady also at the same table. Some social rules were almost reflexive in the fourteenth century.

"And you don't recognize her at all?" asked Jim.

"No, m'Lord."

"What're they talking about?"

"I don't really know, m'Lord. None of them seem to like each other."

Not an unusual situation around the Loud Lord, Jim told himself. He looked at the tent in frustration. From where they stood, they could hear the murmur of voices, but not make out what was being said.

"Wait a minute, Hob. Could you hear what they were saying?"

"Oh, yes, m'Lord. I was right by the table."

"And they didn't see you?"

"I was up near the top pole that runs the length of the tent. There was lots of candle smoke up there. Anyhow, none of them looked up."

"Yes, but—"

"If you'll forgive me, Sir James"—the voice of the QB was still right next to them—"I went around the back of the tent myself, just now, to see what I might smell or hear. I could not hear; but a suspicion I had was confirmed. One of those in there is indeed Queen Morgan le Fay."

"Morgan—" Jim checked himself, his mind suddenly galloping. The thought that came first was that if Morgan was here in the Borderland, which technically was a part of the Drowned Land, and outside Lyonesse, her magic should not work any better than his.

Or would it? He had managed to concept his magic fruits here in Drowned Land territory.

But then, he reminded himself, he had produced the fruits inside his expanded ward. Perhaps she could ward her own powers as well as KinetetE had warded his.

In any case, warded or not, Morgan's magic would not be easily available to her at the moment, and that meant he ought to be able to go right up, close enough to touch her, as long as she did not see or hear him. He needed to hear for himself what was going on right now between her, Agatha, and Cumberland.

"Hob," he said.

"Yes, m'Lord?"

"Come here to me."

"I'm right in front of you now, m'Lord."

"Good. Now I'm going to work a little magic on me and you. It won't hurt and you shouldn't be scared."

"I have no fear of anything, m'Lord," answered Hob's voice, quavering a little nonetheless on the last two words.

"Believe me," said Jim, "this will be interesting magic. Fun magic. You're going back into that tent; and I'm going with you. Only, this time I'll be inside you—you won't feel me there, but you'll know I'm with you, and I'll be moving your body around to where I want to go. Most of the time I'll just be riding in you, listening. Then we'll come back out and I'll leave you. You understand? I don't want you to be frightened if you find me there; don't try to fight my taking charge of what you do. All right?''

''My Lord,'' said Hob with dignity, ''I am your Hob.''

''I know. But a magician is required to say what he's going to do in a case like this. It's an obligation, like the obligations of being a Knight.''

''I understand, m'Lord! It sounds like great sport. I wasn't worried, of course. Just interested!''

''Well, see how you like it. Brian? QB? Hob's going to go into the tent again; and—Hob, how are you going to get in? You don't want to open the tent flap, or anything like that, to alert the people inside.''

''You forget, m'Lord. I just came out,'' said Hob reproachfully. ''I showed you at King Edward's Court once. Any space smoke can go through, I can go through.''

''Right. I remember. You did show me. Here I come, then.''

He reached into his purse for a fruit and came up with the pear, this time; biting into it, he visualized himself like an invisible presence in the general vicinity of Hob's brain—and there he was, a second later, looking out through the little hobgoblin's eyes. They two were now oozing between the stained white cloth of the two tent flaps, which did not part as they passed.

M'Lord, are you there? Hob's thoughts echoed strangely in his mind. *I thought I'd start us out—since you'd never done this before.*

Fine, Hob, he thought back. *Very thoughtful of you. Yes, I'm here and I'm fine. How are you?*

Just the way I always am, m'Lord.

They were inside the tent, still close to the door. Jim looked around him, and saw that Hob had been right: a smelly fog, of candle smoke and perhaps other things, had gathered directly under the highest part of the tent, which was over the central pole that ran the length of it, to hold the sloping cloth sides up. The smoke was thickest directly above the table at which sat a man and two women. Hob's coloring blended in with the smoke, making him obscure enough that anyone catching sight of him in that haze would have to look again, and look closely, to make him out.

"I'm taking over," Jim said; and moved Hob's body down along the center of the roof and just beneath it, until they were only about six feet from the table, looking down through the fog of smoke at those seated there.

The man was Cumberland, all right; and next to his angular face was the narrow one of Agatha Falon, attemptive murderer of her baby half brother. She sat at the Earl's left, her face as merciless as ever; however, it was a strong face in its own way—as strong as the Earl's.

Jim noticed, though, that she looked thinner than when he had seen her in the past; and in spite of the heat that multiple candles gave to the tent's atmosphere, she wore a white, knitted something like a shawl about her narrow shoulders.

On Cumberland's other side, seated as if he would keep the two women apart, at the far end of the table was Morgan le Fay. A pitcher of wine and one of water, with metal wine cups, sat on the table between her and the Earl. No such tableware between the Earl and Agatha.

Still, the Earl dominated the table. That was in character for him. The day he did not dominate would undoubtedly be the day he was dead.

"—and I can't keep coming to see you every Dark!" Morgan was saying in an acid voice. "If you think I'm at your beck and call, think again."

"What else?" said Cumberland, easily enough. "We must needs get together; and I decide when my men will move, Lady."

"I am a Queen! Address me as one!"

"And I am a King, in all but name. We should call each other 'cousin' as Royalty does."

"Fire will take the world before I call you 'cousin,' Cumberland!"

"I am content to wait."

The Earl was obviously in an unusually good mood. Otherwise, he was unchanged, as far as Jim could tell—as much at home here where he should have been out of place, as he would have been in Windsor Castle. The same voice, the same attitude, the same tall, burly, middle-aged body, the same readiness to anger still seeming to lurk just under the surface of his present pleasantness. The same hard-boned, rectangular, long-nosed, Plantagenate face. "You will learn to live in my world, Lady—"

"Highness, rot you, Cumberland!" flared Morgan. "I am a Queen, I say, and down here you are nothing!"

The Earl laughed harshly. The pleasantness was wearing thin.

"Save your breath, le Fay!" he said. "You have things exactly turned about. You may be a Queen in Lyonesse; but here in the Drowned Land you are nothing, and powerless to boot! Whereas I come here with an army that can take both these lands. Moreover, we can return at will by the Witches' Gate to the land above, where you cannot go. You have bought your bull in the marketplace. Now learn to live with it!"

"You are a fool, and sleeping; but I've no wish to wake you, until you have done me the service I require. But ware! Anger me more like this and I will rid myself of you and do without you."

"How?" The Earl laughed again. "Will *you* lead these men I've gathered here for you? I warn you, they are the sweepings of our Western World: bloodstained villains and rascals—not to be led by a woman. In especial, by a woman who has no magick!"

"I have Modred to lead them!"

"Modred!" The Earl laughed again, filling his wine cup from the pitcher; and Jim began to suspect that he was the only one of the three who had been drinking here. Clearly, he seemed to think he was amusing himself in this cross-talk with Morgan le Fay. But Morgan—and surely Agatha must realize it, if the Earl did not—was in deadly earnest.

"Yes, Modred!" she spat out now. "He was one of Arthur's once—how else, being Arthur's son? But all who were once of Arthur's Court are risen from wherever they were put in earth—I know not how, except it is the workings of the Old Magic, and the why of what *that* does is never fully understood—and they all are returning to Lyonesse. But those who would oppose me, there and here, do not stop to think that half of them fought with Modred, before, in the final battles between him and Arthur. These will go with Modred again!''

''Go? Oh, they will go—or they will not go. It makes no difference which. Resurrected knights out of old stories will never win the Drowned Land for your private kingdom. It takes men such as I have outside. Aye, they have good archers in this Drowned Land—but archers alone never won a battle. Only when together with horse and foot, heavy in armor, weapons, and experience, do archers see a victory! But men of that sort, like those I have gathered, need a war-captain to head them—and Modred is none such!''

He laughed again, drinking.

''You plowboy!'' said Morgan with icy venom. ''You plowboy in prince's clothing!''

Cumberland's face was abruptly sober. He stared at Morgan and flung the remaining contents of his wine cup into her face.

She stared back at him, motionless, with the wine dripping from her. She said nothing. Only her face went as white as the face of a harpy.

But Agatha was already on her feet, whipping off the shawl from around her shoulders, on her way to Morgan.

''Highness!'' she said. ''Forgive him, I beg and plead. He has taken his wine too fast. We must not quarrel among ourselves like this, when we are all so necessary to each other; in especial if there is a hope of anything to be done for any one of us. Surely you will not give up your chance for a separate kingdom of your own—all for the sake of one thoughtless gesture on my Lord's part? And even if you did, what of the Dark Powers if we fail in your bargain with them?''

Morgan snatched the shawl from Agatha, and wiped her face with her own hands.

"None can do that to me!" she said in a voice so choked with emotion that she could hardly speak above a whisper. "I will keep my bargains, all of them. But I will have my payments also!"

"Robert—my Lord!" said Agatha, turning on Cumberland. "You have gone too far. Say so!"

Cumberland's big hands were two fists sitting on the table before him. His face was without expression; but with an expressionlessness like that of a cornered animal pausing in its wildness of fighting to be free, and gathering its strength to fight on.

"The blood of kings runs in my veins," he said slowly and deeply. "That blood can never lie quiet under naming such as I have just heard here. I, too, keep my bargains and have my payments—but perhaps I forgot for a moment that it was not a man who spoke me so!"

He and Morgan sat looking at each other, neither averting his or her eyes. There was silence.

"I think we have spoken enough for this time," said Agatha. "I have explained to your Highness that I am only part-witch; but that part of me that is, now smells the lifting of the Dark very shortly. My Queen, your men and horses are at the end of the tunnel by which you came to this tent. We will be better off with no more words this time."

Hob, Jim said mentally, *if the Dark is nearly over, we need to get out, too. I think I've learned about as much as I can this trip.*

Yes, m'Lord.

They left the tent.

"Good! You're back," the QB said, as they appeared in their proper, separate bodies, before him outside the tent; which was now a misty gray shape, its angles blurred by the faint light of a sky beginning to lighten. "While enough of the Dark still lasts, I can take us all out swiftly. Come, Sir Brian."

Chapter 34

The remains of the Dark flowed about them like the rags and tatters of some heavy obscuring mist for the few moments it took the QB to move them back to the home of King Pellinore. When they stopped, the murk had vanished. It was full daylight, though the nearby trees still hid the face of the white sun of Lyonesse.

Jim felt an odd pressure like something heavy leaning against his shoulder, and turned his head to look.

Something was indeed leaning there. It was Brian, totally unconscious but still standing, thanks to the fact of Jim's presence; and now that Jim listened, he could hear a faint but unusually audible sound that was breathing—Brian was asleep and on the very verge of snoring.

Jim's conscience struck him like a body block. In all the times they had gone strange places and without food or sleep before, Brian had been an iron man. He never seemed to think of food; and he never appeared to need sleep.

Now the only amazing thing was that he was still upright. Jim eased slightly away from him, and stopped immediately as Brian leaned dangerously farther. Just short of falling, he slept on.

Jim would have had trouble believing his eyes and ears if it had not been for two things; beginning with the fact that he had once read of a company of English soldiers in World War I, marching into a French village—every one asleep on his feet. At the time, he had sneered at the page of the book where he found this, disbelieving it entirely.

Then, years later, he had also found himself in exactly that situation—for an entirely different reason, but still having to keep on his feet and keep moving. It had been after midnight and he, with others, had been marching steadily since morning.

He had not remembered being out on his feet—just very

tired—but he began to find himself stumbling off the narrow dirt road they were travelling, straying into the rough, weedy ground beside their route. He was aware of this happening several times, and it puzzled him, before his mind woke enough to understand he had been falling asleep—still walking—and, in his ambulant slumber, straying off their route.

Now, he had magically given himself some sleep; but Brian had had none. As a result, for once he had outdone his friend. Understanding followed with a blow to his conscience. He took Brian's arm and shook it gently. Brian opened his eyes.

"Brian," he said, "how would you like to be a dragon?"

"Dragon? Sounds like a merry time . . ." said Brian, and went back to sleep.

"Is he ill?" said the voice of David; and Jim glanced away from Brian for a moment to see the young King standing by and looking concerned.

"No. He just needs sleep," said Jim. He put an arm around Brian as insurance against the other's falling over.

"Can I help?" asked Hob's worried voice from Jim's shoulder.

"No," said Jim, "but he'll be all right. QB?"

He looked around for the QB and found him equally close, but on the other side of Brian, somehow managing also to show a look of concern on his snake's face.

"Yes, Sir James?"

"We were to go with King Pellinore to meet the other Originals and maybe speak to them? Was that the plan? When do we have to leave?"

"Oh, not for some hours yet. King Pellinore will wish to wait for afternoon, when most will be there."

"Then Brian's got time to get some sleep. Would there be a bed inside?"

"Of course," said the QB. "Follow me."

Steering his friend like a sleepwalker—something, Jim suddenly realized, at this moment Brian actually was—he followed the QB into the log building. Inside, it turned out to be rather like a hunting lodge, except for the lack of pelts or mounted heads on the walls. They went down a narrow corridor from the main room, to a door that let them into a very small chamber, almost filled by the small bed in it, and with some child-sized pieces of armor and weapons hanging on the wall.

Jim brought Brian to the edge of the bed, rotated him, and laid him down on it, taking off his shoes, spurs, and weapon-laden knight's-belt. Brian began to snore in dead earnest.

"Well," Jim said, when he and the QB had returned outside to Dafydd and David, neither of whom had followed them in. "He's settled. Four hours or so, if I know Brian, should see him on his feet again, whether he's properly rested or not. How are you two for food and sleep?"

"Sir Pellinore fed us, and gave us a place to sleep, while you were gone," said David. "I, myself, feel no further need for sleep at the moment. But mayhap Dafydd . . ." He turned with a look of concern to the bowman.

"I slept well, Sire," said Dafydd. "Enough that I know my eye is sharp and my aim sure."

"But you, Sir James," said the QB; "if Sir Brian needs sleep so badly, surely you do? And when did you eat last?"

"Oh, Brian can always outlast me in staying awake," said Jim. "And as for eating, I ate—"

He broke off. When had he eaten? When he had stopped to see Angie on the way back here? No. Angie had offered; but he had said he didn't have time.

"—I could eat a horse!" he found himself saying.

"Horse, Sir James?"

"Forgive me, QB. Didn't explain myself well," said Jim. "It's just a saying where I come from—when you say you could eat a horse, it only means you've got an appetite."

"It does not have to be horse, then?"

"No, no. I'd rather not horse, actually. Anything else you've got handy will be welcome."

"Then we must feed you at once, without delay," said the QB seriously.

"Oh, no hurry, either," put in Jim, salivating secretly.

"I will see to it right now!"

The QB went inside. He did not return immediately; but

after a moment, two half-grown black bears came out, walking on their hind legs and carrying trestles, a stool and a tabletop.

Scarcely a minute later a deer pushed the door open from the inside and looked out briefly, before emerging completely. She was a doe, a slim young fallow deer; and she was carrying two otters, perched along her spine. The otters were holding a folded white tablecloth and a large folded napkin between them.

The otters hopped down in a typical otter flowing movement, onto the tabletop, once it had been set in place upon the trestles. They spread the tablecloth, putting the napkin, with a spoon and a large, thick slice of coarse brown bread that had been hidden in its folds, in front of the stool at one end. After that they jumped up once more onto the back of the doe, who moved off a small distance; and, like the bears, turned back to watch the table.

All together, they formed a line of observers; the two otters crouched down, one behind the other, on the doe's back, each gazing at Jim from one side of the doe's neck.

Immediately, four perfectly ordinary, if a bit aged, male servants came out, bringing a pitcher and a wine cup, plus a large pie that radiated warmth as if it had just come out of an oven. They served a portion of the pie onto the thick slice of bread, filled the wine cup, and one of them held the stool so Jim could sit down. Then they also lined up, but at a small distance from the animals; and also stood waiting, evidently politely ready to be of service.

The QB came out, closely followed by King Pellinore.

"Forgive me, Sir James—" the QB was beginning, when Pellinore interrupted him.

"It is for me to beg forgiveness, QB," he said. "Sir James, it is a sorry thing that I must serve you partly with animals. But out in these woods, away from others, it is difficult to get enough serving folk; and the beasts, being young, find much pleasure showing their cleverness to you."

"No, no," said Jim. "I mean, that's quite all right. I like animals—all kinds of animals."

"So do the QB and I—" said Pellinore. "But enough of manners. Let you now eat."

Jim looked at the rough circle standing and watching him. Dafydd and David. Pellinore and the QB. The four human servants. The doe, otters, and young bears. He felt like Exhibit A in a courtroom trial.

But they were all waiting. Fourteenth-century table manners—which ought to do here in Lyonesse—were that you used your fingers for any food they could pick up; and the spoon only for whatever they could not. Gingerly, hoping he would not spill the filling between the two layers of pastry, he broke off a piece of pie and put it in his mouth.

It was, he found, fish pie. He had never eaten fish in a pie before; but that was no reason why he should not now. Also, he found, it was delicious. And he was not merely hungry, he was ravenous. Forgetting his audience, he waded into the food before him, washing mouthfuls down with straight wine—no water to mix with the wine had been provided.

More fish pie, more wine—deftly served to him the moment his slice of bread or wine cup was empty.

He realized finally he could not hold another bite. He was about to rise, with a sigh of satisfaction, when he remembered that the bread, now soaked with juices from the pie, was untouched. It was good manners in the fourteenth century for a passing guest to eat it also, as a compliment to the food. Was it that way here in Arthurian times—perhaps a thousand years earlier? He felt as if one more mouthful would have no place to go; but he would have to at least go through the motions.

He picked up the bread, which drooped like the sodden thing it now was, and took as big a bite as he could out of it. He managed to chew it and get it down. It, too, tasted good; but it was a labor getting that one bite down.

He did, however; and smiled at his audience. They seemed to approve—those that were left. The humans, all except the aged male servants, had all gone off. Dafydd was engaging David in quiet conversation and had led him away a small distance. Pellinore had disappeared—probably to back inside his house, once he saw his guest was being satisfied. Only the QB, the animals, and the elderly servants remained to watch.

The QB was still standing where he had been, but pointedly looking a little away from Jim. The human servants stood motionless, also seeming to look past him, but clearly attentive in case he wanted anything—almost as if there was a large badge with I AM INVISIBLE written on it and pinned to the shirt of each.

Only the animals were still unabashedly staring, as if fascinated by every move he made and totally indifferent to whether he liked their watching or not.

Jim looked at the QB.

"Er . . . QB!" he said.

The QB came over to him.

"Yes, Sir James?"

"An excellent meal," said Jim. "I hope I get a chance to thank King Pellinore."

"There will be opportunity later, Sir James."

Jim glanced at the animals, still watching.

"I don't know how to thank the others . . ." He was a little drunk from the wine. "Fine-looking animals, all of them. Did I mention I like animals?"

"You did, Sir James."

Jim hardly heard him.

"—Do you happen to know an old ballad called 'The Three Ravens'? There's a North England version called 'The Twa Corbies.' "

"I do not," said the QB.

"Too bad," said Jim. He looked at the animals again. "I was just thinking of singing it to them. You know—as sort of thanks and praise for their clever service— *Whoa,* he told himself, *You're drunk* . . . But his mouth went right on talking.

"I thought maybe if you knew it, we could sing it to them together. It's about a knight slain under his shield; and three ravens are talking. They want to eat his corpse; but one points out the dead knight's hounds they lie down at his feet—so well do they their Master keep; and his hawks fly above him so eagerly, there is no bird dare him come nigh; and... you're sure you don't know it?"

"To my disgrace, Sir James, I do not."

"Too bad! It has a great ending. The end part goes—" And to his horror he heard himself beginning to sing:

... downne there comes a fallow doe,
Downne a down, hay downne, hay downne,
As greate with young as she might goe.

She got him up upon her backe
And carried him to earthen lake.

She buried him there before the prime,
Was dead herselfe by even-song time,
God send then to every man—
Such hawks, such hounds, and such a leman

With a down derrie, derrie, derrie, downe downe

"—I think I left out a line or two; and mixed it up a bit, but you get the idea. If you drop by, sometime, I'll show it to you—it's in volume one," Jim said, forgetting entirely that his dog-eared four-volume paperback copy of Francis James Childe's collection of English and Scottish ballads was universes of distance away. He stared at the bears, the otters, and the doe, who between them had just finished folding up the cloth and napkin, picking up the table furnishings, and taking everything into the building.

"Tell me, QB," he said, "how did King Pellinore get these creatures and train them so well? Were they abandoned at birth for some reason? Did he raise them from nurslings and teach them—"

"Oh, no, Sir James! They each—well, the bears and the otters came in pairs—but they came of their own will and offered their services. They are free to come and go, but they stay because they like him and his home."

"Amazing!" said Jim. "Bears, otters, that doe..."

"Both King Pellinore and I," said the QB, "honor the

beasts and love them. We hunt always for the chase, never for the killing—sometimes we hunt each other, for sport—''

He paused. To Jim's surprise, he seemed be hesitating. Jim had never known the QB to hesitate before.

''But your telling me this and singing a part of that song for me,'' the QB went on, ''encourages me to bring up something I have been less than certain about mentioning to you. As you undoubtedly know, we animals generally mistrust humans, all except the Magickians among them.''

Jim nodded. He did indeed know. It had been one of the first facts he had learned in his early days in the body of the dragon Gorbash. He had learned it from either Aargh the English Wolf or Carolinus, or both.

The QB was going on.

''The animals of Lyonesse, many of them, would like to speak to you and ask your advice. I have plainly come to trust you, and the trees have spoken well of you. But I hesitated, because I was not sure if you had the feeling for all of us who dwell in Lyonesse. But now I judge you do. Your song was about one of the few things that animals and humans tend to think about alike—loyalty to what and who they love. Also you sang it with real feeling. Will you honor us all by meeting with some of them? They have wished to know you.''

''Meet—oh, of course!'' said Jim, scrambling to his feet and caught in an emotion that could have been partly from the wine he had drunk, but was also a matter of being both embarrassed and honestly touched by what the other had said. ''When though? We've got this meeting with the Originals—''

''It will take very little time to meet the animals; and we have ample left before we must go and Sir Brian be wakened. The animals can be gathering as we travel.''

''Well, good, then,'' said Jim. He was sobering up fast, but he wished it were even faster. He had not thought of the wild animals which must surely be in these forests of Lyonesse, and he found he very much wanted to see them.

''Come with me, then,'' the QB was saying. ''It were best

you leave your horse behind and go on foot. If you close your eyes I can take the two of us more swiftly."

"Can I come too, m'Lord?"

Hob was so light, sitting somehow securely on his shoulder, that Jim had begun to forget he was there.

"I think n—"

"Indeed, it will be good if Hob is with you," said the QB. "Being small and inoffensive—and no human—he will be a warrant of the friendliness in you."

"Well then . . . yes, Hob."

"Thank you, my Lord."

Jim closed his eyes. He felt the usual small breeze; but this time something else strange seemed to be happening. They were travelling with the QB's special quickness; but on this occasion he had a strange feeling that time itself was going by faster than it should, so that what seemed a minute or two might really be a quarter or half an hour—or even longer.

"You can open your eyes now, Sir James," said the voice of the QB. Jim did so and looked around him.

He was deep in forest, and at the bottom and center of a sort of natural amphitheater, a huge bowl covered with grass and curving up on all sides to wide-trunked old trees standing like guardians at the top edge of the bowl.

All around him were animals of the forest and plains, from tiny meadow mice through shrews, hares, and stoats, to mature bears, heavy-antlered deer, and powerful boars; but with sizes, sex, and age mixed. On the rim of the amphitheater, the lower branches of the old trees were bowed down with birds of all sizes and kinds.

But something more unexpected was there, too. He found himself staring, startled, at—not one lion, but a family of them—a pride led by a large, black-maned male, two grown females, and several half-grown youngsters, two males and one female. They were standing all together, looking at him from a small, clear space in the crowd around them, as still and decorous as a family in church.

It was not believable—all those species gathered together to meet him. Even in this magic-loaded, crazy version of fourteenth-century Earth. This was finally too much—the straw that broke the camel's back. His thoughts whirled crazily like the propeller of an outboard motor suddenly lifted out of the water. But then, rising like a friendly wave, overwhelming it again and slowing it back to its proper, useful speed, came the one explanation which made sense. The one to which he could cling.

This was Lyonesse. Anything could happen here. He remembered the squirrel, boldly jumping from a tree branch onto the pommel of his saddle as he and Brian entered Lyonesse.

But nothing happened anywhere without a reason, he told himself—and that must be true here as well as elsewhere. Find the reason for everything, from the squirrel landing on his saddle to the unreasonable congregation of all these creatures—most of them predators, from weasels to lions . . .

Yet it was against reason for different species of animals to gather peacefully together—or was it?

There were, he remembered, in his world, the breeding islands near the South Pole, where leopard seals waded through penguins, ashore, without harming the odd birds; though the same penguins encountered in the ocean water were immediately pursued, killed, and eaten by the carnivorous seals. Different conditions evidently could produce different behaviors by the same meat-eating seal. But what about Lyonesse would produce something like this, here and now?

Out of a dusty corner of his memory came something he had been told of by a friend who was a wolf researcher. The story of the Mackenzie Arctic wolf, who normally did not join together in packs, but ranged individually over large territories—except for twice a year when the days-long river of migrating caribou flowed to and from the Great Slave Lakes where they gave birth to their young, before returning south again when the winter moved in.

At those two times, these solitary wolves would join together with wagging tails and every other sign of friendship. Then, working together in teams, they would prey upon the caribou while they passed; and this alliance would last as long as the great herds moved by.

A common resource drew them together. But what kind of common resource had drawn together all these here, now?

He had asked that same kind of question about the Mackenzie wolves, at the time he heard about them; and his friend had said even animals of different species were capable of combining against a common enemy, or to defend a common resource. But there was no common resource here . . .

He suddenly remembered what Merlin had said—"*The animals share equally . . . They have their own link with the Old Magic, one we have never understood—but we understand that Lyonesse is theirs as much as ours.*"

The Old Magic a resource? Crazy! No, perhaps . . . just perhaps—beside him the QB moved slightly; and it struck Jim that both the QB and the animals here could be waiting for him to come out of his mental laboratory and pay attention to them.

An awkward realization. An awkward moment. "Look! Lions!" said Jim in a low voice to the QB, to signal his return to matters at hand.

"Of course," answered the QB. "Is not the name of our land Lyonesse?"

"Oh, yes. Of course."

It was full day now, and the white sun shone directly on him in the open spot at the lowest, center point of the bowl. The unwavering eyes of all of them looked at him with the same, direct, unshielded, unblinking stare that the doe, the otters, and the young bears had used.

There was silence for a long minute as he stood there; then a sort of general rustling sound, more like the sound of feet shifting than of vocal cords uttering.

"They have looked at you," said the QB, beside him. "The trees have spoken for you to them and they find you good. They wait for you to speak."

"What am I supposed to say?" muttered Jim. The animal eyes were once again like miniature spotlights steadily on him; and he felt like a fool. At least by now the wine was out of his head.

"They want to know what they can do," said QB.

"Do?" Jim tried to understand. "But what kind of thing do they want me to tell them about?"

"They know the fighting for Lyonesse will come. The trees can do nothing. These are different. They want you to tell them how they can fight."

Jim's reawakened mind leaped and slithered down a slope of possibilities. He tried to visualize a battle—an actual battle—for Lyonesse. A battle with the men he had seen in the camp on the Borderland—against whatever fighting force Lyonesse could raise. The Originals—even with their descendants helping—would be heavily outnumbered. That went almost without saying. But what could animals do against humans, in any case?

Then, abruptly, his mental ground stopped being slippery. It became solid, level, and plain. In the tangle that was a medieval combat, from the small ones he had been in himself to the full-sized battles of one country against another, there were things that teeth and horns and hoofs might do.

Some animals—if they were animals with a purpose—could even be dangerous to that most dangerous of attackers, the partnership of the armored knight, squire, or man-at-arms on his warhorse.

But the odds would still be heavy against any animal, which would need luck to succeed in every case. It was not the sort of thing that these savage innocents should be asked to do—too much like sending men with machetes and knives against machine-gun fire, in his own world.

"You'll tell them what I say?" Jim asked the QB.

"The trees will tell them, in time, in any case," said the QB. "But if you like I will also tell them."

"Good." Jim looked over the animal faces all but carpeting the open space and crowding the rim of the bowl. He spoke, raising his voice, although he knew his words by themselves would mean nothing to them.

"Some of you know how dangerous an enemy a human

on horseback with weapons can be. There's no need for you to face that kind of foe just to help. I'll tell the Originals and all the others I meet here of what a brave offer you've made. It will cheer them on. But I think you ought to think twice about helping."

He stopped. The hundreds of animal eyes looked back at him without change. They said nothing. They did not move.

"I asked the trees not to tell them what you said just now, Sir James," he heard the QB's voice beside him saying, "and I did not tell them myself. Forgive me, but you make a mistake. The lives of those here and all like them are lives of killing or being killed, all their days. They are not like you and other humans, who can afford those things called bravery or cowardice. It is simply that this is their land and those who come are not allowed here. They do not ask you for permission to fight. They only ask how they may do it."

Jim winced internally. That phrase "you and other humans" struck deep. He had been with the QB long enough to come to think of him as one with Brian, Dafydd, and himself, only in strange shape. He had forgotten that it was the animal world a Questing Beast must belong to, when the chips were down. Not his world, or that of any other human. Not even Pellinore's, close as the two of them were.

"All right," he said; and looked at the listeners again. He felt foolish. He was not used to giving speeches, and to begin now to give one to a silent audience of wild animals—He took a deep breath.

"All right," he said loudly—startling himself in face of the complete silence of the faces looking at him.

"Look—" he started again. "None of you are going to be able to win in the long run by going face-to-face with the mounted and armored men. But you don't have to do that to be useful. There are other things you can do. If they set up their tents someplace here in Lyonesse, and there's a Dark before the battle, some of you could gnaw through the tent ropes, so that their covering falls on them in the night and they can't see. They probably won't sleep the rest of the Dark before the battle." The silence continued.

"For those of you who can venture on the field," Jim went on, "remember, a mounted man loses much of his dangerousness if his horse goes down—"

He hesitated. Brian, like most knights, had a special place in his heart for horses. So, indeed, did Jim himself; though not to Brian's extent. But what he had in mind had to be suggested. It was probably the single most effective thing they could do. He braced himself.

"—The horse's legs are the part of him you want to attack. Break or hurt a horse's leg badly enough and he'll fall—particularly if you hit him while he's moving. His rider is going to fall with him. You stoats and weasels might even think about attacking the rider's unarmored parts once he's down. Stags, you know you can outrun any horse in the short distance, even a horse that doesn't have the weight of an armored man on its back. Come up from the back, use your horns, and then turn and run away. Then come back in someplace else and do it again. Boars, I don't have to tell you how to use your tusks—on men or horses."

He paused.

"I don't really need to tell you how to fight best. You know that better than I do. But don't get carried away. Sometimes I'm a dragon; and as a dragon I get carried away. Even humans do that. Some of you may, too, once the fighting starts. Well, don't. Attack in darkness, or where they aren't expecting you, or when they wouldn't be looking in your direction."

Jim hesitated. The silence in which they all listened was unnerving—as if they couldn't hear him, or weren't really listening to begin with.

"But, above all," he went on desperately, "attack! Attack at the edges of the battle. You'll be most useful distracting and disturbing the enemy; and living to disturb them some more; so Lyonesse's own armored men can fight them with an advantage; and the Knights and you together, hopefully, can drive them back where they came from."

He stopped again. He had no more to say; but it seemed to him a very lame way to finish. He stood staring at them and they stayed where they were, staring back.

As the silence dragged out, Jim began to notice furry bodies loping up the slope and vanishing among the trees. Stags started to turn away as these passed. Jim felt an ugly hollowness in his stomach, in spite of his recent meal.

They were all leaving now, with no acknowledgment, no evidence of a response to signal that anything he had told them could be useful.

The stomach feeling deepened as he watched them leave. He did not know what he had expected; but anything would have been better than this voiceless turning away, as if he had been a complete disappointment—disagreement with what he had told them, even anger, would have been better than this—there was a faint rustle all around the amphitheater, as if of last winter's dead and blackened leaves being stirred by a breeze.

"I believe them pleased with what you told them, Sir James," said the QB. Shocked, Jim stared at him, opened his mouth—then quickly rethought the words he had been about to say.

"But you can't be sure,"

"Each will do what he or she wills, of course. But it is my mind that all who were here will be there when needed. However, come now. It is time we were returning, to go to the gathering place of the Originals."

"All the animals . . ." Hob's voice murmured on Jim's shoulder in a tone of wonder, as they turned together to leave the amphitheater behind.

Chapter 35

The Gathering Place of the Originals turned out to be something like an antique picnic ground. Tables and benches sat out in the open, surrounding a wooden structure, painted white—a kind of open pavilion, with roof and floor only, and a ring of pillars that held up the roof. Here, there were more picnic-style tables of all sizes, with stools and stiff-backed, wooden chairs. All of those Jim saw sitting at tables outside or inside the pavilion, sat without touching any chair back—in the same erect posture they would have shown on horseback.

Brian, he noticed, was looking around hungrily. Awakened in time to eat at Pellinore's, he had chosen instead to sleep to the last minute. Now his nose lifted toward those tables with food and wine on them. Jim felt for him, remembering his own appetite for the fish pie and the wine at Pellinore's; but could think of no way to help him.

"Do you chance to see the Descendant of Sir Dinedan we met once, on our way to the Gnarly cave?" Brian asked Jim, in a low voice. "Surely he would remember us and offer us a cup of wine—if not, indeed, we could offer it to him."

There were some obvious Descendants among the Original Knights, moving around or standing attentively, almost like squires, waiting on some of the Originals present; but Jim recognized none of them.

"I'm afraid not," Jim said.

"Well, well," said Brian. "A man cannot always live in a castle. What do we now?"

"We continue to follow King Pellinore, Sir Brian," said the QB.

They had emerged from the forest with their horses, all of them, including the philosophical sumpter horse. Jim felt a little uneasy. He would have liked a little time to get used to the surroundings and the Knights here; but Pellinore seemed to intend to ride right up into the pavilion.

Suddenly, however, the tall King reined in his horse abruptly; and swung himself down out of his saddle as if he was no older than David. He was looking off beside the pavilion, down a leaf-shadowed glade, up which the figure of a younger Knight was coming toward him.

It had seemed to Jim in that first second that Pellinore had intended to go toward the advancing man; but instead he merely stood, suddenly stiff and erect beside his saddle, overtopping even the head of his tall horse. He seemed braced, as if to face the shock of something that would call for all his inner strength. Touched with a sudden feeling of dread, Jim also dismounted; and Brian followed him.

Jim took two steps forward to see if the expression on Pellinore's face could tell him anything; but it was still the same unyielding visage, the same iron expression. Behind him, Jim heard Brian being accosted by what must be one of the two Knights at an outdoor table they had just ridden past.

"Sir James—" began the voice of the QB at Jim's elbow, in a low tone. But before it could continue, the approaching Knight had taken his last step toward Pellinore. Unlike nearly all of the Originals around them, who had come here wearing their knight's belts, but with nothing at them but the customary sheathed dagger, the new arrival was fully armed in chain mail, as were Pellinore, Jim, and Brian. They had come, in full arms and armor—Jim and Brian because it was their travelling costume, Pellinore in token of their errand.

From the first instant of seeing the young man come toward them, the thought that this was Modred, showing up here after all, had clutched at Jim. But as he stared at the approaching figure, doubt began to creep in. The fact that this face was clean-shaven was unimportant. Modred could have discarded beard and mustache by this time.

The QB's attention now seemed to be fully on Pellinore. Jim spoke very softly, under his breath.

"Hob," he said, "could this have been the other man in Cumberland's tent, when you and the QB were outside it the first time? He would have had a beard and mustache then."

"I don't know, my Lord," Hob said, also whispering, from his post behind Jim's head, where he was concealed by Jim's armor.

Jim looked more closely. The clean-shaved face, which he could see in more detail now that it was nearer, was too open and frank to be the one he had half glimpsed in the shadows of the Borderland tent behind the Earl and Agatha. Also, though it and the body attached to it were half a head shorter than Pellinore, it had something like the same amazing breadth of shoulder and unconquerable attitude. And the face was smiling, as if in greeting.

"It is good to see you, Sir Lamorack," said Pellinore harshly.

"And good it is to see you, King Pellinore, my father," said the other Knight.

"Are you well with God and man?"

"Sir, to the best of my knowing, I am."

"My sons were always good men and good Knights." There was still no emotion in Pellinore's voice; but he opened his arms. Sir Lamorack stepped into them—and it came to Jim that the younger man must be grateful for his armor as those long arms tightened so fiercely and strongly around him.

"Come, my father," said Sir Lamorack softly, when the arms let go. "Let the two of us step aside and speak a while."

They went off.

Jim blinked his eyes, which had unaccountably begun to mist. Just in case it was the magic glasses that were to warn him of any sign of color seen in Lyonesse—he had almost forgotten he was wearing them—he took them off and looked at them. But they showed no difference; and when he put them back on, after a couple of quick dabs with a forefinger at the inner corners of his eyes, Lyonesse showed itself as black and white as it had when they were off.

He became aware once more of Brian's voice behind him, in conversation with two other voices. He looked to his right, where the QB had been, but the QB was gone. He looked back and saw Brian standing, facing the table they had just passed, where the two Knights who had been there were also on their feet, and facing him.

The two looked from Brian to Jim, curiously.

"Ah," said Brian, following their gaze. "Allow me to name to you Sir James Eckert, oft called Sir Dragon, Baron de Bois de Malencontri et Riveroak. Sir James, may I name to you Sir Kay, foster brother to King Arthur; and this is Sir Bedivere."

"Honored to meet you," said both of them; and Sir Kay added, "Sir Brian tells us you are also a magickian."

"I am," said Jim. As a knight, manners should have obliged him to be modest. But as a magickian he was almost required to be arrogant. After all, magickians called everyone, including kings, by their christened name. Nor did they hesitate to tell Royalty off if necessary.

"Hah!" said Sir Kay and Sir Bedivere, plainly impressed.

They all sat down on stools at the table and Sir Bedivere filled metal wine cups with a dark wine for Brian and Jim. For the first time Jim looked closely at their hosts.

Sir Kay was not a young man, but his round features gave him an appearance of near youthfulness. His bushy mustache seemed salt-and-peppered in this black-and-white land, which reinforced the effect; but if he was King Arthur's foster brother, he must therefore be close to the same age; and Arthur had been white-bearded toward the end of his life. But then, this was Lyonesse.

Sir Bedivere had a face that could be any age.

"My thanks to you, Sir Bedivere," said Jim, as the ranking member of his own twosome.

"It honors me to be of service to you, Sir. You and Sir Brian are in Lyonesse because of this threat of an Evil called the Dark Powers?"

"That's right," said Jim, tasting the wine, as politeness required, but taking only a small mouthful in view of the drinking he had done at his earlier meal. This wine was not bad.

"We gather they are a thing to be feared," put in Sir Kay, "of the hardest and cruelest of magicks. Would that be also your opinion, Sir?"

"You could say that, Sir," said Jim. "But being Spirits only, anything they take, they cannot hold, being limited in this way as are all immaterial forces. As a result, it is only their creatures and their armed men that would need to be dealt with."

"Hah!" said Sir Kay jovially. "No fear from that quarter. Do you not agree, Bedivere?"

"I should certainly agree," said Bedivere. His was a plain face, but honest-looking in a remarkable degree. A face like that of a farmer who had found himself made a Knight by mistake; but was being the best Knight he could be now that he was one. "Yet I have a foreboding . . ."

"And I would venture to agree with Sir Bedivere, Sir Kay," said Brian. "Not merely because of a foreboding, however. But because I have seen their army in the Borderland of the Drowned Land."

"A large army, Sir?" asked Bedivere.

The conversation was moving out of Jim's territory of expertise.

"Between eight and twelve hundreds of lances."

Brian, Jim realized, must have picked this information up with his more experienced eye, just while they had tried to walk inconspicuously through the camp on the way to its horse lines—before they were stopped. Jim, himself, had paid no attention to how many fighting men the camp had held.

"Gentlemen?" queried Kay sharply. He would be referring only to the knights and squires, Jim knew.

"Six-tenths of them, perhaps," said Brian. "But few of them gentlemen you would sit to table with. They are ruined or sinful men, hedge-knights and outlaws—the scraping of the world's drain ditches."

"But armed and able to fight, I trust?" asked Bedivere. "It were a shame to put to flight no more than a rabble."

"Oh, armed, experienced, armored, and some with squire or page," said Brian; "and such as will fight hard, because for those like theirselves, it is win or die—and having nothing left but their few mortal years they value life."

"A considerable number," said Bedivere thoughtfully.

"Come, Sir Bedivere!" said Kay to him, "to attack *us*? They must be mad, were they twice as many."

"Any such attack will go as God wills," said Sir Bedivere. "And while I think no Knight here would fear death in battle, the arm wearies with killing; and we are not what we once were, in especial without Arthur the King or Lancelot to lead us. You remember how it was with us who were with Arthur in the next to last battle with Modred, the battle at Dover, where he had much greater numbers, but the King, beyond himself with might and passion, his white beard flaming in the sunlight, himself drove them back—and we his Knights followed. But we no longer have him, nor the brightness of Lancelot to set us alight."

"Lancelot will light no lights in his hermit cell, let be how light the lady!" said Kay, with a somewhat coarse laugh. But then he crossed himself. "If sobeit he is still on live—nay, nay—" he added swiftly, for Sir Bedivere's face had darkened and hardened. "I mean no disrespect to his memory. In all but one thing he was the most noble of Knights!"

"Well you may say so," said Bedivere.

"But you, Sir Brian." Changing his attention and his subject somewhat hastily, Sir Kay returned to Jim's friend. "From what you tell us of those armed against us, you must be old in fighting. But, without offense, Sir, may I ask how sure your estimate of this rabble raised against us may be? Have you seen much of battle? Or for that, of spear-runnings?"

"Of battle, only once, and for little time, Sir. But for spear-runnings, since my boyhood, they have been my great desire and delight," said Brian, "and I have had some small success in them."

Jim now knew enough of knightly manners to know that it was now up to him, as Brian's friend, to set the record straight.

"I do not remember, in my time," he said, as slowly and impressively as he could, "the tournament at which Sir Brian failed to carry away the crown." (He had only seen one, actually, at the Earl of Somerset's Christmas party of the previous year.)

"Ah, indeed?" said Sir Kay. His voice dropped a note or two. "Of course, those would all be tournaments in the land above, would they not?"

"They were," said Brian, "and doubtless not to compare with those found here in Lyonesse. Yet I pray you, Sir Kay, if you would do me the honor, you and I might break a spear or two so that you can judge for yourself how much I know."

"Sit down. Sit down!" said Bedivere. "With foes at our

border is no time to be playing amongst ourselves with sharpened lances!"

Both Brian and Kay sat back down on their stools. Wine was poured into cups. There was a little silence.

Jim was tense. It was Arthur who, in the Legends, focused the concept of chivalry to these men. Underneath, in many ways, they were still savage; and Sir Kay seemed all too ready to make trouble.

"What, then," said Sir Kay, breaking the pause once more, "from your experience, Sir Brian, would you say is the most important skill of all in spear-runnings?"

It was clearly a testing question.

"Sir," said Brian, "I would say that it is the skill of a good agreement between the man and his horse."

This clearly unexpected answer startled Jim with the way it abruptly cleared the small invisible thundercloud of growing antagonism at the table. Both Sir Kay and Sir Bedivere leaned forward with a sudden, wholehearted, eager interest, Sir Kay's ready animosity forgotten.

"Why do you place that foremost among all other such skills?" asked Bedivere.

"Because, Sir," said Brian, "if that a gentleman be lacking in it against an opponent whose mount is one with him, not all the other skills put together will avail."

"But surely, Sir," said Sir Kay, and there was no edge to his voice at all now, only open inquiry, "all of us have that skill—so all are equal?"

"Perhaps here in your Lyonesse it is so," said Brian. "I would not doubt that. But consider, Sirs, when the spearpoint strikes, the winner is one who is able to put not only his own weight, but that of his horse, for an instant, behind the blow. I can only say that I have met few indeed in my own experience who could do so."

"But I say again," said Sir Kay, "you must be speaking of somewhat other than what is usually considered in this. Does not the weight of horse and man necessarily go behind the strike of the spearpoint?"

"Many assume so, but no. Not with all possible force, not

without an exceptional, trained horse; and not without much training of man and horse together . . .''

Brian spoke on. He had been deeply concerned from the beginning of their friendship to teach Jim jousting, along with other weapon skills; and he had tried hard to do so. But he had never mentioned the unity of horse and man at the moment of collision until now; and Jim judged that it was subject matter for those much more expert than he would ever be—the graduate level of spear-running, so to speak.

His mind drifted off from the conversation. He wondered where Dafydd and the QB had gone when they disappeared. It struck him he was gaining nothing by sitting here while technical talk of spear-runnings whizzed about his ears. Taking advantage of a slight pause in the conversation, he stood up.

''If you will forgive me, Sirs,'' he said. ''There is something I just remembered I should be about. I will hope to rejoin you a little later—no, no, Brian, there's no need for you to come, too. By all means stay and finish talking.''

Brian settled back. Jim went. Before he had taken two steps they were deep in a discussion of how much there was to be gained by knowing the man you were about to joust with. Kay and Bedivere believed there was a great deal. Brian insisted the notion was exaggerated.

''—There is a gentleman of my acquaintance,'' he was saying as Jim walked out of hearing. ''I cannot claim him as an especial friend of mine; but there is not denying he is a superb horseman and man of his hands. I have met him many a time and oft in the lists and outside them; but never have I been able to learn in those times of any weakness or bad habit in his lance or sword work. He gained the crown at one tourney when my girth broke as he and I rode against each other to see who should win the day . . .''

The words faded behind Jim. He had encountered this same thing in the land above, long since. The gentry could be as tedious as any professionals of his original world when it came to talking shop. Opinions and instances concerning hounds, hawks, hunting practice, and the use of weapons could end up dinning in the ear of someone who had not been raised to live with those things.

Jim roamed through the Gathering Place, noticed as a stranger, but no more than noticed; and as soon forgotten by those he passed. But he found no sign of Dafydd, David, the QB, or Pellinore.

The Gathering Place of the Original Knights of Lyonesse, aside from the Pavilion, had not seemed to have much in the way of walls, or even borders. But now he began to find that even what passed for borders were particularly unreliable, tables with stools seeming to straggle off into unoccupied forest in all directions.

He reached what he thought was an outer edge now; and started to circle around the whole Place—a clever way of seeing all and everyone there, he thought—until he discovered that what had been an outer edge of it some thirty steps earlier had only protruded halfway to the longer area he now walked into, with tables and straight-backed, martial figures talking at them.

But farther around, beyond this second area, the forest closed in again. No tables, no figures, no talking. He wandered into the trees a short distance, however, just to make sure he was not being misled by the immediate greenery and this really was the outer edge of the Gathering Place at this point.

But this time no outdoor furniture and seated Knights appeared, no one. Only on one yew tree he became aware of a squirrel, larger than the one he had seen on entering Lyonesse.

This squirrel clung easily to the trunk of the yew, at a point a little above his head—motionless, upside down, but watching him with up-arched neck and bright, black-seeming eyes. He wondered if it was one of the animals he had spoken to in the amphitheater, earlier.

"Hello there," he said to it.

It said nothing. Neither did it move, though he was within two long strides of it.

Jim's mind went worriedly back to the matter of finding his missing friends and Pellinore. The day was moving on, but he could do nothing until he knew what they had been up to. In spite of himself, a feeling of depression, of being hurried into what might well be the wrong action, was growing in him. Good fighters as these figures of heroic deeds long past undoubtedly were, their idea of armed combat was probably nothing more than a super-melee, each one fighting, berserk-fashion, against the enemy before him at the moment, with no overall direction.

Cumberland would at least have a plan. The English, he recalled, had won at Crecy against the French, using the harrow formation: the archers, protected by ditches and stakes, on both wings, and dismounted men-at-arms—Jim could not see any of the Round Table Knights agreeing to dismount—in the center as spearmen. They had also made use of a favorable ground position.

Here, the question of a plan could not wait much longer. Nor could that of a leader for the fighters of Lyonesse; and though Jim found himself thinking very highly of Pellinore, he could not quite see him as the sort of magnetic general officer who might lead his fellow legendary Knights to victory, fourteenth-century style.

The fact of it was, he felt that he, himself, should be able to think of some way in which they could win against opponents that certainly must greatly outnumber them. The Earl of Cumberland had hardly a decent human quality to recommend him. But Jim did not need to see him in battle to know that the man was no coward. He had commanded—which meant leading in this age—before and would do so now. He would be ready to show the way; and none of those behind him would shirk having to follow.

Even if the Originals had the aid of all their descendants, and even if those, like the Originals, were fearsome fighters—which he secretly believed was not very likely, after meeting the Descendant of Sir Dinedan the last time he, Brian, and Dafydd had been in Lyonesse—they were going to be unreasonably outnumbered and overpowered, in any case. In this mulligan stew of magic and brutal, deadly weapons, he needed some knowledge of a way in which they could be led—what tactics, if any, they could be brought to follow.

But nothing came to mind.

He needed to talk to someone who could tell him more of what to expect from the Lyonesse warriors. What was wrong with him, anyway? Usually he could come up with an idea—but this time his mind might as well have been asleep.

Moved by a wild thought, he looked at the squirrel, who was still there, unmoved, watching him. On impulse he looked for a dead leaf, found none. He reached into his purse for the leaf Angie had given him. "Good magic," she had called it. It was worth a try in this land of magic.

He reached forward to the squirrel and slipped the leaf edgewise into the animal's slightly open mouth.

"Here!" he said, "take that to Merlin and tell him I need to know how to get to Avalon."

"M'Lord?" said Hob excitedly, on Jim's shoulder, "are we going to Avalon? The ballad singer who taught me—"

"Don't talk!" Still watching the squirrel, Jim cut him short.

The little animal had not moved. It was doing nothing about the leaf, either. It was not dropping it, but at the same time it hardly seemed aware the leaf was in its mouth. Even for a squirrel, it did not seem to have much intelligence.

Jim started to turn away, feeling empty inside. He should have kept Angie's leaf. He might as well head back toward the center of the Gathering Place. But before he was completely turned, he became aware that the squirrel was gone. He turned back instantly, but the trunk held nothing now. Strange . . . he had not seen it disappear, and it had still been within his range of vision.

A sudden touch of coldness, like an icicle slipped down the back of his shirt neck, took him.

What if it had been no living squirrel at all, but some creature or creation of either the Dark Powers or Morgan le Fay, sent to spy upon him?

If so, they might now believe he had some kind of working arrangement with Merlin; and that was why he had just sent the squirrel to the tree-bound seer. Squirrels denned in holes in trees well above ground, and such a hole in the tree where Merlin was imprisoned could lead all the way to the ancient magician. That suspicion might slow them down a bit—or it might make them move all the faster to settle things before he actually made a trip to the legendary land of Avalon.

He shook the thought off. Avalon would be unreachable, of course; and anyway, by now the squirrel would have dropped and forgotten the leaf—which at most could only be a reminder of the message, and useful only if it had understood him, which it probably had not.

"—James! James!"

Chapter 36

"James, I say! JAMES!"

Jim turned to see Brian hastening toward him.

"Most heartily do I crave the mercy of your pardon, James!" Brian said, reaching him. "Most thoughtless—most unmannerly of me—to lose my courtesie completely, in a conversation with two gentlemen, neither of whom we know; and let you start off on some task alone when I should be at your side—"

"No such thing, Brian," said Jim. "I was just hunting for Dafydd and the QB."

"Why, they and the lad David went off, even as we met with Sir Bedivere—a solid-thinking, worthy gentleman, though his ideas are somewhat out-of-date—and Sir Kay. But then, their armor, and weapons, also—however, I run on once more. Of course, your back was turned when our friends disappeared; and of course they made no sound doing it."

"I particularly wanted to ask the QB when we might get back together with King Pellinore and speak to all the Originals about getting ready to face any invasion from that small army we saw in the Borderland."

"James," said Brian solemnly, "it is not a *small* army."

"No, of course not. Just my odd way of saying things,

Brian. But, you know, there was a squirrel here just now—''

Jim checked himself, looking at the tall yew tree.

''Well, there was a squirrel,'' he went on, ''one that'd been watching me. Nothing important. I just thought I might send a message through him somehow—''

''Through a *squirrel*, James?''

But Jim's mind had gone back to being helpful again. Ignoring the question, he told Brian about how the QB had taken him to meet the wild animals of forest and plain.

''That must indeed have been a moment to remember,'' said Brian, a little wistfuly. ''Do not think I complain, James, but it has not been my good fortune to be engaged in anything so far on this voyage. Nothing, at least, of the sort that makes good telling around the fire on a winter's night. But indeed''—he brightened up suddenly—''did you know that King Pellinore has animals about his castle that serve like men and women?''

''As a matter of fact . . .'' began Jim, ''I did. They set a table outside for me; and some human servants brought out food.''

''Did they?''

''Yes.'' Jim told him all about it.

''Well, well!'' said Brian admiringly. ''They did? I have always said that you will find better manners in your usual beast than you will in your usual gentleman. Certainly your well-trained horse or dog . . . but my own happenstance with these was no less wonderful.''

''When did you have time to have it? When I went with the QB to meet with the animals in the woods you were asleep, and still asleep when we got back.''

''Ah, yes, but I woke up betweentimes. It has happened to me once or twice before, when I have gone somewhat beyond my usual time of sleep. I woke, James, suddenly; not knowing where I was for a moment. I wished very much to sleep again, but I could not seem to do so, so I got up and went out.''

''All the way outside?''

''Outside King Pellinore's palace. I sat down on his

bench—you recall that bench seat against the front wall of it? And sat, trying to think myself back into slumber, but without success. Still, I must have dozed for a moment—but do not think I dreamed this, James!''

''No. I won't. Of course not.''

''I opened my eyes to see some of the small bears and otters you mentioned, James; one couple of each standing a little apart from the other couple, but all regarding me. It did not come to my mind at first that these animals were servitors of King Pellinore. My first thought was that they had just wandered in out of the woods, though I marvelled to see them stand two and two like that—I was barely awake, for all I could not sleep, you understand—and I did not think to see if there was any other animal there with them.''

He stopped, shaking his head.

''Go on,'' said Jim.

''Ah, me,'' said Brian, with sudden softness, ''I shall never be able to bring myself to hunt a little doe again, no matter how hard the winter. But all at once there was this soft breath in my face, and a young fallow deer was before me, and the end of her muzzle was at rest on my shoulder . . . those gentle eyes looking at me—sorrowfully it seemed, almost—for that I could not sleep; and after a moment, she lowered her head and nudged me under my right arm, nudged me upward.''

Brian sighed.

''It may be hard to believe, James; but I could no more refuse that nudge than I could have refused a polite request from a lady. Once on my feet, I felt her moving to nudge me from behind; and so she pushed me gently to the door of the palace, down a corridor and into the room where I had been sleeping, and so to my bed. I fell on it, ready to sleep now; and rest came to me like instant night. The last I remember were her great eyes, so gentle, still watching, looking down into mine, until I could hold them open no longer.''

He stopped speaking, and sat, staring a little away from Jim as if he was seeing what he had just been talking about. Brian, Jim knew, was not a run-of-the-mill romantic. But once he was caught up by emotion, he was off like a rocket.

Jim had seen him in the grip of emotion before—most notably during their trip to Northumberland, where they two, with Dafydd, had gone to bring word of the death of their friend Giles to his family.

Thankfully, Giles had in fact not died, after all, thanks to his heritage of silkie blood—a fact that had not been known when Jim, thinking so, had had his first run-in with the Earl of Cumberland over the burial. The Earl had been forced to give way at that time, due to the intercession of the young Prince Edward; but Jim and his friends had earned themselves the Earl's enmity.

But having found Giles alive in his home, Jim found himself confronted with the problem presented by Brian's sudden infatuation with Giles's sister, to the point of announcing himself ready to forsake his lifelong love, Geronde. Jim had been grateful when Brian's feelings had evaporated with surprising swiftness, and left no residual effects.

Perhaps the same thing would happen with his feeling about Pellinore's deer. But it was hard to tell. There had been something deep-voiced in the way he told the story of the doe that touched Jim as the gathering of the animals had in his case.

"—But here they are, now!" Brian suddenly interrupted himself, in his usual energetic voice.

"Here? Who?" said Jim, turning to look. Back in the direction of the heart of the Gathering Place, where the ends and edges of a number of tables could be glimpsed among the trees, Dafydd, David, and the QB were approaching.

"Our friends, of course," answered Brian unnecessarily.

"Sir James!" said the QB, "we have been searching for you and Sir Brian!"

"And I've been looking for you. You were the ones who disappeared."

"We did not expect to be gone so long. But you are right, Sir James. We were the first to leave, and without speaking to you. Pray pardon us. But we have news of importance. We three have been to the Drowned Land—"

"In daylight?"

"Indeed," said the QB. "But Dafydd—who insists I call him simply that, rather than by his rightful title as a Prince of that land—wondered why it had been so plagued with Harpies, while Lyonesse has seen none of the creatures of the Dark Powers. And since we had some time in hand—"

"Hold on!" said Jim, "wait a minute! I didn't know we 'had some time in hand.' Did you, Brian?"

"I did not," said Brian.

"I thought King Pellinore would be taking us directly to meet some of the leading Originals," went on Jim, "and maybe we'd even begin to start making plans with them. But he went off with his son; and when I thought to look for the rest of you, you were gone."

"Mea culpa—as you humans say. Once more, the blame is entirely mine. Knowing King Pellinore as I do, I did not stop to think that you would not know. His talk with his son could not possibly be a short one. He will be hungry to hear all that Sir Lamorack may have to tell him. But Sir Lamorack will have to talk cleverly and long on his own behalf if he wishes to bring his father to speak of himself. Yet Sir Lamorack will do so, and succeed; for he and Sir Percival, his brother, greatly love King Pellinore."

"I see. Well, these things happen," said Jim. "I didn't mean to sound—anyway, you're here now."

"But, Sir James, I did not mislead you. We do have some time in hand, after all. Favor me by looking into my eyes."

Jim stared at him for a moment, then concentrated on doing what he had just been asked. It was not the simple matter it sounded. The eyes in the QB's head, at the end of his long, snaky neck, were one on each side of that head; whereas Jim's were side by side in front for binocular vision. But Jim managed it.

For a moment he saw nothing but the glittering darkness of those serpent eyes. Then the darkness seemed to expand, and merge into one image, which brightened until it showed the green land under a yellow sun that was the Drowned Land. The figure of a woman in white was pacing up and down, impatiently, half a dozen feet each way.

He stared at her for a moment.

"Isn't that—" he began; but that was as far as he got before the QB interrupted him for a second time.

"Shall we go, Sir James?"

"Go?" Jim blinked, losing the image, and stared at him for a second. "Go. Oh, yes, certainly."

A slice of darkness came seemingly out of nowhere, to cover them for so short a fraction of time that its momentary appearance hardly registered on Jim; and they were there—Jim, the QB, Dafydd, David, and Brian, all facing the lady in white; who had halted, staring at Jim.

"Well?" she said, challengingly, to him.

"The Lady!" Hob burst out, from Jim's shoulder.

"Yes" said Jim grimly, "Queen Northgales."

"Are you better now, my Queen?" asked Hob.

"I am always perfect—so the Natural or manling—the little one, at any rate—is still with you? Get rid of it so we can talk!"

"Is there a lake nearby?" asked Jim.

"How should I know? Are you planning to drown it?"

"No. I was just going to suggest you go to the lake and jump in."

"Jump in?" She stared at him. "Why? Why would I want to do that?"

"Because then both Hob and I'd be rid of you."

"Sir James, Sir James!" said the QB. "Grant the favor of some small amount of patience . . ."

"Hard to do with this Lady."

"I am a Queen, you dolt!"

Jim ignored her.

"I pray you most earnestly, Sir James," said the QB, "that you wait to hear for a little while."

"King David and I also ask that, Sir James," said Dafydd, unexpectedly.

Jim looked at them curiously.

"Is there more to this than just name-calling?"

"We—the Lord QB, King David, and I—believe so."

Jim looked at the two serious human faces, and at the unreadable serpentine face of the QB.

"All right," he said. "But Hob, don't get close to the Queen over there. Above all, don't let her touch you. Best you don't even try to talk to her."

"But m'Lord! She's so sad!"

"Sad!" exploded Northgales, almost sputtering.

"Sad or not, stay clear of her. That's an order, Hob!"

"Yes, m'Lord." Hob's voice was unhappy.

It's for his own safety, Jim told himself. But a trace of guilt was stirring inside him, nonetheless. He had known the little hobgoblin intimately long enough to know that Hob could not help feeling for anyone or anything suffering, lonely, or even less than joyous. He pushed the guilt from him. There was no time for it now.

"All right," he said. "Then, QB, you explain."

"Briefly, Sir James," he said, "King David, Dafydd, and I came to this land to find out if the invaders were ready to move against Lyonesse, as those of this land whom they had kept watching them reported. Dafydd judged they were; indeed, they had already started packing for the move. But then, checking the landscape generally for Harpies and finding none, we yet found—not the Queen of Northgales, but her—"

He hesitated.

"Simulacrum?" Jim suggested.

Northgales sniffed.

"—But when we stopped to look at her, she became herself as you see her now," the QB went on. "She told us she wanted information from you; and might be willing to give you something in return. We all thought immediately that you should be the one to deal with the matter, so we came and got you and Sir Brian. We thought—"

"Never mind what you thought!" said Northgales. "I'll do the talking. You, James, give me your attention. I have watched you stay safely out of the hands of Morgan le Fay for some time now. You will tell me immediately how you have managed to do that."

"Just tell you—like that?"

"Of course!"

"Why?"

"Because you have been commanded to, idiot!"

"Nothing in return?"

"Certainly not. This beast of Pellinore's must have misunderstood me. A Queen does not bargain. I command!"

"Then long may you continue to do so," said Jim.

Northgales evidently did not understand that this was his answer, at first. Then something that was almost a flush stained her white cheeks for a second.

"Of course," said Jim, "being a Queen, you could always try to make me tell. Go right ahead."

"You'll regret it to your dying day—which may be soon!" she spat out.

"I don't mind. Go ahead—what're you waiting for? Don't tell me you don't have any magic powers here in the Drowned Land?"

"That is false! I have some," said Northgales.

"I'll believe 'some,' " said Jim. "You'd need it to make a simulacrum of yourself, but you might have to personally, physically, convey it here."

"You have no magick, either!"

"I don't?" said Jim. "Then how've I been able to stay safely out of Morgan's grasp all this time—sorry, I forgot. That's what you wanted to find out from me."

"Perhaps. But the idea of my giving you anything in return is ridiculous. You may have magick you cannot use—except to stay free of Morgan le Fay!"

A shrewd guess. Jim winced internally.

"You're wrong," he said stoutly.

"Wrong. How? Do you pretend to have magick in Lyonesse?"

"Of course."

"Ridiculous! You are not of Lyonesse, and so could have no powers there. In any case, Morgan would have taken them from you!"

"She tried. She couldn't."

"Couldn't? That's—"

"She burned her fingers when she tried."

"Burned!" Northgales took a quick, long step backward.

"That's right," said Jim. "Now, do you want to come down from your high horse and start talking sensibly to me or shall we end this little chitchat?"

"*Morgan?* Burned her fingers?" This time the emphasis was on the name of the other Witch Queen.

"Yes."

"I'm not surprised." Reasonableness was beginning to sound for the first time in Northgales's voice. Also a sort of desperation, or exhaustion. She passed her fingers over her forehead for a moment.

"—She is not all-powerful," Northgales said suddenly. "We four Witch Queens were given Lyonesse to rule each in our own place of strength. Where my winds blow, none of the other three can stand before me. But Morgan has improved her powers because her strength was to be with Arthur and those like him, whose spirits in all else control Lyonesse, together with the trees and the Old Magic. Now she thinks she should rule all; and, since that is impossible, she has cast her eyes on this earth about us here."

"But she will have no magick power here, either," said Dafydd. "How can she hope to rule and own us?"

"Ah!" said Northgales, laying her finger to her nose, and peering over it slyly at Jim. "If you want that answer, you must buy it—"

But the finger was trembling. She took it away from her nose and stared at it. "Wet!" Her whole hand was shaking; and now Jim saw her body was shaking also. She wavered on her feet.

"M'Lady!" Hob leaped from Jim's shoulder and started to run to her. Jim dived after him; and caught him just out of reach of Northgales. But she made no effort to reach out her arm and touch Hob; only turned her eyes, now wet and spilling tears, on him.

"Why do you torment me so with your vile concern, little one?" she choked.

"But m'Lord, she needs help!" Hob was still struggling in Jim's arms, trying to reach Northgales.

"You can't help her; and if you touch her, she'll hurt you!" said Jim. "Now, be quiet!"

"No one can help!" Her voice had weakened down to a whisper. "No one. It is this sun—the terrible sun here. The heat, the burning heat!"

"Speak quickly," said Jim. "Tell me what you've come to offer; and maybe I can save you. Quick!"

"I . . . came . . ." It took sharp listening to hear the ghost of a whisper from her white lips now. ". . . to join you . . . against her . . ."

"There's more than that. Tell me—you can't take much more of this!"

"Cumberland . . . to have this land . . . in hold. She . . . to gain Lyonesse above the Knights . . . aid Cumber . . . gainst upper worl . . ."

Her voice went silent. Her streaming eyes closed.

Jim reached into his purse with one hand, with the other still holding back Hob. From the purse he pulled out his pear from among the enchanted fruit there, and took one bite. Like his use of the grape earlier to supply him with the sleep he had lost, it was not what he had planned. But it was worth it.

"*A pavilion!*" he said within himself, visualizing the airy, tentlike structure. "*Shade. Temperature seventy—no, fifty-five degrees fahrenheit.*" The Auditing Department would have no idea what Fahrenheit, Celsius, or Absolute degrees meant in terms of heat or cold, but that did not matter.

He did.

Instantly the pavilion was shading them, the temperature that of the outdoors on a cool but not-unpleasant fall day. He had been tempted for a second to go down to forty degrees; but that might be harmful to Northgales—to be plunged into too cool a temperature too quickly, even though it might be a temperature she liked and was used to.

Chapter 37

The shade and the coolness in the pavilion were pleasant for Jim, whatever good they were doing the now-unconscious Witch Queen.

He and the others watched her. Hob had stopped struggling to be free.

"Grant me the grace of your forgiveness, m'Lord," he said now in a small voice. "I am a poor Hobgoblin, not to know that such as I could not help her as you can."

"Nonsense!" said Jim. "Put that out of your mind completely, Hob. What you can do for people, old and young, is beyond magic."

Still held by Jim's arm, Hob looked up at his face with a doubtful expression. Jim remembered to let go of him. Still staring, alternately at Jim and Northgales, Hob joined the silent semicircle around her.

She had not moved, her eyes were still closed—but no longer streaming tears, Jim saw.

"I think she'll be all right," he said in the somehow strange silence of the pavilion. "Let's wait a minute or two."

They waited; and though time seemed to stretch out, it could only have been a moment before her eyes opened.

She stared at the cloth ceiling over her, tensing.

"Am I in Lyonesse?" she asked.

"No," said Jim. "This is still the Drowned Land."

She relaxed, closing her eyes again briefly, and a long breath came slowly from her lips.

"You thought you were back there and had lost your magick?" said Jim, deliberately pronouncing the word as everyone but Angie, Merlin, and himself seemed to pronounce it.

Her eyes snapped open.

"If I did, it was a momentary weakness," she said; and her tone was trying to be as sharp as ever. But, surprisingly, it had softened. "Still, it—strange, I seem to like this little breath of coolness, warm as it still is compared to my fine castle."

"And you'll need our help to get back to that," said Jim. "Your magick may be waiting for you in Lyonesse; but all the troubles that have also been waiting for you are still there. Are you ready to make a deal with me now?"

"Queens do not do . . . what you just said!" But the sharpness was still not what it should have been, for her. "Queens demand; and if they are pleased with what they get, they reward."

"And magicians," said Jim, emphasizing the word and pronouncing it his way, this time, "don't demand. But they don't give at anyone else's demand, either. You're going to have to talk my language if you want to talk to me."

She turned her head a little and looked away from all of them.

"Send that small, intruding creature away. I cannot bear him, weak as I am now."

"He stays," said Jim. "It's not his fault he loves everyone, even someone like you."

"That is false." She was still looking away from them. "Love is an illusion. Even if it were not, no one could love the North Gales. None ever has. None ever will."

"Look back this way and keep your eyes open," said Jim. "One can and does. He's standing right beside you. Take a good look at him and you'll be able to see for yourself how he feels."

"No. Queens do not take commands."

"I challenge you. Turn and look!"

With that she turned her head, opened her eyes, and looked directly at Hob.

"Admit he lies!" she said to him.

"Oh, m'Lady! My Lord would never lie."

Jim winced internally.

"—And besides," said Hob, his voice rising a little. "It's true anyhow! We Hobs are just made that way. It makes us feel good to make the children laugh. It makes us feel sad to see anyone sad. And you can't do anything about it! I'm going to go on feeling sad for you until you stop making me feel that way.''

''Then be sad forevermore—for all the good it will do you! I *am* the North Gales! No one can love me. I have no lovers, no friends.''

''I'm your friend. If you'd just let me take you for a ride on the smoke, you'd see. You'd feel better. You couldn't help it.''

''But I don't want to feel better, you little idiot!'' cried Northgales, sitting up. ''I *like* the way I am. I *like* feeling as I feel! Oh, take him away—!'' she almost screamed at Jim. ''Take him away and destroy—no, don't destroy him, just take him away from me. He lies. You lie. Love! Idiocy! He can't love me—and what difference would it make if he could?''

''Maybe we better go,'' said Jim. Time was slipping by and he was beginning to give up the idea of getting to any sensible bargaining terms with Northgales. ''Hob—''

''But I do!'' cried Hob—and before Jim could stop him he had darted forward, seized Northgales by the hand, and was trying to pull her to her feet.

She made an effort and got herself up. She stared down at him as he let go of her hand.

''I didn't gain any heat from you . . .'' she said slowly. ''It was as if we were of the same chill—or warm!''

She turned on Jim.

''What is this place?'' she said. ''It is not—not in the land—that land—''

''The land above? No,'' said Jim.

''Then how can magick be working here on me when you can have none here?''

''It's not magic,'' said Jim. ''It's you—'' He checked himself just in time. Name-calling never helped any situation; and he had been on the precipice edge of it. But Hob had shown the way to all of them. Jim stepped forward and grasped Northgales's hand.

There was a hollow feeling in his stomach as he touched her; but her hand felt like any other human hand in his—

somewhat cold, but not excessively so under the autumn outdoors temperature inside the pavilion.

He let go again.

She stared down at her own hand as if it had betrayed her.

"I am lost!" she said. "The gales will no longer obey me. I will be no more!"

"No such damned thing!" exploded Brian. He stepped forward himself, picked up her hand himself, and kissed the back of it in his most courtly manner. "—My Queen!"

She stared at him with wide eyes as he let go. She stared at the back of her hand.

"Of course, the gales will still obey you," Jim said. "Your magic doesn't own you. You own it. You've just uncovered something you've been keeping hidden from yourself; hiding it with your own magic. You don't *have* to steal warmth from anyone else you touch!"

"I am not cold," she said, folding her arms around her and holding an opposite elbow in each hand, as if she held her body like that of any stranger. "I am *not* cold!"

"Right," said Jim. "But we've got to be going back to Lyonesse. Maybe my Lord QB would be good enough to take you—"

"Of course," said the QB. "I will be glad to take the Queen of Northgales—but only to where we are going. From there with her own magick she can go the rest of the way herself."

"Fine," said Jim. "Now, Northgales, for the last time, while there's a moment, what did you want to tell me?"

"I will tell you of Morgan le Fay," said Northgales, lifting her head to look at him like a person awakened suddenly. "I will tell you all I know, if you will help me against her."

"Join us in everything—wholeheartedly join us, you understand—and we'll all help you. But you'll have to help us in turn. As for Morgan, you've already let out that she wants to own the Drowned Land; and in exchange she'll use her magic to help Cumberland in something in the land above. What's she planning?"

"Alas," said Northgales, "that I do not know. But her

nagickal powers are great—especially with those who are lying, and those close in danger of death."

"I don't see it helps us much to know that," said Jim. 'What can you tell us about the other two Witch Queens of Lyonesse, she of Eastland, and she of Out Isles?"

"Much. What do you wish to know?"

"Too much to ask now, I guess, come to think of it," said Jim grimly. "QB, I'm going to delete the pavilion. Will you ake us back as soon as it vanishes?"

"The sun—" began Northgales in alarm.

"It won't hurt you now. Ready, QB?"

The pavilion disappeared. The slice of darkness flashed in and out; and they were back at the Originals' Gathering Place. The seated Knights about where they appeared looked up, startled.

"Farewell," said Northgales, looking at Hob. "Farewell, ittle one. I think . . . I think someday I may have what you call love for you, too."

"Oh, I'm happier now, my Queen," said Hob.

She vanished.

"Hah!" said a hard, bass voice; and Jim looked up to see Pellinore. "Here you are. I had been sure you were with me; out meseems you left, and without a word."

"Come," he went on, without waiting for an answer; and urning, led the way to and up three steps into the pavilion. Its circular floor was crowded with many of the picnic-style ables, of which, at the moment, only one was occupied.

Behind its farther edge sat five of the Original Knights of the Legends. They were all clean-shaven, and none looked to be more than in his forties; but there was an air of authority and experience about all of them.

"Hob," whispered Jim, just in time, "hide!"

Hob dived down Jim's back, between his chain mail shirt and the cloth one underneath. How he thinned himself out to do it, Jim did not know—it probably had something to do with his being able to get through any place smoke could get hrough.

"Sirs," said Pellinore, stopping before the table, with Jim

and the others behind him. "May I make known to you Si
James Eckert de Malencontri, Sir Brian Neville-Smythe c
Castle Smythe, both of the land above; and the Lord QB, wit
whom you are familiar, with the King of the Drowned Lan
and Prince . . ."

—To Jim's surprise, he pronounced Dafydd's Drowne
Land princely title in the unpronounceable language of it
people.

"—from our neighbors of the country next to us. The
land, also, has been under attack from the Dark Powers tha
threaten to attack us."

"Sirs," said the Original Knight in the center of the tabl
the shortest of them there, but with a broad jaw that gave hin
a pugnacious look, "we are honored to meet with you."

"Before you," said Pellinore, half turning to Jim and th
others, "allow me to name Sir Gawain; to his right Sir Cado
of Cornwall, and beyond Sir Cador, King Bors. To Sir Ga
wain's left is Sir Idrus, and beyond Sir Idrus, Sir Berel—al
gentlemen who have fought in their time against Rome."

"Will you sit, Sirs?" said Sir Gawain. In spite of his short
ness he was stocky and looked powerful. He spoke in a cold
level baritone.

Jim and the others, including Pellinore, pulled up stools t
their side of the table and sat—all except the QB, of course
who sat politely on his haunches, his head on a level wit
that of everyone else.

"Sirs," said Gawain, "we five have been discussing wha
is to be done about the force now encamped in the Borderlan
of the Drowned Land, if they should dare to move into Lyo
nesse. We have come to certain agreement on several matters
The one is the place at which they will hope to fight us."

"To know where they wish to hold battle is indeed a usefu
thing," said Pellinore. "Which place have you decide
upon?"

"The Empty Plain," said Sir Gawain.

Heads nodded on Gawain's side of the table—and to Jim'
astonishment, he saw not only Pellinore's head nodding o
their side, but Dafydd's and David's as well.

"Forgive me," said Jim, "but I don't know where the Empty Plain is, or what it's like. Would you tell me?"

"You do not known the Empty Plain, Sir?" asked Sir Idrus, a lean-faced man with dark, bright eyes. All of those on the other side of the table stared at Jim unbelievingly.

"Sir James has been through Lyonesse only once before, on his way to the rock wherein hides Gnarlyland; and on this occasion," said Dafydd, "has been here but a short time—I pray the grace of your forgiveness for my interruption, but I thought it was well to mention this. I, and the King of the Drowned Land beside me, know of it from those of our own people who have ventured a certain distance only into this magick ground."

The looks directed by the others darkened from unbelief to something close to contempt.

"Sir James is himself a magickian from the land above," said Pellinore.

The contempt evaporated, leaving only surprise and respect—with even perhaps a touch of healthy caution mixed in as well.

"Might you tell me, Sirs," said Jim, remembering to be on his best fourteenth-century manners, "why the Empty Plain should be first choice of place for this battle?"

"Only decent place with enough ground for a battle," said Sir Idrus.

"But not only that, Sirs," said Sir Gawain, "but those who would invade Lyonesse have heard, beyond any doubt, that our trees are magick; and they do not wish to be ambushed beneath them for fear of what they may be able to do."

"In fact, however, the help of trees is not needed," put in Sir Bors.

"But these invaders do not know that," said Sir Gawain; "although, in fact, they have been known to reach down their limbs and strangle those who would do evil here."

"It is not much help in battle," said King Bors, "if an enemy or two is slowly strangled while the fighting is going on."

"Come!" said Pellinore's deep voice. "Let us not waste

our time on small things when Lyonesse is threatened. I agre
we all agree, that the Empty Plain is the most likely field
battle, where they will expect us to meet them; and there sha
we be, of course. You have Sir James and his friends wh
are wise in experience with the Dark Powers that are said
be behind this. Let you make use of his knowledge by askir
him what you will while he is here."

"You are much in the right, King Pellinore," said Gawai
"We have decided you shall lead—"

—They might have started out by mentioning that, Jim to
himself—

"—May I ask, then," Sir Gawain was going on, "if yo
Sir James, know who will lead our foes?"

"A knight named Sir Robert de Clifford, Earl of Cumbe
land, Sirs," said Jim. "He's not someone those who will fa
us could love; but he's a . . ." Jim's mind hunted hastily f
the proper word, and in desperation grabbed one at random–
though by his standards it didn't fit. "—a knight of prowe
and experience in war. He'll make a strong enemy."

"If Arthur were still with us, or Lancelot, nothing abo
those who come would matter," said Sir Berel, speaking f
the first time.

"But they are not," said Gawain to him; and turned bac
to Jim. ". . . and you judged their force to be between eig
and twelve hundred of lances?"

"That wasn't my count," said Jim, "but Sir Brian's, wh
is better at such numbering than I am."

"But you, Sir," said King Bors unexpectedly; "as a ma
ickian, surely you would know best of any?"

"King Bors," said Jim, thankful that the name was famili
to him from the Legends, so he could remember which ma
it had gone with, "a knight has rules by which he must liv
if he is to be a worthy knight. Similarly, a worker of mag
has the rules that govern magickians. Those rules I may n
and will not break. I will say no more than that."

"Hah!" said Sir Bors, but added no more.

"Still," said Sir Idris, after a short silence, "that cann

ut bring us to a question that we must ask.'' He looked at ir Gawain.

''Do you wish to be the one to put it, Sir?''

''Since I sit in the center of the table, it is doubtless for ne to do so,'' said Gawain. He looked hard at Jim. ''Sir, we onor you for coming to aid us with word of our enemies nd what other help you will to give. But will you tell us vhy such as yourselves and your friends should come to the id of Lyonesse at all, since you are so far removed from s?''

For some reason, it was the last question Jim had been xpecting. In spite of himself, he fumbled internally, searchng for words to answer it. But while he hesitated, Brian burst ut.

''Sir!'' He threw a quick side glance at Jim. ''The grace f your pardon, Sir James—but, noble Knights all! We may e from another land far removed from here; but there is no entleman worthy of his vows in the land we come from vhose heart does not lift at the name of King Arthur and the dventures of his Knights. It is in his name and yours that ve judge ourselves and each other. How could Sir James and stand idle at distance, knowing the Dark Powers and those hat go with them are attempting to bring trouble to those of he Round Table?''

Three of the five at the table said ''Hah!''; and Sir Cador f Cornwall even went so far as to reach toward the right side f his upper lip, as if to twirl the end of a nonexistent musache, before seeming to appear conscious of what he was oing and dropping his hand.

''Then we are much reasssured,'' said Gawain, ''not wishng, as you can understand, Sir Brian and Sir James, to be eholden to any who offer us help for some light or selfish eason.''

''Of course you wouldn't,'' said Jim, moved enough to orget his attempts to speak in a medieval fashion. ''We honor ou for it!''

''It is not needed that Knights of Arthur's be honored for uch a duty,'' said Gawain, his cold voice spacing out the

words. "Well, then, I think we have all in hand. With thos
recently returned to us from deaths before the Lyonesse w
know now, we will field near three hundred of lances. S
many should suffice. I believe that is all. Our Descendan
will follow us, of course, but it should be our endeavor t
protect them by dealing with the foe ourselves. King Pellino
will lead us; and our friends here will lend such aid of whic
they are capable; for which we offer them thanks. Is the
anything more to be said?"

Jim blinked. These men might be the greatest of warrior
but *three hundred* men against *eight to twelve hundred,* i
man-to-man encounters? It was simply unbelievable.

"There is no way, then, we might draw them into an am
bush?" said Sir Berel, a plumpish Knight, in a slightly wistf
voice. "Against the Romans, Sir Lionel and Sir Bedivere, b
laying in ambush, won much honor, though for a short tim
only. Sir Idrus and myself fell into Roman hands until yo
Sir Gawain, with good Sir Idrus—"

"That was only a small part of the Roman Army," sai
Sir Idrus. "You will remember the full battle was fought an
won later against the Emperor Lucius. We are known not t
be such Knights as to all flee cowardly from the field, whic
alone could draw them after us."

"Nor do I think even that would serve," said the dee
voice of Pellinore, unexpectedly. "Fear of what they hav
heard of the trees, from what the Prince on this table-side h
told me of Cumberland's leman, will keep them on the Plai
She well may be a Witch Queen from the land above; an
knows more of our land than she should."

There was a little silence.

"Further, Sirs," said Pellinore, "if by your choice I am t
lead and command, I shall do so. There will be no ambushe
We must trust as always in God and our good right arms."

Gawain looked at him a little sharply, a sudden, dartin
glance. But as quickly looked away again.

"Lord QB," Pellinore said, "may I ask you if the tree
would be good enough to give warning to you when thes

ndless men enter our ground—and that you will then warn ;?''

''Sir, they will, and I will. You will have time to marshal our forces ready for them in the trees at this end of the mpty Plain, before they can advance in order across it.''

''Ah,'' said Sir Idrus, ''how I remember, when Arthur ;ked for counsel from his fellow kings before going to war ith Lucius, the Roman Emperor. Anguish of Scotland of-:red him thousands of men-at-arms—the King of Little Brit-n so promised as well, as did the Lord of West Wales, Sir ancelot, and others; and all of us of the Round Table prom-ed what we could. Now . . .''

''That was then and this is now,'' said Gawain, rising. This Cumberland who comes against us now has no more ıan twelve hundreds of men, by the word of Sir Brian. I feel ıere is no more needed to be said. We will deal with him.''

He rose to his feet. Jim, aghast that they should break up 'ith no more than had been settled so far, held out a hand most without thinking.

''Sir!'' he said. ''If you will give me the grace of a mo-ıent's word more—''

Gawain checked himself, and stood, but with no particu-ırly interested look on his face.

''There might be a lot to gain, if we think about it just a ıoment more,'' Jim said rapidly. ''Stop and think—the Dark owers have been sending their Harpies over the Drowned and, to whom they are equally an enemy. But the Drowned and has archers of great skill, who might well be willing to ght beside you on the Empty Plain. There is a war formation 'hich has won great victories over much greater forces in the ınd above, using archers on the wings of their line of battle, 'ith the men-at-arms in the center—''

''I honor them that they did so well in that fashion,'' in-:rrupted Gawain. ''Each knight may do as he wishes; but for ıe, I prefer to win my own wars with my own sword and ınce. However, nothing is lost, for you may advance your lan to King Pellinore, who now leads. God be with you, irs.''

He stepped back, walked around the end of the table a
past Jim and the others toward the edge of the pavilion.

The others on his side of the table also stood, one by on
and with a "Good day, Sirs," followed Gawain's departur

Chapter 38

After Gawain and the other Knights had disappeared, Pel
nore listened politely while Jim went into details, from h
student days, of the battles at Crecy and Poitiers in France

". . . also," Jim wound up, "I haven't had a chance to ta
to Dafydd"—he thought for a moment of wrestling with Da
ydd's Drowned Land name and title, and decided against
Pellinore knew who he was talking about—"but I've got
idea of how to use my magic, with Sir Brian's help, to cle
the skies over the Drowned Land so the archers of the Bl
could safely come here. I don't even know, of course,
they'd want to—"

"They would," said Dafydd.

"Thank you, Dafydd—but they could make the battle f
more even and might easily insure Lyonesse winning it."

Pellinore nodded.

"What you say is undoubtedly true," he said. "And tho
Drowned Land archers are no doubt brave, honest fellows
great skill and craft with their own weapon. It would be som
thing for almost any army to consider, as most consider sin
ple, ordinary men-at-arms on foot with spears and such."

There was the faintest of pauses. Jim, who had experience
turndowns from experts in the academic field—and they we
no slouches at that in the academic field—felt one comin
now.

"But to die is nothing for a knight, as you must kno
yourself," went on Pellinore; "and if we cannot defend th
land of Arthur with our own arms, alone, we do not deser
to keep it. Otherwise, how could any believe we had a rig

to it in the first place? God Himself could call us to question, and rightly so.

"But I thank you, Sir James, you, Prince *of the Sea-washed Mountains*"—the translation of Dafydd's Drowned Land title returned to Jim's memory even though its pronunciation continued to be impossible for him—"and these good archers for the willingness to aid us. Now, I must be about many matters connected with getting us ready for the onslaught. All of us will wish to have armor, horse, and gear in good readiness for the moment. Give you all good day."

He left them.

"QB," said Jim, as that individual led Jim, Brian, Dafydd, and King David off the raised pavilion floor in a somewhat different direction from the one in which Pellinore had left, "if I'm not asking for more than I should, did I offend them—King Pellinore and Gawain—with my suggestions?"

"King Pellinore, never," said the QB. "Gawain has always been quick to find cause to be offended, however. Thwarting him in the slightest may cause it. But in this case, if he was, there was no reason for him to be so."

"Thanks," said Jim. "That relieves my mind a bit."

"You are not wholly relieved?" They were outside the pavilion now, among the tables—tables that at the moment were empty. The QB led them farther into some trees that here came close to the pavilion. Once among the trees he spoke again. "You are still concerned, Sir James?"

"We could bring the bowmen to the battle despite these Knights," said Dafydd, "and I cannot point out that the Drowned Land is in danger from these same enemies without seeming—as Gawain himself pointed out—selfish in our reason for fighting with them. But otherwise, I cannot think of any miracle that might save Lyonesse, if they fight alone, for all their prowess."

"Gawain said," spoke up young David, "that their Descendants would be allowed to help. Each Knight must have more than two or three of those, at least, of fighting age, after all these generations that must have gone by since Arthur left them for Avalon."

"But none of those are going to have known serious battle, as just about all of the Knights of the Table Round must have," said Jim. "I don't know . . ."

"Come, James!" said Brian. "Lift up your heart. God is on the side of Lyonesse. Also, those who fight for gain cannot match with those who joy in the fighting, especially a fight for a good cause—and what better than this?"

"Lift—" said Jim. "I forgot! It slipped my mind completely. Brian, I asked you once if you'd like—"

He checked himself. Brian had been out on his feet then and Jim had not seriously expected a sensible answer. On the other hand, he had not thought before asking. Brian was not afraid of anything—that was an exaggerated statement used for anyone else Jim knew, but not for Brian—and the fact he was now happily entertaining the thought of the relative handful of Lyonesse Knights encountering an army of experienced men more than several times their own numbers was proof of it.

"You were about to ask if I would like something, James," said Brian. "Of your kindness, continue. Some wine would not go amiss; and I have not eaten to the filling of my hunger for what seems a great time, now."

Jim still hesitated, although the other three were now also waiting to hear what he would say. Now that he had stopped to think, he remembered that courage was not all that was required in what he was going to suggest—at least not from someone like Brian. Brian had hunted mere-dragons—the larger Cliffside dragons stayed prudently out of his sight—and he knew, as everybody did, that an experienced man in armor on horseback and with lance was more than a match for even the largest dragon.

This last Jim had found out to his own cost, when he had first appeared in this world as a dragon, in the body of Gorbash. He had attacked, head-on, Sir Hugh de Bois, then possessor of Malencontri—and almost immediately died, as a result. Dragon bodies, while immensely strong, and heavy on the whole, were necessarily boned as lightly as possible, to allow them to get up into the air; and Sir Hugh's lance had gone clear through Jim.

But in many medieval minds, Jim knew, there was a sense of horror connected with the concept of a dragon. That could well keep Brian from wanting what Jim was to propose.

On the other hand, there was only one way of finding out. That was to ask.

"It was not of wine or food I was going to ask you, Brian," Jim said. "You were asleep on your feet the first time I mentioned it to you, but what I said then was *'How would you like to be a dragon?'* "

Brian blinked; and then he smiled, a large smile.

"Hah!" he said. "I would like it of all things, James!"

Jim sighed internally with relief. It was what he had expected, of course; but although Brian knew nothing of the danger of what Jim had in mind, Jim felt stronger, knowing the other would be with him. But Brian was speaking again.

"That is, James," he was saying, "I would wish to adventure at being a dragon for some short time. But the time must needs be limited. There is Geronde and our wedding to think of."

"Of course," said Jim, his memory jogged. "Still, I think there would be time . . . actually, something came to mind a little bit back that the two of us might get done—"

Dafydd cleared his throat.

"Er, Dafydd," Jim said, turning to him, "I hadn't thought beyond Brian and myself, because you weren't with us at the time the idea first came to me. I don't want you to think I'd forgotten you—"

"Not at all, James," said Dafydd. "I was within a word of echoing Sir Brian's happiness with your question; but before I could speak, I remembered. I am not a man who loves nothing but his duty, look you. But I was at once minded of the fact of my obligation to my King, which must put dreams of flying like a falcon from me."

"I would be right willing to become a dragon, also," said David.

"It is not for us, Sire, alas. Your kingdom weighs on you; and through you, on me."

"You are right!" said David, straightening up and looking as stern as someone his age could. "I thank you for putting me once more in mind of it."

"M'Lord?" said a small voice in Jim's right ear.

"You'd better stay here, Hob, with Dafydd and his Majesty of the Drowned Land."

"But m'Lord, you wanted me with you at all times in case you needed to send some suddenly necessary word to m'Lady at Malencontri!"

"Did I say that?"

"Yes, m'Lord."

"When?"

"I don't remember exactly, m'Lord." Hob screwed up his face in a frown. "—But we always do it. We did it when you took me to the Holy Land and we had all the trouble with those Djinn—and people; and you did have to send me back to Malencontri then. Remember, m'Lord?"

"No," said Jim. "But in any case this is Lyonesse and the land above, where my Lady is, is in another place entirely. There's no way for you to get there from here."

"My Lord," said Hob, "I may only be a Hob, but I may also have mentioned to you there are some few things we Hobs can do. We can go anywhere smoke can go, though the opening may be too small for the eye to see; and we can find one certain smoke, even if it is somewhere on the other side of the world. At Malencontri, smoke arises daily from wood as it is burned; and I may step from wood smoke here to that wood smoke in the wink of an eye, though all distance and difference of lands lie between."

Everybody was silent for a moment, watching Jim.

"Well, I suppose, if you think you can do it," said Jim, giving in to what he knew very well were some rather shaky arguments; and all the rest of those with him now knew it, too. "Hop up on my shoulder, then, and don't move for a minute—not a muscle."

"Yes, m'Lord," said Hob with suspicious meekness.

Hastily, Jim arranged for his ward to cover Hob in addition to himself. It was essentially the same sort of magic mechanism at work as when he had expanded his ward to make room to work on the magic fruit.

On second thought, he arranged for the ward around Hob to bud off from his ward, if Hob had to leave him for a short while; and then reattach itself automatically when the small Natural returned. Hob need never suspect he was being protected.

"All right," Jim said, "better get down inside my mail shirt, though."

"Huzzay!" cried Hob. "But I'm already there, you know, m'Lord."

Happily, he weighed so little Jim felt him as only a slight pressure against his back.

"That's fine, then," said Jim. He turned to the rest of them. "All right, Brian and I are going to try to find out, from the air, where the Harpies come from. The Dark Powers have to make them somewhere. At the Loathly Tower—you remember, Dafydd—it was in the Tower itself. We'll find them and see what can be done. I want to make the Drowned Land safe for your people again. We'll worry about what more's to be done, if anything, after Cumberland's crew gets here, and the fate of Lyonesse is settled. Your Majesty, Dafydd, will you be here when Brian and I get back?"

"I think I'd best take them back to King Pellinore's home," said the QB; and before Jim could say another word, there was the blink of dark and the three were gone.

"One does seem to get around this land a great deal—had you noticed, James?" Brian said.

"I have indeed, Brian. Now, I'll just make you into a dragon—"

"Should I kneel?"

"It's not necessary. I will be," said Jim, "using a form of magic that takes into account the fact you're already a knight."

"Ah."

Jim fished in his purse for his various magic fruits and

brought them out. They had gathered some dust, but since no one in this medieval time paid any attention to such things, he had gotten into the habit of ignoring them, himself.

He had eaten one grape. Now he thought of taking a bite out of the apple. It was a small apple. If he bit into it now, only a few more bites would remain. He was about to take one, when he felt uneasy. There was no reason to prefer one fruit over another. He changed his mind and took another bite from the pear, instead, visualizing Brian as a dragon.

As he looked up from putting the remaining portion of the pear back in his purse, he saw a dragon before him, one a little smaller than he himself would be as a dragon—which made sense since change size was proportional to original size. The new dragon's eyes were all but shooting sparks.

"THIS IS WELCOME INDEED!" boomed Brian, in a voice that easily echoed the length and breadth of the Gathering Place. As a hum of aroused voices arose from beyond the nearest trees, Jim waved both hands desperately downward before Brian's long, savagely toothed muzzle.

"Don't say anything!" hissed Jim in his loudest whisper. "Nothing until I speak to you!"

A dragon's voice was certainly tremendous—a useful thing when you wanted to chat with another dragon across three hundred yards of thin air while on the wing; but a dragon's hearing was also very sensitive.

Brian nodded.

Jim hastily led Brian out from under the trees, into a small clear spot; then changed into his own dragon-form. Brian smiled dragonishly at him, but kept silent. Voices and movement could be heard approaching.

"Here we go, now," said Jim. "We'll fly."

"How . . . ?" said Brian, in a sort of low-pitched bass grumble.

"You can speak up now. They will hear but we'll be gone before they can get to us. As for flying, just think of jumping up into the air. Your dragon body has instincts"—went on Jim, remembering his own first throat-closing dive from an upper entrance to the Cliffside Aerie—"and those instincts will make this body do what you want. When you jump up as a human, you don't have to tell your knees, *'Now bend, now straighten out fast.'* do you? Just follow me, and the body will fly for you."

Jim took off. Brian took off. The sound their wings made, pulling at the air, must have been quite loud; but they were gone above the trees and it could make no difference.

At about eight hundred feet up, Jim leveled out; then had to hurry on up after Brian, who seemed to want to fly all the way to Lyonesse's white sun.

"You can stop moving your wings now," roared Jim at him. "Hold them out open and steady and just let them carry your weight—remember how a falcon does it!"

Brian obeyed.

"DEAR JAMES—that is to say, dear James," he said, toning down his dragon voice as they began to plane earthward into a rising column of warm air Jim had located, "how can I thank you for this. Who do we fight?"

"Nobody," Jim was about to answer, when he realized this would be a blow to Brian's expectations—also perhaps not correct.

"Possibly the Harpies," Jim said.

"Good!" said Brian. "James, you are quite right. I am flying without knowing how I do it. It is a most delightful sensation—just the flying, I mean. Rather like sailing, without the waves."

"Yes," said Jim. "Watch yourself, though; since all you have to do is want to do something, and if this dragon body you've got can do it, it'll try."

"Surely, since it's something I wish, it would be good to do it?"

"Mostly. But you're not just a man at the moment, you're a man in a dragon body. It might get you into something you should have thought before doing."

"Yes. James!" said Brian suddenly. "My soul! I did not think. Have I put my soul in peril by taking on a dragon shape?"

"No, no. It's the same old soul inside the dragon body, with all your regular pieties and virtues."

"Say rather my many sins . . ."

"See. Didn't I just warn you of that?" said Jim, as Brian raked—or rather, tried to rake—a viciously long and sharp talon through his tough-skinned chest in an attempt to cross himself.

"You did, James. I cannot deny it."

"You're still the same person you always were, no matter what shape you're in. Look at me. I've been a dragon dozens of times."

"You have a tendency, though, to fall asleep at vespers," said Brian. "I heard you snoring several times during the two weeks we were at the Earl's Christmas party. We are none of us perfect, James."

"Naturally," said Jim. "But this damn talk about me snoring has to stop. There were enough others asleep at vespers at the Earl's. It could have been anybody snoring."

"You are quite right, James," said Brian. "I pray for the grace and pardon of your forgiveness for thinking it was you I heard."

Jim glared at him. Brian's dragon face looked back innocently—too innocently; and interestingly so, because a dragon's expression of innocence consisted mainly of wide-open eyes and lips pulled away from the fangs as much as possible.

There was nothing to be done about it, however. Brian had outmaneuvered him on this exchange. Jim made up his mind to lie in wait. An opportunity for revenge would present itself.

"Of course," he said, though it almost choked him to get it out gracefully, "that, too, was natural. By the way, were you wondering where we're going?"

"I was."

"I'll tell you, then," said Jim. "We're going north, to travel along the edge of Lyonesse nearest the Drowned Land, almost as far as we can go."

"Hah!" said the dragon that was Brian. "And what do we there, at our destination, James? I know you said we two would go and find where the Harpies come from."

"That's right," said Jim. "The Dark Powers have to make them somewhere. Harpies can fly, but ogres and Worms and other such—if they have other kinds of monsters—have to do their travelling on foot. So the Dark Powers will want to make all of them as close as possible to wherever they plan to fight."

"But what would they need Harpies and such for, if they have that help from some like Queen Morgan le Fay, Cumberland, and Modred?"

"The man or woman who gave it to them would have to give up his or her will completely before being able to work directly that way with the Dark Powers."

"God forfend!" said Brian, raking his chest again with a talon to make the shape of a cross. Jim winced. "But it is a grace that you know these things, James."

Jim winced. He did not *know* them. It was just that from the first, after spending several years here after growing up in a logical universe and world, he had not been able to keep himself from looking for a logical process at work in this world and time as well.

Certainly, this world seemed almost identical to the universe of his birth, with all the natural laws in place—except where magic appeared to set them aside. But did magic really do that? Or was it something else that required that part of what seemed logical reality here was also something that could mold reality like clay into any shape wanted or needed?

. . . Well, this was no time to ponder over that. In any case, the real marvel was the balancing of forces, or whatever, that allowed ordinary physical laws and magic to coexist.

That coexistence had to mean things like the Dark Powers had to be matched with limitations. If he just knew what their limitations were in this case—

"I think," he told Brian, in the privacy of their being some hundreds of feet up in the air with no one between them and the surrounding horizon to listen, "the Powers have to make their Harpies and monsters fresh each time. I can't imagine them keeping them around until the next time they're needed.

It'd be only common sense to reduce them back to the magic energy from which they were created; and then remake them as needed.

"So, chances are they have a monster-building place close to where they're going to be using them; and that's going to mean close to the Empty Plain, which is in the direction we're headed."

"But the Harpies could be made in some place apart from the ogres, Worms, and such, James."

"It's possible, but I don't think so. I'm beginning to think that in some ways the Dark Powers aren't as bright—I mean *wise*—as we would be, or they would have achieved Stasis or Chaos—"

"Forgive me, James, Stasis or Chaos?"

"Uh—well," said Jim, "they're some things magical that they should have gained by now if they were as wise as we are. The point is, why should they split up the places where they make creatures like that, when the use for them is only to be in a final battle with the present owners of Lyonesse?"

"Why, I know not, James," said Brian straightforwardly. "But doubtless you do."

"Well, I don't actually know it," admitted Jim. "But Morgan le Fay's been watching me and listening to me; so when we heard the Empty Plain was going to be the battleground, she must have, too—if she hadn't helped to decide it should be there in the first place. But, given a day or so, any renegade from Lyonesse could have learned it from one of the Originals and told her."

"You think such matters through fully, do you not, James?" said Brian admiringly.

"No, no," Jim broke in on him. "Well, yes, a little, maybe. But on most things it's just a matter of guessing."

"Ah, you are modest, of course," said Brian; and Jim suddenly realized that all this praise was his friend's oblique way of apologizing for the remark about Jim's snoring.

"It just happens," said Jim, to put an end to the whole thing. "Now we've got to concentrate on finding the place I think is there."

"Does it indeed! Well!" Brian was silent for a moment. "If that is the nub of it, then may I ask how you plan to find it? I have seen nothing but treetops below us since we took to the air."

"It ought to be noticeably different than what's around it—just like the Loathly Tower and the end of the causeway was. Something different enough to spot easily from the air."

"You are right, James, of course. I have not been on proper watch for lack of knowing what to watch for. Now you mention it, is that not a somewhat strange place ahead of us and to our left? The trees seem to end suddenly."

"Let's go higher," said Jim, "and look at it from a little more altitude. Follow me, Brian."

In an explosion of wing movement, they shot up another hundred feet or so, found a second thermal that would let them soar more or less in the direction of what Brian had pointed out, and glided on a shallow downward angle toward it.

"No," said Jim. "This has to be just one end of the Empty Plain."

"Let us take a look at it, however. It is always wise to know your ground before you venture on it."

They went toward it accordingly. In only a few minutes, from this height, it opened before them. It was not a very impressive Empty Plain—not more, Jim judged, than a little over three miles long from its near to its farther end; and nowhere more than half a mile in width. It narrowed in sharply at the middle, like an hourglass.

"I'd expected something bigger," said Jim.

"Well enough for those who will engage here," said Brian. "Less than two thousand men and horses can fight each other in this space with room to spare—though no place to hide and little in which to escape, except into the trees."

"I suppose you're right," said Jim. The Plain was completely surrounded by trees; but there were no deer or other animals to be seen grazing on the black grass of Lyonesse. Unreasonably he was a little disappointed. He had expected more, had expected it to be longer, bigger all over, with something more to justify its name, even in this heavily forested land—something about it that was more . . . empty.

But apparently there was nothing. The closest thing to an oddity about it was the point in the middle where the trees on each side pinched in for a short space; but that really did nothing for its image but add a touch of irregularity.

"All right, Brian," he said. "We've seen it. Let's start circling out from here. Just come with me, again; and help look for anything at all in the forest around here that's different."

They flew outward about the Empty Plain in a spiral under Jim's piloting—a spiral whose connected, circular paths were close enough to one another so that they could connect the new ground they were seeing with what they had already passed over.

"James! James! Look to your right now—" burst out Brian suddenly.

"The gray spot?" said Jim. "Just a pile of rocks among the trees."

"But it is not!" boomed Brian.

Chapter 39

Jim looked again, and more closely, at what had seemed to be no more than some huge boulders or an outcropping of rock in a rare bare spot among the trees.

"Something moved there," said Brian.

"We'll go look, then."

They tilted their wings and wheeled over toward the gray area. They were very close to it when a shape came upward into sight, flapping clumsily. Jim immediately tilted his wings and banked away. Brian followed as swiftly and smoothly as if he had been a veteran fighter pilot, used to following his flight leader for months. It would have been more impressive if Jim had not known that it was the result of Brian's simply wanting to follow Jim—his dragon body had translated that wish into the necessary muscle reactions that took him where he wanted to go.

From a distance and a higher altitude they once again flew back in a circle around the gray area, spiraling cautiously inward toward it.

"A harpy, was that not?" said Brian, as the clumsily flying shape, after beating about in the air just above the rocks for an effortful moment, dropped back down out of sight below the treetop line.

Jim nodded. He moved even closer to Brian, going below the other dragon as they moved, and turning his neck with the remarkable ability of dragons, like some long-necked birds, to turn their heads so as to look almost directly backward. This put his face only a few feet below Brian's and his dragon-whisper bridged the gap to Brian's ears.

"Right! Just hatched or something—looked like it was learning to fly. We'll go up until we're at an angle from where we can look down on it. Then, if it's safe to go look, we'll come in again on a steeper angle; but slowly, until we've got a good view, then turn away immediately."

"And then, James?"

"This must be something like a beehive—their breeding center. We'll try to think of a way to destroy all of whatever's inside," said Jim.

He was not being a human magician right now. At the moment he was only a dragon operating on his innate magic like any Natural. For magickians there was the prohibition on using magick for any aggressive purpose. But he was not really a magickian at heart. He was a magician—and the Harpies were creatures that must be destroyed, if Lyonesse and the Drowned Land were to be safe.

From several hundred feet higher they began to circle, gradually drifting lower to get a better look. Slowly, to Jim's eyes, what had seemed like natural rock formations began to show more like a number of rough domes clustered together, with dark cracks in their bases.

The probably-just-hatched harpy was still in sight, trying to get back in through one of the cracks. This entrance was hardly more than a semivertical slit; and the harpy had to align itself with it to enter. It was blundering about, trying to do this, as they watched.

A coldness formed inside Jim as they saw it finally work its way inside. It was not the creature that was making him wary. It was the thought of the Dark Powers themselves. Surely they would not leave a hive where their creations were made unwatched and unguarded?

He told himself he had been an idiot to come here without a more detailed plan of what he would do when he found the hive. What he needed was another magic device like the color-aware spectacles—a warning signal of any sudden awareness and interest by the Dark Powers in the presence here of Brian and himself. Something like the canaries the miners used to carry into mines to warn them of poisonous gases—or the rose in the old fairy tale that had wilted in the presence of evil.

Back in the land above, he could have made himself such a rose if he had only thought of it ahead of time—if he could figure out how to do such a thing. But now he was in Lyonesse, with his magic locked up inside his ward. He could use it on himself or anything he had with him in the ward, but nothing outside—without breaking the ward open again.

Of course, he and Brian could fly off now, across the border into the Drowned Land, just long enough for him to open his ward enough to let him make such a sensitive rose.

But an unusual, almost superstitious, feeling was with him. *Am I letting the Old Magic get to me in some way?* he asked himself. There was a conviction in him that would not go away—the conviction that, now he had found the Dark Powers' monsters factory, he should not leave it without doing what he could to end it. A clinging certainty that if he left, he would come back to find the Powers at home here, the hive more securely guarded or otherwise impregnable.

But even that was only half his concern. The other half had to do with a feeling of guilt at keeping Brian out of the adventure and excitement that Brian had come here to find

However, the whole matter had turned out to be more magic than military.

If Jim was to have a hope of doing something about this place, he had to have a look at what was inside—where the harpy had gone; and while he could get in himself, with a good chance of getting back out alive, he could not take Brian with him with anything like the same hope.

But there was no point in his dithering around, chewing it over, hoping the answers would come out different than the way they seemed now. The first thing was to break the news to Brian that he would be carrying on here alone. Send his friend away on some pretext? It would have to be a good pretext, or Brian would see through him and insist on doing something foolhardy—like standing guard out here in the open while Jim was inside.

He had it.

"Brian," he said, as they soared along together, Brian above, Jim just below.

"Yes, James?"

"You were right. This is it—where the Dark Powers make all the Harpies and other creatures they plan to throw against the Lyonesse Knights, if and when it comes to a battle on the Empty Plain. Even on foot, ogres and Worms—and anything else of the same sort—could get into position to attack during the battle in no more than an hour's walk."

"We must act, James."

"Keep your voice low. We've no way of knowing what kind of hearing they've got down there on the ground. No, I'm the one who has the magic to meet with whatever magic's here. So I have to stay. But meanwhile one of us has to take word back to Dafydd, King David, Pellinore, and the other Round Table Knights about this; so they can know what to expect. That leaves you as the one to go."

"James . . . ," said Brian, in a voice full of longing, "perhaps you might wait until I return—"

"If I can. I'll have to do what seems necessary under the circumstances."

"Only right to do that, of course. But it would be well for me to be in company with you."

"I'll hope it won't take you too long."

"My word on it," said Brian. "I shall be as swift as this dragon body may be. How is it best to make the greatest speed?"

"Well, you can't be pumping your wings all that distance. Gain a lot of altitude—go up very high—but don't start a fast climb until the sound of your wings won't be heard back here. Remember all the noise we made taking off? Then, from that altitude, glide directly toward where you're going. If you get down too low, you'll have to climb again. If you happen to find a strong tail wind high up, boosting you fast in the direction you want, just climb and glide until you get there."

"I shall do so," said Brian. He peeled off from their spiraling, gliding on a shallow slant away and downwards toward the surrounding treetops for a distance, so that he could climb unheard.

Jim watched him dwindle in size against the pale, bright sky, a little emptiness beginning to be felt in him. He actually would have felt better having Brian with him. It would have kept his spirits up. Against any solid, ordinary threat or danger, nothing could daunt Brian.

It was not that pain or death meant nothing to this friend of his. It was only that for him those two things rated below a number of other, more important, elements of existence such as faith, loyalty, or the avoidance of anything which he would consider shameful in another man.

Meanwhile, Jim told himself, he should be getting busy. If the Harpies were coming from here, presumably the other monsters would, too—but were the Dark Powers themselves at home at this address?

When he had approached the Loathly Tower with Brian, Dafydd, Danielle o' the Wold and the dragons Smrgol and Secoh, the cold, powerful, creeping presence of those Powers had been felt long before they got to it, just as that same feeling had been in his own Hall. It was not here.

Strange.

For a second a hope raised its head within him, that perhaps the Dark Powers' magic would not work here, any more than his, if he had not been warded. But it had to be working if they were making Harpies. Forget that easy way out. What he had to do, now that Brian was safely out of the way, was to see what he could do by himself to destroy this hive—or whatever it should be called—and to do that he had to know what it was like inside.

There was only one way to do that—follow the harpy they had been watching through the crack it had entered. There was only one way to do this—be a harpy himself.

The thought of actually becoming one gave him an ugly feeling inside.

But it had to be done. He swung wide of the spot, planed down until he was out of sight behind the treetops between himself and it, then found the already somewhat amputated pear in his purse, sighed, brought it out and finished it off—visualizing himself as inside and controlling the harpy below.

And immediately that was where he found himself.

"*My Lord!*" cried Hob's mind in his. "*What happened? Where are we?*"

Jim snarled at himself silently. He had forgotten Hob completely. Of course, everything inside his ward included the little hobgoblin.

There had been a time, early in his stay in this world, when he was turning into a dragon whether he wanted to or not; and when he did, everything with him was left behind him—including his clothes. Now, more magically experienced, he could, and did, automatically make the magic to take everything with him. He should have remembered Hob had been brought into the ward for protection from Morgan le Fay.

"It's all right, Hob," he said. "We're just inside the harpy, you and I. It's magic—don't ask me to explain it."

The shock of the change had been considerable, however—even to Jim. In the past it had been enjoyable to fly like a dragon or sift through a place which smoke, but nothing solid, could enter; and he had indeed wondered on occasion what it must be like to be one of the Dark Powers' creatures. He had never stopped to consider that being in a harpy might not feel like being a dragon—or a Hob. Those other two had been living beings like himself. This was ugly.

It was like being in, and part of, something like a piece of machinery—a piece of machinery with life, but life that was both unnatural and unfeeling. It was like becoming that piece of machinery and necessarily being the programmed motor that activated it.

He pushed the feeling from his mind. He had made his decision; it did not matter how he felt.

The harpy was now wriggling its way downward through a narrow, tubular passage, like an oversized wormhole. Jim, taking command of the body, folded its wings tightly to its sides, aligned it with the angle of the walls, and continued to move forward.

But the harpy mechanism was still so clumsily unnatural to him that he overcontrolled. Its body blundered partway up one side of the passage, onto what was evidently a small lump or boss where tunnel floor met tunnel wall; almost becoming stuck for a moment. It was a lump Jim could not see—the tunnel was as lightless as a mass grave, undisturbed for years.

But the lump itself broke off in his grasp, crumbling in his claws. He dropped the debris and pushed himself down the slope. Walls, floor, and ceiling of the tunnel pressed against the outer surface of his folded wings. Unexpectedly, for he was not subject to it usually, claustrophobia took him by the throat.

He realized with a sort of panic that he could not even turn around. He could go nowhere but forward; yet already there was a division in the middle of the passage—a fork opening on two different ways.

He realized that here, at least, he could turn himself, heading one way and then backing around into the alternate way. He hesitated.

He had not come in here just to turn back.

But he had no way of telling which way led where. The tunnel had been leading ever downward, and Jim had felt it was turning toward the interior of the structure. In any case, his harpy body seemed to want to continue now by the left-hand path, which to Jim meant they might be turning back toward the outside.

Instinct, it might be, that was directing the harpy here. It seemed to make the best sense to let the harpy body proceed as it had intended; but Jim found himself secretly pleased by the thought that he might be moving back toward the face of the boulder and the open air beyond. He had not thought that the darkness and the tightness of the tunnel would bother him—but it was doing just that.

He must remember, he told himself, the turns in their succession, in case he had to find his own way back to the opening.

But at the next point where the tunnel forked, the harpy body went to the right. Then left again—or had it been to the right both times before? Of course not. It had been left, right, left—in that order. In spite of being sure of that now, an ugly feeling of losing his way was beginning to grow in him. If he should really get lost here, where the Dark Powers could show up without—

—They were here now!

Like a cold hand, Their presence closed around him. He felt it pushing him deeper into the mechanical, primitive instincts of the harpy, deeper and deeper into the maze about him, deeper and deeper into a creature like itself—

An odd little thread of thought, a brave thread, but trembling slightly in spite of itself, broke the spell, speaking to itself in his mind.

"M'Lord . . . I don't like it here . . ."

Hob! A sudden burst of furious humanity erupted in Jim, warming him, driving back the darkness that had been trying to invade not only his body and mind, but the core of his vital spirit.

"Hang on," Jim thought at Hob. *"We're going back out."*

He had stopped the harpy body from moving any farther. After all, in these situations, it was his mind that was in control, not its. For the first time since he had entered this place, his mind was working completely apart and the way it should.

He reached out his left arm and with one harpy leg felt for a wall beside him. It had been only inches away. He moved closer and leaned against it.

The Powers must know by now he was here—surely They could sense an alien presence in their hive? Yes, now that he felt for it, with the harpy's awareness he could feel Them speaking Their message of destruction to him, so They had to know. Unless . . . unless They thought he actually was a harpy. But They could hardly be that blind . . . his shoulder rubbed against the wall beside him, caught on another small outcropping there, and felt it disappear. He reached out with his harpy leg, slid it again over the invisible wall's roughness, found another projecting part, and closed his claws on it.

It crumbled as the projection earlier had done; and as he tightened his grip on what held, he felt the broken parts in his hand grind together into the smallest of particles. It was not so much like rock as it had seemed to be, but more like old bone, rotted by weather and time until what seemed whole, on being picked up, became only a handful of dust.

Of course. They could not build anything solid or permanent. All Their powers were nonphysical, and They had no physical way to strike at him except through one of Their creatures.

Here there seemed, so far, to be only Harpies; and it might well be that their poison would not harm each other.

But still, They had him—him and Hob—in Their possession, trapped. Why weren't They trying to destroy him with another of Their monsters? But maybe They hadn't had time for that, yet. Maybe . . .

Maybe it was because They still didn't know he was the alien who had intruded here?

Certainly, They were Powers. But "Powers" were all They were.

There was no reason for Them to have the kind of logical mental processes that were needed to add two and two, let alone seek to unravel a contradiction. Their thinking could run *"It's something that shouldn't be here!"*—only to have that thought contradicted by *"But it's a harpy. This is where*

Harpies belong when they aren't being useful.''

Their minds—if Their thinking processes could be called that—could be bouncing back and forth from the one decision to the other, bound into a sort of eternal oscillation about what to do with the element that both was a harpy and was not. He had best not say anything more out loud to help Them to the right decision, though—if his guess was correct.

''Hob,'' he thought, *''can you hear me when I just think? I know you hear the trees; and you've heard Gnarlies and horses thinking, if I remember right. Just tell me 'yes' in your head, if you can . . .''*

He waited, but there was no answer. Of course, he told himself, how could there be? Hob might be able to hear his thoughts; but he most certainly could not hear Hob's.

It was a bitter pill to swallow—little Hob, without knowing how he was able to do it, was so much more able than he was with all his magic . . .

He was an idiot! *Sometimes*—he told himself privately—*you can't see what's right under your nose.*

The invisible ghost—like *him* inside the harpy—reached for his pouch, pulled out the plum, and sternly thought *''From now on I can hear Hob when he thinks at me.''* He hesitated a moment before biting into it.

He thought of his dwindling supply of magic fruits. He had not meant to use them up so quickly, but every use had seemed necessary at the time. They had been intended for that last, desperate moment when, his experience told him, needs would come thick and fast. But he had to get himself and Hob out of here if at all humanly possible.

''Hob,'' he thought, *''do you remember how we came here? Could you guide me back the way we came?''*

He held his breath, waiting for the answer. Maybe this kind of talent was not covered by magic manipulation. But the answer came back promptly and clear in his head.

''No, m'Lord. I thought you'd know.''

''I don't.'' There was a long moment of silence in the dark between them. *''Hob, if you had smoke, could it show you*

the way out—you said in the Forest Dedale, if there was an exit, the smoke would find it.''

''Oh, yes, my Lord. But I don't have any smoke.''

''I know. But you also said that if there was wood smoke at Malencontri, you could go from a fire here to there.''

''Yes, m'Lord, I can do that. Like goes to like.''

''Could you go out now and get some smoke and bring it back to us here, so it could find the way out for us?''

''I'd need some smoke to go from. Like to like it goes. I'm very sorry, my Lord . . .''

So here goes another of the magic fruits, Jim thought bitterly.

''Never mind. Maybe I can find you just a single puff of smoke, magically. If I can, what kind of smoke would be quickest for you to find?''

''There was wood smoke at the place where they had you, Sir Brian, and Dafydd tied up in the tents.''

So there must have been, but Jim had paid no attention. He thought of the open fires before the tents, around which slept those without tents among the Borderland invaders. He remembered them; and he held one in particular steadily, pictured sharply in his mind, focusing down on a short piece of wood with only one end burning.

''Right,'' he said out loud, though he was speaking more to himself than Hob. He mentally fumbled in his purse, withdrew this time the so-far unbitten apple, and spoke to it mentally as he visualized.

''Bring me that piece of wood with one end lit.''

He mentally took a bite of the apple, and put the rest back into his purse. There was a pause in which his purely spiritual human heart nearly stopped—a sound of something approaching was coming up the tunnel. Hastily, he began to back up; as quietly as he could, the way he had come. How close had that last tunnel division been?

There was a sudden flicker of light—so unexpected on eyes straining to see through total darkness, that for a moment he was dazzled. The short piece of dead tree limb he had visualized lay on the tunnel floor against the far wall. Its burning end was giving off small flames that seemed to light the area around Jim like a searchlight.

"All right, Hob," he thought. *"Now—"*

There was a sudden increase of light, and a crackling sound, and flame shot up the wall, brightening as it rose and spread. Jim stared. The flames from the wood had immediately set fire to the wall beside it, and were spreading as if the wall was dry paper.

Jim backed frantically away. For a moment he thought he was leaving the fire safely behind; but even as he thought that, the crackling noise increased. Light blossomed before him, and noise and light followed him as he retreated, backwards, as fast as his harpy body could move.

"M'Lord—," said Hob shakily.

"I know, I know!" said Jim. *"But I can't do anything until I get to a place where I can turn around. Was that just a little way back? The place where we went to the left, this last time?"*

"Yes, m'Lord."

"I can't even look back over my shoulder. Can you see it?"

"Yes, m'Lord. I mean I can't see it yet, m'Lord, but it's only a little way back. This narrow room we're in curves so—THERE IT IS!"

"Whew!" said Jim to himself in relief. He reached the place where the tunnel they had come down had branched. *"Hang on, Hob. I'm going to get myself . . . bent . . . around this place where they join . . ."*

By dint of almost breaking his harpy body in half, he managed to reverse his position. Head first now, he went as fast as he could along the way that should bring them out. Waves of heat and flashes of light were chasing him as he went; and the crackling was now a roaring.

"Now right, m'Lord!" cried Hob aloud. "To your right!"

"No, the first one I took was the left one, coming down."

"But you're going back now. The smoke says go right, m'Lord—the smoke is already going out ahead of us."

Jim did not see it. But this was Hob's area of expertise. He took the tunnel to his right, running like a bent-over chicken on his two harpy legs, rubbing a stream of the so-easily burnable material from the walls as he blundered against them in his hurry to escape.

And suddenly, there was a lit slit of white sky ahead. A half dozen more pushing strides—and they were out.

OUTSIDE! Out in the open air, the cool, the lung-filling, clean air. Jim pulled himself onto the surface of what he had originally thought was a boulder, and sagged there, breathing deeply.

"M'Lord, are you all right?"

"Just fine, Hob," he said out loud, still gasping for air, "and about to be better. Hang on!"

He switched out of the harpy, not needing to use his magic fruit to do so since his natural magic could put him back into his dragon body at any time—a fresh, unexhausted body, brimming with breath and energy—and shot almost straight up like a rocket, feeling Hob now clinging to his neck.

Chapter 40

Jim did not rocket far, however. At a bit above treetop level he checked himself; and began making tight circles on the updraft from the burning hive. He circled, held by a somewhat awed fascination with what he had caused to happen.

He was safe now, he knew. If the Dark Powers could attack him only through Their creatures, as he now was almost sure was the case, he could be in no danger up here. The worst They could do was send Harpies up after him; and he could outfly Harpies with—loosely speaking—one wing tied behind his back.

Besides, he doubted They had any Harpies to spare at the moment. If there were, their owners would want to keep them for the encounter between the Earl's small army and the Lyonesse Knights.

Fire had apparently reached all through the hive now; but

ı an odd, irregular fashion. Most of the great, stonelike struc-ıres that had made it up looked untouched on their surface; ut all were spouting flames from side or top in what seemed aphazard fashion. But now, a flame ran up the side of one uge boulder shape, and continued to burn fiercely and spread . . it was hard to believe the whole Nursery was a made ıing. Creating it must have been a gigantic task.

"M'Lord," said Hob in a uncertain voice, behind him, 'did you use magick to make the rock burn?"

"No," said Jim—and was about to go on to say that he ad simply been a complete damn fool. But he checked him-elf in time. It might relieve his feelings to admit the truth; ut that would simply transfer the load of his uncomfortable motions to Hob, as unasked-for confessions usually did to ıe one who heard them.

"I thought it was stone, too," he told Hob, instead, "but was something the Dark Powers just made to look like tone; and whatever it was made of caught fire from that bit f burning wood I summoned."

Privately, he was thinking of the nests made by wasps out f chewed-up plant fibers, or the strands a spider produced rom its own body to make a web. The Dark Powers could ave somehow produced some creature which could build the ock-appearing Nursery in some similar fashion.

He checked his runaway thoughts, realizing his mind was rying to escape what he was forcing himself to watch.

"It's burning up all over," said Hob, craning his head out rom Jim's, so that Jim could see him from the corner of his ye, staring at what was below. "There's our harpy: and see ll the other strange . . . beasts."

"Yes," said Jim emptily, looking down with him. Crea-ures of all sorts of shapes and descriptions were coming out f the bases of the great boulder shapes; and some of them vere huge.

There were ten-foot ogres, like the one Jim, in the dragon ody of Gorbash, had fought at the Loathly Tower; and Vorms as thick as main-line sewer pipes.

But there were also others that Jim had never seen or imag-

ined before. Such as a great flat thing like an enormous land
going flounder, with a massive head owning two mouths fu
of jagged teeth. It was legless and seemed to move by throw
ing its whole body forward—as if it wanted to crush an
opponent as much as to slash them to death with its teeth . .
and there was a sort of great serpent that struck at the sur
rounding rock shapes it passed as it fled from the fire.

These four types were the most numerous. There wer
things of other sizes and shapes—but no other flying one
except the Harpies. Most of them, however, seemed to hav
come forth only to die—or at least collapse. They made thei
way only a little distance from the aperture from which the
escaped before sinking to the earth and lying still, or fallin
over and moving only feebly.

It was, thought Jim as he watched, as if they had only
small hold on an imitation of life; and the mere act of escap
ing the flames had been too much for them.

All together, though, Jim's blunder seemed to be more tha
a small help for those of Lyonesse—that was, if the Dar
Powers had to take some time to replace them. He had starte
out with the thought of seeing what could be done to dela
or bother Them. He had never expected to be able to do thi
much damage.

His next step now was take a look at the Borderland in
vaders and see how close they were to actually showing u
on the Empty Plain—

"Sit back straight up and take a good hold, Hob," he sai
harshly. "We've got to get going."

"But m'Lord—what about the harpy?"

"The harpy?" Jim looked down. The harpy body he ha
been in—strangely familiar from his having been in it, an
evidently equally so to Hob—had pulled itself perhaps a
much as fifteen feet out onto the round, rock-colored surfac
by the slit from which they and it had escaped; and so far a
least, the fire had not followed it. At first glance, Jim ha
assumed it was already dead; but then he saw its body shive
slightly—as if it wanted to move farther, but did not have th
strength.

"Never mind the harpy, Hob," he said. "It's done for any-
ay; and we've got to go."

"But my Lord, it's your harpy!"

There was an emphasis on the word *your* that did not es-
pe Jim. In this world the relationship between any two in-
viduals was a street than ran both ways. The serf, tenant,
rvitor in the Castle (or whatever passed for a castle) owed
rvice and life to his overlord. But that overlord owed him
return—defense, the right to justice against others, enough
adership and forethought so that the lesser one did not
arve. That and a host of other duties according to such
ings as past practice and established custom. There was no
ee lunch.

The harpy's body had been used by Jim. As Hob saw it,
m owed it something in return. And everyone from Brian
—probably even—Morgan le Fay would have agreed with
m. There were those, of course, who did not honor such
bts. They filled up the ranks of the men led here by Cum-
rland.

"Can't we go down to it for a moment, my Lord?"

"Yes. All right, Hob, we'll go down."

Jim descended, accordingly, to beside the now-still body.
ob leaped down immediately; and tried to put his arms
ound the disproportionate head with a madwoman's face.
he harpy pulled back its lips, exposing the vicious poison
ngs, but did not have the strength to reach out and bite him.

"We're here, Lady," said Hob to it softly. "We're here
ith you."

The harpy abandoned its attempt to bite, but stared at Hob
ith eyes like black fires.

"Just rest," Hob was saying. "All things come out all
ght. Just rest. Close your eyes . . ."

To Jim's surprise, the harpy's eyelids flickered down, flick-
ed up, half closed, then closed. It lay still; and then another
rong shiver ran through its whole body and wings. The shiv-
ing stopped, and it relaxed. The wings drooped, the head
gged—until its sharp chin touched the gray surface; and as
m watched, a slow change came over its fierce face, as even

that relaxed . . . relaxed, until it looked sane, almost happy .
and asleep.

"It's dead, Hob," said Jim softly.

"I know, m'Lord," said Hob, slowly taking his arms fro
around the head. "Good-bye, Lady." He looked up at Jir
"Do we go now, m'Lord?"

"You're a better man than I am, Hob," said Jim as he to
off.

"My Lord? Is there someone else with us?"

"No," said Jim. "Forget I mentioned it. It's part of a li
from a poem a man wrote and I read—a long time back."

"But I'm not a man, m'Lord. You know that." Hob
voice was puzzled. "I'm a Hob."

"A very good Hob. Never mind. It doesn't matter—so
of talking to myself, anyway."

Jim had to climb to almost two thousand feet to find
current of air moving toward where the Borderland camp wa
or had been. But from that height he could see it was no
deserted; ugly with litter, but deserted. He looked away to h
left.

The Empty Plain was still empty.

Mentally drawing a line from the camp to the Plain throug
the thickly leaved treetops, he began to glide down towa
that line at its Borderland end.

He reached that point with surprising swiftness; and turne
to soar along above the treetops beside the imaginary line h
had drawn. For some little distance he saw nothing; and the
there was movement visible below him on the ground. As h
went, the movement began to have the purpose and shape o
men and horses moving together in a single direction, thoug
spread out from each other some little distance.

Cumberland's force was indeed on its way from the su
rounding woods into the Empty Plain. How could they be s
sure of their destination, he asked himself; and the answ
came back immediately.

Of course. Morgan, Modred, or any of that inclinatio
could have told them of the Plain's existence and led the
to it.

Meanwhile, they were under the trees, and the trees—for ey were now over the border into Lyonesse itself—were a reat. They probably knew that; but even if they did not alize the trees could reach down with their limbs and rangle them, plants could not move that swiftly. The men ould have to pause, or at least go very slowly, to be in such anger. Those moving below Jim now were probably safe as ng as they were in constant movement.

But—it was puzzling. On several occasions his sharp ragon-hearing picked up shouting voices from below; and e caught glimpses of what seemed to be individuals running different directions than their general line of march.

But he could not get any closer without being seen; and he anted to keep himself unseen, if possible, until he had to ow himself as a dragon. If he went any lower, among and etween the trees, he risked being seen. Best to head direct- back to King Pellinore's home, where Brian and the others ould be waiting for him.

He tilted his wings and peeled off, not wanting to use his ings to climb until he was beyond the hearing of those be- w. Once he was, he beat up some four hundred feet, found tail wind blowing in the right direction, and began riding .

It seemed almost too leisurely a way of going when the nemy was already on the march; but there was not a great eal he could do to hurry it up, unless he wanted to climb in opes of finding a stiffer breeze.

It would be a gamble. He had learned from volleyball that atience also had its place in winning any victory. He turned way from the Plain and soared on.

When he came within sight of Pellinore's log-built home, e saw that Pellinore himself was just about the only one issing from the crowd around its front door. The space here Jim had eaten now held not only Brian—easily rec- gnizable to Jim, still in his dragon shape—Dafydd, King avid, and the QB. But there were also a number of other en, all wearing clothes that looked as if they would have een the Blue of Dafydd's Color, if Jim could have seen their

tint. They had quivers full of arrows slung by their sides an
longbows over their shoulders.

Jim landed with a thump, turning himself back into hi
human shape immediately. As an afterthought, he used
small bite of the plum to turn Brian back into a human, als
The archers stared.

"James!" said Brian, as they gathered around him
"Damme, but it's good to see you! I should never have le
you cozen me into leaving you alone there. But you took n
hurt?"

"Not a scratch," said Jim, deciding to say nothing abou
the crawl in darkness in the narrow tunnel. "But I was righ
about that being the breeding place of the Dark Powers' mon
sters; and by sheer luck—no credit to me, an accident re
ally—I set fire to it. So the numbers of those that bred ther
have been reduced certainly by, at a guess, more than half."

"I wish I had been with you, though."

"Brian, the fire was actually just an accident. I might no
have started it, if there'd been someone sensible with me."

"My Lord was very brave!" said Hob.

"Nonsense!" said Jim. "It was Hob who was very brave."

"What did Hob do that was brave, Sir James?" asked Kin
David, pushing his way through the inner ring of people tha
had formed around Jim.

Jim opened his mouth to tell them of Hob and the dyin
harpy, than decided it would not play well to this particula
audience. The word *bravery*, here, meant flashing swords an
desperate battles.

"He went right into the breeding place with me, all th
way," said Jim, "and he would have been the only one wh
could have guided me back out. I'll tell you more about th
fire some other time, maybe. I hurried back; because after
left the breeding place, I flew over the route from the Bor
derland camp to the Empty Plain. The invaders are just mov
ing into the Plain, now!"

"We know, Sir James," said David.

"Oh?" said Jim, a little dashed.

"The Blues are foresters and hunters from birth, James,"

ıd Dafydd. "Pellinore agreed to let us use them to keep ıtch on those who come. As scouts. We have had some of ːm coming and going at all hours to tell us how the progress the armed men goes; and if from time to time, they have chance to put an arrow into one of them, while being be- nd sight and capture by those with him, that does no harm, her."

"That's right, I did see some of them milling around as if mething had just happened to them. But I didn't think there ıs time to stop and find out what was going on. Your bow- ən are taking a real risk, though. If any of them are caught that bunch—"

"They will not be caught," said Dafydd. "Any who did ɔuld not be wearing Blue and with us now. All those now ling to the Empty Plain will see is one of their number lling from his saddle. By the time they stop and find out ıy, no man will know from what direction the arrow came. ır Blues are like me, James, not men of great dispute; but ːy know how to send an arrow when no man is looking, en he who will receive it. Also how to shoot from cover d move quickly to safety."

"Well . . ." said Jim, knowing he ought to praise this; but rn between that duty and his vision of an unsuspecting rseman, toppling from his saddle, dead before he even ew what killed him. Somehow, man to man with swords lances, it was different. Which Pope was it, in or about the irteenth century, who had condemned bows—he had pos- ɔly been thinking of crossbows—and their missiles as weap- ıs unfit to be used against fellow Christians?

". . . that should slow them up some," he finished.

"Ah, yes," said Brian happily. "But do not fret, James. ıere will still be plenty of the hedge-knights left for us."

"True!" said Jim, as heartily as he could. "King Pellinore agreed on this, you say."

"Most excellently so!" put in young David. "But he still ıshes we of the Drowned Land to stand aside when time mes for battle."

"Yes," said Jim. "But maybe there're other things you

can do than giving the lives of your people for them in batt in a different land.''

''But none so noble, Sir James.''

''True, your Majesty. Oh, Dafydd,'' said Jim, ''have yo any idea from these Blue scouts when the invaders will g to the Empty Plain?''

''If they continue so, the Lord QB believes they will arriv before the next Dark, having traversed the forest by day light—for fear of the trees, they may have planned it so.''

''Or,'' said the QB, speaking up for the first time, ''she Gore—Morgan le Fay—may have counseled them when start and how fast to travel to make it so. Possibly Modre could likewise have done; but only one who has lived Lyonesse would know how long the day may be—it varie from time to time, as you have seen.'' The QB's words be came careful, like the steps of a man on a safe path of ston crossing a quagmire. ''—at the wish, many think, of the O Magic.''

''Is it going to be different this time, QB?'' Jim asked.

''The trees say so. This, Modred could not learn from then Morgan could. But she does not commonly speak to the tree and they to her only when addressed. So I believe her n better counselor than Modred in this.''

''What about the Knights—and Pellinore? They kno about this, of course. What are they doing?''

''Why,'' said the QB, in a tone of mild astonishment someone in a raincoat, going out into a downpour, migh show upon being asked how he would keep from getting we ''they are arming; to meet and defeat the incomers as soo as they arrive.''

''Arrive?'' Jim found his mind was not as sharp as should be. ''But they're already there. Where are th Knights?''

''James,'' said Brian, ''you are acting most strangely. Hav you a fever? All these simple questions. The strength of Lyo nesse will be on the Plain at any time now. Look you, Cum berland has brought footmen with long spears to stop th horses. They must march last, as usual, and once here, be placed in formation. There is time!"

"Of course," said Jim. "No, no fever. I'm just a little stupid for some reason . . ."

It was getting difficult for him to see the others and anything beyond them. A sort of milky mist was thickening before his eyes. "I think I should sit down, though . . ." he heard his voice saying from a distance.

He looked around, but through the rapidly thickening milkiness could not even make out the half-log bench Pellinore had sat on. He felt his arm taken, and made out Brian's face behind it, leading him somewhere. He stumbled like a man newly blind.

His eyes closed in spite of himself. He fell.

He opened his eyes again and looked up into the white sky. His vision was perfectly clear and he felt his usual, clear-thinking self. Evidently, he had only been out for a minute or two. He looked to tell Brian and the others that he was all right; and saw only the two young bears, the two otters—both pairs sitting on their haunches—and the fallow doe on her feet, just raising her head from grazing on the grass.

All five animals looked at him solemnly, the doe with what seemed to be a touch of sympathy—but then her soft eyes could hardly look at anyone in any other way.

No one else was in sight.

There crept into him the first small fear that not a little time, but a lot, had gone past. It grew. Where was he anyway, besides outdoors here?

Chapter 41

He raised his head. He was lying on Pellinore's half-log bench. Now that he was aware of it, he realized it was a very hard bed indeed; and his body was still a little numb, both from pressing against it and because his inner temperature had dropped with sleep—

Sleep!

He rose with a jerk, and considerable effort, dropping his feet to the ground below the bench and sitting up with his back against the logs that made up the side of the building. Something light slid off his chest and floated to the ground. It was a piece of grayish, thick paper, much like the kind Angie used at Malencontri to keep their accounts. Bending, he picked it up.

At the bottom there was a very clumsy drawing, made with what obviously had been a stick of charcoal. Above that, it was a letter, in ink, from Angie. He began to read it, greedily.

Jim: Are you all right? I got worried. I don't know why. I tried to call you the magic way you showed me. But I couldn't seem to reach you or you weren't answering, or something. So I'm going to use the magic paper that Carolinus gave me for emergencies, when you were gone to the Holy Land. He never told me not to use it anymore, so I'm using it. If you get this, Jim, and you're all right, let me know. Or send Hob, or something. I've got to hear from you!

I love you, Angie

"Good God!" he said. Both his hands went automatically to his chest, as if there were breast pockets there, but they encountered only his chain mail shirt. He realized he had nothing to write with, and pulled his poignard from its sheath on his right hip.

He held it up before his eyes.

"You're a pen!" he told it. "A ballpoint pen with ink in it. If you can't be that, turn purple. I'll find something you can be!"

Nothing happened. He cursed to himself, realizing he had forgotten he was in Lyonesse, where his magic would not work outside his ward. He hastily reached into his purse, and pulled out the first thing his fingers found that was not a coin. It was the remainder of the plum, which he ate from its pit, telling it to change the poignard.

The poignard stayed a poignard for a second or two, then almost with a visible effort became something that at least looked like a ballpoint pen, except that the ball on the end was about a quarter the size of a golf ball.

Jim cursed again—then got himself under control.

"Never mind," he said, "I've changed my mind. You're a quill pen—a right-handed one, mind, so your feather end doesn't stick in my eye. Also, give me a pot of ink."

The change was made. Jim wrote on the space below the scrawly drawing.

Dearest,

I'm just fine, only it's very busy at the moment. The Knights of the Round Table are just about to fight the Earl of Cumberland, who is somehow involved with Morgan le Fay, who wants the Drowned Land for her own personal estate or kingdom and hopes to get it by helping the Dark Powers to get control of Lyonesse—put like that it doesn't make sense, I suppose, but I can explain it all to you later. Right now I have to find Brian. I'm healthy, rested, unhurt, and in fine spirits, all the better for hearing from you.

Take care of yourself. I'm here at the home of King Pellinore with a couple of young bears, two otters, and a fallow doe. Everyone else gone, evidently. I'll have to find Brian and the rest. You take care of yourself. I love you and I'll be seeing you very soon. Never worry—remember my magic. I can alway protect myself with that. Hob's all right, too.

I do love you and miss you.
See you soon.
Jim

He waved the paper in the air to dry the ink, turned ink pot and quill pen back into a poignard and sheathed it; and was about to return the paper to Malencontri and Angie when he remembered the drawing. He looked more closely at it.

As well as he could make out at first glance, it showed a horizontal stick figure that was probably supposed to be a person, but looked more like a skeleton, being held at the shoulders by a standing stick figure. After that was the shape of a knight's shield with some sort of drawing on it that must represent a coat of arms painted there; and beyond it, two more stick figures, crossing swords with each other.

Underneath the whole thing were three badly printed words—*notte wak cum.*

Jim shook his head over it and went back to trying to puzzle out what was drawn on the shield. It had definitely not been done by Angie. Between the blurriness of the charcoal stick and the ineptness of whoever had drawn it, it was not easy to decipher; but if there was a key to the drawing it was there. If he knew who the shield identified, he could probably guess the rest.

There was an *X* on the shield, with some peculiar shape below it. That had four legs, so it must be an animal—and abruptly the scrawl above the forward end of it gave him the clue he was looking for. There, attached above the forward end, were what looked like some tree limbs sprouting.

Of course. Those were antlers. That meant the creature was a hart, a male deer.

The whole thing abruptly fell into understandability. It was Brian's arms, which he was used to seeing with a colored background—which, of course, could not be rendered with a piece of charcoal. The *X*, then, was a saltire cross, on what were essentially the arms of the Nevilles of Raby, Earls of Worcester; and the hart "lodged sable" showed that Brian's father had been of cadet stock to the Nevilles.

The figure holding the horizontal one still puzzled him for a few moments longer before he realized the vertical one was supposed to be shaking it—as you shake someone to bring them out of dreamland. The words below, then, backed this up: "notte wak . . ." or "I could not wake you up." And "cum," the last of the message, could only mean what it said:

"Come find us!"

But where were they?

Almost absently, Jim made the cabalistic scrawl with his fingertip over the sheet of paper, and it vanished, automatically on its way back to Malencontri. The magic that had driven it here would take it back again—it was not anything that he had produced, so he did not, happily, have to dig further into his dwindling stock of magic fruits to return it to Angie.

Too late, he remembered Brian's sketched message on the same paper. Angie would be able to interpret that as well as he had been; and it rather contradicted his assurance that things were busy but there was no danger in sight.

So he should get another message off to her as soon as he had the means, reassuring her by more or less showing that there had been no need to be concerned.

Meanwhile, if he interpreted Brian's drawing correctly, the battle between Lyonesse and Cumberland, representing the Dark Powers, was about to begin—undoubtedly at the Empty Plain. He should get there as soon as possible.

"My horse," he said out loud, trying to think of where he had last put or seen Gorp.

The otters and the bears merely continued to look at him. The doe paced over to him and nuzzled at his chest in a comforting gesture.

"I'm afraid you can't help," he said, stroking her soft brow, "but thanks, anyway."

She pulled away from him, walked over to door of the log building; and, raising one foot, struck at it with her hoof, twice. The sound of the hoof against wood was surprisingly loud in the general quiet.

She put her foot back down and stood where she was. Several moments passed; and then the door opened. An elderly human servitor looked out. He had evidently had a strong young face in his time; but time had put deep parentheses about the corners of his mouth and eyes, and other lines in his forehead. He looked at the doe, who turned her head to look at Jim.

"I've got to leave," said Jim.

"And you need your horse, Sir knight?"

"Yes. Have you seen him?"

"He is around the back in the stables," said the servitor with just the tinge of inflection in his old retainer's voice that said Jim should have taken that for granted at the home of King Pellinore. He looked beyond Jim to the corner of the building and shouted "Horse!"

He looked back at Jim.

"He must be equipped first, Sir," he said; for someone who could not easily guess that his horse would be taken care of here, might also be ignorant of the fact that he needed to be saddled and bridled before appearing. Jim wondered how Pellinore's white horse had managed to appear immediately, saddled and bridled. Perhaps a horse stood ready for the owner of the place at all times.

Gorp appeared—saddled, bridled, and with Jim's lance upright in its boot. He trotted agreeably up to Jim with as much decorum as Pellinore's white horse had done, then spoiled the effect when he stopped by reaching down to snatch a mouthful of grass.

The servitor held Jim's stirrup. Jim mounted.

"Am I right?" he asked the man. "They've all gone to the Empty Plain?"

"Yes, Sir. Not more than the time between terce and sext."

That wasn't too bad, thought Jim. Terce was the canonical third hour and sext was midday—hopefully, noon. Three hours. It would take nearly that time to get the host of Lyonesse together and ready for battle.

"—The doe will show you the way," the servitor was saying.

"Er, thanks . . ." In the fourteenth century it was customary to reward those servants of your host who had been helpful to you; but Jim had no idea what the customs here in Lyonesse were. He didn't want to offend anyone if trying to tip him would seem like an insult. Anyway, there was nothing compulsory about the practice. He would let the question go for now—maybe there would be a chance to make it up later.

The doe was touching noses with Gorp. She headed off into the woods and he followed her.

It took them no more than perhaps forty minutes to reach the Empty Plain. Apparently Pellinore's home was closer to it than Jim had guessed from the air—or else Lyonesse, along with its other strangenesses, had places whose distances apart changed from time to time.

They came out at the near end of the Plain, which itself stretched roughly northwest to southeast. The forces of Lyonesse were at the northwestern end—not important, thought Jim, as the doe led Gorp toward it, unless the battle lasted toward sunset. Then the white sun would begin to get in the eyes of the Lyonesse Knights, and be at the back of their opponents . . . and it was already past noon.

At first glance it seemed that every armed man the land could produce was already there. Gorp followed the doe without question; and she led them straight to Pellinore.

Pellinore was standing with a small crowd of older Knights around him—Originals all, no doubt. But not more than a dozen feet off, Jim, with infinite relief, saw Brian, Daffyd, and King David. He rode past the doe, who was gently pushing through the crowd to get to Pellinore—her appearance there evidently creating no surprise among the Knights. A moment later Jim had lost sight of her for good; for when he turned to look Pellinore's way again, she was gone.

There had been an air of excitement in the gathering of the Lyonesse forces. Jim was familiar with it in Brian, just before a battle or a contest, where it always showed itself in his eagerness and high spirits. Those of Lyonesse—the Originals in particular—seemed to belong to the same emotional family in this. Dafydd was just as bad, judging from his constant search in the Land Above to find bowmen and wrestlers to compete against—but he hid it behind his pretence of lazy indifference to everything up there.

Jim himself always felt the pit of his stomach drop at the prospect of any serious fighting. In fact, he had to be hit a couple of times before that feeling disappeared and he could do whatever he was capable of in putting out his best effort.

But Brian's reaction now was right in line with his usual behavior.

"James!" he cried boisterously, as he caught sight of Jim approaching. "You woke! You're here! May all the Saints be praised! I knew you would not miss the chance of such a noble victory."

"You think Lyonesse can win, then?" said Jim, reaching them.

"With my Blues, here, there would have been no doubt of it," said Dafydd.

"Win! Certainly!" said Brian. "What are ruffians like those to the gentlemen of the Table Round? We will sweep them from the Lyonesse earth!"

"You're going to fight with the Originals?"

"Why, yes, James! That is to say, they go first, of course. The place of honor. It is their Lyonesse and their right!"

Out of the corner of an eye, Jim caught sight of a somewhat stout knight—his helmet off, showing a half-bald head—waving both fists as he talked to Pellinore; evidently demanding something. Whatever it was, Pellinore seemed unmoved and adamant about not yielding.

"Cumberland's men are here now, then?" said Jim.

"See for yourself, Sir James!" said King David, waving outward toward the emptiness of the Plain.

Jim looked, and after a moment made out a dark line of what must be armed and ready men. They seemed at least five miles off. He shaded his eyes, trying to see better.

"They're much closer than they seem, Sir James. It is a trick of the eyes that the Plain makes, with that small in-pinch of the trees about it in its middle. Behave yourself, Plain!" said the QB, who had not been in evidence up until now.

For a moment the line of men seemed suddenly to jump closer—close enough that Jim could make out men and horses as individuals. He was almost sure he recognized Cumberland, but just then the Plain suddenly picked up its illusion of distance again; and he had not recognized anyone else.

"Where's Modred?" he asked, reminded of that individual, "and Morgan le Fay?"

"Morgan le Fay is planning to be with us, of course," said the QB. "Where else should she be on such a day? But so far no one has seen her. As for Modred, you have barely missed him. It was said he had expected many of the Knights to rally to him. They did not. He left, saying he would go arm himself and return—but he has not."

The dark line of enemy fighters had seemed impressive to Jim. He glanced about at the Lyonesse Knights. They had seemed a good number as he came in; but looking at them now, he could not convince himself that their forces were in any way equal to those of the distant men.

"They aren't moving toward us," said Jim—for that much at least he had seen in the moment when they appeared close, "—and we aren't going forward. Is there a chance the battle might not happen."

"Never fear it, James!" said Brian. "Our foes are merely sorting out who shall ride where in the first line; and who, if any, shall be in the lines to follow it. If it weren't for this damned Plain, seeming to hold them off at such a distance, I could tell a great deal from a closer study of how they set themselves. Not only whether their strength lies in the center of the van, or on the wings; but also who leads what division and perhaps much of what skill he has by the way he sits his horse and argues, or does not argue, with those he will lead."

"Well," said Jim. His doubts of the success of Lyonesse arms in this situation were beginning to grow. Not only were the Originals so much fewer in number, but they were rather old—not only in their actual age, since they must date back to the fourth century A.D. or something equally antique—but they all showed physical signs of aging. The half-bald stout man, for example.

Also, they had to be out of practice. Sir Bedivere had said that they no longer fought among themselves. How true that was, Jim did not know. There had been that moment when Sir Kay made the joke about "light" and Lancelot, when Jim—from his Land Above experience—was sure Bedivere was entirely ready to fight Kay over it.

Maybe Kay's quick backdown had settled the matter. But in any case, they could be badly out of training for a combat like this—perhaps centuries out of training and only remembering their glory days when they were younger.

"Well," said Jim, again, "we can go take a look. Are you ready to be a dragon again, Brian?"

Brian beamed.

"Most ready, James!"

"Then, here we go—QB, will you explain to Pellinore or any of the Knights who might be worried by our change of shape and flying off, that it's all in their good cause. You can also reassure them I'm not going to use any magic while I'm gone—this is a knightly situation, not a magickian one; and, being a knight myself, I understand how the two must be kept separate."

"I will be glad to do so. Thank you, Sir James, for telling me that," said the QB.

"No call for thanks," said Jim; and added—forgetting how he had carefully used the word *magickian* so as to be understood by the Originals—"a magician's duty. Come, Brian." He took a very small bite from the magic apple.

Instantly, as two dragons, they took off—the roar of the wings attracting the general attention of everyone about them, as Jim had foreseen.

"We'll circle around behind Cumberland's men," said Jim, when he and Brian had reached a height where they could talk without being overheard on the Plain below. "If they see us going off in another direction out of sight beyond the treetops, they'll stop worrying about us. Then we circle, gaining altitude until we can come back in overhead so high they won't be sure we aren't birds of some kind."

Brian nodded.

"I doubt there are dragons in Lyonesse," he said.

"Probably not. I'd have sensed them if there were," said Jim. But a realization of this had not occurred to him before now; and he privately made up his mind to gain even more altitude before they made their return above Cumberland's force.

The maneuver went well. They came back at what was probably over a thousand feet above the enemy, emerging into sight on a long curve that became a spiral above the Plain,